HUSH
HUSH

HUSH HUSH

LUCIA FRANCO

Page & Vine
An Imprint of Meredith Wild LLC

Paperback ISBN: 979-8-9895288-9-9

For Keena and Jill, this story wouldn't have been nearly as fun to write without you guys.
Thank you for the hysterical memories.

Chapter 1

"Where are you coming from, all dolled up like that?" I rub my sleepy eyes then reach under the throw pillow for my cell phone to check the time. It's 4:04 a.m.

"Shit, Aubrey, I'm sorry," my roommate says. "I didn't mean to wake you up. Go back to sleep."

The walls of our apartment are paper-thin, making it almost impossible to get a good night's sleep. Then again, I'm used to it.

"It's not a big deal." I sit up and reach over to turn on the lamp on the end table. I must've fallen asleep on the couch.

"These shoes are killing my feet." Natalie plops down on the opposite end of the couch. Her head falls back, and she turns to look at me. "I'm so worn out," she groans. "I can't believe how late I got home. How the hell am I gonna get up for class in the morning?"

"I don't know why you always keep such an early schedule," I say, my voice groggy. "You should see if you can change it up and take some night classes."

Natalie carefully tugs off her fake eyelashes and drops them on the coffee table in front of us. "You know I can't. I have to work."

This is a usual thing for us. "No, you don't. I don't even know why you do."

"Because I'm not going to be a little rich bitch and rely on my parents, only for them to get mad when I don't heel and take everything away. Fuck that."

I chuckle. Today is the first day of our senior year at Fordham University in Manhattan, and not much has changed since we met as freshmen. I'm still a broke college student here on a full scholarship, and she still has tons of family money but refuses to use it. Being complete opposites, I didn't think we'd get along at first. She's Hollister and I'm whatever's cute straight off a Goodwill rack. I can get lost in the latest romance bestseller; meanwhile, Natalie only reads anything with glossy pages and celebrity pictures. She's rap and I'm pop. Carmine's Italian vs. Chef Boyardee. The list is extensive, but our taste in guys and the lack of filters on our tongues were enough to make us click, and we've been best friends ever since.

"I guess I see your point."

I didn't, really. People with her mentality rile me up. Coming from nothing, and I mean dirt-poor nothing, it's hard to process why anyone would want to struggle when they didn't have to. Still, I love her.

Natalie turns and lies on her back. She places her head on my lap and looks up at the ceiling. "Trust me. Money doesn't make you happy, Aub. All it does is cause more problems," she says, her voice low, empty.

"I'd give anything to not have to worry about living expenses or if I'll even have enough to get a few extra things from the grocery store." My body can only take so much nasty, cheap soup and day-old coffee.

"You need a new job," she states.

Another thing we do all the time.

After fulfilling the first-year requirement of living in the dorms, Natalie immediately wanted to move out, and she'd wanted me to move with her. I didn't have the luxury of leaving since I couldn't afford to live on my own, and my scholarship included room and board on campus. But Natalie insisted I didn't have to pay and begged me to move with her. I didn't like taking handouts from anyone, so we'd made a deal. She covered moving expenses and rent, and with my small part-time job at the laundromat,

I paid the utilities. After the second year, I had a handle on my studies and a second paying job. Not that I like it, though—I hate watching kids.

"Tell me about it," I say. "Come Friday, I'll be stuck with the two little monsters all damn weekend while their parents take a vacation to Martha's Vineyard. I shouldn't complain, though. The money is good."

She laughs as she removes her diamond hoops and places them next to her fake lashes. "I don't know how you deal with crying kids after school and work. I'd rather strap a mattress to my back."

"I need the money, Nat. I don't have a choice. I wonder if I can give them NyQuil all weekend." I laugh when her eyes widen. "I'm kidding!"

My parents had died in a four-car pileup on the Southern State Parkway on Long Island when I was seven, and my grammy raised me and gave me what she could, which wasn't very much. I'd gotten a job at the local pool as a lifeguard as soon as I was old enough, and then during the winters, I worked as a hostess at an Italian restaurant. I even filled in as a dishwasher when they were short-staffed. Whatever money Grammy didn't need for bills, I socked away. But now those savings were gone—living in the city isn't for the poor or the middle class—and I need to figure something out.

Natalie sits up and pulls off her five-inch Louboutin's. The red-bottomed, black lace-up pumps are sexy as hell. I want a pair, but I know I'll never be able to afford them. She drops the shoes on the overshined waxed wood floor like she's taking off cheap work boots.

"I can't believe you walk around serving shots in those heels all night. Aren't you afraid you're going to ruin them?"

"It pays to wear them."

One corner of her mouth pulls up as she reaches for her purse on the floor. Her hand disappears into her clutch, and then she takes out stacks of hundreds banded together. She throws each one at me. My eyes get wider and wider as I catch them. I count eleven.

"Where did all this come from?"

"That's a week of work."

"Get the hell out of here. One week?" This was more money than I made in a year. With one stack of these bills, I could get everything I desperately needed right now but couldn't afford. "Why are you walking around with this much cash in New York City?"

Natalie walks to her room and returns with a familiar book. I hand her back the money after she sits next to me and flips open a weathered dictionary about nine inches thick. The middle is cut out, leaving a big, empty square. She places the money inside then closes it and stacks it in between the books on the coffee table. No one would guess it's a fake, and no one would think to pick it up. I came up with the idea when we'd wanted to hide something that held value in our dorm, and it's a tactic we've used ever since.

"Don't worry, no one knew. I carry a clutch for a reason. It's the perfect size to hide under my armpit. Once my coat is buttoned, no one can tell."

"What if you get mugged?"

She eyes me like I'm stupid. "When? While I'm sitting in a cab? I know better than to walk these streets at night, Mom."

Ever since I started the part-time nanny gig a year ago, her new thing is to call me Mom when I worry about something she does. The little monsters call me Mom too, but that's a different story.

"You could've gotten a crazy cab driver, like in the movie *The Bone Collector*." I get cozy under my blanket, and Natalie climbs under it at the opposite end. "Go straight to the bank. Don't leave that here."

"I'm going after my first class to put some away. It's not like I can deposit it all at once. The bank would make me fill out paperwork then question where it came from. I have to deposit small chunks at a time."

Interesting. I didn't know that. I check the time on my phone. My alarm will be going off in a couple of hours, a little earlier than normal. I need some extra time to get ready for the first day.

"When you're ready to quit changing shitty diapers and wiping snotty noses, let me know. There might be an opening coming up where I work."

I giggle at her suggestion. "I can't be a shot girl. For one, I can't afford to wear the clothes you do. And two, I'm not clumsy, but I know I would drop the tray on someone. I'd end up having to pay for it all, too."

Natalie shifts on the couch. "The money is so good, though. You just gotta leave your morals at the door."

"To serve shots?"

She's quiet for a long moment and I think she's asleep, until she says, "When you're ready to make money—and I'm talking about money like what you saw tonight, money you could use to help Grammy out with—let me know."

I eye the dictionary and think about the stacks of cash I'd held. After all my necessary expenses for the month are paid, I deposit whatever money I have left into Grammy's bank account. Even though I'm struggling, my grammy lives on social security and needs the money more than I do. The winters have been brutal the last few years, and if my little scraps of cash help pay her heating bill, then I can do without.

As sleep overtakes me, I think about Nat's offer. The cash she brought home. The simple luxuries I could treat Grammy and myself to with money like that. I'd get her a flat-screen TV and get rid of the 80s monstrosity in her living room. I'd replace my cheap winter coat that hardly does a thing to create a barrier between the cool air and myself. Maybe even new boots to keep my toes from going numb when the temperature drops. If I made that much cash, I could finally get Grammy out of the shack she lives in.

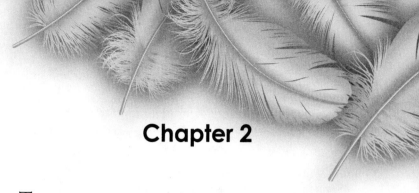

Chapter 2

Two classes complete, and I'm in dire need of a huge serving of caffeine to get through the rest of the day. There's a little hippie coffee shop a few blocks over that Natalie wants to meet at. I have about an hour and a half to spare before my next class.

Walking inside, I spot my best friend immediately, wearing ripped jeans, white Converse, and a peachy pink shirt she's tied into a knot on the left side of her hip. No makeup or jewelry, hair in a messy bun, she's a stark contrast to what she'd looked like early this morning. Natalie is already sitting down with two coffees and a muffin that I know is vegan. She's into all that healthy clean-eating shit.

I drop my books to the floor, and she slides one of the drinks my way. I give her a grateful smile, cup the hot mug in my hands, and take a sip. I sigh, making a scene about it. She knows how I love my coffee.

"You didn't have to get me a coffee. Thank you."

She shrugs it off. "I don't know how you drink coffee like that."

"It's just some sugar," I smirk. I have a terrible sweet tooth.

"It's sweetened condensed milk and cream of coconut. Just thinking about it hurts my teeth."

"Try it." I hold the cup out to her, but she shakes her head as if I'm offering up liver and onions.

"No thanks. I'll stick to my lavender cappuccino."

She's obsessed with drinking lavender coffee and swears it's helped with her anxiety, but I call bullshit.

9

"Lame," I say and take a sip. "How were your morning classes?"

"They'll be easy breezy. The professor for my Law and Society class is hot as fuck. I might have to try and bone him," she says, wiggling her brows. "The man is a walking sin, and I'm not exaggerating. He shouldn't be allowed to teach."

"Sometimes I think you were a guy in your previous life."

"I probably was. I didn't see a ring, not that it matters, but he was wearing a white Henley that I could easily see his tats through. His chest and back are covered in ink." She all but drools.

I laugh, hoping she doesn't fall into a puddle at her chair.

"Just his chest and back? No sleeves?"

Now she has hearts in her eyes. "Both arms, babe," she says. "And he was wearing these slate gray slacks that hugged his fine ass." She mock whimpers. "And his boots ... He looked fresh off fashion week. If I didn't know the name of the class, I wouldn't be able to tell you what it was about. I couldn't stop staring. I want to do bad things with him."

"You and all the other girls too, probably."

"I'll cut their eyes out with my nails if they look at him."

Natalie takes a sip, eyeing me over the rim. I know that scheming look. She keeps reminding me my birthday is coming up.

"No," I say immediately and put my coffee down.

"But it's your twenty-first birthday, and I want to take you out."

"I'm sure I have to work."

She levels a stare at me. "I know you don't. I already checked your calendar. You have Mom duty this weekend, but your birthday weekend is wide open," she announces and smiles.

"I'm going to see Grammy."

Natalie isn't impressed and gives me a droll stare. I can't help but laugh again. All we ever do is laugh.

"All weekend long? Stop lying. See her during the day, and then you're mine that Saturday night. We won't hit the clubs until at least ten, and then you'll have Sunday to recuperate. If you want to spend all day with her, fine, but at night you're mine, and I'm taking you out. And before you say anything else to find a way out of it, I'm paying for everything and dressing you up." She smiles.

I groan in protest. "Nat, I don't want to."

"That's too bad. You live in the greatest city in the world. You don't have a boyfriend, and you're turning twenty-one. We're going out," she states firmly, not taking no for an answer.

"I need a boyfriend."

"You don't have time for a boyfriend," she counters.

"True, but after a night of drinking, I'm going to wish I had one."

"Then hook up with a rando in a bathroom and move on."

I tip my cup toward her. Wouldn't be my first time. "Not a bad idea."

"So it's a deal?" she asks, and I don't miss the eager tone in her voice.

"Do I have a choice?"

"No."

I lick my lips and look out the window toward the hustle and bustle of the busy street. I glance back at her. "Only if I can wear those heels from last night. Then I'm game."

Her eyes light up. "Deal. You can have them if you want."

A laugh escapes me, and I look out the window again. "What do you think she does for a living?" I ask, pointing to a bystander on her phone. She's dressed in a business skirt past her knees with a matching blazer.

This is a game we came up with. We people-watch and try to guess what they do for a living.

"She's new to the city, or else she wouldn't be looking up at the sign like she's reading a language she doesn't understand. She probably tells people she's in marketing, but she's really a temp receptionist for a small business that's going to crumble next month and she doesn't know it."

I nod, and she says, "Your turn. What about him?" She points to a guy in line for coffee.

He looks like every other suit in the city. "He works on Wall Street and actually has money. He doesn't fake it."

"How can you tell?"

"His watch is a dead giveaway," I say, looking at what looks to be a Cartier. I saw a blue one in a magazine once and fell instantly in love with it. I never forgot it—or the seven-thousand-dollar price tag. "You and I both know that suit is not from a corner store or off the rack. It's tailor-made to fit his body and screams wealth. I bet he's terrible in bed."

She drags her gaze down the length of his body. "He has a nice ass, though."

I can always count on her to notice a man's body. I point to a runner.

"He's a P.E. teacher for underprivileged kids and loves his job."

"Come on. A tourist?" I ask, unimpressed after she points to someone taking random pictures of the concrete jungle. "What about that one?"

"He sleeps with his uncle."

"Natalie!" I laugh and cover my mouth. I look around to see if anyone heard her. One person is staring at us.

"What?" She shrugs and sips her java like she was only talking about the weather. "I bet he bones his cousins too."

"You're so bad," I say with a smile. "Okay. Last one, and then I have to head to class."

Her eyes scan the throngs of people, trying to find the best one. "That one."

"A struggling musician with a killer voice. Oh, and he has a muse who walks around naked."

Her eyes light up. "Nice! Okay. Text me later. I might have to work tonight, but I'll try to be quiet when I get home."

"You don't know if you have to work yet? Like you find out at the last minute? That's weird."

She doesn't look at me. "I think I'll buy you some noise-canceling earphones."

"But then how will I hear my alarm?"

She pauses. "Good point. Okay, scratch that. I'll just try to be quiet."

We hug goodbye, I thank her for my coffee, and then we go our separate ways. We might attend Fordham together, but we take completely different classes and our schedules don't usually line up. I'm majoring in Developmental Sociology, and she's still undecided, or so she says. I think that's just to piss her parents off, though. I think she secretly knows but doesn't want to tell anyone.

After a full day of new classes, all I want to do is go through my syllabi and prepare for the semester. Instead, I'm hurrying around my room looking for my uniform because duty calls and my bills need paying. Between crying babies, shitty diapers, and washing and folding strangers' clothes at the laundromat, this education better pay off.

Got to love New York City. It's the only city in the world that can make dreams come true while eating you alive at the same time.

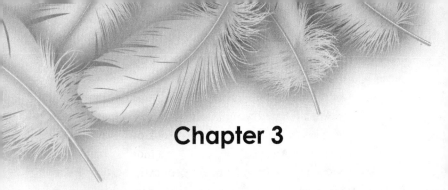

Chapter 3

The first couple weeks of school are always so much more exhausting than the rest of the year for me. Adjusting to new classes, homework, and two jobs, I guess would be tiring for anyone.

The stress of life and reality. Welcome to Adulthood 101.

As I sit on the bus watching the world pass me by, a feeling of nostalgia settles in my heart. Queens is where I was born and raised and is the only home I've ever known. I may have been all around New York City and Long Island, but that's the extent of my traveling. I've never left the state of New York.

I breathe in the familiar neighborhood and take in the exposed brick homes and black wrought iron fences. I don't get to see Grammy as often as I'd like because of my schedule, but when I do, I make the most of our time. She's the only family I have left, and I plan to spend all day with her. I know she'll have made my favorite chocolate kiss cookies and she'll insist on giving me cash for my birthday. She tries every year, and every year I turn around and deposit it right back into her account.

Two more stops and the brakes squeak as the bus pulls to a hard stop just a block away from Grammy's. I can already smell the sweet pastries as I walk up to her little unit. Her barred windows are open, and jazz music fills the air. One of her cats is perched on her stoop, and I bend down to pet the fur ball. She purrs and raises her ass in the air like a little hussy.

"Grammy!"

I step over the threshold. This isn't the greatest part of Queens, and the door needs to be locked at all times, yet hers never is. Grammy says she grew up never worrying about that and she isn't going to start now. She's a stubborn woman.

"My Aubrey." She pulls me into a tight hug. The woman is just over five feet and as strong as an ox. I look over her shoulder and see a new creature, one that wasn't here a month ago.

I pull back. "Gram, did you get another cat?"

"I don't find the cats; they find me." She smiles, and I give her a warning look. "What? They need food and a warm home. I give it to them."

"Someone is going to report you."

She waves her hand away. "They can go bend over."

I giggle. My grammy isn't one to ever curse.

Placing my purse on the table, I look around, and my brows furrow. "How many do you have?"

"I stopped counting."

I draw in a deep breath and frown. "How does it not smell like kitty litter in here?"

"I have nothing better to do with my life at my age, so I keep my house clean and change litter boxes often. Then I go to bingo. Enough about me. How has school been? How's Natalie doing?"

I take a seat at the little dinette table and watch as she bustles around the kitchen wanting to feed me. The cushions are covered in plastic, and the Formica counter is peeling at all the corners. For a woman in her late seventies, she's light on her feet. She attributes it to the cheap red wine and the fact she doesn't have a man in her life. She pays three dollars for the bottle and only allows one glass a night. She says it's because her cats need her.

I wasn't going to argue with that. I tell her all about the classes I'm taking, the professors, and of course, Natalie, whom she loves.

"Seems like you have your work cut out for you this semester. Think you can handle it?"

"Oh, yeah. It's nothing new, really. The classes are a little harder and I took on an extra one, but I think I'll be fine."

Her eyes soften, and I catch a little water in them. "Your parents would've been so proud. I know I am."

I look down. I miss them more and more every day.

Grammy fills me in on all the neighborhood gossip—who she can't stand, which of their dogs are always shitting on her lawn, who's sleeping with whom, and how she's got one person down the street trying to convert her to veganism and another always preaching about God. She refers to the last two as a Jesus freak and a plant-eating hippie. Her New York accent is so strong that it makes her storytelling animated. She might not have much to do, but she sure has an interesting group of people surrounding her.

She places a plate of fresh-baked cookies in front of me. The little thumbprints with a chocolate kiss right in the center smell divine and are my favorite. I pick one up and pop it into my mouth, sighing over the sugary softness. I watch as she reaches under the kitchen sink for a large bottle then places it on the counter. She retrieves two tumblers and pours us each a drink of the clear liquid. I lean over to sniff it when she sets the drink down in front of me. The scent singes my nostrils and burns.

"I didn't take you for a day drinker," I say.

"Aubrey, I have waited for this day for years."

I chuckle and eye her. "To have a drink with me?"

"Yes. You're twenty-one now."

She must've assumed I've never tasted alcohol in my life, which is cute and naive of her. I'm in college, of course I have, but I'll let her believe I haven't.

I lean over to smell the contents again, and my face pinches up. "What is this?"

"Sambuca."

"Do you just sip this?" I ask. I've never had it before.

She sits down in front of me and raises her glass. "You're going to shoot it."

My brows raise up. "A shot?"

"Yes," she says, like it's obvious.

I glance at the glass. "That's more than a shot. That's like two big shots."

She ignores me and wishes me a happy birthday. "Cheers, my sweet granddaughter!" She taps her glass to mine.

Grammy finishes her drink before I even sip mine, and I gawk. Bringing the glass to my lips, I cringe from the smell, shut my mind off, and take the shot—or shots. I'm not sure what she poured me.

Goose bumps coat my arms, and I shudder tasting the nasty liquor. It reminds me of black licorice and tastes hot—disgusting—but I smile anyway like I like it.

"I don't know how you drink this," I say as she refills my glass.

"That's a good girl," she says then shoves more cookies in front of me.

It doesn't take long for the alcohol to stream through my veins and make me smile a lot. I turn into a giggly happy drinker every time. I'm not a huge drinker due to school and work, but I can hold my own. I tell her how Natalie wants to take me out, and Grammy thinks that's generous of her.

"I'm glad I got to be the first to have a drink with you on your twenty-first. Now, be careful tonight, and don't do anything I wouldn't do," she says. Before my parents died, I'd heard colorful stories about her that I couldn't make up even if I wanted to.

Grammy walks into her bedroom and is back in a couple of seconds holding an envelope and a box. She hands them both to me.

I groan. "Grammy, I told you not to get me anything."

"Oh, quiet your mouth," she says. Her eyes glisten, and it makes me feel good to see her so happy. "And I didn't really get you anything. It was your mom's."

I stare at her for a moment as tears well in my eyes. I don't have much to remind me of my parents since I was so young when they passed away. Exhaling a breath, I open the box to reveal a rose gold necklace with a charm inside. My finger strums the thin chain, and my heart breaks a little bit at seeing it.

Grammy leans over and places her chin on her hand. "I remember seeing her wear it, and I asked why in the world she would wear a horseshoe when she'd never even ridden a horse in her life. Actually, she was never in a ten-foot radius of one, now that I think about it. Anyway, she said she didn't know why, just that she loved it at first sight. Your dad bought it for her. She never took it off." She pauses. "After the car accident, that was one of the few items recovered. Her diamond earrings were missing, as well as her watch. They were probably stolen at the scene, but that was still there. I've held on to it ever since."

My chin quivers. Grammy takes the necklace and stands up to place it around my neck.

"I read years ago that a horseshoe is supposed to protect from evil and negative energy, if you believe in that sort of thing." Her voice softens. "She'd want you to have it."

"Thank you," I say, my voice just above a whisper. Tears blur my vision, and I quickly wipe away the fat drop slipping down my cheek. "It's beautiful."

"Open the card when you get home," she says, and I nod. Her phone rings, and she shuffles across the kitchen to answer it.

I know what's inside the envelope. It's a heartfelt message that will probably make me tear up, along with fifty bucks. I've saved every card she's given me, and this one will go in my sentimental box too. A quick glance at the clock on her stove makes me realize it's been hours since I got here. Time always flies when I'm with Grammy.

"Yes, Francis, I said I was coming to bingo, so cool your cucumber." She winks at me. I hear the eagerness in her voice as she talks to her friend while she picks at cookies. Her sweet tooth is just as bad as mine. "I'll be there to pick you up. I haven't forgotten.

I'm not the one with Alzheimer's—you know that's Annabel—but maybe you need to have your head examined because we just had this conversation this morning."

She hangs up, and I stand. It's going to take me about an hour to get home, and I still need to eat before I go out. The last thing I want to do is drink on an empty stomach.

"I love you, Grammy. Thank you for today."

"Thank you, honey. I loved today, and I hope you have fun tonight. Be safe. Let's do this again now that you're legal, and bring Natalie with you too. Here, take these," she says and shoves a tin toward me that I know is packed with various cookies she baked.

We say our goodbyes, and I walk the block to the bus station. Inhaling the fresh air, I take my cell phone out and call my best friend.

"Nat?" I say and hiccup.

"Yeah, girl."

"I think my grandmother was trying to get me drunk. She gave me two double shots. I think I'm tipsy."

She laughs. "Gotta love Grammy. Let's do this!"

Chapter 4

"Damn, Gina, you look fine as hell," Natalie says in her best Martin Lawrence voice.

I grin at her *Martin* reference because it's too hard not to when she's being funny like that. Natalie and I are 90s sitcom junkies.

"Oh my God! You are so embarrassing," I say, exaggerating a little. We fuck with each other all the time.

"Seriously, girl, you look good. Give me those shoes back," she jokes.

I look at myself in the mirror. Lush, dark curls surround my face and drop past my breasts. My rich chocolate eyes flicker against the light. Spellbinding, an old boyfriend once called them, like I could read the darkest secrets in his soul. I line my plump, Cupid's bow lips in red then fill them in with a matching shade. I turn to the side and run my hands down the gold minidress Natalie insisted I wear. The dress is sleeveless with a deep slope between my breasts, accentuating my full-size Cs. It hits a little higher than midthigh and has a revealing open back. With the gorgeous black high heels that sealed our deal to go out, my legs look even longer, and I stand at about six feet tall now. I could be every man's wet dream.

"I clean up well, don't I?" I say, feeling so sexy.

"You sure do."

I look over at Natalie, who's adding a few last-minute curls to her platinum hair. Her bright-red, lacy strapless dress is sexy and even smaller than mine. Being a shot girl, she's used to wearing dresses like that. She has the seductive temptress style down and wears it well.

"Aren't you worried your boobs are going to pop out?" I ask.

Stunning navy blue eyes stare at me through the mirror. Her mouth pulls to one side, and she says, "They're supposed to look that way." She flashes me a wink. "I used double-sided tape. Trust me. They're not going anywhere."

Natalie is confident and outgoing. She embraces her sexuality and gives no fucks. I love that. She lives to make men crawl on their knees for her.

"Wing my eyes like yours when you're done?" I ask. She always has the perfect Adele wing, and I want it too.

Once we have our faces on and our hair styled to perfection, we take a ton of selfies, and then she reaches into a drawer and pulls out a little baggie.

"It's time to pregame," she says, dropping a pill into my hand. "We're celebrating this birthday in true New York City fashion— with a few shots and some Molly."

I've only done Molly a handful of times. Every time I did, all I wanted to do was dance the night away and have insanely hot sex.

"I'm gonna need to find a hot rando tonight if this is what we're doing."

Natalie takes out the bottle of tequila and pours two shots. She eyes my body. "That won't be an issue for you. And if you don't see a rando you want, I got your back. I have a couple of friends who are dying to bang you."

Natalie is a wilder version of me and makes for hysterical memories. She likes to party hard at the clubs. Her nights usually end with one shoe missing and her earrings long gone while she sits on a dirty curb eating pizza in the city. Or with a few guys in her bed. Whatever she's in the mood for.

"Cheers, bitch," she says and raises a shot to me. "This is going to be the best birthday ever!"

I'm glad I had a huge dinner so I won't get drunk too quickly. I want to remember as much as I can of this night. We both take a pill and wash it down with a shot. I place the back of my hand to my mouth and grimace over the shock of tequila. A shiver works down my spine. She waves her fingers at me and takes my mini red Solo shot cup to fill it again.

"You're fucking crazy," I say and take another shot. "Holy shit, my throat is burning."

"You love it," she counters, and I shrug. I do love it.

I'm a little anxious. My chest flutters with eagerness as I anticipate the effects of the Molly. This is why I rarely experiment with drugs—I'd want this high all the time. Everything will be tingly, and I know that constant rush will arrive soon that I'll never want to end. We take one last shot then walk downstairs to a town car waiting to take us to the Meatpacking District.

"Natalie, there's no way we're getting into this club," I say as we pull up to a dark building about twenty minutes later. It's a little after midnight, and I can feel the bass pounding through the closed doors. The tequila is streaming through my veins, warming my body. I'm feeling really good. Too good.

She gives me a sly look and grabs my wrist. "Watch me."

I chuckle. "This is gonna be good."

One of the trendiest and most exclusive clubs in the city is 1 Oak. It's where celebrities hang and the infamous after parties are usually held. I have no idea why she thinks we'll get in. I have no doubt we're going to be refused once we actually get to the front, if we even get there. There's always a line, and it never seems to move. The drinks are expensive as hell—we're not talking twelve bucks either.

We stride up to the front, and all eyes are on us. Natalie struts like she's on the runway. I'm not a shy girl, but the alcohol and pill are making me more confident than ever. I feel good, sexy, ready to conquer the world.

"Natalie, my beautiful leading lady. Always a pleasure," the massive bouncer says.

I eye him up and down. He looks like he was born on steroids. He brings his wrist to his mouth like he's in the CIA and whispers into it. He doesn't do a very good job at keeping his voice low—it's impossible when there's a deep hoarseness to it. He presses the earpiece in his ear and nods before responding with something about VIP.

"Clive, my sexy Dominican. I hope to see you later?" Natalie says flirtatiously and leans in to palm the side of his face and kiss the other cheek.

His eyes are hungry. Clive gives her a look I feel is one only she would understand, and then he turns to me and rakes an I-want-to-fuck-you-and-then-never-see-you-again look down my body. I let him look and don't withdraw. I like the attention he gives me.

"Bring your lady friend with you, and we'll make it a night we'll never forget."

Her chuckle is airy as she says, "Keep the drinks flowing, and anything is possible."

He raises a brow and looks intrigued, but I know she's just playing the game and giving him what he wants. He grins and opens the door for us to enter the club.

The hip-hop thumping from the speakers makes me want to get on the dance floor immediately. Excitement rolls down my arms as I take in my surroundings. Strobe lights flash over the bronze interior, a large, crystal clear chandelier hangs from the center of the room, and white orchid arrangements fill the four corners. The room is crowded, but at a comfortable level.

I'm in awe. I've never been inside a nightclub that exemplifies class and sophistication. I'm suddenly in love with the idea of being here.

"Told ya," Natalie smirks. We hit the bar first.

"How'd you do that?" I ask. She lifts two fingers to the bartender and orders us drinks. I have no idea what she orders, and I really don't care.

"You know I never kiss and tell."

It's true. She never lets her lips flap and always thinks before she speaks.

"Nat, I want to know. This is an exclusive club!"

She gives me a droll stare and leans in so she doesn't have to scream over the booming music. "My dad knows people, and those people know me."

Though I've never met him, Natalie's father is supposedly a well-known big shot lawyer in the city. They all claim to be a big shot.

"I thought you didn't really talk to him."

"Not often, but I use his name when I need to. This is one of the businesses he used to rep. He saved the owners' asses big time, and they're basically indebted to him forever."

I don't buy her story, but I don't question it either. Natalie isn't the type to use her parents' connections when she doesn't have the best relationship with them to begin with. When she wants to tell me the truth, she will.

The drinks are placed in front of us with a wink from the bartender. I don't ask what's in it. I just take a sip. The sweet liquor is like candy on my tongue and goes down too easy, loosening me up. I exhale and my skin tingles, my heart fluttering with anticipation. I'm feeling good, like I'm high on a cloud, when "Promises" by Calvin Harris and Sam Smith plays through the speakers. My eyes widen.

"I love this song!" I scream, and Natalie laughs.

"Drink up. Let's go dance!" Nat yells.

We finish our drinks and then head to the dance floor. I sway side to side allowing the alcohol to work its way through my veins as I wait for that impending rush from the Molly to take me higher. Tonight I'm letting go and having fun. Come Monday, I'll be back on the grind.

Lights are dimmed and the laser lines slow down until the beat drops. The DJ spins the music into a perfect fusion of hard-pounding bass and edgy techno. The sounds rip through the speakers, and we lift our arms in the air and roll our heads back, letting our bodies move to the rhythm. I explode with euphoria, the rush finally here.

My head is hazy and I'm soaring on another level, chasing the feeling of ecstasy. A blissful smile tips my lips, and I'm suddenly so happy Natalie talked me into going out. It's not often I get to do anything for myself, not with working so much and going to school.

Lost Boyz mixed with Jay-Z blend into the music. Natalie taps my shoulder, and I look at her. She points to something behind me, and I turn around to look. Fucking hell. I recognize the face behind the DJ table. DJ DiModa. He spins breakbeats and old-school hip-hop. He's the fucking scratch king of NYC.

"Shout out to my homegirl, Natalie, and her friend, Aubrey. Happy birthday, babe!" he says, the mic pressed to his mouth. Holding the headset to his shoulder, his arm swiftly shifts back and forth until the beat drops again, and he lets go.

"What the fuck! No way!" I scream in absolute shock. "How do you know him?"

I'm beginning to think my best friend lives a double life and I've just been given a little glimpse.

Chapter 5

The music slows down, and just as "Into You" by Fabulous comes on, I feel a body sidle up behind me. He places his face to the column of my neck, and his scruffy beard teases my heated skin, causing tingles to wash over me. I lean back into him, feeling the warmth of his body pressed against my back. A lazy, feel-good smile curves my lips, and a purr escapes my throat.

Natalie takes my little clutch purse to free my hands. My eyes roll shut as I let myself go. Having someone's hands all over me while on Molly just makes everything feel that much better.

My dance partner wraps his muscular arms around my front as I lift my arms and wrap them around the back of his neck. He towers over me, making me feel small and petite. Our bodies move in perfect harmony, hips swaying to the sensual rhythm of the music. He settles one hand on my stomach—his fingers splayed out make his hand appear large—while the other lands on my hip, giving it a good squeeze.

"I've been watching you dance all night. The things I want to do to you," he says, and it sends chills down my spine.

My nipples harden and I press my ass into him, grinding into his hard cock. He growls against my neck then peppers kisses down the column of my throat. A soft sigh escapes me. There's nothing like having the power of making a man fall to his knees with need that gets me going. He pushes his hips against me and I push back. I wouldn't be surprised if he's on some kind of pill too. In my experience, it's more like who *isn't* on something at a club in New York City.

The mixture of drugs, music, and the touch of his hands gripping me fill my veins with hunger for more. Our bodies continue to move in unison as if we're two lovers on the dance floor. Everything feels divine, and I turn around to face him.

He's cute, good-looking.

He'll do.

His eyes are glazed over, like I'm sure mine are, and the desire is as thick as the air between us. I work his body like a stripper pole. He watches and his gaze darkens. I give him a seductive smile.

"Tell me what you wanna do to me," I say, my voice husky.

"You want to know?" he says and then growls. "I'd rather show you."

He guides my arms around his neck and pulls me close, taking control. He grinds his hips against mine. His nostrils flare, and I inhale a deep breath from the ache building between my legs. He moves one hand to the small of my back and clutches my neck with the other, kissing me ruthlessly, savagely. I melt against him as he fucks my mouth, giving me a preview of what's to come.

The dancing heats up between us to a dangerous level. I can barely breathe with the way he's consuming me, stroking me with his tongue, taking me higher and higher. He shifts one of his thick thighs between my legs, and I grind on it. A purr escapes my lips, and I press down harder, squeezing him. My minidress shifts a little higher on my legs. I hope my ass doesn't show, but at the same time, I really don't care. All modesty goes out the window when Molly arrives.

My nipples ache to be touched, and my panties are sticking to my needy flesh. My rando for the night takes my hand and places it between us, leaving me no choice but to palm his length over his jeans. My lust for him intensifies, and I give a little squeeze.

"Come on, big boy." I press my breasts into his chest. "Show me what you got."

We slam into the men's bathroom, and he locks the door

behind him. His gaze tracks me like a predator across the small room and my heart hammers against my ribs. Goose bumps dance down my arms. I like the hunt. I sink my teeth into my bottom lip as he nears closer. I want him on me, devouring me. I want him to take control and make me forget my name.

Rando spins me around and shoves my stretchy dress up to my waist, and then he gives my ass a good, hard slap. I grab the counter and arch my ass a little higher in the air. Anticipation electrifies my veins as I look at my reflection in the dirty mirror. My eyes are glossy and my cheeks are flushed. I look high as hell. The sound of a zipper catches my ears, and I watch while he unzips his jeans and pulls his cock out.

"Condom," I say, breathless.

"No shit," he responds.

He pulls out a foil packet from his back pocket and rips it open with his teeth then rolls the condom down his thick length. Grabbing my hips, he roughly yanks them back so there's a deep sweep in my back. With one tug, he rips my panties off and drops them to the floor. He swipes his hand between my thighs and his eyes light up.

"You're so fucking wet. This is going to be good."

He grabs his cock and angles it at my entrance then drives into me in one hard stroke. I fall forward, my elbows hitting the marble counter, and I gasp from the intrusion. The pressure feels good, just how I like it, but I need a second to adjust.

"Oh, no, babe. You hold yourself up and fuck me back."

His dirty talk is all I need. What a little hussy I can be when I party.

I push myself up and thrust my hips back. He grabs my hair, wraps it around his fist, and gives it a good tug. I grunt. He's so deep at this angle that I can't tell if I love it or hate it, but then I look at us in the mirror and watch our joined bodies slap into each other, and I answer my own question. We line up just right, and for once I'm happy to tower over most women. His hand slips to the front of my pussy, finding my clit. Thank God he knows where it is and how to circle it with precision. A loud moan rolls off my shameless lips. My thighs quiver with anticipation as I thirst for more.

"Those fucking heels kill me," he says, thrusting in so deep that I draw in an audible breath. That produces a smile from me. For eight hundred dollars, they better fucking kill him.

My gaze drifts down to my shoes, and even I have to admit that I look good in them.

"Damn, you can fuck," he says. "Most chicks just lie there."

"How boring," I respond, and his hips pick up speed.

Our thighs slapping against one another and the sound of heavy breathing echoes throughout the bathroom. He grabs my face and turns it toward him. Our tongues meet, and that's all we both need to push us over the edge. My guy releases my hair and wraps his strong arm around my waist to hold me to him while he teases my clit. I love being held down and restricted. I rear back so he plunges harder, deeper. A few more thrusts and he's rolling his hips into me slow but hard, making us both come at the same time. I whimper at the feel of him twitching inside me. He grunts, and I can tell he's relishing in the pleasure just as much as I am.

"Gotta love fucking on E. Nothing compares," he says, pulling out once our pleasure subsides. I almost fall, but he grabs me to hold me up. "Especially with a chick as hot as you who can take cock like a pro."

"Tell me about it," I say, trying to catch my breath. "I can go all night, especially with a man who knows what he's doing," I counter.

He shoots me a wicked grin as he pulls the condom off and drops it into the trash. He picks up my ripped panties and dumps them too then places his cock back into his pants just as I push my dress down and fix my hair.

"How about we have a couple of shots then get back on the dance floor?"

I smile at him. "I'm down for that."

We walk back to the bar with his arm around my shoulders like we're dating and find Natalie talking to a stranger and throwing back shots.

"Ohhhh, I see you got a birthdaygasm with a hottie." She's grinning from ear to ear and slides my purse to me.

"It's your birthday?" my rando asks. "Tell me you're legal."

I laugh. I can't help it. I've always been told I look young for my age. "Twenty-one today."

"Thank fuck," he says and waves for a round of shots.

"Ready to hit the next club?" Natalie asks after the shots are delivered.

"Where are we off to?"

"Marquee."

Natalie's rando groans. "I never get into that club."

"That's because you don't have a female with you," Natalie says, and I look at her in confusion. "Marquee doesn't usually let a man inside unless he has a girl. They have strict rules," she clarifies.

"Guess it's your lucky night," I say to her guy. I pull my own man in for a kiss and then look at Natalie. "He's with me all night."

We take one last shot then walk downstairs to hail a taxi to West Chelsea. It takes ten minutes to get to Marquee with traffic, and just like at 1 Oak, we're ushered to the VIP section.

We spend the rest of the night dancing and drinking, with a few rounds of hot, drug-induced sex in the bathroom.

"What's your name?" my rando asks as we part ways.

"Felicia." It's been fun, but like hell I'm giving him my real name.

"I'm never gonna see you again, am I?"

"Nope," I chuckle.

"Damn," he whispers. His grin is so fucking cute, I almost want to give him my real info. "Well, thanks for one hell of a night."

"Thanks, guys, for the drinks and orgasms, but we gotta go," Natalie says playfully, and we take off in a different direction.

We walk a couple of blocks, giggling over nothing, while trying not to trip in our heels over the uneven pavement. If we weren't as drunk as sailors, it wouldn't be an issue, but right now I'm seeing triple and I wonder just how bad my best friend is.

"How many fingers," I ask as we reach the end of the sidewalk. We're waiting on the light to change so we can cross the street. As wasted as we are, we'd probably get caught and ticketed if we jaywalked, or worse, we'd get hit by a car.

Her face pinches up and she squints. "Hmmm. Both hands!" she says happily, and I bust out laughing.

I had four fingers up.

About thirty minutes later, we stop at one of the many pizzerias open all night and order slices as big as our heads. My mouth waters as I watch the counter boy remove them from the oven. The smell of cheese bubbling and toasty crust baking in the brick oven that New York City is known for almost makes me sigh. He plates two greasy slices and sets them in front of us.

"This is the best fucking pizza I've ever had in my life," Natalie slurs after she takes a bite. She acts like she's making love to it.

I laugh so hard at the sound of her moans that my vision blurs with unshed tears. Lifting the steaming slice to my mouth, I take a bite and white-hot heat scorches my bottom lip. A loud gasp flies out of me. I immediately rear back, letting go of the flimsy slice and dropping it to the plate.

"Fuck!" I swipe my drink and wrap my lips around the straw. The pizza is so piping hot that I burned my mouth. Once I feel like my mouth has recovered from the shock, I blow on the slice to cool it down the same way I do for the little shits I nanny for.

I can feel Natalie's eyes on me and turn to look at her. She's staring at my mouth, trying not to laugh but fails miserably.

"I bet I look like I have herpes now," I grimace with a shake of my head. Nat doubles over in laughter. I end up laughing too.

My lip is swollen and pulsating. I didn't take note of how hot my slice was, even though I watched it come straight from the oven. I glance around the pizza joint we're sitting in. Somehow, we ended up in the touristy part of the city, a place we try never to be. I guess we were too distracted and laughing to realize how far we had walked. Times Square is great for people-watching, just not at three in the morning when the creatures of the night come out to play. But something is missing ...

Frowning, I glance between us, then scan the countertop. "Where's your purse?" I ask as I fish my phone out of my clutch.

Natalie looks at me, but her eyes drift over my shoulder. "What purse?"

This birthday is by far the best one I've ever had, pizza-herpes lip and all, and I have my bestie to thank for it.

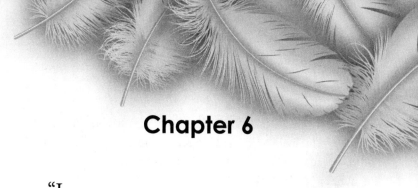

Chapter 6

"I fucking hate you," I say, holding the side of my pounding head.

There's too much light in the living room, and it's causing a throb in my temples. I turn over on the couch and bury my head under a pillow. We both couldn't take a step farther to our rooms last night and had crashed here.

"Today is going to be the worst day ever." Natalie chuckles then whimpers.

"What time is it? I feel like we've been sleeping all day."

"I don't know. I can't find my purse."

"That's because you lost it," I respond, my voice muffled from being under the pillow.

"At least it wasn't my shoes this time. Give me your phone so I can cancel my cards and order a new cell."

"You're not going to even try to find it?" I ask, groaning, and move the pillow off my head to stare at her. My head is killing me, but I won't bother with an aspirin. It's not like it will help the hangover anyway.

Nat pops up on her elbows. "Aub, do you remember all the places we hit last night?"

I hesitate for a moment. "Nope."

"Exactly. And it's New York. I'll never get any of it back."

Getting out of bed with a groan, I make my way to where I threw my phone last night. I swipe it off the counter and turn around. The room tilts, and I lose my balance, hitting the floor with a thud.

Natalie laughs hard and then jumps up, holding her crotch.

"I'm going to pee my pants!" She runs from the living room with her knees locked together.

A few minutes later, she's back, and I'm still on the floor dying.

"Do you have your weed pen? The only way I'm gonna get rid of this headache is with weed." When she doesn't respond, I look up at her and ask, "What?"

"Why didn't I think of that?"

Natalie retrieves the pen from a drawer in the kitchen and inhales deeply before handing it to me. I take a few hits and pass it back.

"You have the worst pair of raccoon eyes I've ever seen." The black smeared makeup around her eyes makes her look like it was done by a toddler in the dark.

"You don't look so hot either, *Felicia*."

I giggle at the fake name I gave the guy last night. At least she remembers that. I flip the screen on my camera app to look at my reflection.

"Jesus Christ." My eyes widen. "I look like I had an exorcism."

Natalie takes another hit and holds it for a second then exhales, a dense cloud of smoke forming in front of her face. "Nah, you just look like you got some good D."

I purse my lips and nod. "It's true."

"We seriously need our own reality show," she announces, handing me back the odorless pen. "Wicked senses of humor. Check. Dirty minds. Check. New York City is our playground. Check. Shamelessly hot. Check. Epic bitches with low principles ..." She looks at me and raises a brow. "Double check. What's not to love *and* want? We can't be epically fucking amazing without all of that."

All I can do is shake my head and inhale one last time. That's all I really need. Once it kicks in, I'll be good to go and the pain will be gone.

"I think he had the biggest dick I've ever seen in my life," I say.

She chokes, and then the coughing comes. I throw her a water bottle that's been sitting on the table for a week. She misses, and it hits her head. I burst out laughing, which causes her to laugh even harder. She can't sip the water because she's in between coughing and laughing so hard.

"You don't even know, Nat. He rammed that shit into me. Thank God I was flying high and loose as a goose so it wasn't bad. I can't imagine banging him on the regular. I wouldn't be able to walk after."

She drinks half the bottle and exhales a huge breath like she just came up for air.

"They don't call it the Meatpacking District for nothing."

"No, they don't."

"Lucky you. My rando was thick, but he was so short. A chode."

Frowning, I look at her. "Did you just make that word up?"

Natalie gawks. "You've never heard of a chode?"

I shake my head. Thankfully it's already feeling lighter. "What the hell is it?"

"A chode is a short but fat dick."

Oh God. The giggles kick in again, and I can't stop laughing. She follows suit. We're so lame.

"You're a chode," I say, grinning from ear to ear. We're both hysterical over the word.

"Okay, Ram Jam."

"What the fuck?" I laugh harder.

We recount the night and then crash for hours. I wake up and stretch my arms above my head and yawn. It's dark outside, but I'm feeling a million times better. A little smoke always helps ease the tension and stress, and it's the best hangover cure.

My stomach growls obnoxiously loud, and I realize I haven't

eaten anything today. I'm suddenly craving greasy, fatty food, but I don't feel like going anywhere alone. Sitting up, I reach for my phone to check the time. It's only a little after seven. I decide that since Natalie took me out last night, I would return the favor and treat her. Neither one of us left the apartment today, but that's because we were too incapacitated to leave.

"I'm seriously not looking forward to tomorrow," I say an hour later. I'm dreading school.

We're at a tiny diner a couple of blocks away. I typically hate the smell of diners. They remind me of old people and baby powder, but every so often we find a little hole-in-the-wall diner where the food is amazing. Like the one we're at now. It doesn't smell bad, and all the dishes around us look appetizing. Our food is brought out and placed in front of us. My stomach is still a mess, but at least my head is fine. Natalie, on the other hand, looks torn up.

"Aubs, no one looks forward to Mondays," she says and stuffs three tater tots into her mouth.

I stare at her in morbid fascination as she mixes up a disgusting concoction of mustard, ketchup, and a ridiculous amount of black pepper. "You're so gross."

She dips a tater tot into the sauce and holds it out to me. "Try it."

I pull back and grimace. "No fucking thank you. Where did you come up with that idea anyway?"

"When I was high."

A chuckle rolls off my lips. As hard as Natalie parties, she's on top of her shit. She holds down a job and is in the top of her class, not that she has much of a choice when it comes to school. Her parents would rain down on her if she got anything less than a B in any of her classes.

"Remember that time I was eating salty popcorn with flan frozen yogurt? How I dipped each piece of popcorn into the flan and acted like it was better than sex?"

"I can't erase the memory from my mind even if I wanted to. It's seared into my head for my next ten lives. Let's not forget that it was vegan flan you had, which tasted repulsive. Man, you were so into it though. Flaaaannnnnn." I drag out the word the way she did that night.

Natalie looks like she's ready to choke me over my reenactment. Her expression kills me, and I start laughing. I love being around her. All we do is laugh and have fun and live in the moment. Natalie doesn't give two shits about much in this world, and I find it encouraging. For the most part, I feel like I'm like that too, but I do have those few moments when I hesitate and overthink. She never does though. Once her mind is made up, that's it.

I take a bite of my greasy burger that's topped with a sunny-side up egg and think about my week ahead. "I really don't want to fold clothes tomorrow or deal with screaming babies on a Friday night. Ugh. Kill me now."

"So why do you do it?"

"I may hate the job at the laundromat, and being a nanny, but I have bills I have to pay. Beggars can't be choosers."

"Where I work, you could easily quadruple your week's pay in one night. I could probably get you a job. You'll make a ton of cash there under the table." She hesitates. "You just have to be really open-minded before you go in and not overthink where the money is coming from or what you're doing to get it."

"Why do I feel like there's more to being a shot girl than what you're telling me."

Natalie finishes the last bite of her tofu burger, wipes her fingers on the ketchup-smeared napkin, and tosses it on her plate. She turns toward me.

"Growing up around the white collars, I've learned that everyone is hiding something. People can be devious in their pursuit of riches. Trust me when I tell you I've heard the conversations my parents had at their parties. Money is money however you get it. Dirty or clean. And once you get a taste, there's no going back. You'll do whatever it takes to get more. A stock trader on Wall Street isn't going to tell you what his secret is to make the big bucks. He'll only tell you part of the secret and take the rest to the grave. It's like giving a helping hand. Only your hand is wet, and you're going to slip out if you don't find a way to pull yourself up. You're only going to get so much help, you know?"

I consider her words.

"But how does one live with themselves by screwing people over to get ahead?"

Natalie pulls her tangled hair into a messy bun. I can tell she's still being vague.

"Listen. You want to make it? Sometimes you have to lie to Paul to steal from Pete. And if you really want to be a cut above the rest, you have to cheat on Pat and fuck his friend, Paco."

"I think it's rob Peter to pay Paul. I don't remember anything about fucking friends."

"Okay, Ram Jam. Same difference. Why do you have to be a smarty pants? Money is money, and I want as much as I can get, however I can get it."

"Pot calling the kettle black. You get better grades than I do," I say.

"Sometimes I wonder if my parents made a large donation to the school for me to attend. I didn't even apply to Fordham."

My eyes widen. "Are you serious? Is that even possible?"

She shrugs. "Money always walks. Anything is possible, Aubrey," she says, drawing out my name.

I pay the bill, and we both get up to leave. I'm stuffed and I know I'm going to sleep like the dead tonight, which is what I need so I can be prepared for school tomorrow. The fresh air helps revive me as we walk back to our apartment.

At one of the street corners, there's an older man standing with a cardboard sign in one hand and a Styrofoam cup in the other. It's hard to read the chunky block writing, but I get the gist of it. I reach into my pocket and pull out whatever's left and drop it in his cup. I don't have much, but I like to give where I can.

"My stomach is so full," I say, holding myself when we round the corner.

"I look like I'm about to give birth," Nat says, rubbing her belly.

I chuckle and look at her bloating midsection. Natalie is my height and just as thin.

"How far along are you?" I joke. She jabs me playfully with her elbow. "I can't wait to pass out. This week is going to be long. The first week back to school always is." I pause. "Thanks for last night."

"Will you stop thanking me," she says jabbing me with her elbow again.

"I'm sorry, but I had so much fun and I want you to know that I really appreciate it. I got to let loose and not stress about life for once."

She's quiet for a moment. "You could live like that, party all the time, and rarely ever spend money doing so. You'd give up your laundromat and nanny jobs real fast."

I shoot her a glance. "Sounds tempting, but the nanny job pays really well. I can't give that up."

"Not better than what I make. What you make in a week, I make in a few hours."

"By being a shot girl?" I ask, my voice raised. I don't hide my skepticism. "Where the hell are you serving shots to get the kind of money you speak of? And how much are these shots anyway?"

"If I tell you, promise you won't judge me?"

I'm confused. "For being a shot girl? Why would I judge you for that?"

A sly smile curls the corners of her injected lips. "What if I told you I've never been a shot girl in my life?"

Chapter 7

We're back to our place, showered, and ready for bed. The day was a complete waste, but I don't feel guilty about it. Going out like I did last night and living the VIP life is something I never do and probably won't be doing again anytime soon.

Glancing around Natalie's room, I take in the wall she recently redecorated. White lights are strung from corner to corner, and pictures of friends—no family—hang from clothespins. There's a minibar with a tall lingerie dresser next to it. She loves to paint, so her artwork hangs in the empty spaces. It's all very shabby chic and gives nothing away to this mysterious life I never knew she apparently had. I scoot under the comforter and wait for her to finish putting on her pajamas. I'm curious about this job offer she mentioned. A shot girl job that isn't a shot girl job, and pays better than both my jobs combined? Sign me up! The wealth in New York City is astounding. I'm a shameless paper chaser. I'm willing to try anything at least once.

"Listen," Natalie says as she climbs in next to me, "if I tell you about my job, I don't want you to shoot me down. I want you to take time to consider it, then give me your answer. It's not for the delicate Debras of the world, but keep in mind that you won't make money like this anywhere else. I think you could handle it or else I wouldn't have mentioned it to you. This is a mind-over-matter job, and it requires the utmost discretion. You don't talk about it. Kind of like *Fight Club*."

I frown. "Is it legal?"

She shrugs like she isn't sure. Her mouth bunches up, and I

already have my answer. I'll take that as a no.

"Depends on who you ask. I have a license for what I do," she says, but her voice is raised, like she teeters on the edge of what she does being considered right or wrong. I'm going to go with wrong.

"Okay. Illegal. Got it. Next."

"It's not illegal, though, like strippers use it."

My brows bunch together. I just stare because I have no damn clue where she's going with this. I'm about to tell her to spit it out already.

"Are you a secret stripper? A streetwalker? It would make sense with all that money."

New York strippers get paid big bucks, but only if they're good. Some even travel to put on shows.

"No," she says, sitting up and crossing her legs. Oh shit. She's about to get serious.

"Don't tell me your nighttime secret name is Stardust, or Muffin, or Destiny, or Trixie."

Her head falls back and she laughs.

"I'm serious! They always have funny names. Have you ever met a stripper named Betty? Only the classy ones are called ..." I hesitate as I try to think of a tasteful flower. "Magnolias. They're called magnolias. Like it's a step above carnation or something."

She can't stop giggling hysterically. Probably because she knows I'm right. "Have you ever been in a strip club?"

"I grew up in Queens. How sheltered do you think I am?"

"Good point." She pauses and blows out a heavy breath. "I want to tell you this, but I don't want you to think any less of me, and this definitely could make someone second-guess a person's morals."

Whatever she has to say must be hard for her to voice, so I immediately get serious with her. "I swear I won't view you any differently. You're my best friend, and there are very few things that could ruin that. Your job would never be a reason to make me look at you in any type of negative way, I promise. You don't do anything without motive, so whatever you're doing, I'm sure you have a reasonable excuse. Unless it's like murder or something."

She kind of offers me a smile, kind of doesn't. At least I know it's not murder, and I feel a little better about that. She rubs her eyes with the heel of her hands and releases a jagged breath. The last thing I would ever want to do is hurt her with judgment.

"Nat, tell me."

Like the true Manhattanite that she is, she starts talking a mile a minute, like she's had twelve shots of espresso and a bump of cocaine in the bathroom.

"So what I have is an Adult Entertainment License. It's a requirement to work in adult clubs, but I don't strip. I mean, I could if I wanted to, but I don't have the strength to hold myself up on the pole the way strippers do. I've tried it. It's so much harder than it looks. I had bruises everywhere, and I was sore for days. Plus, I just don't have the grace most exotic dancers have."

"When the hell did you do that?"

"About two years ago."

My brows shoot up to my hairline. Eyes wide, I'm flabbergasted. "Two years ago? Where was I?"

She shrugs. "Not important."

I put my hand up. "Um, excuse me, but I would've liked to know when my friend tried working the pole and I didn't get to laugh while watching her."

This time she smiles so big that I end up smiling too. I was being serious. I would've totally watched her and cheered her on.

"Girl. *It's so hard.* One day we should take a pole dancing class together just so you can see."

The idea intrigues me. "That actually sounds fun. Wait. So you went to a strip club?"

She shifts uncomfortably. "Not necessarily. I went to a club called Sanctuary Cove and tried it there."

My face twists in confusion as I try to think if I've ever heard of it. Despite Manhattan being one of the most densely populated cities in the world, it's actually really small.

"I've never heard of that place."

She shakes her head. A few blonde strands fall in her face, and she brushes them behind her ear. "You wouldn't have. It's an extremely discreet club for the filthy rich and powerful. The elite of Manhattan, the cream of the crop. You have to be invited to join. It's very hush-hush. I had to sign a nondisclosure agreement. The only reason I'm telling you is because I think you would be a good fit. Kind of. I guess we'll see."

My forehead is starting to throb from bunching my brows so hard.

"Nat, what are you involved in?"

She worries her bottom lip. "What if I told you that you could easily make about twenty grand in a couple of hours? Fifty thousand in one weekend? That in one month, you could walk away with over one hundred thousand dollars?"

"I'd say you're full of shit but to sign me the fuck up." There's a flicker of light in her eyes. "Tell me everything."

"What I do is ... Basically I ..." She stalls then exhales a slow breath. "I fulfill men's every desire. Women too, if they swing that way. Sometimes a spouse is involved, but only through clearance first."

The urge to giggle is strong, but judging by the serious look on her face, it's probably not the best time. "At this place called Sanctuary Cove?"

"Or wherever they want to meet. I'm told where to go based on what the client wants. It can be a bit more inconspicuous that way."

What she's describing sounds like an underground club. I also know most underground happenings are typically illegal and eventually get busted. Still, I'm curious about it. Being told I could make a minimum of twenty thousand dollars in a few hours sounds preposterous and too good to be true. But that would be hard for anyone to turn away. I shouldn't be intrigued, but I am, and I want to know more.

"Who's they? Who tells you where to go? I'm confused. How do you meet these men and women?"

"Through a woman named Christine."

"And what does Christine do?" I ask, enunciating every word like I do when the toddlers I nanny cause trouble.

"She sells your dignity."

I tip my head to the side. "I'm serious."

"She sells a good time with very happy endings," Natalie says.

I laugh because that isn't what I expected.

"Oh, God. Do you give massages? What's so hush-hush about that? Honestly, that's lame, Nat."

Her eyes lift to the ceiling and her lips pucker to the side. "I guess you could say I go the extra mile with my job."

I exhale an exasperated sigh. I'm getting peeved with playing twenty questions only to get one-word answers.

"Can you just be out with it already? You're killing me here."

She averts her gaze to the ugly wood floor covered in her clothes. She has to know by now that I wouldn't judge her, if that's what she's still worried about. Her head falls into her hands.

"I've never said this out loud." Her voice is muffled as she sits staring at her crossed legs. "I didn't think it would be this hard, and now I sort of wish I hadn't even brought it up."

I lower my voice to a more sympathetic tone. Whatever she's about to tell me is big, and I want her to know her secret is safe with me.

"Said what?"

"What I do for the money I get. No one knows, Aub. It's definitely nothing to be proud of, but it has to stay a secret, even if you decide what I do isn't for you. Promise me."

Nodding, I try to lighten the mood.

"Fine. Deal. Scout's honor. Be out with it already and stop beating around the bush. You know I'm good for it," I say.

Natalie picks up her head and looks straight into my eyes. She takes one deep breath, then slowly exhales, her lips forming an "o."

"I sleep with men for money. I'm good at it. Really good at it."

I blink and debate with how I'm supposed to receive her words.

Naturally, I spit out a joke.

"Nat, are you trying to tell me you're a rent-a-hoe?"

Chapter 8

Her mouth twitches as she tries not to laugh, but she does in the end. I know I did the right thing, even though I'm stunned as fuck.

"Yes, I guess I am."

Lines crease my forehead. "For real, though? Do you really sleep with men for money? Like get paid to have sex with them? Men *and* women?"

She nods, and I'm floored.

"I'm an escort. A one-stop shop. I don't cuddle or give foot rubs, but if you name your price, I just might."

I stare at Natalie, lost somewhere between speechless and stunned because it's almost too crazy to fathom that what my best friend just told me she does is real.

I take her in, really look at her. From the outside, she's a Manhattan princess. Flawless, creamy skin, big round midnight blue eyes, legs for days, wears all the top-notch fashion designers, *and* has a hefty trust fund. She has the perfect life and will never want for anything. I'm dumbstruck as to why she feels the need to sell her body for money.

What's even more mind-blowing is that she thinks I'm a good fit for something like this. I mean, I have nothing against escorts—sometimes you gotta do what you gotta do—but I don't know why she would think I would be a good candidate.

"Say something," she says, her voice a low whisper.

"You're a dirty little freak," I joke. "For real, Nat, how the hell did you get involved in that? Do you have a pimp?"

"No, no pimp, but there is a house mom—a madam. Madam

Christine. She owns and runs Sanctuary Cove."

I burst out laughing because she can't be serious right now. She has a madam? No way. Now I know she's making this up.

"This is starting to resemble a Lifetime movie with a bombshell twist," I say, which makes me laugh even more. "I can already see the tagline for the commercial—Manhattan princess by day, seductress hooker by night."

Except she jumps from her bed and marches over to her tiny closet in her pajamas. Natalie looks mad, but I know she's not. She's about to prove a point.

Natalie bends over and digs into the back of the closet. She pulls out a tattered black suitcase and drops it to the floor. She unzips it in a flurry, throwing the top back, then unzips a smaller suitcase stashed inside. She reaches in and takes out an ugly ass, bright green and orange stuffed dragon. She walks back to the bed and holds the toy out for me to look at. It looks like something she won at a fair.

I'm appalled at her savagery when she rips the head off. Natalie turns the dragon over, and money falls out of its neck onto my lap. My jaw drops. I hold my breath as all the humor between us fades. There are stacks and stacks of fifty- and hundred-dollar bills, and they're all tightly wrapped in money bands. The bills are clean and crisp, not crumpled together. I start counting in my head. There has to be somewhere around fifty thousand dollars here. Maybe more.

"This can't all be from giving a few blow jobs."

I finger the money, fanning it in front of me in awe. The scent of freshly printed money fills the air. This is a lot of cash to hide in an apartment, let alone for a college student to have. She isn't making this from being a shot girl, that's for sure. Natalie crawls onto the bed and sits next to me.

"I'm an escort for the rich. A high-end escort."

"What does that mean? You're a prostitute?"

She confirms my question with a nod.

"It means I really am paid for a good time. Whether it's sex or acting as just a companion, an hour for a quickie, a whole weekend under someone's control, or arm candy at a Saturday brunch event, I get paid for it. I do whatever they want. I have my limits, and I only do what I'm comfortable with."

"You're a classy Vivian. Julia Roberts would be so proud." I kid, not knowing what else to say. "Where do you find these men?" My voice is a low whisper, as if we're going to get caught.

"I told you. Madam Christine finds them."

"You weren't kidding about her?"

"No. Every transaction goes through her. She sets the date up based on what the client's needs are, what her girls can do, and when. We're paid in cash at either the end of every job or at the end of the week. All this"—she nods with her chin toward the cash in my lap—"is from last month. I've been trying to open a deposit account offshore to hide it."

My mind is spinning with question after question. I don't know where to start. Mainly I want to know why she does this.

"Where does she find the clients," I ask, my voice low.

Natalie looks at me. Her eyes are like an open book. All I can do is stare. This is a huge pill to swallow.

"They're members of Sanctuary Cove. Doctors, lawyers, real estate moguls, businessmen—they're the richest of the rich. Some come from old money, some work for the government. Some are self-made billionaires. Half of the time the clients just want a few hours away from their hectic lives."

I just stare in astonishment, trying to process her words. I wonder what they want the other half of the time.

"Okay, so it is prostitution, but it's not. As you can see, I don't give twenty-dollar blow jobs," she says and gestures toward the money. "These men, they're usually married and not looking to have a romantic affair that could ruin their image. They want a no-strings-attached rendezvous while keeping their families whole. They want gorgeous women who can dress up and hang on their arms, not ones wearing clear high heels. I don't call it a hookup, and date is a far stretch from the truth. Depending on what my client wants, I give it to him—or her."

"Don't you feel bad, though? Like having sex with a married man?"

Natalie shakes her head, and the look in her eyes tells me she really doesn't feel bad.

"No, because I'm not soliciting them; they're coming to Sanctuary Cove. The clients have already set their minds on hiring an escort. Madame Christine gives them the reassurance of confidentiality they need."

I can't deny that this is all fascinating. I'm intrigued more than ever, but this kind of lifestyle isn't for everyone. I'm pretty positive it's not for me. Still, I'm curious.

"But why would someone pay this much money for sex when you can get it so much cheaper on the corner?"

"Aubs, the amount of money in this city is sickening. People will pay for anything if they want it bad enough. And they want the confidentiality we offer. The women at Sanctuary Cove are screened and tested regularly to work there. So are the clients. When I told you this job was hush-hush, I wasn't kidding."

"But don't the wives ask where the money is going?"

She laughs, but it's more of a mock. "No. These men have secret accounts they keep from their wives. They're sneaky as fuck and know how to play the game. Plus, the wives are set up so nicely that they're never going to question a thing. They get stipends every month and live in penthouses with butlers and chauffeurs."

I ask the one question I need answered most. "But why do *you* do it? You don't need to."

She falls back on the bed and drapes an arm over her forehead. "I knew you were going to ask that. It was by accident, really, and

I'm not going to get into the logistics of it, but it happened after I had a huge argument with my parents. Even from a young age, my life has been so controlled and planned by them. You know I'm at this school because of them, and you know I take the classes I do because of them, because they're setting up the future they want for me. They say one day I'll thank them, but I won't. I've always hated school. And I don't want to follow in their footsteps. Never have."

"But you're twenty-two. Why do you even stay in school if you hate it?"

She levels me with a stare. "Because if I don't do what they say, I lose my trust fund. I'm not willing to risk that. Plus, you need a degree to do anything these days, so I figure it can't hurt to get one from an Ivy League school on my parents' tab."

She has a point, and I can't fault her for that one. "But from what I've seen this weekend, you have a lot of money to live on your own. Why don't you?"

"You see my taste. I love luxurious things. Plus, you're my bestie. I have fun living with you." She pauses. "My goal is to stack as much money as possible, that way I'll be able to retire fresh out of college. I have two hundred grand sitting in the bank in a personal account right now. I need to deposit this, but I can't. I've already raised red flags at my bank, which is why I need an offshore account."

I gawk at her. That's a lot of money for having sex.

"And your parents have no idea?"

She shakes her head. " I still withdraw money from my trust or just swipe my debit card to make it look like I'm using it."

"Two hundred grand," I repeat. My voice is a whisper as I stare at the sex money. "How? How long did it take to accumulate this much?"

Natalie shrugs one shoulder nonchalantly. "A little over a year. There's money to be made in this city, and once you start making it, it becomes addicting. This is what they call hush money."

I fall back onto the pillow, trying to sort out my thoughts and process all the information Natalie just threw at me. My mind is stuck on the number figures she's talking about. It's tempting now when she explained escorting the way she did. There's a lot I could afford without the stress of how I was going to get through the month. Forget the flat screen for Grammy and my simple luxuries. I could move her to SoHo and take her on a *Pretty Woman*-inspired shopping spree.

My head is still spinning when Nat says, "The real question is, how much are you willing to sell yourself for?"

Chapter 9

I tap my pen on my desk, staring in a daze at my white-haired professor. I should be focused on what he's saying, but my thoughts keep going to my best friend's surreptitious identity.

Who is Natalie at night? There's no chance in hell she uses her real name. We both rarely give out our real names when we go out for the night. So who is she? I know she's not a Betty or a Trixie.

More importantly, how does she actually go through with the deed? A one-night stand is understandable because there's a mutual attraction—usually encouraged by liquor—so it works.

But this is something else. This is literally being paid to have sex with a stranger.

I can't wrap my head around how someone has sex for money if they're sober and normal. I mean, I know it happens all the time, but I never really gave it much thought until now. I'm fairly certain I'd be as dry as the Sahara Desert if I was paired with an eighty-year-old man. I have a feeling my body would not spread like oil when the time came to do the job and I'd be more like frozen butter. I shiver at the thought. There's no way his wrinkly dick would just slide in. I wonder if he has to take his dentures out to have sex.

Manhattan is the city that never sleeps, riddled with unlawful activity on every block. Everyone hustles. Everyone is always on the go. And everyone is trying to make a quick buck. I've always loved that aspect of living here. But how many of them are willingly selling sex? I'm shocked by how in the dark I've been about this secret life Natalie lives. I never thought to ask if there was more to what her job required. Why would I? Now I can't stop thinking about it.

Sitting in the last twenty minutes of class—aptly titled The Study of Deviance and How It Relates to Power and Class— has me putting serious thought into Natalie's offer. Is she suggesting I become a Vivian? I'm not sure I have the ability to relinquish my body like that, and I wonder why she thinks I could. I glance at my watch. If I hurry back to our apartment fast enough, I might catch her before I need to leave for the laundromat. I want to ask her a few more questions. I'm not looking forward to going to work. That place smells like dirty jock straps, but it helps pay the bills, so I try not to complain too much.

Class lets out, and I quickly gather my belongings. When I step outside, I'm greeted by the mass of people and the scent of sewage lingering in the air that never seems to disappear. It's a little cooler, so the smell isn't as disgusting as it is in the summer. I dodge and swerve around the picture-taking tourists and make it to our apartment pretty quickly. Not before dropping some change into a cup, though. What can I say? I have a bleeding heart. I take the stairs two at a time and race down our floor to the end of the hall. Unlocking the door, I walk inside to see Natalie getting dressed.

"Hey, girl," she says casually, like she didn't just ask me if I'd be willing to sell my body for sex last night.

"Hey."

"What's up?"

I drop my books on the table and follow her into her room. I eye her. She's wearing a stunning nude cocktail dress with a sweetheart neckline and tons of flashy rhinestones. It's glitzy and glamorous and screams money. She looks amazing and pulls off the style like it was made for her. Teardrop dangly earrings with no necklace finish off the attire. She looks like a goddamn supermodel.

"Going to work?" I ask.

She gives me a side smile, and there's an impish look in her eyes. I almost think she likes what she does.

"I am, but it won't be a long night. I have to attend some ritzy dinner on the Upper East Side, where the plates are about two thousand a person." She rolls her eyes. "Who pays that much for a dinner?"

"Do they donate it to charity? Usually that's why, like they'll donate half."

"I have no idea. Probably not. The richies I know rarely ever give back."

I make a little noise because she has a point.

"So there's no sex tonight?"

"I always expect sex. Any man, even if he isn't paying for sex, is going to expect it at the end of a date. It's just the way it goes."

"I have to ask you something," I say, and she shoots me a quick glance. "What makes you think I can do what you do?"

"Because you love sex and you don't have an issue with one-night stands." She's not wrong. "And you really need the money." Valid. "You wouldn't have to stress about how you're going to pay for you or Grammy, and you wouldn't have to work so much. Depending on what your hard limits are, you could literally work one weekend a month, and even that would bring in way more than you're making now. But I wouldn't expect that because Madam Christine demands we work a minimum of seven days a month. Those seven days a month, Aubs, you can live comfortably and stress-free."

But not morally free, and I'm not sure I'm okay with that. Selling my body for sex makes me feel a little dirty.

I watch as she takes out a long coat from the closet and places it carefully on her bed. Even the coat is top quality, and for a minute, I'm a little envious.

"How do you just lie back and take it, though? That's what I don't understand."

Doing what Natalie does takes a special breed of people to let modesty fly out the window. I like to consider myself sexually liberated, but now, I'm not so sure. I've had plenty of one-night stands before and never felt ashamed. I always woke up with no regrets, unless it was one of those random mornings when I woke up to a face only a mother could love.

"How every girl does it. Alcohol."

I raise my brows. I'd have to be plastered. "You get drunk? How do you keep yourself from getting sloppy?"

"Not drunk," she says, putting a few condoms and her makeup compact into her cute clutch. I wonder if she brings a variety of sizes. She throws in lip gloss and a few cash bills. "Enough to take the edge off. I usually take a Percocet too."

Now my eyes are huge. While I see why she would need to have a drink or take a pill to get through the night, she works a lot and it's easy to get addicted. That's not something I have time for, let alone want. Natalie sees my surprised look then takes out her bottle of liquor.

"I don't take the pills all the time. Just depends on what is planned for me. I always take two shots of vodka though, and that's enough to loosen me up. For instance, tonight is an easy one even if it ends in sex, so I'll just take the shots. I'm expecting limo sex."

"Where do you get the pills from?"

She gives me a deadpan look. "Aubrey, this is New York. I can walk down any street and into a dark corner and find them. Even in a hippie vegan bread shop. But these I get from the lady of the house. That way I know they're not fucked with."

"Do you use a fake name?"

Natalie pauses then pulls out the chair from the desk. She sits down and looks at me.

"There are three rules when you get into this line of work that you have to live by. One, you keep your personal life separate. Two, you never reveal your true identity. And three, don't get close to a client. You separate that shit, because all these men want is sex and money. That's it. The client is never going to leave his wife, and if he does, it sure as hell isn't going to be for you." She pauses to lick her lips. "Everything is a lie and has to stay that way because some clients can get a little obsessive. I know a girl who fakes a New Zealand accent so well you would never think she's from the States. Yes, I use a fake name. I go by Natalia, and they think it's exotic. Ignore the increasing number of men you sleep with. Do not count them, do not think about it. Just count your bills all the way to the bank, and nothing more. It's like a normal one-night stand, but you're being paid for it. That's how I see it."

"Do you get to pick your men?"

"No. They're paying, so they pick. I never see them in advance. I just go where I'm told."

I grimace. "I bet they're all old and ugly. I don't know if I can willingly fuck that, Nat. I need a little attraction." I hold my hand up and pinch my fingers together.

She laughs. "That's why you have your vodka glasses on."

Now it's my turn to laugh.

"You'd be surprised, though. Most of the clients are middle-aged, and yes there are much older ones, but they're not what you're thinking at all. Not the high-paying ones. A few have drug problems and want to do rails off your naked body. Some have strange fetishes. They come from all different backgrounds, and for the most part, they've got their shit together. They're well-dressed and work out too, but there are a few who could lay off the carbs. Money talks, and if a client has it, and he's invited into Sanctuary Cove, Madam Christine isn't going to say no to anything he wants. There's a lady for every client's needs."

"Have you been with all of them?"

"Oh God, no. Usually, when a client finds one lady he likes, he requests her often." She pauses to apply a soft pink lipstick. "Listen. I won't push you into this, but the offer is on the table. I know Madam Christine would love to have you. You have the looks and the body, and you're not afraid to put out. I will pay for your identification card, your STD test—"

"An STD test?" I ask.

"Oh, yes. We're tested before we start taking clients and then regularly after that. So are the men. Using protection is ingrained into your skull, but you have the option to forego it. I never forego. Wear a rubber, or you're not passing go."

"I mean, that makes sense. Catching a disease is not on my to-do list."

"In addition to paying for that," Natalie continues, ignoring my disease jab. "I'll give you five thousand dollars. No. Ten thousand—"

"Nope." I shut her down. "Not going to happen."

"Just shut up and listen to me. I'll give you ten thousand. Put five aside for bills and Grammy since you'll be quitting those two jobs of yours that you're going nowhere with. Take Grammy out to eat and buy her something nice. I don't care. I'll take you shopping with the rest of the money and help you get new clothes. You can't be wearing Goodwill cast-offs. You need Versace, Prada, a little Diane, and Chanel. That shit costs money, and as you can see, I have plenty of money, so take it."

It's almost too good to pass up when she lays it out like that.

Natalie stands up and grabs her purse then slips her beige coat on. She buckles it around her waist, looking like a total babe. Her face is on point—natural yet sensually seductive—and her ridiculously tempting tall heels match her coat and dress.

"Would you call those fuck-me heels?" I jokingly ask.

She glances down then back at me. "These are 'don't cha wish your girlfriend was hot like me' heels."

Shaking my head, I follow her out of her room. "I can't believe I ever thought you were only a shot girl dressing up like that."

She chuckles and then says, "I mean, it's not impossible. Lots of shot girls dress up like this. I feel bad for lying to you about it, though."

I brush it off. I probably would've lied too.

"Natalie," I call as she reaches the door. "Sink or swim, right?" I say when she looks over her shoulder at me.

"For me, tonight, it's spit or swallow." She winks and gives me two air kisses before she leaves me standing here with my jaw dropped.

Chapter 10

I'm on my way to class when my phone vibrates in my pocket. I take it out and smile at the name on the display.

"Hey, Grammy," I answer.

"My sweetie, Aubrey. Just checking in to see how you're doing."

My heart softens. I love her so much.

"I'm walking to class right now actually. Not excited for the weekend because of the little monsters I'm going to be stuck with, but I'm good for the most part. How are you doing?"

She starts coughing, and it's one of those relentless coughs that sounds like it's deep in her lungs. My brows furrow together. Someone shoulder bumps me, and I keep walking. "Are you sick?"

"No," she says without hesitation. I bet she's in denial. She always is when she's sick and refuses to go to the doctor. "I just have this cough I can't shake. Nothing else. And, Aubrey, I told you, if you keep talking about God's children like that, you're going to give birth to Satan's child."

I bust out laughing because she's far from religious. Grammy's sarcastic, but with a coating of honey.

"I'm not having kids. Problem solved."

"You bite your tongue. You better make me a great-grammy before I die."

Laughing, I round the corner and am hit with a gust of wind that slithers around my neck. I pull my jacket tighter and shiver, feeling the crisp fall air slowly make its descent upon the city. Fall and winter are the absolute best in New York. There's no place better than here during the holidays.

"We'll see. Maybe Prince Charming will roll up in a broken-down white creeper van and whisk me away to his dungeon. He'll impregnate me, and I'll bear six sons for him before he's off with my head. But hey, you'll get your grandkids, even if they're never allowed to leave his mansion tucked away in the woods that even GPS can't pick up."

"Aubrey." She pauses, and I pull the phone away to hide my snicker. I can see her puzzled face in my head. "Where do you come up with this stuff?"

I chuckle. "I have no clue. How about I finish school first, and then we talk kids?"

She makes a sound under her breath and coughs again. I can't help but worry like a stressed parent. She raised me. Now it's my turn to take care of her.

"How's your oil? Do you have enough for the start of the season?" I ask.

The last thing I want is for her to freeze during the winter, so I need to make sure she has enough oil to turn her heat on. I saw on the news last night that this winter is estimated to be one of the coldest yet, with record-breaking temperatures.

"Will you stop it. Save your money. I don't need a thing."

She never asks for a dime, but that doesn't stop me from giving it to her. Just like she's done for me my whole life.

"You know I'm going to do it anyway," I say, walking up to the lecture hall.

"You're just like your mother, you know," she says softly, as if she's reminiscing. "When she made her mind up about something, that was it."

I run my fingers over the rose gold chain I've yet to remove since it was placed around my neck. "Do your cats need anything?"

"No, sweetie. They're plenty stocked and you know I would feed them before I would feed myself."

Just to be safe, I'll make an extra deposit today after class. Thank God today's payday. After this weekend, I'll have almost a thousand from watching the spawns, on top of folding clothes at the laundromat. It'll be a tight month, but I can survive on ramen until next payday.

You wouldn't have to if you'd take Natalie up on her offer.

I shake it off and tell myself that I'll worry about it later.

"I'm about to run into class now, but if your coughing persists, will you please make an appointment to see the doctor."

"Focus on your studies. Education is everything," she says, her voice raised, completely ignoring me.

I just smile. "Love you. Bye."

"Love you too, sweetie."

***

"I won't be here this weekend," I say to Natalie.

We haven't seen each other much this week, but that is normal for us once school starts back up. We both work and live the college life, just trying to get by. Or at least I am.

She looks up. The room is dim, and she's sitting with her legs crossed on the couch. Her hair is tied into a messy knot at the top of her head, and she has a pencil dangling between her teeth. She looks so innocent under the white Christmas lights.

"The devils?"

I fight a grin. We both have names for the two kids I nanny. They're the cutest boys, but I swear the minute I turn my back, they turn into the *Problem Child* on crack times two. At that point, I'm ready to build my own pipe and ask for a hit of whatever they're on. Call me MacGyver. The jack of all trades.

"Yup. I had a feeling they'd need me all weekend after I took off last weekend. I swear, why have kids if you have to hire a nanny all the time? It doesn't make sense to me," I say and head to my room to pack.

I don't bring too much and try to keep it light since I'll have to carry my duffel bag to the subway then transfer onto the Long Island Rail Road, where I'll be picked up from the station closest to their house. The Schneiders live in Manhasset, and their French Normandy Tudor-style home that looks like it was made for a fairy tale is priced in the millions. Suburbs for the wealthy and dull. I can't even imagine having a home like that.

"You know how rich people are," Natalie says when I return to the living room. "But my dad would never let a nanny in our house. We had maids and shit, and occasionally a babysitter. My dad was all about my mom being a stay-at-home mom. He was adamant that she raise me. It's probably why I'm close to my mom and not my dad."

"That's still kind of nice, though, you know? I mean it sucks your dad is the way he is, and in some strange way, it makes sense why you work where you do. You take back a little bit of control in your life and possibly your future too. Though, I have to be honest, I think this route is a little extreme to show defiance. But hey, whatever works for you."

"You could have the same control too, you know," she says, her voice silky as she reminds me of her suggestion. As if I could ever forget my best friend asking me to join her in being a rent-a-hoe. "That offer still stands."

My lips flatten. If my grammy knew about this, she'd say it's the Devil's work. Probably is.

"I just don't know if I can do it."

"You had more one-night stands your first year in college than I did, and I wasn't selling the goods. You have nothing to lose. I know you can totally do it, but I would never want to push you into this lifestyle either. That being said, the ten grand is yours."

I huff out a laugh. "You just gotta remind me of that money, don't you?"

She shrugs casually. A one-night stand and getting paid to

have sex really aren't the same, but in a strange way, they are. My shoulders slump forward. The choice weighing down one hand more than the other.

"Even if I decide to do it, I can't take your money."

She glares at me. "You will take it, and you will use it. No returns. You'll need the cash to start up anyway."

I worry my bottom lip. My heart beats a little faster than usual, and a surge of adrenaline pushes through me.

"What if I pay it back to you with my first ... job?" I didn't know what to call it.

Her eyes light up when they shouldn't. She shouldn't want me to do this with her, and she shouldn't encourage it, but I'm a willing adult who can make sane decisions. I let out a loud, dramatic exhale. I can't believe I find prostitution tempting, but I do, and I'm kind of ashamed about it.

"Deal!" she yells. I feel like she's just saying that to tide me over.

I cast her a look, the same one I give the boys when I scold them. "Calm down. I didn't agree to anything yet. I'm just asking questions and weighing my options."

Her smile curves up like the Grinch. "But you will."

I throw my duffel bag over my shoulder and walk toward the door, mentally preparing for a long-ass weekend.

"I'd say don't do anything I wouldn't do, but now I don't even know what that is anymore," I say.

Natalie's chuckle is light and airy, and she responds in a husky voice I didn't know she was capable of. "I'll share all my secrets for the right price."

Shaking my head, I smile as I walk out the door.

Chapter 11

"Thank you for coming this weekend, Aubrey. My wife and I could use the break. I had three major surgeries and need to get away for a bit to shut my mind off."

"Of course. Anytime you need me, you know I'm here for you guys. Working and raising two boys requires a village," I schmooze. "I miss those two little nuggets."

"They miss you. They've been writing your name all over the walls with Leslie's lipstick. Of course, they can't actually write, but we tell them we love it anyway," he muses with a dreamy smile on his face.

I try not to stare at Mr. Schneider too much as we drive to his house, but now I can't help but wonder if I could have sex with him for cash. I don't find him attractive, but he's not the ugliest man I've ever seen either. He's average and looks to be in shape. He always wears black, though, so I can't tell if he's flabby or not.

Natalie said some of the men have fetishes. What if I get one who wants me to wear a strap-on and call him Uncle Bobby? That might be a hard no for me.

"We're going to need you to get the lipstick off the walls," Mr. Schneider says, like he's daydreaming about Uncle Bobby.

"Nothing a magic eraser can't remove," I respond, my appeasing robot personality kicking in. What the fuck! Why wasn't his precious wife watching the little shits so they didn't hijack her makeup? Why can't she clean up the mess her kids made?

Fuck my life.

The moment we pull up the driveway, Spawn One and Spawn

Two run outside in their sagging cloth diapers, along with their mother. I get out of the car and open my arms to them. Their faces are covered in dirt and there's snot running down their noses into their mouths, but I hug them anyway, because they really are the cutest fucking kids. They're a mess, but this is because Leslie likes to teach the boys through playing. They jump in muddy puddles in the rain, have action figures with no faces, and all-natural, biodegradable toys. No Playmobile for these tots. It's all wood and peasant clothing. I don't really get it, but that's not my problem. I just do what I'm told, and they pay me well. It's a good system, and I try not to ever ruin a good thing.

"We've all missed you," Mrs. Schneider says. Leslie really is a nice woman, just a doormat kind, and I find it annoying. "You're here until Sunday night, correct?"

I smile at her and nod. Her eyes are full of relief, and I can't help but wonder what she'd do if I put my two weeks in.

"I'm all yours." I turn to the little monsters. "I heard you guys drew me some pretty pictures. Ready to show me?"

They don't really speak, but they understand what I'm saying and reach for my hand. I get by because I understand their mumbles.

We walk inside, and I look around. My jaw drops the moment we reach the living room. I try to mask my reaction, but it's a serious struggle. There are shades of pink lines everywhere. I feel like Leslie purposely gave them the makeup now as a fuck-you for leaving her with her spawns last weekend. I have my work cut out for me.

Saturday morning, I wake up and realize Mr. and Mrs. Schneider never called to check on their kids. While the boys sleep, I scrub the walls again, this time with an old container of bleach. I had to go on a scavenger hunt to find it, as the Schneiders only use natural products.

Once the boys get up, my day is filled with chasing toddlers, making airplane sounds so they eat a few bites of food, and changing handmade diapers that I have to wash immediately after. I make sure to run the boys ragged by playing with them outside for hours so the fresh air knocks them out. After the day I've had with them, I'm so tired. All I want is to go to bed as soon as they do.

Sunday comes, and I've yet to hear from the Schneiders, which is strange because they always check in. Aren't they curious how their kids are faring? They haven't picked up one phone call from me.

"Um, Nat, the parents still aren't home."

It's six in the morning, and I call her first thing. I don't even bother making coffee, even though they have the best-tasting coffee I've ever had.

"See, you wouldn't have that issue if your new name was Sparkles."

Her voice is groggy, and even though I'm worried about where the hell these people are, I still laugh.

"The prospect is looking brighter, that's for sure."

"What are you going to do if you haven't heard from them by late afternoon?"

I glance around the quiet house, searching for an answer. "Well, I obviously can't leave the kids alone. What can I do?"

"I think if you don't hear from them around noon, you should start blowing up their phone. This is a little crazy. They didn't tell you where they were going?"

I glance out the kitchen window, hoping to see their car pull up any second.

"I didn't ask. It's none of my business. I just find it so incredibly rude to do this. Like it makes me never want to come back here, the way they've left me in limbo."

I sigh, deciding I would text them around lunchtime, telling them I have an emergency with Grammy. Surely they would understand.

"Tell me what you did last night," I say.

"A man in his thirties."

My brows raise. Doesn't seem too bad. "That young?"

"Yeah. Every once in a while you get a spring chicken. He wanted to hit the hottest clubs and fuck all night long."

"That's it?"

"Yeah, I mean he was doing coke off my boobs so he *could* have sex all night long—I hate sex on coke—but I got eleven thousand dollars for it, so I'm not complaining."

My eyes pop wide open. "If you get eleven thousand, how much does head bitch in charge get?"

"Christine gets a cut, but for everyone it's a different price. It really depends on how long you've been doing it, what you do, that sort of thing. Last night cost the client twenty-two thousand, and he pays for everything too."

"I just don't understand why he would pay so much for that. An eight ball is a couple hundred dollars. Why pay twenty grand more than necessary? This whole thing blows my mind."

She yawns, and I'm starting to feel bad for waking her up. "Money isn't an issue with the clients of Sanctuary Cove. The wealth is astounding. They know what they're getting, so they know their money is being well spent in their eyes. Do I look like a hooker to you? No. It's an illusion they're after, and we're paid top dollar to give it. Ludacris said it perfectly—men want a lady on the streets but a freak in the sheets. The girls are clean, and we're totally discreet."

"When's your next date?"

"Tonight. I have to get naked while the client plays his guitar in front of me."

"And then have sex?"

"No, he just wants someone to be his muse while he writes songs. I can't tell you who it is, but he's a heavy hitter in the entertainment industry and filthy rich. You'd die if you knew. I was starstruck at first."

My jaw drops in shock. I'm still staring out the window, hoping to see the champagne Jag pull up.

"If I guess, will you tell me?"

"Nope." She chuckles. "He's hot as sin though and has requested me a few times now. We've yet to have sex, but let me tell you, our chemistry is off the charts. He's younger than most men at Sanctuary and in great shape. He's got tattoos on both arms. And the way he looks at my body while he strums his guitar, I swear he can read my soul. One of these days, we're going to fuck, and it's going to be insanely hot." She sighs, and I swear I can hear longing in her voice.

"I thought you weren't supposed to get close to the clients."

"Aubrey." She clears her throat, and I hear her blankets ruffle. "When you fucked the guy in the bathroom on your birthday, were you close to him?"

"Well, no."

"Did you bang him because you thought he was hot?"

"Yeah."

"So how is this any different? The only difference is that I'm getting paid for it, and honestly, who cares if no one knows anyway? Just because I want this musician to strum me like he does his guitar doesn't mean I need to be emotionally or romantically attached to him. I just want to see if he's as good as he puts off. I want to know what he feels like inside of me and if he's as good as the tabloids say he is. Coming isn't a top priority—the client always comes first, figuratively speaking—but I'd still want to if I could."

I pull back, utterly confused. "Wait. What? What do you mean you can't come? How do you hold back?"

"That's a rule of Madam Christine's. We're not allowed to have any sort of pleasure until after the client is fully sated, not that you'll really want it anyway because you'll be so focused on rocking their world for that cash. Having an orgasm isn't that easy when the pressure is on and you have to create the best experience for the client. Your priority is to give them a moment they'll never forget."

I blink rapidly. My head is spinning with all the dirty deets Natalie keeps throwing at me. Now I have even more questions than I started with. Orgasms hadn't crossed my mind yet, but I just assumed they happened. On the one hand, I'm okay with that. It helps me believe that my self-respect is still intact. On the other hand, I'd feel dirty and used, because I know myself and I'll probably end up orgasming if the client is hot.

"So you've never had an orgasm with a client? Not once?"

"Oh, I have plenty of times, just not often. You're not going to be able to every time. The clients are not what you think, and they expect you to do all the work. It's what they're paying you for, after all."

I'm quiet for a moment. Eleven thousand dollars was her cut. That's big money right there, and I suddenly want a piece of it.

"Nat?" I say after a few beats of silence. My voice is a little shaky because I'm about to sell my soul to the Devil.

"Real recognizes real," she says with such a heavy Bronx accent in the back of her throat. "Say no more. I got you, girl."

Chapter 12

"I quit!" I yell as I walk into our apartment and slam the door shut. It's after midnight, and I have to be up early for class in the morning, and I'm just now getting home. I don't even have time to shower because I need to study for a huge test tomorrow.

"I almost put out an Amber Alert for you. What the hell happened?" Natalie takes a sip from her coffee mug, and I chuckle under my breath. I'M A HOOKER ON THE WEEKENDS is printed in bold black and red lettering on the side of her mug. How have I never put two and two together? Then again, that's Natalie's personality, so I didn't even think twice.

I plop down onto the couch and blow out a stressed breath. "You don't even know. First of all, the Schneiders never answered any of my calls, and I sent text message after text message to no avail. I even went as far as telling them Grammy fell down a flight of stairs and was in critical condition so I needed to get to the emergency room. Crickets. I started to think they were never coming back, until they strolled in like nothing happened four fucking hours later. I had to keep my cool, though, because they still needed to pay me, and I wanted my money."

"Are you fucking shitting me? I would've left those monsters alone and dipped out."

"Of course, I wanted to just walk out, but I couldn't do that. It's not the kids' fault their parents are ignorant assholes. But it gets better."

"I can't wait to hear this."

"They only wanted me to use lemon juice to clean off the

71

lipstick from the walls. I'd rather muck a horse stall. I found an old container of bleach in the basement and switched to that. Lemon juice wasn't cutting it. Oh, and the cloth diapers they use because they're worried about the environment? They wanted me to wipe off the shit from the diapers first before throwing them into the washer. Fine. I agree with that. I'm all for saving the animals and being a tree hugger, but you will never catch me putting literal shit into my washing machine."

Natalie's face pinches into a scowl of disgust. It's exactly how I feel.

"So Mr. Schneider takes me to the railroad station, and as he hands me my pay, he proceeds to tell me he's short by five-fucking-hundred dollars."

"You can't be serious," Natalie says, and her jaw drops.

"As a heart attack. He said he'd give it to me next weekend. That was the icing on the cake. I take care of his kids all weekend, and he can't even pay me in full!" I take a deep breath. Just thinking about it again gets me all worked up.

I crack my neck, and the sound echoes throughout the room. I was supposed to be paid eight hundred for the weekend. I got three.

"They've done this before, but this was just the straw that broke the camel's back."

"Fucking losers." Natalie rolls her eyes at the lunacy of the situation and shakes her head. "So, do they know you quit?"

"Sure do." I smile as I think about Mr. Schneider's shocked expression. "He told me he'd see me Tuesday and Thursday and then the weekend again and that I needed to make sure I could fulfill those dates indefinitely. He'd give me the rest of my pay then." Natalie's eyes bulge, and I can feel her anger. It's as hot as mine. "Once I had the cash in my hand, I told him he'll never see me again and to bend over and say please because that's what it feels like to get stiffed my pay."

"Bend over? That's the best you could come up with?"

"Of course, now I have better comebacks since I've had time to stew. The kids were in the car, and I didn't want to curse in front of them. But you know what's funny? His face went pale white, almost as if someone actually told him to bend over."

Natalie covers her mouth. "No way! You're kidding me!"

"I wish I was. He looked so shocked. He didn't drive off for a solid minute after I got out of the car."

"That's amazing. I wish you would've been like, 'Go fuck your mother,' but sometimes you like to keep it classy, and I get it. You're the nice one in this relationship."

I shrug. For the most part they were nice to me while I worked for them, but that was because I was taking care of their kids. They shouldn't treat the hired help like shit, definitely not the nanny anyway. When I look back on it and think about all the things they had me do on top of watching their kids, how they had little to no concern for the train schedules I needed to catch, or the few obligations I needed to fulfill, like leaving by a specific time. I was just another pebble in their driveway for them to kick around.

I yawn and stand up. "I'm gonna hit the sack. I'm exhausted."

"Later, Sleeping Beauty," Natalie says, and I walk into my room and get settled into my bed.

I turn over onto my side and curl up into a ball, pulling the covers tight to my chin. The horns and whistles and the police sirens don't bother me anymore. The noise is almost like a lullaby that soothes me to sleep. Later on today, I'll need to see if I can pick up a few extra shifts at the laundromat, and then I'll deposit the rest of the money, save for like a hundred bucks, into Grammy's account.

"I got you an interview," Natalie says quietly.

I pop up and turn to face her standing in my doorway. My heart begins beating faster than usual. I'm both excited and nervous—definitely more nervous than anything.

"Already? I figured we'd talk about it first. How? When?"

She flips on the light. "Ah, I thought we already did talk about it."

I frown and try to steady my heart rate. "Not really. I mean, I just thought we'd talk more."

"There's nothing to really talk about. After we spoke earlier, I called Madam Christine and told her about you. She said to bring you in when you're available, which means ASAP. Like later today after class and shit."

My eyes widen. "But I have to work at the laundromat today," I say, a little panicked.

"Obviously you're gonna call in. You can't miss this interview."

I gawk at her. "But what if she doesn't like me? Then I'm out two jobs. I can't risk that, Natalie. Can you just reschedule it to tomorrow?"

She shakes her head. "You won't be out. Trust me. She's going to take one look at you and hire you on the spot."

My face scrunches up. "One look? What kind of interview is this? Like, what's she going to ask me? Who gets interviewed to be a call girl?"

"Relax. She isn't going to ask you to get on your knees and make you demonstrate how big of an O you can turn your mouth into."

My lips twitch, and I lie back down under the covers. Natalie always knows how to make a stressful moment funny.

"I'm just nervous. This is a big thing. I'm more nervous about it than anything else."

"It's a huge deal, so I get it. Christine has this sixth sense about it, where she can look at a girl and know if she'll work out immediately. After I sent her a picture of you, she said to bring you in as soon as possible. Trust me, you need to be there all dolled up like you're going on a date. You need to dress like *Natalia*. I've got just the outfit for you, and I'll do your hair and makeup."

"What will she ask me?" My voice gives way to my anxiety. I've held quite a few odd jobs over the years, and never once have I felt butterflies like this. Am I really going to interview to be a sex worker?

"She'll ask you things like how many guys you've been with, are you cool with one-night stands, what kinds of days or nights you can work, what your hard limits are. Stuff we've talked about before."

My heart is fucking racing. I'm not sure I can do this. The thought is making me ill. I'm never going to sleep tonight.

"What's my name going to be?"

Natalie muses over my question.

"Carlita."

I roll my eyes. "Okay, forget I asked. How about Maeve?"

"Meh. Sometimes Christine gives the girls names. Let's just wait and see."

"How do I know what my hard limits are?" I ask. I feel like I know, but then again, there's some wild people in the world doing things I don't find to be a turn-on.

"She'll have a checklist for you. Don't be afraid to check them off either, because the last thing you want to do is get matched with someone who wants you to pee on them or wants to pee on you."

I lean up on my elbows and look at her in mortification. There's no way. Just the thought causes a sour taste in the back of my throat.

"I'm just kidding," Natalie says playfully. "Madam Christine runs a classy business. It's one of the top-rated in New York City. Think of it as the couture side of being an escort. Only the streetwalkers pee on people."

My forehead creases. That doesn't help at all. "Seriously?"

She gives me a bored stare. "Do you really believe that people pee on other people?"

"I believe people will do anything for money, so, yes. And I also think people like really strange things that I don't."

She rubs her hands together and inhales. "We'll have a shot of vodka while you're getting ready. That'll help bring down the nerves. Make sure you come straight here after class. We'll need about an hour to do hair and makeup and then take a town car to Chelsea."

"She's in Chelsea?"

It doesn't surprise me that she's on the West Side in such an upscale part of the city.

Natalie nods. "It's a huge converted warehouse. I think she paid around a cool million for it—in cash, mind you—and then upgraded the fuck out of it. Wait until you see it. The way she designed it looks like a penthouse suite." Her face lights up, and for a split second, my apprehension turns to anticipation. "There's a cigar lounge just for the men. We're not allowed in there, but they can watch girls dance in these little cages. It's kind of sexy, if you ask me. The lights are turned down low, so their faces are never shown. I don't dance, but the girls can wear masquerade masks if they want extra privacy. There are also rooms to rent with private entries if it's just an afternoon quickie or a place for you to get ready if you don't have time to go home. There's even a kitchen with private chefs. She really spared no expense for this devious business."

I nod, still flustered as a hen in its cage.

"Don't stress too much. It's not as bad as it seems. Look at it this way ... you could be giving blow jobs to smelly truck drivers for twenty bucks."

Chapter 13

Another Monday where class is a bust.

I'm having a hard time focusing this morning due to the lack of sleep. I tossed and turned all night with tons of questions weighing on my mind, different theories, and of course, the shame.

My mind is a maze with three entrances but no exits. My stomach is a knotted mess cramping together as I sit in a freezing lecture hall. Riddled with guilt, I almost pull my phone out to message Natalie to tell her I'm not going, but something inside of me holds me back.

As soon as class lets out, I grab my books and briskly walk to the first coffee shop I can find. I'm going to need something a little stronger to make it through the rest of the day. I stand in line inhaling the dark aroma and already feel a little better. There's something about the smell of brewed coffee that just makes me feel good and instantly calms my nerves.

The doors behind me are open with customers streaming in and out, the street air cooling down the little vintage shop. This is what I love about living in the city. There's something new to experience every single day.

"I'll have a triple shot with your medium roast, please." I'm out of one job and called in sick to another. This could be my last decadent cup of java for a while.

"A woman after my own heart," a man says from behind me as I reach into my purse for my wallet.

I turn around and look up into a pair of dark chocolate eyes. He's about my height, with lashes as thick as soot and a jawline that could sharpen knives. I'm feeling a little shy and pull my books tighter to my chest.

"Desperate times call for desperate measures." I smile at him. "It's Monday, and I'm on a mission to take over the world."

"I'll have what she's having," he says to the barista and pulls a hundred from his money clip then reaches around me to drop it on the counter.

"Oh, no. Here, let me give you money," I say and fumble with my purse. A book slips from my grasp and drops to the floor. I'm not a clumsy kind of girl, so this just embarrasses me. I watch as he reaches down to pick it up, and his green scrubs catch my attention. I'd been too busy staring into his eyes to notice anything else.

"The coffee is on me," he says like it's the end of the discussion. "And because"—he leans back to look at my textbooks—"you're studying at Fordham and could probably use the caffeine."

"You guessed that by a three-second look at my books?"

The twinkle in his eyes causes a flutter in my stomach. If I wasn't in such a rush to make it to my next class on time, I might try to strike up a conversation with him.

"No, it's just the closest school nearby."

"I usually get coffee cold, but I need a good swift kick to my ass today. I love it with sweetened condensed milk and cream of coconut—shaken, not stirred—but not a lot of places carry that."

He studies me. "That's an interesting concoction."

"It's rich and creamy and has a pleasant aftertaste."

Heat blossoms under my cheeks. I don't know why I said all that.

He places his left hand into his pocket and says, "How about I take you to your favorite coffee shop tonight and you can introduce me to this drink of yours?"

Blunt. Forward. I like it. I almost take him up on the offer, when I remember I have an interview tonight at a whorehouse. I'm pretty sure no respectable man would ever allow his girlfriend to sell herself. Not that we would immediately start dating or anything, of course.

The man reaches around me and grabs the coffee off the counter then hands it to me. Our fingers brush, and my stomach flips backwards. God, I hope I don't act like this with clients. He reaches for the other cup and takes a sip, his eyes boring into mine over the rim like he's trying to get a read on me. It's a little thrilling.

"I can already see you're going to decline. How about we meet back here tomorrow?"

I smile and shake my head. "No."

He's staring at my lips. "Do you come here often?"

Persistent. I like that. "Thank you for the coffee," I say, then step around him.

I peer over my shoulder as I walk out of the coffee shop. Just like I expected, his gaze follows me until I'm out of his view.

I take a deep breath. I'm sure coffee with him tonight would end just as strong. But right now, with a twenty-page paper due in a few weeks and my potential new job that requires me to spread my legs, the last thing I need is a man.

***

I can't believe I'm going through with this.

"Okay, make me look like every man's wet dream."

Natalie chuckles. "That isn't hard. You're already a neck-breaker."

I smile. I never know what to say when someone says I'm pretty. Thank you? I'm not blind. I was blessed with the best parts of my parents—small mouth with pouty lips, big doe eyes that are a deep brown to almost black, and a pimple-free complexion. I know I'm pretty but wouldn't go as far as to say I'm gorgeous. That's just being extra.

"Thanks, girl," I say. "Now give me a shot."

My nerves are already worked up, and we aren't leaving for

at least an hour. Natalie hands me a shot in her favorite red Solo shot glass.

"This is like a double, you ass. I can't be drunk when I walk in there!"

She brushes it off. "You won't be drunk, trust me. You need to relax, and this will do the trick. All the girls do it. No one walks in there straight and sober. It's impossible."

Natalie makes a good point, but that still doesn't loosen the knots in my stomach.

"Here's to getting my groove on." I toast then take the shot.

Natalie gets to work, putting all this shit on my face I don't typically wear. She moves fast with a steady hand, winging my eyes, applying heavy mascara, and giving me rosy cheeks. She finishes me off with red, glossy lipstick.

"Really? Red lipstick," I say. It's the color of a fire hydrant. "All trick girls wear red."

"Yeah, because men fucking love it," she retorts, and I shrug. Fine. She would know more than me anyway.

I look alluring, yet still a little innocent, and it works for me. My skin appears flawless, and I need to know what she used so I can buy it too. Natalie doesn't do much to my hair—just straightens it and adds some soft curls at the ends. She applies some shiny stuff to it, making it look really healthy. I want to run my fingers through it, but I know she'll only slap my hand away.

I feel my body relaxing as the vodka works its magic. My shoulders aren't as tense, and I'm a tad more confident than before. I'm sure that will change when I step inside Sanctuary Cove.

"Jesus, Nat. If you ever decide to stop being a hooker, you should definitely look into the hair and makeup field, because you killed this. I look like a goddess."

I stare at my reflection in disbelief. I look like a sultry and dark version of myself. I have to say, if I wasn't so lazy with makeup, or cheap, then I'd rock this look all the time.

"You're welcome," she says proudly. "Now, let's dress you up!"

Natalie pulls out a couple of dresses and places them on her bed. She studies each one, taking turns looking at me then the dresses. She finally decides on a black scrunched dress with spaghetti straps. She says something about it being a bodycon. It's a minidress made to stick to a body, and that's exactly what it does when I put it on.

"Your boobs look fantastic," she says.

I look at them in the mirror and silently agree. The top isn't anything special—it just sits straight across—but since I have full breasts, the dress makes me look insanely tempting. I love the way I look so much. I actually feel sexy. She hands me a pair of peep toe nude heels then brings my hair to my front so it drapes over my chest, twisting the ends to keep the curl.

"I'm impressed. I didn't think I was going to look like this, but I have to say, I would totally do myself."

Natalie giggles and slips into a V-neck dress and soft-pink heels.

"Not for nothing, but I didn't expect escorts to dress so ... tastefully? It helps wash the grime away."

"Let me guess. You imagined patent leather or some vinyl shit." She gives me a droll stare.

I bite my bottom lip, guilty. "Kinda. You can't blame me. People don't usually think classy and sophisticated when they think escort. They think trashy prostitute with no morals or self-respect."

"That's because this is New York and we're a different breed. Prostitutes are strictly for sexual satisfaction. Escorts are for entertainment purposes with a glamorous look that just happens to come with the sex benefits. Now, listen. When we get there, I want you to walk in with your shoulders back and your chin up, but no resting bitch face. You want to look tantalizing and juicy and feel comfortable in your skin. Shy is fine—we don't want insecure, which I know you're not, so *do not* cower when she starts to grill you. Got it? Good."

I feel my nerves climbing again, but I push them down. I can do this.

"What's she going to say to me?"

Natalie hands me a coat and then puts one on herself.

"She's different with everyone. No two people are the same, so I can't really say." She checks the time on her phone then looks at me and says, "Let's roll. Our car is waiting."

Here goes nothing.

Chapter 14

Posh. Opulent. Rich.

Sanctuary Cove is nothing like what I anticipated. I wasn't sure what I was expecting, but this was definitely not it. I guess I expected to feel sleazy when I walked in, the air to smell like sex and sweat. Despite Natalie's constant reassurance, I still wasn't sold ... until now.

Our coats are taken at the door by an older man who resembles a nightclub bouncer, and when the door closes behind us, I can't hear any of the noise from the busy New York City streets. Soundproof. We're immediately plunged into a world of decadence.

Smelling of jasmine with just a hint of cigar smoke, the air caresses my senses. I recall Natalie telling me there's a cigar lounge somewhere in here but it's one of the areas where women aren't allowed. Probably a good thing. I think I'd feel like a piece of meat with lions preying all around me, waiting to attack if I walked in there.

Taking in my surroundings, I revel in how beautiful this place is, and it helps ease the nerves in my stomach. The floor is white marble, and in the center of the entrance is a circular table with a beige tablecloth of thin chiffon ruffles draped to the floor. It's gorgeous and catches my eye immediately. There are mini tea lights on the gold tabletop, along with a massive flower arrangement. It looks like a tree, but moss curves around the branches. There are tons of white orchids drooping over, giving the room a romantic feel. White hydrangeas finish off the arrangement at the base. It's elegant, and if we were anywhere else, I would've taken my phone out to snap a picture to post on social media.

"Remember what I told you," Natalie says quietly under her breath, and I nod. "Act like you're worth the ten grand an hour," she says. "Madam Christine loves a confident woman."

I mimic Natalie, walking like she does—my legs crisscrossing one in front of the other, the way runway models do—into what looks like a private room.

I swallow down the giant knot in my throat as we step inside where Natalie's boss is waiting for us. My eyes lock with who I presume is Madame Christine. Anxiousness steamrolls through me. My heart is seconds away from jumping out of my chest, and I'm afraid I'm going to slip in my heels, something I never do. Exhaling a heavy breath, I blow out all my fear and let the liquor soothe my nerves.

Christine immediately rakes a hard stare down the length of my body, assessing every inch of my nearly six-foot height. She watches the way I walk, takes in my hips, how my breasts bounce, then looks at me. Her gaze gives nothing away. I can't get a beat on her. We stop in front of the high-top table she's standing at. While Christine's not as tall as me, she's giving off the impression she's someone you don't want to be on bad terms with.

"Madam Christine," Natalie says, her voice raspy, "I'd like to introduce you to my girlfriend, Aubrey Abrams."

"Aubrey, it's a pleasure to meet you." Her voice is soothing, kind of sensual.

I give her a demure smile. "You as well."

"Tell me something about you that no one would know."

I blink, unprepared for her question. "I love jazzy blues music."

"Something else."

"I like reading stock trading books."

She raises a brow. "What else?"

"I'm not a huge fan of tattoos."

"Why not?"

"They're a waste of money and half the time they look like shit."

She's quiet. I get the impression she either wants me to offer more or I've offended her with my tattoo comment, which was not my intention.

"I take that back. Tattoos depend on the artist and how much money someone is willing to spend. But most people are cheap. They want everything for nothing, and because of that, in twenty years it's going to look like an abstract blob of color."

"If you had the money, and the right artist, would you get one?"

"No."

"Why?"

"I'm a broke college student. I don't like to waste my money on things that aren't necessities."

"So no handouts were given. You had to work for what you want."

"Yes. My grandmother struggled to raise me, and now I do everything in my power to make sure she no longer has to struggle, even though she hates that I do."

"Where are your parents?"

"Dead."

"Both?"

"Yes. They died in a car accident when I was very young."

"So you go above and beyond for your grandmother because she's the only family you have left."

"Always."

"Where were you working before you came here?"

I correct her. "I'm currently working at a laundromat, and I was a nanny for a family of twin boys on Long Island, but I recently quit."

She angles her head just slightly, her eyes narrowing. "Why did you quit?"

"I felt taken advantage of, and the husband kept underpaying me. He'd have an excuse why I couldn't get my full pay and would have to wait until the following week. I don't like when people mess with my hard-earned money."

She makes a little sound in the back of her throat, and I feel triumphant. By her reaction, what I said seems like something she wanted to hear. I didn't say that just for her benefit, though. It's how I feel on the inside.

Madam Christine pushes off the table and waves her fingers for us to follow her. I take in her backside, and I'm a little surprised by how amazing she looks. I have no idea how old she is, but she doesn't look a day over forty. I'd wager she's much older, though.

We walk into a room that reminds me of a place where boudoir photos would be taken. She shuts the door, and I take in the room in awe. Lush and soft, inviting. My favorite part is the blush pink, lilac gray, and ivory strings of pearls that hold back the long slate gray curtains.

I turn around to see what we're doing in here when Christine walks up to me. She's a few feet from me, and her eyes roam my face.

"Strip."

My eyes shift to Natalie, and Christine snaps her fingers in front of my face.

"Don't look at her. She won't be in the room when you're with a client. Strip."

I blink, taken aback. Natalie and I dress in front of each other all the time, but I wasn't expecting this.

I've also never just *stripped* for anyone before, so there's that.

Looking Christine in the eye, I hand Natalie the little clutch she let me borrow then pull down the thin straps of my dress. My breasts spill out, and my nipples instantly pucker from the chilly air. She doesn't hide her wandering eyes and focuses on my raspberry areolas. Her lingering gaze oddly makes me glow with arousal. She makes me feel sexy under her traveling gaze. I wasn't expecting this reaction. I arch my back a little and push the dress over my hips and step out of it, debating whether I want to leave it on the floor or hold it up for her. I'd hold it up for a man, but I don't want her thinking I'm cocky. Pushing it to the side, I stand tall, my breasts full but perky.

She lifts her eyes to mine and raises a brow, waiting. I know what that means.

Hooking my thumbs into the black lace of my thong underwear, I push them down and step out of them. All I'm left in are Natalie's five-inch black heels. I don't even have jewelry on because Natalie insisted I didn't need it.

Madam Christine steps back, and I swear I can feel her eyes on every square inch of my skin. It's like she's taking inventory and pinning my physique to memory.

"Spread your legs so they're shoulder-length apart. Put your arms behind your head."

I breathe in slow and do as she says, my pulse thrashing in my neck. All I want to do is look at Natalie to make sure this is normal, but the rustling in my veins tells me not to.

"She needs waxing," Christine says to Natalie without taking her eyes off my body. "Wax everything."

I shaved pretty well, so I'm not sure what she means, but okay. I've never had waxing done before. Mainly because I couldn't afford to.

Christine steps closer and places two fingers under my breast. She taps gently, watching it bounce, then places her palm against my nipple and gives me a squeeze. I draw in a silent breath. My stomach tightens.

"What size are you?"

"Thirty-four C, or D, depending on the bra."

"Beautiful," she says and cups my other breast, giving it the same treatment.

She places both hands under my arms and then drags them down to my waist and around my jutting hips, slowly lowering herself to the floor until she's on her knees.

"Waist and hip sizes."

"My waist is a twenty-six. My hips are thirty-three."

"Do you work out?" she asks, eye level with my pussy, and I want to die of embarrassment.

She's looking up for my answer, but all I can think about is how I'm turned on seeing Christine on her knees.

I lick my lips. "No," I respond, my voice a bit raspy.

"Why not?"

"I can't afford a gym membership."

She doesn't say anything and continues running her palms to my backside, cupping my ass cheeks. Looking over her shoulder, she says to Natalie, "Go to a Pilates or yoga studio, not a gym. I don't want my women looking like men. Clients want soft and supple. Some like to think they can break a woman or overpower her, and we give them the illusion they can."

I wish Madam Christine would tell *me* these things directly instead of pretending I'm not here.

"That's all for now, Natalie. Thank you. Please see yourself out. I need to speak with Aubrey alone now."

I look frantically between both of them, wondering what she needs to talk to me about alone while I'm buck naked. Natalie gives me no clue. She just nods and excuses herself from the room.

Christine remains on her knees, and once the door closes, she does the same exact thing to my pussy that she did to my boobs. A little gasp escapes me as she taps on my bare lips. She looks up to watch my reaction, but I give nothing away. I do my best to remain as cool as a cucumber even though my stomach dips, and a strange sensation cultivates inside my body that I don't know how to process.

"Have you ever been touched by a woman?"

"No." My answer is a whisper on my lips.

Something gleams in her eyes, and I have no clue how to read it. My heart is pounding against my rib cage. Christine uses both her hands to spread my lips apart. Jesus Christ ... I swallow hard as she eyes my pink clit.

"If a woman wants to be with you, are you willing?"

Fuck. Fuck. Fuck.

I've never really thought about it. I'm not opposed to being with the same sex, but I don't know if I want to. I've always loved men and their masculinity. Alpha males are the best. Their strength, how dominating and strong they are—they light my blood on fire. Yes, there are women I find downright stunning, but I never stopped to ask if I found them sexually appealing in that way. I swallow thickly and give her the answer I know she wants to hear.

"Yes."

Her face softens and she looks pleased. "That's good to know."

Christine stands up and walks behind me, her nails grazing over my hip. "Have you ever kissed a woman?"

"Yes."

"How many men have you been with?" she asks, her hands covering my breasts, massaging them. Her chest is to my back, and my eyes widen as she fits her body against me. Her breath tickles my neck. I've never had a woman touch me like this before, and I'm not sure what to think because I actually like the way it feels.

My back arches of its own accord, and I lean into her touch. "I don't keep count," I say, a little breathless.

"Give me a roundabout number, Aubrey. Three, nine, twelve?"

Blunt and to the point.

"Over twenty. I prefer one-night stands. I'm not a relationship kind of girl, and I'm not just saying that in the hopes you hire me.

I just don't do boyfriends."

There's a purr in the back of her throat. Madam Christine tweaks my nipples, pinching and tugging. Her touch is sending a zing straight to my throbbing pussy. My arousal coats my inner thighs. I want to squeeze my legs together to ease some of the ache, but I can't.

Her fingers spread, and she slowly skims her hands down my stomach, leaving a trail of heat in their wake. My eyes roll shut, and I focus on her touch, my body simmering with a craving for more.

When I leave Sanctuary Cove tonight, I'm going to crucify Natalie for not fucking warning me first that not only would I be getting touched by Madam Christine, but that I would *like it* too.

Chapter 15

"What about anal, Aubrey?" Christine says, her tone a sensual caress down my neck. For a second, I wonder if she'd like to strap one on and test me out.

I blink rapidly while her hands move over to my hips and down to my inner thighs, just grazing past my pussy to tease me. She gives my inner thigh a squeeze, and my body lights up like it's the Fourth of July. I let out a little sigh. Her grip loosens, and my skin tingles. I'm aching for her to move higher, to touch me where no woman ever has. Her hand on my opposite thigh moves in circles, torturing me in the same manner. Just when I think she's going to continue teasing me, she shocks me by delving her fingers into my pussy.

My hips jolt back and press into hers, and I let out an obvious sigh of pleasure. Christine plays with my folds, stroking them both equally, building my desire.

"Anal, Aubrey? Answer it."

Fuck. I'd forgotten she asked that. My hips tilt into her touch and a rush escapes my lips.

"No," I say, and she glides two fingers up and down my embarrassingly wet slit, rubbing over my clit.

I try to focus on something, anything, other than how good she's making me feel, but it's impossible. There's something erotic about the way she, a woman, is touching my sex. Like it's forbidden, and that makes it much more desirable.

"I appreciate your honesty," she says, stroking me slow enough with just enough pressure to make my body tremble on the edge of desire. "I can't tell you how many girls lie, and when they're paired up with the wrong guy ..." She clucks her tongue. "Aubrey?"

"Yes?"

Her fingers slow down then speed up, her attention on my clit just right. I'm breathing heavily, and my eyes roll shut.

"Do you want to come?"

Swallowing hard, I lie. "No."

"If I keep playing with your wet pussy, are you going to come?"

I squeeze my eyes shut. "No." That would mean I'm okay with all of this. I can't tell if I want to be or not.

She rubs harder and faster until I feel the orgasm climbing, but I try desperately to force it down.

"Are you sure? Your thighs are quivering and your lips are swollen. If I finger you, will you orgasm?"

I wish she'd stop talking to me like that, purposely taunting me with her sexy voice. My body feels like a blazing inferno ready to combust. No man who pays for sex is going to do this, or even talk to me in a filthy manner just to see me orgasm. In my experience, all men think about are themselves in the heat of the moment, on that cusp of completion, so I don't understand why she's doing this. I draw in a deep breath.

Two fingers circle my clit faster in response. I gasp as she simultaneously hits the right spot and presses her lips against my shoulder blade. My nipples harden, and she reaches up to tweak one until it burns.

She steps in front of me then. I watch as she leans in to wrap her red lips around one of my nipples. Through my shock, I can see why red lips are necessary now, because the sight before me— the way her mouth is moving on my breast—is enough to make me orgasm.

She gently tugs on my nipple with her teeth and a moan

escapes me. My lips part and my back bows, arching from the brazen desire running through my veins. She runs her tongue over the sensitive nub, and another little whimper pushes past my lips. I want her to give the same treatment to my other breast now.

"If I told you to lie on the lounge chair and spread your legs, would you?"

I have no idea why she's doing this to me, and at this point, I honestly don't care. All I can focus on is the pleasure streaming through my blood.

"Yes." My response is a breathless whisper.

"Good. Now do it."

I'm momentarily stunned, and I blink a few times before my legs carry me to the chair. I lie back and position myself like she said. Legs spread wide, my arousal drips down to my ass. My breathing is low, heavy, as I watch her walk over and drop to her knees. Her hands run up my calves, and I widen my legs even more. She knows how to touch a person and make them crave things they've never had. My teeth dig into my bottom lip, and I'm in absolute shock as she leans down, flattens her tongue, and drags it up my wet pussy.

When she asked if I'd ever kissed a woman, I didn't realize she'd meant like this.

"*Oh*" rolls off my lips.

My hips press into her face as her tongue sweeps across my clit. A moan rumbles in the back of my throat, and a rush of wetness seeps out of me, spurring her on with the hard stroke of her tongue. Chills rake my body, and the pleasure is all too much for me to handle. I run my fingers through her soft hair, and her hands push into my thighs as she licks my pussy better than any man ever has.

Christine lifts her eyes to mine, and I realize that I like watching her lap at my swollen pussy. She inserts two fingers into my sex and focuses her tongue on my aching clit with utter perfection. She's a fucking pro—obviously—and should teach classes on this, because my orgasm is still hovering at the surface, and it didn't take much time to get there.

I clench around her digits, and a ragged sigh drips from my lips. My thighs are trembling, but she doesn't let up. Her fingers fuck me just right as her tongue works wonders. Fisting her hair, I push her face into me as ecstasy steamrolls through every vein in my body and I release into her mouth.

Madam Christine pulls back and our eyes meet. Her mouth is coated in my pleasure. Leave it to a woman to make me come harder than I ever have with a man.

I stare at her in wonderment, her eyes on mine and her lips shiny with the remnants of my orgasm. On a startling impulse, I lean forward and capture her lips with mine. Climbing over her body, I force her onto her back. She goes willingly, her hands immediately roaming over my back and through my hair. Our legs sandwich each other's. Our tongues swirl together, and I taste myself on her, which only turns me on more.

Her dress slips to her hips and I tug it out of the way. I plunge my hand between our bodies, and a new sensation ignites in me at finding her bare. I've never had sex with a woman before, but I find myself wanting to so desperately now.

My needy fingers play with her wet pussy, and I marvel at feeling the contours of skin so similar to my own, yet so different. A little nervous, I tentatively slip two fingers inside her, and she clenches around me. Her teeth dig into my bottom lip, and her hand grips my ass. Then she's riding my fingers, and it's by far one of the most erotic things I've ever done in my life.

Her tongue twirls around mine, and she grinds her clit into my hand. We both moan into each other's mouths, and I want my clit on hers. I pull my hand away and grab her hips to position her just right, my carnal instincts kicking in.

Oh. My. God.

Never in my life have I felt anything like this. My skin breaks out in a heated shiver as our clits rub together. It's all too much, and I fucking love it.

"Make me come with your pussy," she says, her voice sexy as lace.

I nod and do as she asks.

Our supple bodies are pressed together, moving in harmony. We clench and grind on one another. The sounds erupting from her tell me she's loving what I'm doing, which only encourages me more. I slam my hips into hers, and heat prickles my skin. Our thighs are slick from our building desire, and our swollen lips rub back and forth, back and forth, until we both come together in blissful ecstasy.

"I must say, I wasn't expecting that," she pants against my mouth. A small smile tips her lips as our orgasms fade.

Banging my potential boss was the last thing I expected walking into Sanctuary Cove.

"You're going to make a lot of men happy," she says, releasing a sated sigh. "You can dress now," Christine says, and it's back to business.

I stand, a little unsteady, and pull my dress on as she walks over to a jewelry box on the counter. She flips it open and takes out a Wet-Nap then wipes her fingers off.

"Did Natalie tell you that you are not permitted to come until after the client does?" she asks, slowly licking her lips. I wonder if she can still taste me.

"No, I wasn't aware of that," I lie. Natalie wasn't supposed to tell me a thing, and I didn't want to throw her under the bus.

"That's the last time you will come first while working for Sanctuary Cove. Our focus is on making sure the clients' needs are met. They always come first, and not just sexually. Do you understand?"

"I understand," I say, my voice hitching in the back of my

throat.

Christine looks at me then crooks two fingers and signals for me to come to her. Her eyes bore into mine as I close the distance and stand in front of her.

"There are a few simple rules to follow. If you can heed them, you'll do very well here. I already know which clients would love to have you."

I nod. I can't decide if I should be happy about that or not.

"Birth control is an absolute must, and I'm not just talking about condoms. I have both condoms and the pill here if you need them. STD testing is every three months. All clients and working girls are tested. It's up to you whether you want to use condoms when the time comes, but you will always carry them with you."

This line of work is already risky and probably knocking off ten years of my life to begin with. Why wouldn't every working girl use both birth control and a condom? Even for a blow job? I'll definitely be using a raincoat each and every time.

"You're allowed to deny two clients a month with no questions asked. Any more than two, and we'll need to reevaluate if you should be here or not." Christine pauses to allow her weighted stare to sink into me. I get the point quickly and nod. "When you agree to see a client, you show. I have a no-refund policy. If you're a no-show, that's an automatic termination. I don't give second chances."

She's a no-bullshit boss. I can respect that, even if she does make my heart quake with intimidation.

"You never reveal any personal information, and under no circumstances will you get close to a client. The rules are simple. I can make you rich, but it's all in how you play the game. Play wisely, dress the part, and you can come out on top. And know this ... I have eyes and ears everywhere. Do you understand?"

"I do," I respond, looking her directly in the eye.

"You'll be given a thousand dollars for today. You have two

weeks to get your license and testing done. You also need to fill out the hard-limit sheet so I know what you're not okay with. In the meantime, you'll go shopping with Natalie's help. You'll start a workout program and get the waxing done. Don't shave for a few days, as the hair needs to be long when you go." Her eyes roam my face. "Your skin is nice, but it wouldn't hurt to have monthly facials."

Jesus Christ. I can't believe I'm actually going through with this.

"Quit the laundromat tomorrow."

"Done."

"How do you feel about the name Valentina?"

"Perfect," I say, even though I don't care for it. I'll get used to it.

"Good. I'll see you in a few weeks. Oh, and Valentina? I'm not your friend. You'll do well to remember that."

Christine excuses me, and I step out of the room to find Natalie sitting in a chair. She stands and walks over to me.

"You will not be sorry about this," she says excitedly then takes my hand and leads me back to the esthetically perfect, jasmine-scented foyer.

We retrieve our coats and step out into the chilly air then quietly make our way to the town car waiting for us.

"You knew, didn't you?" I accuse her once we're settled in the back seat.

Natalie struggles to keep a straight face as she asks, "What's your new name?"

"Valentina. And you're such a fucking asshole! I hate you."

"It's all part of the process." Natalie's face lights up, and some of my anger fades. Natalie is the kind of person who wouldn't harm a fly, so it's hard to stay mad at her for long about anything.

"Oh my God. Warn a bitch next time."

"If I told you, then you might've backed out. Plus, I'm sure you got an amazing orgasm from it, so technically, you're welcome."

I release an exasperated sigh. She's right. I probably would've backed out had I known what was waiting for me, but ...

"You could've given me a side-eye, some kind of signal, a warning. Anything. I was dying in there."

Her lips pucker and her body trembles from her restrained laughter. "Nope. I wanted you to experience it the same way I did."

I shake my head and face forward. The corners of my mouth curl in a small smile. I'm so torn on how to feel.

"You know I'm down for just about anything under normal circumstances, but I never expected to fuck my potential boss during the interview process ... and actually like it."

Natalie's eyes widen and her jaw falls slack. "You guys had sex?"

I nod. "She went down on me too. I never ever thought I would go that far with a chick, but holy shit it was fucking hot and I was so turned on."

"Then I say you came out on top," she jokes.

"And I still think you're an asshole."

"I love you too, Valentina."

I laugh over the name. Valentina sounds like I should wear something seductive and lacy, maybe the color red. I muse over the idea for a moment. Maybe it could be my signature thing.

"Oh! Check your pocket."

Frowning, I pat my coat pockets and feel something on my right side. I slip my hand inside and pull out a black envelope. My brows draw together as I open the flap and withdraw crisp hundred-dollar bills. Twelve of them.

"How the hell did she do that?" I ask, perplexed.

Natalie leans into my side. "Oh, she gave you a tip. She must really like you."

I roll my eyes toward her. "You know, we've seen each other at our worst, naked and shit, hungover, crying over boys who ghosted us, but now you've got me hooking and banging my female boss," I say like I'm exasperated, but she knows I'm not. "This means you're stuck with me for life. That shit makes us stronger than blood sisters."

She chuckles. "We're *wet* sisters."

I fake gag. "Don't ever say that again. It sounds like incest."

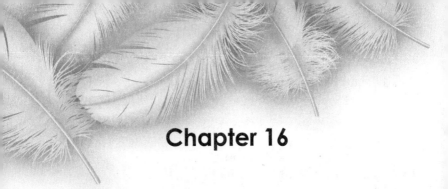

Chapter 16

"Ready for your Brazilian?"

"Do I have a choice?" I ask as I look around the posh salon. All the white ostrich feathers and pastel pink walls are relaxing and give off a glamorous vibe. "I've never had one before."

She gives me a naughty smile that makes my stomach flip. I have a sinking suspicion I'm going to hate this. She'd given me two Tylenol an hour before, and even though it's chilly outside, she insisted I wear a dress under my jacket.

"You're going to love it."

The lady at the counter shows us to a back room, where I have to undress.

Lying on the table, I place the sheet over my body. "Man, if I didn't know any better, I'd say you love seeing me naked."

Natalie rolls her eyes. "Nothing I haven't seen before," she says. "After this, we'll do your facial and then a mani-pedi. I usually come about once a month."

I grimace. "I have to do this once a month?"

She nods, crossing her arms in front of her chest. "Trust me, you'll want to."

There's a knock on the door, and in walks a woman who looks to be in her mid-thirties.

"Natalie, a pleasure as always." They exchange amicable smiles, and then she turns to me. "Hi, Aubrey. I'll be your waxing technician today. I see it's your first full-body waxing, so I'll try to make this as painless as I can."

She explains the process, which only makes me more nervous.

"For the next forty minutes, your vagina and body belong to me. Let's get started, baby girl."

I can't help but burst out laughing. That was the last thing I expected to hear. New Yorkers are known for their animated and blunt attitudes. There's a uniqueness about them, a seventy-thirty blend of take-no-bullshit attitude and humor in their words.

She raises her brows, and I respond to her questioning look. "I'm sorry. I've just never done this before."

She purses her lips together, and they twitch with entertainment. "Oh, this is gonna be fun. I'll go light and start with your armpits, brows, and upper lip. Then we move on to the goods."

The technician prepares her supplies and then waxes the three places she mentioned pretty quickly. My top lip is a little sensitive and hurts the most. There's a slight burn but nothing too bad. I do love the idea that I don't have to shave under my arms now.

"You mind if I shape your brows? You could use it," she says like they offend her.

I just nod. She plucks pretty quickly and even uses some string that looks like floss.

"Oh, Aub, they're looking good," Natalie says, impressed as she leans over to inspect them. "There's a nice arch now and they're thin. Not huge, overgrown bushes."

"Hey now, I didn't have bushes."

Her eyes drop to mine. "You had more hair on your forehead than I do on my pussy when it grows in."

"Hmmm ... It's true," the technician chimes in and agrees.

They weren't that bad. I tweeze them. I just don't know how to shape them. The technician hands me a mirror, and I look at them. The shape gives my face a totally different look.

"They look good. Better," I say, and the woman glares around the mirror at me. "They look fucking amazing, and I feel like the ugly duckling that just turned into a swan," I amend.

"Good." She moves to stand at the end of the table. "Now, pull your knees up and put your feet here like you're at the gyno." She guides my feet to the sides. "Yes. Now let your legs fall open."

A twinge of embarrassment heats my cheeks.

"We'll start with your ass."

I slam my knees shut. "My ass?"

"We're waxing that ass too." Natalie smiles at me.

"For what? No one goes back there."

"When that ass is in the air, and men look at it wanting to fuck it, you want it looking good. You don't want them to see a hairy jungle. It's about to be your second-best feature. Now open up, pull your knees back like you're about to give birth, and let the woman do her job."

What the fuck? I'm at a loss for words. I've been around the block a few times, but I've never had any complaints about how my ass looks when it's in the air.

"You're such a bitch," I say to Natalie. "You love to see me tortured, don't you?"

Exhaling a sigh, I do as she says, even though I feel extremely exposed. This is probably tame compared to what my new job will entail so I need to get over my embarrassment. Based on what Natalie tells me, anything is possible.

"If there's an award for being the worst best friend, you win it," I say.

She's standing behind me, and I can hear her trying to stifle her laughter. "This is another moment you would've run from had you known what was waiting for you."

I angle my neck to look back at her. "Do you see the position I'm in? Not even my gynecologist gets this up close and personal with me."

"Get used to it." Natalie lifts her chin toward the technician. "She's gonna be up close and personal with your goodies often."

I shake my head and pull my legs back farther so the technician can apply the wax. I could probably use a little modesty, but it's too late to practice that now. This is one for the scrapbook—I know we're going to look back on this one day and laugh. My embarrassment begins to tamper off, and I relax slightly.

"Take a deep breath," the tech says as she presses two strips of cloth to my ass and then rips them both off.

My eyes shoot wide open, and my butthole puckers like there's a circle of fire surrounding it. All I want to do is squeeze my legs shut from the warmth spreading over my skin. The technician applies some salve, and it immediately cools the heat down a little.

"Shit, that hurt."

"We do anal bleaching, by the way," the woman says casually, like she's ordering two sugars in her coffee.

My eyes take in the pretty garden picture on the ceiling panel that's supposed to take my mind off things. Anal bleaching? The fuck?

"No, thanks. I think I'm good."

"Suit yourself. Place your feet down and drop your knees."

The woman applies the gooey wax to my inner thighs and bikini area. She tells me to exhale before she rips off one side then quickly moves to the next side.

I squeeze my eyes shut, and my back arches from the heat searing my flesh. Goddamn, that hurt, and she's not even done. Grabbing the sides of the table, my fingers curl around the edges as I try to steady my breathing. Warm wax is placed on my mound, then on the actual lips, moving them to the side for what I'm assuming is to get all the fine, little hairs.

"This is gonna hurt, isn't it?" I glare at the stupid picture above me, hating it. My heart is pounding against my ribs, and I'm seriously dreading this. There's no going back now because the honey-looking goo is already on and has to come off somehow.

"Ready?" the woman asks.

"Nope."

"Good," she says then rips one side off.

I fucking see stars.

Shock surges through me, and bile rises to the back of my throat. Tears fill my eyes, and I'm in utter agony.

"Oh my God. I think you ripped off my vagina!" The pain, oh hell ... It's brutal and unlike anything I've ever felt before. I just want to cup myself the way a guy does when he gets kicked in the balls, and I can't.

I barely have time to catch my breath when she's holding the skin down to rip off the other side, and then the one on my mound.

"*Fuck!*" I cry, drawing out the word. "My vagina is on fire! Get the hell away!" Rug burn times eighty million on my vag.

Natalie is laughing hysterically, and I silently vow to smother her in her sleep tonight for this.

"No more." My breathing is heavy.

"You're done anyway," the technician says then cleans up so she can give me a facial. "You can dress now. If I were you, I would wear loose-fitting clothes for the rest of the day. Tomorrow you will be fine and smoother than a newborn baby. Trust me, you'll be excited to come back next month."

Somehow, I highly doubt that.

"Do I have any flesh left?" I ask, my voice cracking.

They both chuckle, and I die a little inside. My goodies are both on fire and numb at the same time. I sit up and reach for my dress, not even bothering with my thong. Now I know why Natalie said to wear a dress.

"It will be easier next time," Natalie says.

"No," I spit and lie back on the table. "I feel victimized."

"Just wait and see," she says, eyeing me.

I get the feeling she's trying to tell me something. The woman steps out of the room to grab some products, and Natalie leans in to whisper in my ear.

"When you get paid for those first few jobs, you'll be back here doing everything because that money is going to be your biggest motivator. Mark my words. Plus, there's no maintenance and it's really nice. The men love being with young girls, and a smooth vag looks fresh and new to them."

"Men are fucking creeps."

"Eh. Doesn't bother me. We all have our fixes. I just want their money."

I shake my head and let out a breath. I really want that money too, but I don't think anal bleaching or waxing my ass is necessary to get it. Then again, I guess I'll find out. I've come this far. Who knows what I'll agree to next?

After my facial and mani-pedi, we stop at a bar for a drink before heading to the apartment. I haven't been out since my birthday, and now that I'm legal, I don't have to use my fake ID. We both have schoolwork waiting for us at home, so we decide to stay for no more than an hour.

"Why are you walking like that?" Natalie asks, laughing, as we walk down the street. "You look like you went horseback riding bareback style, all bowlegged and shit."

I roll my eyes at her and laugh. My walk isn't that exaggerated, but I definitely don't walk like I'm about to take the runway either. I'm still panty-free, and even though it's chillier than before, it feels good against my fiery privates.

"It feels like I did," I say and open the door to the bar.

We order our drinks—gin and tonic for Natalie, Sprite and tequila for me—and find a quiet booth in the back. I can't cross my legs without it feeling uncomfortable, but after a few sips, the alcohol coats my veins and dulls the pain.

"I'm not supposed to tell you this because it's a test—I wish someone had told me—but Madam Christine is going to assign some test Johns to you."

My brows bunch together. "What does that mean?"

"You're going to get some guys who are going to be extremely aggressive and come on to you hard. They're going to put heavy moves on you and provoke you," Natalie warns. "It's a test to see if you can handle yourself and the clients. There's no saying how many you're going to have, but you'll know when Christine's done testing you."

I take another sip and let her words sink in. "How will I know which is fake and which is real?"

"I would expect at least two, but I've heard she's sent up to five. I think that's her max."

I take a sip and let her words sink in. "Are they going to be violent?"

"No," she says, and I feel a little relieved. "Madam Christine doesn't stand for violence. She always does an in-depth background check on all members before she lets them near any of her girls, and she runs follow-up checks every three months, so don't ever worry. She makes sure it's a safe environment for everyone."

I was already uneasy about this secret world of high-end escorting, but now I'm wondering if I should sign up for self-defense classes.

"It's not as bad as you think. You're going to be nervous as hell thinking they're all test Johns until you find your way. Just don't take too long. She's quick to fire girls, too."

I take a long sip. "No pressure, right?"

"You got it. That's why you take two shots and a Percocet before you go and pretend you own them—unless you're hired to be a sub and say, 'No, Daddy' That's a different story."

I almost choke on my drink stifling my laughter. "You've had to do that?"

"Once. He had a wicked fetish and made me use a pacifier, but I got thirty thousand out of it, so who cares?"

My eyes widen. I can't fathom that kind of money.

I glance around the dimly lit bar, wondering if any of these white-collared men have daddy dom fetishes. It could be anyone, really, and I'd never know.

"How long were you with him?"

"The whole weekend. Half the time the Johns take Viagra to make sure they get their money's worth. Oh! And here's a tip—before you go on any appointments, use spearmint spray to relax your gag reflex and coat your goods in coconut oil for easy access. Both make a huge difference, unless, of course, he's got a small dick. If that's the case, you lick it like a Dum Dums lollipop and pretend he's got an anaconda hanging between his legs. No working girl wants a big dick. It's too much work and requires hazard pay. I'll make sure you have some travel sizes for your purse too. Give a great blow job, and you got a client for life, er, ah, for however long you want, I guess." She makes a face when she realizes this should never be lifelong work.

"Tricks of the trade, huh?" I say, finishing off my drink.

She laughs and her eyes light up. "Girl, I've got enough to write a book."

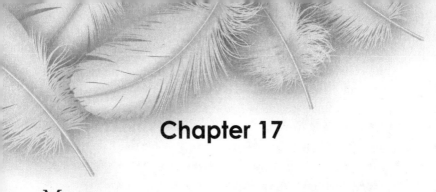

Chapter 17

My phone vibrates in my lap, and I glance around the auditorium to see if anyone else noticed it. I'm in the middle of class and don't want to offend the professor.

Swiping the screen open, I read a text message from Natalie. She wants to meet for shopping after class, but since I still have another class after this one, I let her know I'll see her in about three hours. The one thing I won't do is sacrifice my education for anything. Say the escorting works out for a couple of years and I get ahead financially ... It won't last forever the way a degree will. I need to play my cards right so I don't fuck myself in the end.

When my classes are done for the day, I drop my books off at the apartment, then take the subway to meet Natalie uptown. I got a clean STD test, which I knew I would, and got my adult entertainment license; I even signed up for Pilates where Natalie goes. The last thing on my to-do list from Christine is to shop for proper attire.

I walk into a store on Madison Avenue, and Natalie already has a few bags in her hands. Stella McCartney, Carolina Herrera, Fendi, Prada—all places I never thought I'd shop at. I've walked past them countless times over the years, but I've never let myself step inside any of them. No sense looking at what you'll never own, right?

"Hey, girl. I started shopping already," Natalie says cheerily. "I've got a bunch of stuff picked out for you."

"That's awesome. I love your style, so it works."

"Thanks to my mother," she says and flips through bright-red, high-waisted miniskirts. As usual, her makeup and clothes are on point. "My mom should've been a fashion designer, or at least a celebrity stylist. I think she missed her calling in life. She has incredible taste and always looks fresh to death. She has inside intel on what all the new trends will be, and then she tells me." Natalie hands me a handful of cocktail dresses that are insanely elegant and scream wealth. "Let's go to the back and try these on."

I don't care about new fashion trends, but I guess if I'm diving head-first into the sex trade, I probably should. Wealthy men know class when they see it. These clients want arm candy to show off, something that'll make other men envious of them. I can't do that with a skirt from Target.

I try on one dress and try not to gawk at the price tag. I step out of the fitting room, and Natalie's eyes roam my body for two seconds.

"We'll take it," she says. "Next."

Natalie says that for all the dresses, and it starts to worry me. While she held true to her word and gave me ten grand for taking the Sanctuary Cove job, I don't think it's going to be enough, so I speak up.

"Even with the money you gave me, Nat, I can't afford all the dresses and whatever else you already bought."

She smiles at me, always so friendly and sweet.

"I got you into this, so I'm going to set you up. It's only fair. After your first job or two, take me out or buy me a sexy pair of shoes, and we'll call it even."

I tilt my head to the side. "Nat—"

"Nope. Let me do this. And I'm sure I'll want to borrow some stuff anyway, so it's really for both of us," she says like it's final then hands me a gorgeous pair of metallic gold Manolo Blahnik sandals. There's a band of amber crystals across the toes and a thin ankle strap. Stylish. I could dress them up with a black dress or dress them down with a pair of jeans.

I don't even know how many more shops we stop at, but I now have my own beige and black Burberry coat, shoes from Prada, delicate gloves by a designer I can't even pronounce, and a flowy blood orange and deep-green floral scarf dress that I'd never, ever in a million years wear, but it happened to fit perfectly and I loved it at first sight. Natalie insisted it would be good for a brunch event. Something about my dark hair and milky complexion working well with the colors. Everything is glamorous and exquisite, and I'm suddenly excited to wear them. We hit Bergdorf, Saks, Tory Burch, and even some little boutiques for jewelry before we take an Uber back to the apartment since we have so many bags.

"Welcome to the lifestyle of the rich and shameless. If we're ever given a reality show, that's what we'll call it," Natalie says, and I laugh. "You never wear personal jewelry. Nothing that can link you back to your real life or holds personal value. When you step out of the town car, you become Valentina," she says. "You forget your real world. You're there to do a job. It's no different than any other job, really."

I swallow, knowing it is different.

I take my purchases to my room and hang up the clothes as Natalie checks her phone.

"Your phone is vibrating," she says.

I reach for my back pocket and frown when I palm it. "No, it's not."

"Your Valentina phone."

My heart drops.

I walk to retrieve the phone Madam Christine had sent over for me the other day. Swiping it open, my hand is shaking as I read the text message from her.

I glance up and meet Natalie's gaze. Instant nerves consume my entire being, and I feel like I'm going to be sick. I knew this day was coming, I just thought I'd have more time to prepare.

"Two hours," I say. "I have two hours until my first job."

Natalie's bright smile annoys me. I want her to panic with me, but she's acting like a kid in a candy shop.

"How exciting! Good thing we went shopping!"

My eyes widen and my chest rises and falls heavily. "But it's a school night. I have school tomorrow," I say, making any excuse to talk myself out of going. I don't think I'm cut out for this after all.

She stares at me, blinks long, and then laughs so hard that she has to reach out to steady herself from falling over. I'm so glad my freak-out amuses her. I prop my hands on my hips and just glare at her.

"Okay," she says, trying not to laugh. "Stop being dramatic. You're not ten. You can stay out past your curfew. I asked and got approval. I promise you won't get grounded."

I tie my hair up into a messy knot. I'm starting to sweat. "You're a dick. How come she didn't tell me sooner?"

"She didn't want you to panic or have the time to back out at the last minute. She sprang it on you just like she does with everyone. The first date is always the worst because your nerves are all over the place. It's better this way, trust me. When I was told when my first job would be, I had a week to stew on it, and it was the absolute worst. My stomach was so messed up that I couldn't stop going to the bathroom. I was sweating, and I had the shakes."

My jaw drops as realization dawns. I remember her not being able to go to class for three days because she was stuck in bed. That was about two years ago.

"Oh my God! You told me you had the flu."

Her blue eyes widen with confirmation. "Yes, that's when it was."

I frown, brows pulling together. "I don't remember you dressing up and leaving."

"I got lucky. You were with your grammy that night, but while I was getting ready, it dawned on me that I was going to need a cover story, and that's how I came up with shot girl."

I apply weight to my heels and just stare at her.

"I can't believe how stupid I was—"

My Valentina cell phone vibrates in my hand again. We both look down.

"Oh, that's Christine. Answer it!"

My fingers tremble a little, but I slide the screen open and bring the phone to my ear.

"Hello?"

"Valentina?"

Pulse thrashing, I can barely hear her. It's so strange being called that name. "Yes?"

"Christine here. You'll have your first job tonight. I expect you to accept."

I shoot a glance at my best friend, who can't seem to stop smiling. My knees are shaking. "Yes, of course."

"Wonderful. I'll send all the information. Check your text messages. Going forward, text message is how we'll communicate, so make sure you have this phone on you at all times." She pauses. "You're not to bring your personal cell phone with you, and do not give this number out. Do not text or call anyone who is not me from this line. It's strictly for work."

I lick my lips and watch as Natalie pours two shots then snaps a pill in half. "I understand."

"Do not bring any identification with you. You won't need it. No debit cards, nothing that can link you to your true identity."

"I won't."

"Wonderful. Remember the rules. I'm aware of your hard limits—I'll never pair you with someone you're not comfortable with. Whatever he wants is something you've already agreed to."

I swallow the lump in my throat, wondering what I'd agreed to because my mind is a clouded mess and now I can't remember. "Thank you."

"Come by tomorrow afternoon for your payment."

My brows shoot up, and I'm filled with unjustified excitement over getting paid for sexual acts I haven't even committed yet. Actually, I don't even know what I'm being paid for, and I feel like that's something I should know beforehand, but I don't ask. I'll ask Natalie. Maybe she'll know.

"I'll see you then."

Just as I'm about to hang up, she says, "Oh, Valentina?"

Dread forms in the pit of my stomach. Her soothing voice is starting to make my insides turn to mush. "Yes?"

"Remember, I have eyes and ears everywhere. Don't disappoint me."

"I won't," I respond quietly then hang up.

I look at the black screen, blinking, thinking, overthinking, before I lift my gaze to Natalie.

I don't say anything. I'm too nervous. I'm not sure what to say anyway, but she's one step ahead of me and hands me a shot then half of the pill she just split.

I stare at the clear liquid, contemplating my life choices. I could turn around now and walk away. I could say no. I could find another job, a normal job, but instead, I find myself saying, "Spit or swallow, right?"

We clink our shot glasses together as Natalie says, "I'll cheers to that."

Then we throw back the shots together.

Chapter 18

The black town car pulls up in front of the Empire Hotel, and I make a mental note to thank Natalie for her special pre-work brew. While I'm nervous as fuck, my knees aren't shaking and I'm not sweating or on the verge of a stroke.

Before I left the apartment, Christine sent one more message listing my price for tonight.

My jaw had dropped when I read the text.

Eight thousand for two hours.

Eight. Thousand. Fucking. Dollars.

For a high-priced booty call.

As I step out of the car, I can't help but wonder how much Madam Christine is making off me if this is my cut.

Exhaling a deep breath, I enter the hotel and walk through the building, keeping my focus straight ahead to the elevator. There's no wait, and I get on and take it all the way to the top floor, where my John is waiting at the rooftop bar.

The elevator dings, and Natalie's parting advice to be confident, to act like I own the place, filters through my mind. I put on my best sexy, come-hither face, even though I'm shaking like a leaf inside and my stomach is tensing up, despite my pre-show cocktail.

There's a doorman right when I step out, and he asks for my name.

"Au—Valentina."

Fuck. I already made one mistake. He doesn't seem to notice it. Unbuckling the belt, I hand him my new Burberry coat and look down at my attire. A little black dress works for every occasion. Except mine is strapless, shapes to my body, and has a chiffon bow at the center of my breasts. Even I can admit I look like sex on a stick in this dress. Let's hope he's a boob guy, because I've got these babies on full display just for him. Everything Natalie put together for me makes me feel beautiful with a hint of seduction. Not too trashy, just enough to get the job done. She said I'm a walking wet dream, and at the moment, I kind of feel like it.

Holding my clutch, I push forward and step outside into a private oasis that doesn't seem to fit in the middle of the city. Rat Pack music is playing, and I can feel the bass vibrating through my body. The music isn't loud, but it's enough to drown out the busy city below.

I feel at least eight pairs of eyes on me as I walk slowly, looking at each one of the men, trying to find my John. When I talk to Madam Christine tomorrow, I'm going to see if she can give me a description for my next job so I don't feel completely blind.

My heart is about to pump out of my chest when a man rises from his seat and walks toward me. This just got one hundred percent real. I feel like I'm going to throw up.

Cue the fucking nerves. I'm rooted in place. Swallowing hard, I nervously bite my lip, unintentionally looking a little innocent and seductive at the same time, but he seems to like it as his eyes flicker with lust. The man has to be in his fifties, and he screams old money. He's not attractive, but he's not horrible either.

"Relax," he whispers into my ear as he takes my hand and pulls me into a tender embrace.

I nod and try to steady my heart. I need to remember that he's a test John and that Christine has eyes everywhere.

"You look beautiful," he says and kisses my cheek.

I pull back but keep my hands on him and peer up through heavy black lashes that only multiple coats of mascara can give. "Thank you," I reply sweetly. "You look pretty handsome yourself."

I have no idea what possessed me to say that, but I guess I should show interest, right?

He guides me to where he was sitting and takes a seat. We're side by side, our knees almost touching. My dress rises up a little. It's just enough to entice, which he seems to like. Outside of this escort life, I do love the attention of men, and I do like seeing desire in a man's eyes, so seeing his lust helps a little. Maybe this won't be so bad.

His heated gaze travels the length of my legs and then lingers. I may have only just started doing Pilates, but I've always thought I have nice legs, and the five-inch heels just add to the appeal.

"Would you like a drink?" he asks.

"Sprite and tequila, please."

He places our order, getting a scotch for himself.

"Have you ever been here before?" he asks.

I glance around the swanky outdoor lounge. "Can't say I have. I didn't expect it to be so chill. Do you come here often?" I realize my question makes it sound like I asked if he brings escorts here often. I quickly rephrase my words. "It's a perfect place to unwind after work."

Jesus Christ! I'm dying inside with nerves. Where's my fucking drink?

He tilts his head to the side. "It's actually the only place I enjoy coming to after work. Tell me, what do you do?"

A test question. I eye him and go with the first thing that pops into my head.

"I'm a preschool teacher."

His eyes lower, and I swear I hear him growl. I decide from here on out that's my job ... well, my job within a job. The last thing I ever want to be is a teacher, so it works perfectly.

His weathered eyes flicker again, this time with hunger, and I have him pegged. He likes his girls looking innocent and young. Perfect.

Our drinks are finally brought over, and I just want to suck mine down, but I wait for him to take the first sip before even touching my glass. I have to take it slow anyway since I already had two shots.

"You love children?"

I shake my head. "Not really," I joke, and he laughs.

That makes me feel good. I look around, wondering if anyone knows what I'm doing here, but he stops me.

"No."

My eyes snap to his.

"Your eyes stay on me," he says in a harsh, low voice, and for a second, everything inside of me freezes. "Do not look at anyone else. You're here with me."

I lick my red lips, and his gaze falls, following the motion. "You're all I see," I say. It's not my best line, but short and simple seems to work.

We make useless conversation until we finish our drinks, and the next thing I know, he takes my hand in his as we walk to retrieve our coats from the doorman and head straight to the elevator.

He's on me before the elevator doors even close, and it freaks me the fuck out. We fall into the corner, and I hit my head against the wall. He doesn't seem to notice as he grabs my breasts and gives them a painful squeeze. I whimper, taking it. My breathing labors and my clenched hands find his shoulders. I'm stiff but trying to go with it like a virgin on prom night. He sinks his teeth into the curve of my neck, and I tense up again, while his other hand brazenly reaches under my dress and cups my pussy to the point of pain. I almost grunt. Instead, I grit my teeth and wonder how we're going to have sex when I'm as dry as sandpaper and shaking inside.

"Fucking wet, just like a real whore should be." His tone is filled with malevolence, and he's not at all the pleasant guy I was having a drink with outside seconds ago.

I frown at his statement then remember Natalie had me use coconut oil as a lubricant before I left, and some of my anxiety eases.

Treat him as a one-night stand.

He's all over me, putting his full, suffocating weight on me. The elevator doors open, and then we're power walking to his hotel room. Thank God I know how to walk in heels and I'm not tripping over my feet. The closer we get to the door, the more anxiety grows in my stomach. I push it down and tell myself this will all be over soon. This has to be a part of the process. Right? I can't imagine anyone selling their body for money is comfortable with it the first time ... or first few times.

Eight thousand dollars. You're going to make eight thousand dollars.

We're in his room faster than I can blink, and before the door can even shut, he shoves me against the wall. My head smacks it, and I reach up to grab it. I'm going to end up with a fucking concussion before the night's over. His mouth is on mine, and all I taste is menthol cigarettes, which is interesting because outside I could only smell the kerosene from the lanterns.

He's mauling me, smothering my personal space. I can't seem to get a good handle on things as he takes control in a sloppy manner. He yanks the top of my dress down and my breasts spill out. Cool air breezes over them, and something inside me wakes up when he roughly grabs my bare flesh. My stomach hardens. He twists my nipples past the point of pleasure, and I smack his hands away. Taking a deep breath, I use force and push him off me, but I don't do it like I'm disgusted, even though I am. I do it as if I'm so sexually frustrated that I can't even bear foreplay. I act as if I need his cock inside of me right now, this second ...

And it does the trick.

I can play this game too, asshole.

He pulls back and glares at me as if he's offended, but I move quickly and shove him against the wall. I cup the front of his pants, finding his cock already hard. I give it a squeeze over the material and run my palm up and down. If I can find a little control, I think I'll be okay. He's average-sized, which instantly calms me because I know he won't hurt me. I've had bigger.

Leaning into his body, I bite the side of his neck the way he did me.

"Hard for me already, baby?" I say, my voice that of a kitten purring.

He pushes me back, and this time I almost stumble in my heels.

"Get on your knees and suck me off, you slut."

I'm not really into the whole degradation talk. It's not my style. Being called names like slut, whore, or skank have never turned me on.

But for eight thousand dollars, it can.

He shoves me down to my knees, and I unbuckle his pants to free his erection. My hands shake a little, and I hope he doesn't notice.

I put my hand out. "Condom, big daddy."

I want to die over my choice of words. Not from humiliation, but because I've never spoken to a man like this before and I find it comical and embarrassing for him. But of course, I don't show that.

He slaps a condom in my hand, because no fucking way am I giving him a blowjob without protection. I roll it on him. He's not even in my mouth for three seconds before his meaty hands find the back of my head and he's ramming his dick down my throat. I have the strongest urge to bite down because of how he's acting, but I really don't want a swift kick to my face. He's pumping his hips obnoxiously fast and grunting, yelling obscenities about how I'm his dirty little slut who better suck him harder. My eyes start watering. Thank God my gag reflex is on point.

Yeah, this isn't going to work.

I pull back so he pops out of my mouth so I can peer up at him. I start stroking him, twisting my wrist.

"Let me show you how good I can be," I say, my voice husky and seductive. "Let me satisfy you, baby." His intense stare disturbs me, but I show no fear, stroking him hard and slow. He gives me the slightest green light, and I lean in, making it my mission to give him the best blow job he's ever had.

It doesn't take long before his body is pliant and soft and he's feeling everything my tongue has to offer. He starts moaning and slowly moves his hips in conjunction with my mouth. His heavy sack in the palm of my hand is tightening up. Just when I think he's about to come, he pulls me back gently and looks down. My lips are swollen as I look up at him. Eyes glossy, he's either on drugs or he loves what I'm doing to him.

"Take your clothes off," he says, panting for breath. "I want you back on your knees. Spread your legs and arch your ass back so I can see that filthy pussy in the mirror while you deep throat my cock. Then I'm going to fuck you like the good little slut that you are."

So much for weaseling my way out of having sex on the first night.

Chapter 19

I don't take a town car to Sanctuary Cove. Instead, I walk the couple of blocks to clear my mind, wondering if people will know what I've done when I stop in front of the doors.

I didn't get a chance to follow up with Natalie last night when I got home. It was well after midnight and she was already asleep, so I took a shower, scrubbing my body until it was bright red, and then I crashed. She sent me a few text messages earlier when I was in class, but I couldn't respond. I know she's dying to know what happened, and I'm eager to tell her all about my first night as a professional hooker. I still can't believe what happened myself, and I need to talk my feelings out.

I send Nat a quick text to meet me for dinner at a little Mediterranean place we like, and then I steady myself before ringing the doorbell.

Shooting a glance over my shoulder to see if anyone is watching, I make eye contact with an older woman who looks to be in her sixties slouching against a brick building. Her coat is stained, and she's surrounded by tied white plastic bags that probably contain her entire life. The sorrow in her gray gaze is unsettling, and I have to turn away. She could easily be my grammy. One social security check short, and Grammy could be out on the street. No. I would never let that happen. That's why I'm here. For her, and for me.

The same doorman from last time welcomes me in. He dips his chin in acknowledgment and takes me straight to Christine's office. Another lavish room that looks fresh out of an issue of

Vogue. She's sitting behind a desk going over paperwork when she glances up. Our eyes meet, and I'm reminded of what happened the last time I was at Sanctuary Cove. Heat flames my cheeks. I'm a little tingly thinking about my first full girl-on-girl sex. I can tell she's thinking about it too by the way her lusty eyes rake down the length of my body.

I know I'm not dressed in Sanctuary Cove attire, but I was just in school for six hours, and the distressed jeans and cropped I HEART NEW YORK sweater work for me right now. My hair is in a cute ponytail, and I only have a touch of makeup on, making me look more natural than anything.

The corner of her mouth curves just slightly, causing a flutter in my stomach.

"Valentina, it's a pleasure to see you," she says, her voice silky. She gestures toward a chair with her hand. "Take a seat."

"Hi," I say, a little shy. I'm not sure if I'm supposed to address her as Madam Christine or just Christine.

"So, you're a preschool teacher."

I pale. Not a question, but rather a statement, and it makes me edgy. She doesn't seem bothered by it, but she isn't amused either. I can't tell if I'm in trouble or not.

Swallowing, I hide my panic and offer a timid smile. "It was the first thing that came to mind and something I'd never, ever do, so I figured it would be okay. I don't even want kids."

"Of course. It's good to have a cover ready when you're asked questions."

"I can change it if you like. I can be a pastry chef or a florist. Whatever you like."

She shakes her head. "It's not necessary. Were you nervous?"

"Yes, very."

"Once you start doing more jobs, it'll get easier, if that's what you want," she says, never breaking eye contact. She doesn't even blink.

I nod. "Yes."

I feel like I'm under a spotlight. Trying to remain collected is proving to be harder than expected.

Christine reaches into her desk and pulls out what looks like a prescription bottle. She gives it a little shake then hands it to me. There's no label, no instructions, but then, why would there be? It's clearly not from a doctor.

"Take one an hour before each job."

I reach for the see-through orange bottle. "What is it?"

"Percocet. Natalia said she gave you one, but I think you need a stronger dose until you're more comfortable. If you run out, just ask me for more."

My gut tells me there's more to what she's saying than she's letting on. I can't help but wonder if the test John had complained.

"Did I do something wrong?" I ask quietly.

Her lips purse together, eyes flashing with the hidden truth. "No, but I don't want my girls to act like amateurs. You've fucked plenty of men. You shouldn't tremble when you're touched or grunt like an animal. Men pay a lot of money to be a member of Sanctuary Cove, Valentina. They want seasoned women." Her gaze drops with her voice. "Act like you fucking love it, even if his dick is small and you can't tell if he's inside you or not. Make him feel like a king, like you're giving him the best sex of his life. Do not moan like a porn star. Remember how you moaned and whimpered under me? That's how it should be for the client. If you have to imagine my tongue on your pussy, then so be it."

I flush and glance down. My body warms, and I'm instantly hot in my sweater. I knew she wasn't happy with me. I sensed it, but all I can do is nod.

I *did* shake, I *was* nervous, and I may have sounded a little off last night. I guess I was focused on what I was supposed to do and how I was going to impress him that I didn't realize it would backfire on me. I didn't know if I should make noise or not. I didn't know if I should let him do what he wanted or if I should take control, if I should show interest. I'd simply viewed it as my first night on the job and tried to learn as much as I could on the fly.

"I understand. It won't happen again."

Her eyes are blazing. A weak person would cower, but I steel myself, forcing an unwavering gaze back at her.

"I don't give a lot of chances."

"I like a good challenge."

Something flashes across her face as she slides an envelope across her desk toward me. She keeps her French manicured nails on it to keep me from grabbing it.

"Do not deposit that into a bank account all at once. A little at a time, or try to pay cash for anything you need. Some girls open offshore accounts, and that's something you can look into if you should need to." She lets go and sits back.

"Thank you," I say then slip it into my bag. The envelope doesn't feel as thick as I assumed it would, but I can't wait to count it. I won't be able to until I get home, though. Flashing money like this in New York City is a sure way to get mugged.

Christine hasn't taken her eyes off me. "How many days a week do you want to work?"

"I'll take whatever you want to give me. Weekends I'm free for anything at any time. The weekdays will have to be evenings."

"Are you willing to travel?"

I consider her question. "I don't see why not, if it doesn't interfere with my classes. Is that a common thing?"

She doesn't answer me. "I'll text you with your next job. Do you have any questions?"

"No," I say and stand. "Thank you for the second chance. You won't be sorry."

Right before I leave, she calls my name, and I look over my shoulder.

"He did say you can suck cock better than anyone else

here. Trust me, he's been with most of my girls. Take that as a compliment." Her lips twitch. She seems proud.

At least I'd done something right.

Before I jump back on the subway, I stop at this little Dominican place and order the most popular dish on their menu to go. I pay for it and walk outside, handing the Styrofoam container to the woman sitting in the same place as before, along with a crisp hundred-dollar bill. So many people go hungry in this city, and my heart bleeds for them.

Nearly an hour later, I'm finally sitting down to eat with Natalie.

"She said that?" she asks, listening intently. "I mean, she's usually hard on everyone at first until they find their own way."

I nod. "What do I say to that? Like, thanks? I'm glad to know I give a good blowie? I think I need to work on my O game. Apparently I don't know how to fake it." I exhale, frustrated. "Nat, he sounded like he had an entire carton of Newport cigarettes for breakfast. He was grunting and making noises like he was dying. It made my skin crawl. How do you fake it to that when you keep looking over your shoulder to see if he's about to stroke out?"

Natalie is laughing so hard she has tears in her eyes.

"That's terrible," she says when she catches her breath. "I guess you just focus on the money. That's what I did. You're getting paid to perform. The better you are, the more you get. And once you start raking in the dough, you'll want more and you'll work even harder to get it. You'll forget how awkward escorting is."

I glance across the street and watch someone jaywalk. "Did you feel dirty after? Shameful?"

She nods, cupping her hair behind her ear. "Yeah, I did, but that's normal. It took, probably, a handful of times for the grime to wash away. That feeling doesn't ever go away completely. Escorting gets easier the more jobs you take. Thankfully they're clean-cut men and not dirty slobs. The way I see it, it could always be worse."

I rub my arms, holding myself. "You have a point. I just hated how I felt last night when I got home. I felt so sleazy and dirty. I stayed in the shower until it ran cold."

Natalie takes a sip of her water. "That sounds about right. It'll get easier ... unless you don't want it to? A lot of girls don't return, which is understandable."

"No, I do. I can do it again. Sex isn't a big deal to me. It's just sex, you know? No-strings-attached sex, like any other time, except I'm being paid. The cash shouldn't change anything, but it does," I say, and she nods in agreement. "I just have to not be so nervous and panicky. I think I was focusing too much on the rules and what I should and shouldn't be doing."

"Being a high-priced prostitute is not for the faint of heart, which is what you are. Like you kind of have to have low principles to do this."

"Or be poor and not want to struggle for the rest of your life."

She tips her glass of water toward me. The ice cubes clink together. "That too. Why do you think so many women strip? The money is good and quick, and they want security."

As we eat, I muse over Natalie's words. I wonder if it really will ever get easier, if I'll get to a point where I don't feel as disgusting afterward. At least a little. I can't imagine anyone ever feels normal working in the sex trade. I'd think one would feel an array of emotions even long after they stop. But I also think it could give a sense of strength having gone through a chapter of their life no one is truly proud of to talk about and still come out on top.

"I think I've come up with a solution. If I don't feel differently after six jobs, I'm going to walk away and just go back to working myself to the bone rather than boning everyone else to take care of myself and Grammy."

"If that's what you need to do, then do it. I think it's a good idea, honestly. What are you going to do about this O issue you have?" she asks, dipping warm bread into the seasoned hummus.

"No clue. Practice?"

Her eyes light up, and she's grinning from ear to ear. "Can I be there to laugh at you while you try?"

I bundle up my straw wrapper and throw it at her. "You're an asshole. Of course."

The check comes, and for once I pay for it with ease. It makes me feel good that I can, and then we head back to our apartment together.

Once we're in and the door is locked, I take out an old book and Natalie helps me carve out a deep square for my new money. Eight thousand dollars, just like Christine promised. I wrap the hundreds in stacks of thousands and use a black marker to write the number one on each band to represent my first job, then I place the banded stacks in the book and close it.

Living in a city rich with sin and opportunity, I was always under the impression that if I can make it here, I can make it anywhere.

And I will.

Come hell or high water, I refuse to be another statistic that New York got the best of.

And yet, that's what I feel like I am quickly becoming. A working girl with no set business hours, on the corner just trying to make a quick buck to get by.

Chapter 20

I frown at my phone while trying to get to class on time, wondering why Grammy isn't picking up. She usually gets up before the sun rises to feed her cats, so it's highly unusual that she's not answering her phone. A shoulder bumps into me, but I keep going, mumbling an apology. I can't be late, but her not answering doesn't sit well in my stomach.

I decide to try her again after class.

Social Science Statistics. I chuckle to myself. I feel like most of my classes were a forewarning of my new job and I just didn't know it until now.

After the two-hour lecture, Grammy still isn't answering, which only worries me more. This isn't like her. She always answers or calls me right back. Despite the anxious feeling I can't shake, I stop to buy a pretzel from one of the nearby street carts to appease my rumbling stomach before I go to my next class. I contemplate skipping class to hop on the subway so I can check on her when my phone lights up with her name. Relief courses through me, and I answer the phone midchew.

"Grammy, where have you been?"

"Oh, sweetie, I slept in. I can't believe what time it is. I woke up to the cats crying, and one of them was licking my face."

I grimace. I hope I never wake up to someone, or something, licking my face. "You never sleep in," I say.

"I guess my body needed the rest. Are you okay? I saw a lot of missed calls on my caller ID. Now you have me concerned. Is something wrong?"

I take another bite. "I'm fine. Everything's okay. I just wanted to make plans to take you out for Thanksgiving, but then you weren't answering and I got worried."

"Aubrey." She almost seems exasperated, and that makes me smile. "You don't have to mother me."

"I know. Anyway, I want you to pick any restaurant."

"That's a month away, and it's not necessary. I will cook."

I knew she'd say that. She loves to be in her kitchen.

"Nope. I'm taking you out this year, so pick a place by the end of the week. That way I can make reservations. Now that I've heard your lovely voice, I can breathe again and head to my last class. Love you."

"Love you too, sweetheart."

Hanging up, I chuck the pretzel wrapper into the trash and slip my phone into my purse—never my back pocket—and walk a couple of blocks to one of the many tall concrete buildings that make up the best city in the world. I feel a hundred times better now that I spoke to her. Stepping inside the lecture hall, I take a seat.

As the class quiets down, I hear my cell phone vibrating. I sit up and reach into my bag, thinking it's Grammy calling me back, only to realize it's my Valentina phone.

I still. This weird blend of anxiousness and dread swirls around in my stomach. I'm excited, but I'm not. I shoot a glance around the room to see if anyone is watching, but no one is.

Placing my phone in my lap, I slide my thumb across the screen to unlock and read the message. It's short and to the point.

Another job. Fourteen thousand this time. And it's at Sanctuary Cove.

My eyes nearly pop from my head. Holy shit. What the fuck does the client want for that amount of money?

Apprehension comes with the territory, but it's churning in my gut and hardening the food I just ate to stone. Fuck, I'm nervous. Natalie was right. It's only two days away, and if I had known a week beforehand like she did, I probably would've canceled.

Fourteen. Thousand. Dollars.

Natalie was right. The money is starting to change my tune.

I cross my legs, my foot bobbing. My fingers are jittery, and the anticipation is making me edgy. I can't tell if it's a warning sign, just performance anxiety, or the fact that I know it's wrong and I'll end up in hell for this.

I take a deep breath then send Madame Christine a reply, agreeing to the job. After that first asshole, how bad could this one be?

***

"Natalie," I blurt into the phone. "Nat? Are you there?" I repeat, my voice filled with urgency. I'm so disturbed right now I can barely form sentences. "Where are you?"

"Just getting home. What's up? You sound sketched."

Relief courses through me, and I close my eyes. I hear her keys jingle in the background and then a door shut.

"That's because I am! Break out the bottle. I need to tell you what the fuck happened with this client. Never in my life ..." My voice trails off. "I just got off the subway. I'll be there soon."

"On it," she says then hangs up.

I didn't bother with a town car for the ride home. Instead, I had the driver drop me at the nearest subway entrance, and then I walked underground to jump on the train and took that to my usual stop. It was faster, and I felt better being surrounded by normal people.

I climb the flights of stairs leading to and from the subway in record time wearing four-inch strappy Tom Ford heels. At this rate, I'm going to have the best legs on the block just from the station stairs alone. One of them is over a hundred and fifty feet below level. Meaning a lot of fucking stairs.

Natalie must've heard my click-clack coming down the hall because she's waiting for me with a double shot of tequila the second I throw the door open. I drop everything and reach for the mini glass. I don't wait for her. I tip it back and let it burn the back of my throat. The hair on my arms rise, goose bumps coating my skin from my wrist to my shoulder. I wave to her for another one.

"Damn. I can't wait to hear what happened with this John."

"He was the biggest fucking weirdo I've ever seen."

She clucks her cheek and hands me another, then takes one for herself.

"I'm sure I have some stories that'll make your head spin."

My eyes narrow. I'm not sure she can top this story, but in a strange way I hope she can. Maybe that would help me feel better about all of this. I swallow the second shot, then yank off my pumps and drop them to the floor in a clunk.

"He had a serious Hannibal Lecter fetish."

Creases form between her eyes. "What do you mean?"

I walk into my room, needing to get out of these clothes. As Nat follows me, I consider the odds of surviving a bleach bath.

"What I mean is"—I pull down the straps of my beige dress, the one he requested I wear because it's the color of my fucking skin—"I had instructions to walk into a room at Sanctuary Cove and lock the door. The room was freezing, like it had to be thirty degrees. I found the John sitting in the dark, buck naked, with a fucking mask on his face, Natalie. The one Buffalo Bill wears in *Silence of the Lambs*. I almost ran from the room. He scared the shit out of me."

Just thinking about that moment again makes my heart fucking hammer against my ribs.

Once the dress is on the floor, I reach into my dresser and grab a baggy shirt that goes to midthigh. I unsnap my bra and let that fall too. Tugging the shirt over my head, I sit on my bed and pull one knee up and just stare at her, trying to figure out where I should start. I'm still shaking. I feel like I need a hug and for someone to tell me it's going to be okay while they rock me in their arms. I also desperately need a shower, but I have to get this out first.

"What did you do when you found him like that?"

"For one, he had his dick tucked between his legs, so I didn't even see it," I say, and Natalie looks concerned. "I froze because I literally thought I was going to die or be mauled by some freak in a leather mask with a hidden dick."

She chuckles then. "You're kidding me?"

"I wish I was. He poured a glass of red wine the moment I walked in. I would later realize it was Chianti. I don't know why he was pouring it, since there was no way he'd be able to drink through his mask. Anyway, he doesn't even say hi, he just gives me a blank fucking stare while he's petting a dog."

She frowns. "A dog?"

I nod fervently. "Yeah, like that cute, fluffy white one in the movie. So he tells me to strip. No biggie," I say, shrugging casually. "I do, but he's talking slow and asking me to strip really slow, like extra slow because he yelled through the mask for me to turn around and bend over to touch my toes." She acts like this is nothing shocking, and so I continue, though I'm extremely exasperated while I'm telling her. "He asked me to spread my cheeks and push. Push, Natalie. Push as in you have to take a shit or something. I assumed he had a butt fetish because who asks for that?" She's starting to laugh now, but I don't find it funny. "The whole night was mortifying and extremely demeaning. All I could think about was how I wanted to tell Christine to never book me for him again. Of course, I didn't because I got fourteen grand from the date." Nat's laughing even harder now. She gives me a knowing look. "I wanted to die. Thank God I got that awful waxing."

"Wait ... Did you push?"

I flatten my lips. "Of course I did. I wanted that money. I could see him over my shoulder. Once I started pushing, he reached between his shaved legs and started playing with himself."

She covers her mouth, fighting the fit of laughter trying to break free. "And here I thought I had worse stories than this."

Brows raised high, I hold up my index finger. Here comes the worst part. "Then, *then*, he grabs a bottle of lotion from God knows where and starts rubbing it on his dick. He stands and rolls a condom on. I thought the condom would slide off since he lathered himself up first, but it didn't. So I bend over and silently question what I got myself into when the next thing I know, he's literally ramming into me so hard I fall forward and separate from him. I hit the fucking wall."

"Ram Jam strikes again!" she yells, laughing. "Did you really fall?"

I nod, lips puckered together. I feel the liquor warming my veins and my shoulders relaxing a bit.

"Yes, my head hit the wall then fell to my knees. I probably have a bump." I reach up and touch my head, feeling for a lump. "I wasn't doing anything but bending over at the time, so I had nothing to hold on to when he rammed me with his vanilla bean–scented dick. I was so caught off guard that it took me a second to get up. Apparently, I didn't move fast enough, because he grabbed me by my hair and told me he wanted to wear my skin because it's supple and soft. First of all, what the fuck? And second of all, what man says supple?"

"Buffalo Bill," she says, smiling.

"You know the rule that we can't come until the client does? It won't be an issue with guys like this nut job. I was able to block the sex out real easy this time. Any more clients like him, I'm gonna dry up permanently and become a sister of God. Anyway, he fucks me while making these slithery snake sounds and when he was done, he made me rub lotion on him. Like all over his body. So I did."

Her jaw drops. "Okay. You're making this up."

"Hand to God, I'm not."

"Keep going."

"All I kept thinking was that I'm getting paid good money for this or else I would've run from the room the second I stepped in. He had me put what looked like an old bottle of Bath and Body Works lotion all over every inch of his skin, while still wearing the mask. Mind you, he's hairy as fuck, so it's triple gross. Then, he made me rub lotion on myself. I didn't want to put it on my skin, but of course, I did it anyway. He told me to go really slow over my nips and vag, and then he freaking asked me if he could suck my toes." I exhale a stress-filled sigh and shiver in revulsion. "I wasn't sure how he would with a mask on but then he took it off specifically for my toes. You know how I feel about feet, but I let him anyway, because hello, money. Once he was done, he asked if he could pretend shave me with the dull side of a butter knife."

Her eyes widen, and the laughter dies down then, her expression turning worried.

"Of course I do, but at one point I felt like in his mind he was peeling off my skin because his eyes rolled into the back of his head and his dick got hard. Once he shaved the lotion off my body, I cursed myself when he said to put the lotion on both of us again. Again! How much lotion does one man need? Nat, I was already sliding off the plastic-covered couch. I didn't want to lube us both up again. The cream he used had a really strong scent."

"Plastic?" She looks confused.

"Yeah, he had a clear plastic cover on the couch, like people did in the sixties. I was slipping all over it and sweating at the same time."

"That's bizarre."

"Yeah, so I shake my head, telling him no more lotion. I

didn't want to be fake shaved again, and I knew that's where he was going. He got too close to my goods with the butter knife the first time. I wasn't taking a chance of "accidentally" being cut the second time."

Natalie's face falls and she pales like I just told her I'd killed the guy. I know we're not allowed to reject Johns, but there are some things that I'm realizing I *will* say no to. Rules be damned. I feel like Christine would be understanding since he used a knife on me.

"You told him no? Tell me you didn't." Her voice is full of dread.

"Yes, I did. I was nervous with that fucking knife! He even 'shaved' my back and got extremely close to my exit zone. Once was enough for me. Don't tell me you would've said, 'Yes, please give me more.' How do I know he wasn't going to cut me with it?"

She purses her lips. "You have a point, but I wouldn't be surprised if he goes to Christine."

I pause for a moment, thinking about the finale of imposter Buffalo Bill's creep show.

"He won't be going to her. You can trust me on that."

Her brows furrow. "What do you mean?"

"When I told him no and I shook my head, he legit said, 'It puts the lotion on its skin, or it gets the cock again.'"

I pause and take a deep breath, wondering what I did to deserve the John I got. Natalie covers her mouth, trying to not laugh over the worst night of my life.

Lowering my voice, my shoulders slump forward, and I say dejectedly, "I got the cock again."

Chapter 21

I didn't hear from Madam Christine for an entire week—a blessing in disguise if you ask me. She probably knows the last test John she sent me is certifiable. I would bet a whole job payment that none of the girls want to work with him.

Natalie said Christine did this sometimes. If the client is more demanding than the others, she would sometimes give them a few days to recuperate before texting them with a new job. It is her own way of being nice, I guess.

So far I'm two for five. The first job wasn't bad, but that second lunatic was enough to make me want to walk away, beaucoup bucks be damned. However, I'm not the type to give up so soon either, so I'm sticking to my original plan of taking five jobs. Christine might be giving me an assessment, but I am giving her one too.

Which is why I'm currently walking into a private event in Bryant Park, looking for a man with salt-and-pepper hair standing at a table with a drink. I thought it would be difficult, but I spot him immediately from behind and stop in my tracks.

He can't see me, but I can see him. He's tall, thankfully taller than me, and built like an ox. Hair dusted with heavy streaks of silver—way more than the salt-and-pepper Christine described— he appears much older than I am. He's dressed in a tailored navy-blue suit, casually leaning against a tall, round table with a snifter in his hand. There's something suave about the way he spins his glass, the amber liquid hardly moving ... Then I catch sight of the thick gold band on his finger.

Married. Naturally.

Natalie did say ninety percent of her clients are married, but was it normal for them to attend public events like this without their spouse? And wear their wedding ring?

Exhaling a deep breath, I strut toward him, mentally preparing myself for another one of Christine's decoys.

Personal test number three, here I come.

Licking my freshly painted red lips, my nerves are suppressed by the Percocet I'd taken earlier. I'd skipped the vodka shots since the pill is strong enough on its own. I figured I'd have a drink with my John anyway. The last thing I want to come across as is wasted.

My stomach flutters with anticipation as I draw closer to him. I shake my fingers out and then place a hand on his back, feeling his strength underneath his suit. He stands tall as I move around to face him.

"Valentina?" he asks, his voice making something inside my belly swirl like the smoke trails of a cigar.

I smile and nod in response.

"Fuck, you're stunning. You're ... I have no words."

His voice is low and in the back of his throat, and it washes over me like warm caramel. He doesn't enunciate his Rs, which tells me he's a born-and-bred New Yorker. Men—not boys—with heavy New York accents are my weakness. It's sexy as hell and gives me goose bumps every time.

His eyes rake the length of my body. I feel like he's picturing me naked. I'm okay with that. He takes my hand into his and pulls me close to him, kissing my cheek like we're old lovers.

This is probably my biggest—and if I had to guess—last test from Christine, based on what Natalie told me. I hope so, anyway.

Not only is his body solid as a brick against mine, but he smells divine. His cologne is like an aphrodisiac, and I want to bathe in it. I catch the slightest hint of lemon and some fancy wood with a dash of bergamot, which I happen to love, even though most people hate it. Sophisticated, yet sexy. On top of smelling delicious, he's rocking a full beard and mustache that *just* works for him. His cornflower blue eyes take in my face like he's pleased. My smile deepens. I feel smitten by him.

Christine sent me this silver fox on purpose. I know she did.

Too bad I'm going to crush her test.

"Hello," I say, my voice a little husky.

I almost want to look away when my cheeks flush with heat from his gaze. He laces his fingers with mine, the seductive brush of his skin making my stomach dip. His thumb gently strokes the top of my hand.

"I'm James Riviera," he says, unable to tear his eyes from mine. "Are you cold? Let me give you my coat."

He goes to break our contact, but I step closer and place my hand on him. Heat sizzles beneath my fingertips as my palm moves across his broad chest, letting him know I'm okay. My body acts of its own accord, surprising even myself.

"There's no need. I'm not cold."

His brows furrow. "Are you sure? I don't mind."

My eyes soften at his concern. I like that he's considerate. I'm not cold, and liquor usually warms me right up anyway. I'm so glad I didn't have those shots before I left, but for the love of God, he needs to get me a drink before I faint to the ground. Something tells me my nerves will never go away with any of these jobs despite what Natalie said, especially not when the client is actually attractive. And James ... He's a hunk of a man making my blood simmer with lust at first sight.

James slides his drink toward me. "Cognac?"

My smile is a bit shy, and I hope he doesn't notice.

"I've actually never had cognac before."

He tilts his head to the side, his striking gaze taking me in. "Try mine. If you like it, I'll order you one. If not, you can order whatever you like."

As I bring the lowball glass to my lips, I hesitate just as James leans in to whisper, "I'll give you my coat whenever you wish, but I'm glad you declined. It would be a shame to cover your beauty. That dress compliments you. You remind me of the Greek goddess Aphrodite."

Time to put my game face on.

My lashes fall to my warming cheeks. His fingers tighten around mine. He's still stroking my hand, and there's something sweet I find about that. His compliment makes me feel sexy. I was excited when I got to put the dress on this morning. It's the orange and green scarf dress I'd fallen in love with when Natalie and I had gone clothes shopping. The material floats across my legs, and the top fits my breasts just right.

"Aphrodite? I think you can do better than that."

The corners of his eyes crinkle. "Peitho. Goddess of seduction and persuasion." He pauses. "She was handmaiden to Aphrodite."

"James ... I bet you say this to all the girls," I say coyly.

The top two buttons of his crisp white shirt are undone, and I catch a glimpse of his chest hair.

He shakes his head. "I don't. I don't sugarcoat either. I'm very close to asking who designed it so I can have customs made for you. I bet you could entice the Devil himself in it."

My brows lift and I turn around, giving him a view of behind. His gaze intensifies as he takes in my backless ensemble, and a pleased smile slips across my face. The dress sits just above my tailbone, leaving my back mostly bare, save for the thin, crisscross strings holding it together at the shoulders. James groans deep in the back of his throat like he's in a state of bliss seeing me like this, and fuck, that was hot. I know I shouldn't feel this way, but I do. The way he's looked at me in under a few minutes makes me feel absolutely gorgeous inside, which is something I didn't know I needed until this moment. His reaction veils the revulsion I was feeling for myself earlier, and I relish in it.

"You're trying to kill me with this dress," he says, leaning in toward my ear. "You are so fucking sexy, princess."

Princess. I giggle on cue. I hate that nickname, but it works with the way he says it.

"I'm glad you like it. You look pretty dashing yourself, if I'm being honest."

I make sure my eyes slowly eat up the length of his body, showing him that I actually mean what I say.

He leans in closer, his beard tickling my neck. James whispers against my ear, "It's a good thing we're in public right now, or else I would be ripping that dress off you."

It's another line I'm sure he says to all the girls, but I take the compliment anyway. I need all the praise I can get.

"I'm happy you like it. I'm in love with the floral print and material."

James clears his throat and gestures to my hand still holding his drink. "I want to know what you think of the cognac. Tell me what you smell and how it tastes on your tongue."

I glance at my hand. I'd forgotten I was holding the glass, but I find it interesting that he's trying to have a real conversation with me.

Our eyes meet, and I smirk from behind the rim. As I swirl the liquid around, it coats the sides of the glass the way any good alcohol should, and the fragrance hits me quickly. "Is that lavender?"

James almost looks proud. "Lilac."

"That's the last thing I expected. I know there's some spices, but I'm not sure which ones. They remind me of holiday baking."

"Fair enough."

I can't stop smiling, and I realize with surprise that I'm actually having a good time. Taking a sip, I decide I'm going to be humorous about it. I lick my lips like I'm trying to be sophisticated and whip out the best English accent I can muster.

"The smoothness is a surprise. The light notes of oak reveal candied fruit that's been stomped on with bare feet, then scooped into a barrel made from eighteenth-century wood. There's a pleasant aftertaste. Out of five stars, I give this spirit a four-point seven."

His blue eyes are gleaming. I'm going to call it early and say that he's happy with my performance.

"Aye, sir. What say you?"

His mouth twitches. "Did you just switch from English to Scottish?"

I pause for a moment then burst out laughing. A breeze of wind rustles my hair. "I dinnae ken whit ye, mate."

He's positively ecstatic now, and I love that he is. I did switch accents without realizing, but he seems to think it's funny. If only every job were this easy.

"Dinna fash yer pretty wee self."

"Where did you come from?" he asks, the corners of his lips curving upward. James takes my hand and guides the drink to his lips, his gaze not wavering from mine. We hold the glass together, and he takes a deep sip, his Adam's apple just making an appearance from behind his silvery beard.

"The loins of my father," I say with the faux English accent.

James barks out a lively laugh, and then I'm grinning with him. It wasn't a fake laugh either, but one that's good-natured.

"Well, you aren't far off. It's originally from the nineteenth century and aged for twenty years. I'd rather buy a bottle of Rémy Martin and ditch this event just to hear your opinion of it. Unfortunately, I have to stay and suffer through it. At least I'll have you with me."

I sober up and glance over my shoulder at the lavish brunch dresses and oversized hats, the pricey suits and Gucci loafers. Contrary to the other richies, James seems almost bothered by the glitz and glam surrounding us.

"How long are we here for?"

"A couple of hours. Is that okay with you?"

I blink, surprised he's taking my feelings into consideration. After all, he's the one paying big money for me to be at his beck and call, so it's not like I'd have any say in the matter anyway.

His shoulders are tense, and I realize with a start that I *want* to soothe him. I smile and slide close so our bodies are touching, and then I take our joined hands and wind them around my back so he has to hug me. He gives my fingers a squeeze. His eyes shift back and forth like he's studying me. My heart is beating a little faster than usual, sending an array of sensations through me.

"I'm here for however long you want. So tell me, what's this shindig about?"

His lips twitch and he unwinds. I can feel the tension in his shoulders loosen.

"It's an event to celebrate the most influential personalities representing New York City, the ones who will be recipients of Super Lawyer. It's for the attorneys who provide vital support to the community with the way they collaborate and create change. It's considered an honor to be invited, since less than five percent get a nomination."

My brows raise. "You're a lawyer?"

He nods. Another dime-a-dozen attorney in New York City. I should've known just by looking at him, but he didn't seem pompous at hello, so I was caught by surprise.

James leans into me and lowers his voice. "It's basically a snooze fest and I'd rather be anywhere but here, but since I'm a partner, I have no choice."

I focus on the way his mouth moves, how he enunciates his words in the back of his throat in true New York fashion. I find that insanely attractive.

James finishes the drink with a final sip. He lifts his arm in the air and waves for the waiter to bring us two glasses, then pauses. "Did you want cognac, or would you like something else?"

"No, I'll have what you're having. Thank you." After he gives the waiter two fingers to place his order, I ask, "Have you ever been a Super Lawyer?" I don't even know if I ask that correctly because I've never heard of it.

James nods.

"How do you become one?" I'm curious. I'm not a dumb girl, but this mumbo jumbo talk isn't common knowledge either.

"It's a four-step selection process based on specific indicators and how many points are accumulated. There's research and evaluations." He pauses, and I watch his Adam's apple bob. "I've been one for ten years in a row, which isn't normal."

"Wow. That's impressive."

He studies me. "What do you do?"

I decide not to use the preschool teacher job after the way Madam Christine had reacted and go with something else instead.

"I'm a pastry chef."

"So you're sweet and good with your hands?" He lifts one brow, and I chuckle.

"I'm sweet where it counts," I reply, making sure he gets the point.

As he's about to respond, a man who looks older than James makes his way toward us with a woman attached to his side. James's arm tightens around me, stiffening in protection. I eye him warily, but his focus is on the stout man closing the distance.

I feel a vibration rumble in his chest and try to ease his tension by grabbing his hand and squeezing it in silent support. He gleams down at me, and then much to my surprise, he kisses my forehead. "Ignore everything he says. Got it?"

I nod.

"Ah, James. New flavor of the week?"

Unintentionally, my fingers tighten around James's. I wonder if this little egg-shaped man is part of the test. The creep's comment rubs me the wrong way. I look at the man. His black eyes greedily roam my body. I quiver inside, and not in a good way. I don't like being called a whore. If men can sleep around and get away with it, so can I.

I'm going to assume this Humpty-Dumpty man is referring to James's playboy ways, since he doesn't know me from Adam. I also have to remind myself that I signed up for this, that I'm not being forced into anything. It's a choice I made, and idiots like him come with the job.

Grammy always said you attract more bees with honey, and I know how to kill 'em with kindness better than anyone else.

Chapter 22

"Philip. Can't say it's a pleasure seeing you here," James says tightly. "This is Valentina, a friend of mine."

Philip's wife, or I assume that's who's next to him, is staring me down, but I don't show her any attention. I just glare at Philip, wishing I could stomp on him with my shoe.

"Of course her name is Valentina," the woman says then offers me a forced smile.

I ignore the jab and instead compliment her hideous hat that's so big it could give her husband shade. It reminds me of the ones worn at the Kentucky Derby.

"I love your hat. It's so ... wide."

"A custom design from a friend Suzanne Millinery."

Whoop-de-fucking-do, whoever that is.

Philips says, "Is that how you congratulate a fellow nominee? You should be offering a bottle of your finest to us to celebrate. After all, I got the deal on one of the biggest clients my firm has ever seen. Possibly bigger than the Wilson Energy one you closed."

Pompous ass face.

James runs his tongue over his bottom lip. I notice the slight grin tug at the corners of his mouth. My heart pumps faster. This silver fox is controlled silence, and that's a major turn-on.

"A five-hundred-dollar bottle of cognac is reserved for people I actually like," he says.

Philip grunts in reply.

"I think it's an honor to be recognized, honey," the woman with the hooked nose says. It's like she's trying to soothe a child, only she looks frightening. "It's a big achievement and shows the years of success you've had." She turns to me, and her eyes soften like I'm a total idiot. "It's for lawyers who display excellence in their field."

"I'm aware, thank you very much," I reply with a sugary voice. "James acquired his first nomination early in his career." I look at James. "You've had, what? Ten now?"

His eyes meet mine, like he's pleased with my response, and it makes me feel giddy inside. Thank goodness I asked what a Super Lawyer is. He looks at Humpty-Dumpty.

"You didn't get a bigger client, Philip. You obviously haven't been made aware yet, but Packer Resources and I came to an agreement. We signed off on the documents early this morning. I secured the deal." James says, lifting his glass toward me in a silent toast. "We both know I'm simply better at what we do. I always have been."

Philip noticeably pales and his wife looks constipated. She quickly excuses herself after apparently spotting friends.

"How much are you paying for this one?" Philip asks, nodding with his chin toward me.

This one? I grit my teeth, reminding myself that my job title alone is a target, and that I need to work at not being offended. For Philip to immediately attack me, a stranger, because he didn't get his way, says everything about his character. What a sore loser. I hope James chews him out because I sure can't.

"Some things you can't put a price tag on," James says. "The interest you take in my personal life flatters me."

Philip's eyes harden. "I'm not interested in your personal life," he says with a bite.

"You always want what I have. Stature, notoriety, a beautiful woman on your arm. My position at the firm. You give yourself away when you belittle people, especially women."

I try to conceal the smile threatening to spread across my

face, one Philip unfortunately takes note of. I like the way James handles the situation—reserved and one step above the other asshole.

Philip's gaze on me turns to a glare, but I don't flinch. I might still be a little unsteady on my feet with this job, but if there's one thing I'm confident about it's myself. I eat men like him for breakfast.

"You know this isn't a movie, right? You're not going to get lucky in the end and marry the rich man. You're going to wake up a cheap whore tomorrow, looking for your next meal ticket." He glances at James, then looks back at me. "When you're done with him, come find me so I can show you the way you're meant to be used. I'll even pay double."

Oh, that sets me off. Before I can think better of it, I respond, my voice low. "Philip, you can't afford me, and even if you could, I still wouldn't touch you with a ten-foot pole. I can see why you'd want to be with me after seeing your washed-up, haggard wife, though. I bet you can't even get your little pecker up with her. But when it comes to James, no one has *ever* fucked me the way he has. The rumors are true. He's hung like a stallion and fucks like a beast."

I smile, wanting to pat my shoulder. I'm pretty proud of myself for that one.

Philip's cheeks burn with obvious anger, and I feel satisfied that he looks like he's about to explode. He's a fucking prick. Straightening his back, he turns and stalks off with the stick still in his ass.

James doesn't say anything. I'm almost afraid to look at him. My stomach churns. I'm certain he's going to report my behavior to Christine. It's going to suck getting fired from escorting for running my mouth, but at least it was worth it.

"Finish your drink. Let's go," he says low and near my ear, and my heart plummets. I was actually having a good time until that fuckwad came over. I close my eyes and exhale through my nose, upset I let that asshole get the best of me.

As he buttons the middle of his suit coat with one hand, his gold watch flashes in the corner of my eye. I look over and catch a view of a tattoo on his wrist where his cufflinks are. I'm surprised that a man as polished as he is has a tattoo, but as I move to get a closer look, he drops his hand.

James finishes his drink in three large gulps. I do the same. Taking my fingers between his, he walks us out of Bryant Park, and I'm thankful for my long legs that let me keep up with him. His gait is wide with determination and purpose. Probably trying to dump me as soon as possible.

My stomach is twisted with anxiety as I look ahead and see a gray Rolls-Royce parked at the curb. I wish I hadn't said anything. As we reach the car, I decide I want to apologize, but James spins me toward him and grabs both my cheeks then smashes his mouth to mine in a fierce kiss. He doesn't ask. He just thrusts his tongue between my lips and kisses me hard.

I'm momentarily stunned. This is the last thing I would have expected, but I quickly react and kiss him back with the same intensity. The fine hair of his beard tickles my lips, igniting a fire and sending heat straight to my core that I wasn't expecting. His tongue caresses mine with dominating strokes, causing my heart to race in response. I reach for him, gripping the lapels of his suit, but he pulls back and breaks the kiss. Here it comes. My heart is pounding. I'm going to get the boot.

"I've never had a woman talk about me like that," he says. "Not in public, at least."

"I'm sorry. I'm so sorry. I know it was out of line—"

"Don't apologize. I like seeing a woman able to hold her own. The shy and mild don't do it for me."

I look back and forth between his eyes and notice they've darkened to sapphires. "You're not embarrassed? Mad? Reporting me to Christine?"

A look of confusion crosses his face. He rears back. "Why would I be embarrassed?" Taking my hand, he brazenly places it on his rock-hard cock. "Does this feel like I'm mad, Valentina?"

My cheeks heat at his boldness, but I love it. I purposely run my fingers down his length, and his eyes flicker with lust. What I said back there apparently wasn't a lie. He *is* hung. Jesus.

"I spoke up when I shouldn't have. I talked about the size of your dick in a public setting at a work-related event." My body starts to shake, thinking about all of the money I'm about to lose. Christine made it clear she doesn't do refunds.

The corners of James's lips twist into a hot smirk. "I'm keeping you. I like that you have no problem standing up for yourself. Confidence and having a brain is a fucking turn-on. And as you can tell, I *am* hung like a fucking animal. And I do fuck like a beast. I hope you can handle me. Philip is a bastard and needed to be put in his place."

James places his hand at the small of my back and ushers me into the back seat. He follows and sits next to me then shuts the door. I sit, tongue-tied for a moment.

"I'm so confused right now. I thought you couldn't leave. Wait. You're not firing me?"

"Le Bernardin, please," James says to the driver, then he looks at me.

My gaze drops to his mouth. My red lipstick is smeared across his lips—a stark contrast to his beard. I reach over and wipe it with my thumb then rub my fingers together. I look up to find his eyes fixated on me. Blinking, I give him a timid smile.

"You looked like you were wearing lipstick. It was on your beard too, but I got it off."

* * *

Three hours later and half a bottle of delicious cognac gone, I'm way more than tipsy. Though it's a smooth, refined kind of tipsy that gets the heat flowing through my veins. I like it, but I'm not sure of it. I'm relaxed, sated, and I don't have the urge to get my eagle on. I guess this is the kind of boozing that wealth buys, not vodka by P. Diddy that makes me want to dance naked.

We're sitting next to each other in this underground, private room at an upscale restaurant I've never heard of. Our arms are touching, and I'm leaning into him, more comfortable in the moment than I ever imagined I would be with a client. We talk about the firm where he works and the type of law he practices, our favorite foods, and what we read. He reads books about stock trading like I do and loves Italian food. Though, I don't know nearly as much about the stock market as he does. I tell him about my love for romance novels and any food that isn't ramen. He doesn't care for the law he practices, but it makes him good money, so he stays. Small talk drives me crazy, but our small talk doesn't *feel* like small talk. Our conversation is easy, almost too easy for us.

I throw my legs over his muscled thigh so my high-heeled feet dangle between his. James hasn't taken his hands off me since we got here, and I wish I didn't like that. There's an air about him that fascinates me. I like being next to him. I like the sexuality he oozes, the way he looks at me with hunger. James makes me feel wanted, not like I'm a doll to be played with. I study him. There seems to be nothing I can find wrong. I'm curious to learn more about who he is.

As he leans over to pour another glass of cognac, I stop him. I'm not supposed to get drunk, and since I'm not used to this warm, relaxed, alcohol-induced body high, I feel like I should slow down.

"No, no more for me. Thank you, though."

He grabs the bottle by the neck and says, "We're not done yet. We still have half a bottle left."

My eyes widen in shock. "You want to finish the bottle off?"

He looks at me like I'd just asked an obvious question. When he responds, he makes it more of a statement.

"Yes, we are."

My stomach is a cluster of knots. "James, I can't get drunk."

"You're not going to. I'm going to feed you, and then we're going to sip and talk. I like talking to you, Valentina. I'm not ready for our time to be over."

I smile softly, and his gaze falls to my lips. If only all my jobs were like this. Then maybe there wouldn't be the constant battle between morality and survival raging inside of me, and it'd be more like two old friends hanging out.

James says he likes a girl who speaks her mind, so I decided to test it out by asking him a bold question. I pray it doesn't backfire.

"Why are you wasting five hundred dollars drinking a rare bottle of cognac with someone like me? I'm just another girl trying to get by selling her body to the highest bidder. Philip is right. I am a whore—"

His eyes darken. "Don't call yourself that."

"Why did you bring me here instead of to a hotel?"

He studies me. "Would you rather go to a hotel?"

No.

"I want to do whatever you want, but I'm confused. Most men in this situation don't just want to talk. They want their dicks sucked."

Chapter 23

The lines around his eyes deepen as he observes me. James isn't bothered by my question—he doesn't even flinch. He studies me without saying a word.

I take in the width of his broad shoulders. His suit jacket is long forgotten, tossed to the side like it doesn't cost more than ten bucks. Masculinity seeps from every inch of him. I want to run my hands all over his body. The silent power he exudes has me aching between my legs. My gaze falls to his chest, and I wonder what he looks like under the crisp, white shirt. James looks downright edible in business attire. I drag my tongue over my bottom lip. I'm usually a touchy-feely drunk girl, so holding back is a challenge. The craving I have for him itches under my skin.

I blink a few times, confused by my thoughts. I sit up a little straighter, reminding myself that this is nothing more than a job and that I'm paid to give an illusion. This spell with James will end when we part ways tonight. Tomorrow I'll wake up Aubrey Abrams, and I'll be taking another college exam. I'll probably get a text message from Madam Christine by noon regarding my next job.

"Life is too short, Valentina. You can't put a price tag on happiness."

He hands me a fresh glass and pours one for himself. I can smell the lilac and breathe it in.

"You've made me feel alive today. I'm not stressing about work, what emails I need to respond to before the night is over, what I'll go home to. There's no pressure sitting on my chest, no anxiety to riddle my nerves. I'm not suffocating in this rat race city like I typically do. He shakes his head and takes a sip. Memories are created by impromptu moments, and those are priceless to me. Like right now. Maybe years from now you'll come back here, and it'll spark a reminder of our time together. You may not remember everything that happened this day, but you'll feel it in your bones and smile. I'll remember how I shared a bottle of cognac one Saturday afternoon with a gorgeous woman who mouthed off to a rival lawyer from a very large law firm. Money can buy a lot of things, but it can't buy moments, and those are priceless. The five hundred dollars was worth every penny when spent with you. I'd do it again in a heartbeat."

My lips part in awe, my gaze unblinking. There's a fluttering around my heart that I've never felt before. I'm moved by his words, and I cling to them like they were exactly what I needed to hear. Of all the things he could have said, this was the last thing I expected to fall from his lips.

James sets down his glass, then removes a cufflink. I watch as he rolls up his white sleeve, revealing a maze of intricate, colorful tattoos that I marvel over. This wasn't done by just any corner shop, but by a true artist who charged a boatload of money. These won't turn into blobs of ink like I told Madame Christine. James turns his arm over, and I see a quote amid the designs, tucked away so that only the people he chooses to show can see it.

"Life is a collection of moments," he reads. His voice is as rich as the cognac. I lean closer and he says, "When I'm six feet under, my story will still be here because memories don't die. They'll live on forever."

I have an overwhelming urge to kiss him in this moment. I know I can't just do that, not unless he asks for it. Instead, I place my glass on the table next to his then roll up his sleeve as far as his thick forearm allows and take in his art.

"Are these all moments?" I ask, my fingers tracing over the

lines. I want to study his ink and unravel who this man is.

He widens his thighs, the material tightening around his legs. "Yes. Everything on my body has meaning."

Our eyes meet, and I start breathing a little heavier. "You have more? Can I see?" My eyes drop to his chest, and I wonder what he has hidden under his shirt. "I want to know about all of your moments."

I wait, but he doesn't move. When I glance up, he tilts his head to the side, his blue eyes focusing on my mouth like he's deep in thought. With his other hand, he places his knuckles under my jaw and lifts my mouth to his so slow that it takes my breath away.

James is a taker, and he slips his tongue between my lips without waiting for approval. I kiss him a little differently, not so detached in the way I am with the other clients or one-night stands. I stroke him with passion, letting myself revel in his kiss. I don't hold back. My hand on his ink moves, my nails delicately dancing over his skin. His kiss is potent, igniting a hunger in me. I rise, and he's already moving his hands to my waist so I can straddle his hips.

With my chest pressed against his, I devour James with the same intensity he does me. I give him all I've got. My fingers thread through his hair, and his hands skim up my backside to cup my neck. He applies pressure, and my body becomes pliant. I'm weak from his kisses. I love a man with strength, and the way he's gripping my waist and neck makes me melt inside. I roll my hips into his, purring when I feel his erection straining against his zipper. He groans, and I feel the vibration against my breasts. This connection between us isn't like my other jobs or quickies with randos. This is different. My panties are actually damp. I'm turned on by James. I want him more than I ever thought I would want a client. My head is too hazy to tell if what I'm doing is for him, or myself. James pulls back and breaks the kiss.

"I had other plans for you today, you know," he says, his voice hoarse and low, and God, I fucking love it so much. I love the way he's looking at my mouth as he talks to me. "I'd planned to just fuck you until you couldn't walk and then send you on home, but something tells me you're the kind of woman I'll need to spend hours upon hours pleasing."

"I think you drank too much," I giggle. "Why would you want to spend hours pleasing me? It's my job to please *you*."

James looks at me, his hips still purposely moving into mine, teasing my pussy. It's a slow, decadent roll, and I give back just as good as I'm getting. His eyes are heavy, and his hand on my lower back guides me into him as if we're having sex. I place a hand on his chest in an attempt to stop the climax that's building inside me and catch sight of another tattoo. My fingers move the collar of his shirt to get a better view, and I see that he has quite a few tattoos there. They all have meaning to him, he'd said, and I'm curious to know more.

"Because your pleasure is what turns me on. I can't fuck someone who doesn't feel as good as I do and get off on it. I need to feel you come on my cock. I need to see how you look, the expression on your face when I'm fucking you so hard that you beg me to stop. I want your back to arch so my dick goes deeper and I can feel your cum soaking my cock. I need to feel your pussy contracting as I come inside you. If you don't feel what I do when I'm fucking you, then there's no point. I can make you feel things you've never felt before, Valentina, but only if you let me."

He pauses, and I'm fucking breathless.

No man has ever spoken to me like that. I suddenly wonder why I've never been with someone older.

"I want you to feel as good as I do when we fuck, and trust me, we will. I'll never just expect you to satisfy me without making your time with me just as pleasurable. I want you to take as much as I give." His eyes shift back and forth between mine. "I don't know what it is about you, but I want the moment."

Leaning in, I kiss him harder than I'd ever planned to kiss a client, tugging on his bottom lip with my teeth. His words. Fucking hell, *I like* the way he talks to me. James has made it clear that he's a take-charge kind of guy, wanting to give and receive in the same fashion. I think about how he captures life in moments, and I realize that's something I want to start doing. This job gives me that opportunity. Maybe I can even make moments with Grammy too.

I also want to give *him* a moment he'll never forget, so I deliberately kiss him like I'm making love to his mouth and not just some cheap whore riding his cock. Kissing him deep and provocatively slow, I show him I'm as good as he thinks and maybe even a little better.

Reaching between us, I run my fingers over his bulge. His legs widen farther in his seat, and the material of his pants pulls tight so I can get a good feel of his cock. A little moan escapes me. Something tells me he would be good in bed.

James grabs my wrists and places them behind my back, securing them tightly. My eyes roll shut, and I whimper at the feeling of being restrained by such a strong man. He threads his fingers through my hair with his free hand and gives it a good tug, breaking our kiss. I arch my back and push my breasts forward. He doesn't hold back as he bites one of my pointed nipples through the fabric of my dress.

My thighs clench, and I let out a soft moan. James releases my nipple and licks a wet trail up the column of my neck, his teeth nipping my flesh along the way. His fingers loosen their hold on my hair, and he guides me up to meet his gaze. Our eyes lock, and something flashes in his, almost like awareness, but I'm not sure. Exhaling through parted lips, we breathe into each other. I'm turned on, wanting to come just like this.

"That look right there is what's got my dick hard. Your body responding to my touch. When you feel good, I feel good, sweetheart. It's that simple," he says, his voice raw and hot.

I love the way he talks. He's so New York and has that natural swagger to him, even when he's simply speaking.

I have to get my bearings and get his focus off me. It's too much, and I don't know where to go from here. I wish there was a handbook for times like this. Then again, how often is someone in my line of work actually attracted to their client?

"James, let me make you feel good," I say, a little breathless. "I bet I can make you feel better than anyone else ever has."

I tug on my wrists, but he holds them tighter. A shiver rolls through me. Under normal circumstances, I'd be filled with panic, but for some reason, I'm not afraid of James.

James smirks. "I bet you could, but I bet I can make you forget your name. Tell me something, Valentina, do you like being restrained during sex? If I secured your arms and took power over your pleasure, your thoughts, your body, so that all you can do is feel what I'm doing to you, would you come?"

I swallow hard and take note of the devious grin growing on his face. My hips are still rolling over his, his cock stroking my clit just right. God, I want to come.

"I bet you would come hard," he states, his voice breaking me down.

I know I would. My eyes threaten to flutter shut and my heart leaps. I don't like the thought of it ... I *love* the thought of it. But doing something like that requires trust between two people, and it's not something I'd ever give to a client. It's not something I'm allowed to give a client. And I don't have an issue with kinky sex, but he isn't going to handcuff me to a bed or practice shibari on me. I made that explicitly clear to Christine when we went over my hard limits.

"You're a conqueror, aren't you, James?" I ask, my voice a husky whisper. "You like to control? Do you want to dominate me?" His eyes flash with something wicked, and a smile spreads across my face. "Unfortunately for you, I don't have a submissive bone in my body, which I'm sure you've already noticed. A meek and docile person I am not."

His fingers on my neck press into my skin, just hard enough to elicit a soft sigh from me.

"Weakness and submission are not the same thing," he says, his voice low. "Submissive women are strong women. They just want someone who's stronger than them."

"And you think I'm strong?" I bluntly ask. "If I kneel at your feet, will I have to walk behind you too?"

Chapter 24

"I like a woman who challenges me." James grins, his eyes heavy with desire. He waits a few seconds before he speaks again. "How about we finish this bottle and see where the night takes us?"

I nod and get off his lap to sit next to him and right my dress. I'm glad he suggested this. I stare up at the gold-tiled ceiling, wondering what I'm doing and how I got myself into this predicament. He hands me my glass, and I down it in one gulp. I hand it back to him for another.

"I feel like I need a cigarette, and I don't even smoke," I say, sounding out of breath. He chuckles and refills my glass. I continue staring up in a daze, confused. "Honestly, James, my clients before you were total whack jobs. None of them left me so turned on the way you have, and none have declined me like that either. It's a hit to my ego," I joke. I turn to look at him, but he's already studying me.

"You get turned on easily?" he asks as he adjusts his bulge. He looks so fucking hot when he does that. It looks painful, though, so I'll have to try again to relieve that for him. It's why I'm here, after all.

"No, not too easily, unless I'm really drunk. Then I turn into a twenty-dollar hooker instead of a twenty-thousand-dollar one." I pause, laughing at myself. Luckily James doesn't seem bothered by my crude humor and laughs with me. "I usually think too much and can't shut my brain off any other time. Plus, this isn't a regular nine-to-five job, so it's a little different for me." I pause again, wondering why I even said that. "How old are you?"

"How old do you think I am?"

"Early forties?"

"Fifty-two."

My brows raise in surprise. "You don't seem like a normal fifty-year-old."

He brushes his free hand down his beard, his chuckle robust and deep.

"How old are you?" he asks.

I debate lying as I take a sip of cognac but figure there's no harm in him knowing my age. "Twenty-one."

"Really?"

"Yes, really."

His brows furrow. "Your real name isn't Valentina, is it?"

"Why are you here with me and not your wife?" I counter, blatantly eying his gold band.

His mouth twitches, but it's his eyes that give him away. "Fair enough. I guess there are a few things we're both not willing to talk about." James takes a long pull on his glass. "You know what I do. I'm your typical New York bloodsucking, money-hungry lawyer. What do you do?"

"I told you. I'm a pastry chef."

"Oh, yeah? What's your favorite dessert, Valentina?"

I blank, hesitating for a moment to think. "Tiramisu."

"Liar."

I take a sip then lick my lips. "Macarons?" I offer, trying not to laugh.

He smiles, and it warms my belly again. "Those are cookies," he states.

I lift my glass and toast to myself. "And I hear they're fabulous."

He's grinning from ear to ear now, and I can't help but smile too. It's like everything he does is contagious, and I feel that fluttering in my chest again. He's fun to talk to.

"You've never had one?"

"Nope. I have a bad sweet tooth, but I've never had those."

"What do you do?" he asks again.

"I'm a librarian." He's not impressed. "A shot girl? A florist?" He doesn't say anything, and my humor fades. Against my better judgment, I decide to get real with him. "Do you want me to say prostitute, James? Because that's what I am. But you already know that."

He doesn't even flinch. "I want the truth."

I frown. "Why? What does it matter? Is this a test or something?"

He doesn't say anything, just sits there waiting patiently.

"I'm in college."

"Which one?"

"One in the five boroughs. Take your pick. There're tons. I'm just your *typical* struggling college student, raised with very little means. I have to work myself to the bone for everything I have, and now I'm trying to support the only family I have left. Selling my body makes me more money in one week than I would make in six months at a respectable job, and since I've always liked sex, mainly one-night stands, I'm making my peace with this line of work."

"You have commitment issues," he states, curiosity in his voice.

I look him dead in the eye and tell him how I really feel. "No, not really. I've just never found anyone I actually want to give myself to long enough, someone who can handle me with my odd sense of humor, warped vision of the world, and not be offended easily. I'm also young and I don't care to be locked down just yet, if I'm being honest. Not to mention I have family to support, so my free time is limited anyway."

"So then the idea of being trapped worries you," he says, and

I notice that he's twirling his wedding ring as he speaks.

My chest tightens. "It does, but I don't know why. Seriously, what man is going to want me anyway after he learns I've been around the block the way I have? He's going to have to be willing to look past *all* my imperfections, including my body count. I'll be lucky if I ever find him."

"But what if the right one comes along and gives you all you ask for?"

I shake my head and purse my lips together. "It won't happen. I don't go out much, and I'm not going to meet someone like that in my line of work, that's for sure."

"Understandable you feel that way, but say you meet someone in a coffee shop and they're able to give you that?"

"Then I'd say it's happenstance, but I don't believe in that."

He seems amused. "Of course you don't. You know, subs are seen as an equal."

"That's great," I snap sarcastically. "I'm not looking to be dominated by any man, but name your price and I just might." I wink then get serious. "You don't see me as an equal, and you never will."

His forehead creases. James seems hurt by my comment, but I don't let it bother me.

"Why do you say that?"

"You're paying me for a good time and nothing more. What man is ever going to see a hooker as their equal? I'm below you."

He shakes his head then takes a sip of his drink. "You don't get it, do you, Valentina? I'm not like every other Joe Schmo out there. I don't give a shit how many partners you or anyone else I'm with have had. I see you, and everyone I meet, as an equal. I don't look down on people because of the job they take to pay their bills. We're not so different as you think. Job titles don't mean anything to me. They never have. Who am I to judge? I care more about who you are inside, your character, and how you treat people when no one is looking. There's not a single person in this world who's honest in their business. Not even a fucking priest walks the straight and narrow line. They're fucking little boys in the confessionals. You want to go toe-to-toe all night? I'm game, sweetheart. Name your price, and I'm all yours." He smirks. "I win all my cases."

That gets a rise out of me, but I'm not angry. He's feeding my words back to me, but playfully, and I'm okay with that. I also like that he is.

"Cocky much?" I say.

"I won't apologize for who I am."

I exhale a breath through my nose and decide to change the topic. James was probably born with a silver spoon in his mouth and grew up in a penthouse with a private entrance and butlers. He probably never wanted for anything. He'll never understand my struggles in life.

"Tell me what your tattoos mean."

James unbuttons his shirt and pulls the material from his pants, letting it hang at his sides. I despise myself for admitting that he looks sexy like this, but damn, he does. He's got abs, but they're not pronounced like the washboard kind are. His remind me of the ones you get from actual hard, back-breaking labor. It takes everything in me not to marvel over his toned, ink-covered body and run my hands over him. But the best part is he doesn't have much chest hair. I love that. I can clearly see each stroke of the ink pen, the beautiful colors and shades of the rainbow. It's mesmerizing. One of his arms is completely inked, along with his chest and one side of his neck. He tells me he's leaving his right arm for something special that hasn't happened yet but that he'll know when it does.

If someone would've told me this is how my Saturday as a call girl would go, I'd have laughed in their face. Today was nothing I expected, yet somehow everything I needed.

James tells me story after story about his tattoos as I point to each one. He's traveled around the world and has met extraordinary people. He's had moments and conversations he says he never wants to forget. He's all about preserving time, and I'm curious to know why.

I'm a little envious and can't help but wonder if I'll ever get to be as worldly as he is. I hope so. I've heard there are a few clients who will pay for companionship, and I'm wondering if he's one of them.

"Life is beautiful," he says at one point. "There's so much to see and experience. It isn't as bad as everyone makes it out to be. We're lucky to be alive. The way I see it, it could always be worse."

There goes my chest fluttering again. James doesn't have an ounce of arrogance when he talks. He seems like he just wants to share things with me, and I find myself absorbing every single word that falls from his lips.

"You're a fascinating man, James," I say, then finish my glass. "What's your passion in life?"

I pull back. "Getting a little deep, are you?"

James doesn't say anything, but just waits for me to answer. I lick my lips nervously and debate how honest I should be.

I decide to go with it. Call it liquid courage.

"I'm not sure exactly ... All I know is that I have this need inside me to help people, ones who are less fortunate like me. My parents always gave to the poor, and it's something I still do, even though there have been many times when I couldn't afford to. I still give back with my Grammy every year." I pause, expelling a breath. "I want to help people. I just don't know how I will yet."

His gaze is intense, and it tugs at my heartstrings. "We essentially have the same passion, but for different reasons."

"Oh really?" He doesn't seem like he was ever poor.

"Yes. I see the way you're looking at me, and I'll let it slide. You, more than anyone, should know looks can be deceiving. I didn't always have money, and I worked fucking hard to get where I am. I do believe good fortune comes with good practice."

Hours have passed, and the bottle on the table is now empty. I have no idea what time it is, probably close to midnight. We picked at food and talked as if we were close friends catching up. I know the night has to be coming to an end, but I don't want it to. I'm not ready to say goodbye. A part of me hopes that James will request me again in the future.

"You make me want to pack a bag and hit the road and see where it takes me."

The way he smiles causes a storm of emotions to surge through me. James is seemingly overflowing with happiness.

"You should do it. Go alone and experience the world for what it is."

I look away, feeling the longing at his words. "Maybe one day," I say softly. "I've never been outside of New York."

His brows rise in surprise. "You're kidding me."

I brush off the melancholy pressing on me. I don't want to ruin the mood.

"I'm young. I have time. I'll probably be single for the rest of my life anyway, so I'll get to go everywhere I want," I joke with a smile. "Maybe I'll buy one of those luxury conversion vans and start living on the road. Sounds kind of fun, actually."

Finishing the contents in his glass, James stands and buttons his shirt. He puts his suit jacket back on then offers me his hand.

"Wanderlust is a real thing," James says as we make our way outside to the parked Rolls-Royce.

I didn't see him pay the check, so I assume he has a tab. Wouldn't surprise me.

"I'm always ready and willing to hop on a plane and leave." He hesitates. "Though life doesn't usually allot for that."

"Tell me about it," I respond.

I can't help but feel like James is trapped by something or

somewhere he doesn't want to be. Like he has no way of escaping. The way he talks with longing and aspiration nudges something in my gut.

James looks at his watch then back at me. "Don't take the subway or a taxi. Let my driver know where you need to go, and he'll take you home."

I nod and don't tell him I'll be switching cars anyway. I don't want to risk my residence being found out.

James steps closer. "Thank you for today, Valentina. It ended up being more perfect than anything I've had in a while."

"It was perfectly imperfect," I say, smiling. "And why are you thanking me?" I pat his chest. "I should be thanking you for today. I got to mouth off to an attorney, drink expensive alcohol in an underground swanky restaurant, and make out with a hot-as-fuck man who happens to be old enough to be my dad. What's better than that?"

James barks out a laugh. "You just had to go there, didn't you?" He's positively radiating, and it draws me to him more.

"I say it like it is. Sort of like you," I respond through a toothy grin.

James pulls me close so I'm flush against his chest. His head dips at an angle. I react automatically and lift my lips to meet his.

There's no breaking any seams. Our tongues automatically seek each other's, and we both hum in unison when they meet. Like we've been waiting for this. In a way, I have. His body is strong, and he makes me feel protected in his arms. I grip the lapels of his jacket as he deepens the kiss with so much passion and intensity that I forget I'm supposed to be Valentina. I kiss him with everything I have in me. James doesn't seem to be the kind of man who does anything half-assed. I briefly wonder if he fucks the same way he kisses.

My heart is pounding against my ribs, and for a moment I forget we're standing by the curb in the middle of Manhattan as we kiss goodbye like two lovers who only see each other.

Chapter 25

I don't focus on when Christine will message me. If James was unhappy with me, then I would've heard about it by now, which I haven't. Instead, I lose myself in schoolwork the next couple of days and start on the twenty-page paper due before winter break on the consequences of socioeconomic disadvantage across three generations.

There's a two-hour gap between my classes, so I go to my favorite little coffee shop again a couple of blocks away and order a hot coffee. The temperature has dropped considerably, and I'm in need of something to warm me up. I'm sitting at a small, round table scribbling notes when a shadow is cast over me. I glance up, and recognition dawns in my eyes.

"Hey, you," I say and smile, pleasantly surprised. I don't actually know his name.

He gestures to the open seat across from me in silent question, and I nod.

"I've been here a few times but just figured I missed you. I wondered if I'd ever see you again." He pauses. "I'm Daniel."

"Ah, a name to go with my coffee aficionado. I'm Aubrey," I say. "Thank you, again, for that cup. You really didn't have to, you know, but thanks."

He shrugs subtly, and it's cute. "It's just coffee," he says. "But I did hope you would come back here more often."

I laugh and take in his scrubs under his coat. "I take it you work around here?"

"I'm a doctor over at Mount Sinai. I just got off a thirty-hour shift."

My brows rise. Impressive. "You're a doctor."

He nods. "A cardiologist."

"That's incredible. How admirable of you. How are you even standing right now?"

"Why do you think I'm here? I'm getting coffee then going home to crash until tomorrow. Someone called out, which would've been fine, but we had a trauma come in and a dozen patients were admitted and prepped for surgery."

My mouth turns downward. "Wow. That's a long day."

Daniel's name is called, and he stands to grab his drink off the counter then comes back to me.

"Let me take you out sometime." He doesn't ask, just states it, and I like that.

Even still, I smile up at him regrettably. Given my new line of work, I have to say no. It's not something I'd imagine he, a doctor, would be okay with.

Daniel reads my indecision. "You can't say no. What are the chances that we ran into each other again?" he says.

But what if the right one comes along ... Say you meet someone in a coffee shop ... James's words filter through my head. I'm not one to believe in fate, but it does seem serendipitous that out of the 1.7 million people in Manhattan, we're able to run into each other again.

"Come on. Give me one date. Just one. Let's see where it goes."

I purse my lips together and concede. "Fine. One date, Daniel." I give him my cell phone number. "And by the way, I don't put out on the first date, so don't try and get frisky."

He seems taken aback by my comment. I'm totally joking.

Oh well.

***

"You have three options," Daniel says.

It's Friday night, and I'm not really looking forward to a dinner date after my last-minute Valentina job. I can still smell the distinctive scent of cocaine that dusts my breasts. Sweet and a little floral. The client licked off the remnants so there shouldn't be any left, but I can still smell the powder. He was an easy wham-bam-thank-you-ma'am, let-me-snort-some-rails-off-your-body-while-I-come quickie. He kept offering me lines to do off his dick, but I declined politely. Not my style. But it did make me wonder how Madame Christine finds these guys with fetishes I didn't know existed. He seemed to enjoy every second of my time he bought and came four times in that hour. I didn't even come once. I couldn't get off. Christine had texted me earlier in the afternoon. One hour, eight thousand dollars. How could I say no?

"We could go to a nice candlelit restaurant and order a bottle of wine," Daniel continues as I take in his appearance.

The last two times we've met, he was in light-green scrubs. Tonight, he's dressed in black dress pants and an eggplant-colored, button-down shirt with the sleeves rolled up. His dark hair is messy and loose, perfect to run my fingers through.

"If you don't like that option, we can go to a sports bar and eat greasy burgers and drink beer." His eyes gleam with excitement, and dammit I start feeling it too. "Or we can hang here and do shots then stumble to get pizza."

"Wow, Daniel, you really know how to woo a lady," I say, my tone full of sarcasm, and I fan myself like I'm hot. "The choices are difficult. How will I ever choose?"

He chuckles, and I feel it in my bones. A shiver travels down my spine as my smile grows.

"I feel like I'm supposed to go for the first option, but ..."

Daniel's shoulders shift and he purses his lips. "It's respectable." He doesn't seem too keen on the idea, even if it was his suggestion.

"I'm not really a respectable girl."

He lets out a boisterous laugh, and I find myself laughing with him. If he only knew just two hours before, I'd had a John's dick deep in my pussy.

"I say we do shots and get pizza. Call it a hunch, but I have a feeling we both had a long week and need to let loose."

"I like your style," he says and turns to the bartender to order two shots of tequila.

The shots are set in front of us a moment later, and Daniel boldly takes my hand and licks the space between my thumb and forefinger then dusts it with salt.

"To new beginnings?" I suggest when he hands me a shot glass and a lime.

"To new beginnings, and those shoes you're wearing that are fucking killing me."

I grin, loving the sound of his thick, brassy city accent, and we tap glasses. We lick the salt, down the shot, and suck the lime.

Three shots in, and I feel *too* good. Not drunk, but I'm not far from it. Daniel's holding me to his side, embracing me while we stand at the bar and talk. I'm slightly taller than him in my heels, and while he's not built with muscle, he's not soft either.

"You smell good," I say, feeling the liquor coat my veins. "I want to take a bite out of you."

Daniel laughs, and it's good-hearted. "You're so cute. Want another shot?"

"No, but you should have one."

I'd taken half a pill earlier before my job, and I'm still flying high and feeling great.

He eyes me, and I'm grinning. I can't help it. When I get like this, all I do is smile and laugh.

"I have a feeling you're a bad influence. Like that one friend who is always encouraging her friends to do bad things when they shouldn't."

I give him a sly smile and pretend to zip my lips. "I don't kiss and tell."

He brings my chest to his. My low-cut dress pushes my breasts up, giving me ample cleavage.

Leaning in near my ear, he says low and deep, "What if I want to kiss you?"

Instead of waiting to see if he does kiss me, I grab his face and plant a hard one on his lips. The people surrounding us at the bar roar, hollering and chanting. I smile against his mouth, and Daniel's hands roam my back, stopping at my hips. He's gentle, considerate. Breaking the kiss, I look at his mouth and start giggling.

"What?" he asks, looking confused.

"You have huge red lips slanted across your mouth," I answer, trying to contain my laughter.

He's surprised and wipes his mouth off with a napkin.

"So tell me about you. I feel like all we've done is talk about me."

I give him my old nanny job details. It's the perfect cover. If this thing between us goes anywhere, I can always say I have to babysit if Christine texts me with a job.

"I don't even like kids," I say, then add that I'm majoring in sociology with the goal of either going into law or something related to helping children and families.

His eyes are filled with laughter as he watches me. "That doesn't make any sense. You don't like kids, yet you want to make a career out of working with them?"

"Well, I guess I kind of like them. I just don't like babysitting them for long stretches of time. And it's not like I would be working closely with them if I made a career ..." I stop and give him a droll stare. "Would you want to babysit someone else's kids for forty-eight hours straight?"

Daniel grimaces. "Not really. Do you want kids?"

"Whoa, Daniel. We just met. Slow your roll. I'm not ready for my own little monsters yet. You didn't even get to second base."

"You're such a sarcastic ass," he says and laughs. "Why do I have this feeling there's never a dull moment with you around?"

I playfully bat my lashes, and he tugs me closer to his side again, leaving his hand to rest on my hip.

We chat about our upbringings. He comes from a large family of accountants, and I, well, what more can I say about Grammy other than she's a saint. I learn he's a Mets fan, which causes us to teasingly argue because I'm a Yankees fan, and there's no better team than the Yankees. We talk for a while about everything and nothing until we get the check and he pays, and then we walk across the street to grab a couple slices of pizza.

The night is fun. No stress, no pressure, just easygoing conversation that I didn't realize I desperately needed.

I take the train back home with my mind focused on Daniel. I can't remember the last time I had a real date and try to jog my memory. The only thing that comes to mind is my time with James, but that doesn't really count.

James.

My heart lurches just thinking about him and how incredible that day was. I wonder if he'll request me again. He'd wanted to create a moment to remember, and that's exactly what he did.

I fall asleep the moment I get in my bed. My thoughts filled with James. Daniel. James and Daniel with me sandwiched in the middle. Mmm ...

Chapter 26

"Nat. Nat, wake up," I say softly, shaking her. "Wake up."

Natalie rolls onto her side. Her blonde hair is matted to the side of her face, and she's looking at me but not really seeing me. I think she came home after I did last night.

"Is someone dead?" she asks, her voice groggy.

I frown. "No."

"The building on fire?"

"No."

"A shooting or attack outside?"

"What the fuck? No."

"Then why are you waking me up so early on a Saturday?"

"I need a day with my bestie. It's been too long. Get your ass up and let's go."

She groans and sits up, her loose waves falling around her shoulders. She rights her wrinkled shirt, but her shorts are on inside out, and I laugh.

"Long night," she says, her voice like sandpaper.

"I can see. Get up and shower. I want to hang out with you today, and it's on me."

She smiles as she rubs her eyes. I hand her weed pen to her, and she takes a hit. She offers it to me, but I decline.

"Come on, wake and bake with me."

"Nah, I'm good. I feel like I'm still high off that Perc from last night."

Within an hour, we're sitting at Tipsy's, a nail salon that serves drinks. We're both sipping on mimosas while getting a pedicure together. Next are manis and facials.

"I'm glad you woke me up. I have a full week ahead of me and could use this." She smiles happily. "What's on the agenda for today?"

"I want to go shopping. I need a new winter coat and some new jeans, bras and shit. I want to take advantage of the fact that I don't have to micromanage my money for once. Now I make enough to fully take care of Grammy and spoil myself if I want."

Her eyes light up and she smiles widely. "You know I live to shop. Working a lot lately?"

"Enough that I now have a chunk of money socked away. I'm not going to spend it all, obviously, but I need some new things." I pause, thinking. "I can't tell if Christine's still testing me or not."

I think back to James.

"Do you think she'd send one to me"—I lower my voice—"who wouldn't want a happy ending?"

Her brows angle together like she's confused. "Ah, maybe? I doubt it, though. Wait—you mean you didn't have to do anything after? Like ... nothing?"

"No, nothing. I tried, but he didn't want it. That's weird, right? We did kiss, and it got hot and heavy, but he didn't let me take it further. Maybe he got performance anxiety," I joke.

"I mean, all men want sex, or at least a blowie, so that's a little weird to me. Maybe he just really liked your company."

I pause, thinking about our time together. "Honestly, I think he just wanted to hang out—"

"What was his name?" she asks.

"John," I lie. I don't want to find out Natalie's been with him too or that she finished him off when he wouldn't let me. I'd rather not know. "He has red hair, like flaming red, and pasty white skin. I think he said he was a doctor? Sound familiar?"

"No, but there's a lot of clients I haven't met yet. A lot of them use a fake name because they don't want to get caught cheating."

"Yeah, this one had a ring."

She nods. "I had a feeling you were going to say that. They have no shame in sticking their dick in any hole. I swear, I'm going to be single for the rest of my life after I've seen how men can be while working there. They think they're God's gift to us. I'm convinced they're all liars and cheaters. Meanwhile, we're just counting the minutes until their pencil dicks are spent and pray we don't end up with a roast beef vagina one day."

I giggle when the nail technician looks up at us. Natalie looks so sweet and innocent ... until she opens her mouth. We both apologize.

"We'll both be single for the rest of our lives together."

She high-fives me. "Faking an O has never been easier."

"For real," I say. I'm pretty sure I have that down now after practicing in the shower one day when Nat wasn't home.

After our spa treatment, we do a little shopping for a couple of hours then decide to stop for lunch.

"So I went out with Daniel last night."

Natalie's eyes widen around her vegan sandwich, sprouts hanging over the bread.

"You went out with coffee guy after your job? No way."

I laugh, nodding. "I did. My client literally just wanted to fuck while he got high, so he was in and out, and I was done pretty quickly."

"Nice," she says. "Quick and easy money. Do you think you'll see Daniel again?"

I shrug one shoulder, dipping a fry into ketchup. I wouldn't say my night with Daniel was earth-shattering, but it was fun and I could see myself hanging out with him again.

"I guess if he calls I wouldn't say no. He's so relaxed and nice, and he's adorable. I think I might've been a little too outspoken for him, but he went with it. He's a doctor."

"Like every other person in this city. If you're not a doctor, you're a lawyer or stock trader."

I agree. "It's true. Or they're models and singers."

She laughs. "Was it strange seeing him after a job?"

"Not really. Is that weird? I thought I would be bothered, but it didn't bother me at all. What does that say about me?"

I fill her in on the rest of the details from my date and how I lied about my profession.

Natalie takes a sip of her ice water. "What if it gets serious, though? Like, what if you guys get intimate? How are you going to tell him you sleep with men for money?"

I stare at her and wonder the same thing. The truth is, I don't know. I don't know how any man would ever be okay with something like that. Just thinking about it makes my chest hurt a little. I wonder if I'm ruining myself for anything serious in the long run. A relationship is built on trust and acceptance, not lies and deceit.

I'm such a fucking hypocrite.

"Unless it gets serious, I don't think I'm going to tell any guy. How can I? Would you be okay if your man was selling his body?"

"You know it's not the same. Men don't get heat for things the same way women do. It's okay for them but not us."

I sigh, instantly annoyed. "I know."

"Would I be okay with it, though?" Natalie says, musing over my question. "I guess I'd be okay with it as long as he isn't having sex for free, because then that's totally cheating."

"Do you ever get the same client twice?" I ask, curious, wondering if James will ever see me again.

"Oh yeah, when a guy likes you, he'll request you. I have repeats all the time."

I pause for a moment, panicking a little as I think about my first few clients. "Oh man, really? I hope I don't get that Hannibal guy again. He freaked me out big time."

"Girl, I already told you I can make your head spin with

the jobs I've had. I never reject any of them, though, and I'll do whatever is asked of me. The money is too hard to walk away from. It's addicting. I've been doing this for over two years now, and I've made over a million dollars. How do I walk away from that? I swear I get high from chasing paper."

My jaw drops. I blink. I stare. I'm in utter shock. Two years and a million bucks? No way. She's lying.

"Close your mouth. You're gonna catch flies in there," she says.

Lowering my voice, I lean in and say, "A million dollars? You've made a million dollars? You're lying. What kind of shit are you doing, Nat?"

She shakes her head. "It's not always like that. My time is valuable. You want a weekend with me on a yacht in Jamaica, where you're entertaining potential clients so you can embezzle their money and shit? One hundred grand, and I'm yours. And that's just my cut."

I'm speechless. While I can see how she's addicted to making that kind of money in a short period of time, I can't wrap my head around how she's able to do the work, perform, and still brush off the client's wild obsessions like it's nothing. I feel like my humanity is being chipped away with each client I've had so far, except one.

"How many clients have you been with?" I ask.

She looks me dead in the eye. "I don't count. I refuse to, and you shouldn't either."

"How do you not lose a little piece of yourself every time?"

"Every day when I step out of the apartment to meet a client, I wonder why Jesus is walking next to me when the Devil is right behind me."

Natalie feels the same way I do, only she disguises it better. Much better. I'm kind of relieved.

I swallow, then admit how I really feel. "Sometimes I feel like when I leave a client, they slice a piece of me off and light it on fire."

She crosses her arms on the table and leans on her elbows. "At first I did too, but after a couple of months, it became normal for me and I got comfortable. When I get a text, I shut my brain down, I get dressed, and I become Natalia. Not everyone is capable of doing that, but high-end escorting is a lucrative business, and I want my piece of it." Natalie pauses, no shame at all in telling me how she feels. "I'd never push you to keep going, but every girl feels the same as you in the beginning. The indecision is a killer—it'll get to you—but that's normal. What you're feeling is because you're *allowing* the men to take a piece of you. Don't allow it. Shut that shit down. You're not doing anything different than an investment adviser on Wall Street who's about to fuck his client and take their money. This job can only make you feel negatively if you allow it to. Don't allow it. When you leave our apartment, you become Valentina. Separate yourself."

I nod, folding my cloth napkin and placing it near my plate. It's the indecision that gets to me every time, but then the cash is placed in my hand and I start singing a different tune. I remember that I'm doing this because I desperately need the money. It's a choice I'm making for me and for Grammy.

"Listen, I'm going to get real with you," Natalie says, looking into my eyes. "Don't kill me."

My stomach drops, and I prepare for the worst.

"The only way you're going to fully accept this is to recognize that at the end of the day, you're just another woman selling her body for money. Acceptance is what silences the thoughts in your head because you're honest with yourself. The way I see it, I'm just being paid for the one-night stands I would've had anyway, so what's the difference? Some are just less exciting than others. I'm a whore who happens to wear Versace. So are you. That's the harsh reality. What really changed my perspective is that I use my sexuality and beauty to my advantage. There's nothing wrong with doing that either. Look at the Victoria's Secret models. They sell sex on the runway. Those women know they're gorgeous, they know they have killer bodies, and they make millions of dollars a year because of that. Same goes for the actors in Hollywood. Why is what we do any different? Use your beauty and sexuality to your advantage. The buyer already wants you."

Natalie is right. My views held me back, and now I know why. I hadn't considered models and actresses to fall into the same category, but she's not wrong. They're selling the product using sex appeal. Hollywood is known for selling sex, even at a young age.

My biggest fear isn't losing Aubrey. I know who I am. It's having the strength to accept Valentina in the same magnitude as I do myself.

The guilt and shame of who Valentina is stares back at me every morning when I look in the mirror. She's why I feel filthy. If I can learn to love and accept Valentina as I do Aubrey, I'll be okay.

Chapter 27

The holidays always create a buzzing feeling of enthusiasm in the city. Everyone is alive with spirit. The crammed streets are adorned with strings of lights, the shop windows decked with items no average person can afford. Even so, that doesn't stop the smiling faces from pushing forward. The hustle and bustle is exciting, and I love that the snow flurries bring a sense of wistfulness. The icy air invigorates every passerby with optimism, and when the tree goes up at Rockefeller Center in a couple of weeks and the lights are turned on, the city will come together, and it makes my heart happy. Like everyone is one and equal. There's no divide. No looking down on anyone.

After my girl day with Natalie, I did some serious soul-searching and finally let the negative views I was holding onto dissolve. Separating my feelings between Aubrey and becoming Valentina was key. Once I did that, the stigma that came with the job wasn't nearly as bad.

I kept the jobs to a minimum during the weekdays. Between homework, Grammy, Pilates, and the new clients, I was busy enough, but I wasn't stressed about being Valentina. I was also smoking more weed to sleep at night, but that was another story.

The jobs I had lined up each weekend weren't bad—quick blowies, some kinky sex that could actually be fun if I wasn't focusing on trying to please the client, and of course a few questionable fetishes that made my skin crawl. I was adjusting.

The next text I got from Christine said I needed to wear red lingerie and that I would meet my client at Sanctuary Cove. Since

I didn't own any, I went after class and bought a spicy little one-piece that made me feel sexy the minute I pulled on the lace. I loved it so much I bought one in black too.

I add loose waves to my hair for a sultry look while I wait for the Percocet to kick in, but I skip on the vodka. The rooms are stocked with alcohol, so I'll pour a glass as soon as I get there, then wait in the shadows for my next victim to arrive.

I kid.

***

I'm about to take another deep sip when the door flies open and startles me. A breath hitches in my throat as the man bursts into the room. I take in his height and build, then I tip the glass to my lips and take a long pull on my drink. Anticipation swirls in my belly and a grin I know he can't see curls my lips.

James.

I guess he wasn't a test John after all.

My body glows with lust at the sight of him. I'm warm from head to toe, tingly and hungry for this man I thought I might not ever see again. He makes my heart pound just being in the same vicinity as him. He's so much older than me, experienced, yet he's buying *my* time and paying *me* for sexual acts.

Our eyes meet and his gaze holds mine. He looks like he's had a demanding day at the office. He rips off his suit jacket and throws it on the lounge chair then rolls up his sleeves to reveal the stunning colors that decorate one of his arms.

James walks past me to the bar near the window. I can taste the aggression pouring out of him, and I lick my lips, eager for what's to come. He stops in front of the bar to pour himself a tall glass of what I assume is cognac. The blinds are half-mast, shades of darkness slice across his large body as he downs the amber liquor while staring at me the entire time. I gulp hard, feeling my desire for James rush through my veins. I can't break my gaze from his.

"Take the coat off, Valentina," he orders, his voice rough and brass. It sends a shiver down my spine. I tell myself to block out my attraction to him, but it's too hard. I love his voice.

I watch as he pours another glass, the liquid splashing up the sides. His heated gaze takes in the length of my body while I unbuckle my belt and remove my coat. I drop it to the back of the chair I was sitting in to reveal the shamelessly tempting piece of lace I paired with black strappy heels that lace up my calves.

His eyes flicker with appreciation, and I revel in knowing he likes what he sees. A seductive smile tips my lips, and he notices. I don't deny that I'm pretty. I have great breasts, and in this ridiculously expensive ensemble, they're lush and supple, and his eyes are focused on them. I look like a sex vixen.

James slams his glass to the table and advances on me. He eats up the ground in a few steps with his long strides. My heart jumps, and I take a nervous step back.

He gives his head a firm shake. "No. Don't walk away from me," he says, and I freeze. My heart races in anticipation from his demand.

James palms the back of my head with one hand and grabs my ass cheek with the other then slams his mouth to mine in a brutal kiss. The taste of cognac on his lips provokes me, leaving little bites of heat in its trail. He doesn't ask. He just takes like he has a right.

His demanding passion ignites something hidden within me, and I kiss him back, wrapping my tongue around his and seductively stroking him to show just how good I can be. James growls, and I feel the vibration against my chest. His fingers dig into my bare skin like they're little bites of pleasure. I moan and he devours my mouth, fisting my hair as he consumes me. His hips press into mine, and I feel how hard his cock already is. *Yes.* James is everywhere, his hands all over my body like he can't get enough.

Breaking the kiss, he uses his teeth to tug on my bottom lip until it pops from his hold. I gasp, feeling it.

"I've wanted to feel your pretty lips around my cock since the first time I saw you. I want you on your knees and sucking me off until I come inside that sexy mouth of yours," he says, lifting my chin so our eyes meet. "And I want you to swallow every single bit of my cum. Do you understand?"

My lips part, my breathing labors. He sees it and his eyes lower, becoming heavy. Wetness seeps from me over his demand, and my body reacts with wanting to please him. I want to do exactly what he says.

"Suck me good, Valentina."

My insides turn to mush over his order. I nod. I fucking plan to.

My body is burning for him as I reach between us, tug on his belt, and undo the button on his dress slacks. With my blood flowing, the tension is so thick between us that I know he feels whatever this is, too. I push his pants over his hips and cop a good feel.

Fuck. I'd love to know what he'd feel like inside of me.

I can barely fit him in my hand, and I panic for a second, wondering how I would actually fit him inside me, assuming that's where this is going to lead tonight. Thank God I'd used the coconut oil trick before I left the apartment.

James steps out of his pants as I quickly remove his shirt and drop it to the floor. Placing my hands to his wall of a chest, I push him back until he falls into a chair, completely naked with his legs spread wide. His cock is erect between his hips. My mouth waters, eager to please him. I allow my gaze to roam his body the way he did mine, taking in every inch of his glorious six-foot-plus height. For fifty-two, he's in incredible shape with the body of a professional football player and the power to snap me in half if I wanted him to.

This is why I love men—and sex—so much. A man's body is something I can stare at all day and never grow tired of. I think about all the things they're capable of doing to me, the power and strength they wield, and it makes me weak in the knees.

"Your body, James. Fuck." I sigh and lick my lips, wondering where the fuck Valentina is, because that was totally an Aubrey comment, and this is Aubrey lust oozing out of me.

I'm about to lower myself to my knees when he stops me. "Get over here," he says low, almost a growl, and I feel it in my bones.

I'm not really sure where he wants me to go since he's in a chair, so I climb onto his lap and straddle his hips, feeling his erection pressed between us. A rush of pleasure washes over me like hot honey. I want his cock inside of me now.

James slips the thin straps down my shoulders, tugging my top with it. My breasts spill out, and he immediately takes a nipple into his mouth and bites down, his sharp teeth sending a shock straight to my core. A gasp escapes me, my mind blanking for a split second. His tongue laps around the hard point, and I draw in a pleasure-filled breath. I think about what Natalie said the other day about using my sexuality to my advantage, and I decide to do just that.

Cupping the back of his head, I press him into my chest and rock against his hardness. My hips move painfully slow, like I'm having sex with him while giving him a lap dance. He shows the other breast the same attention and then licks a trail up my neck, allowing his teeth to pierce my skin. A sigh rolls off my lips. God, his hands feel so good on my body.

James pulls my hair, exposing my neck as he peppers kisses all the way up to my waiting mouth. We both get lost in each other. His kisses are like foreplay. He's aggressive with his actions, greedy with what he wants and how he'll take it, but skilled enough to know how to give pleasure and make me melt under his touch. I don't have to have sex with James to know he's not a gentle lover.

I also don't have to have sex with James to know it would be the kind of sex I'd like and want more of.

I break the kiss and slide down his body until my knees meet the plush carpet. I'm about to show him what he missed out on the last time we were together. Gripping his length in my hand, I twist my wrist a few times up his shaft, then take him into my mouth and go as deep as I can. James's entire body slackens and he leans back, his hips relaxing.

His hand finds the back of my head, and I peek up at him. Jaw flexed, there's a thick vein running down his neck that leads to the most gorgeous, intricate set of ink. James looks down at me, his eyes darkened with hunger. There's something about pleasing a man and seeing him drown in pleasure that encourages more from me. It awakens my desire for his pleasure. And with the way James is looking at me, I want to give him so much more.

Closing my eyes, I focus on stroking his cock with my tongue, sucking him deep as I try to block out the desire climbing inside of me. His hips are shifting back and forth, and his breathing deepens as I pull up with a pop of my mouth and then take him even deeper.

"Fuck, Val, your mouth." He moans.

Val. I like that. I suction my mouth as tight as I can and feel him twitch. I squeeze his shaft tightly, twisting, and his thighs flex.

"Take it all, sweetheart," he orders, and I do, wanting to make him feel good. "That's right, swallow it."

James starts coming, and I take a deep breath, knowing I'm not going to be able to breathe for a few seconds. I go all the way down to swallow and suck at the same time.

"Holy fuck," he draws out, gritting his teeth as he thrusts his hips into my face.

Before I have a second to swallow the last drop and wipe my mouth, he's lifting me up and throwing me onto the bed. A gasp gushes from me, and James is crawling up my body and kissing my mouth. He drops his weight, and my eyes close at the feel of his body on mine. James is strong, big, and the way he dominates me through a kiss consumes my whole body. He grabs my leg and lifts it up, hoisting it over his back. Fingers at my pussy, he slides the lingerie aside and thrusts two inside. I clench around him unexpectedly and moan in utter desire.

"James," I whisper, holding the back of his neck.

He's pulling my flesh into his mouth, the fine hair of his beard provoking my senses. My heel digs into the mattress, and my hips roll into his fingers.

"I'm about to fuck you senseless," he rasps against my neck.

God, his voice ... It does things to my heart and makes my body tremble.

"No condom," he says, but I'm not letting him fuck me raw.

James pulls away and slides down my body. He climbs off the bed, and I watch in confusion as he walks over to a table and pulls open the drawer. He reaches inside and takes out a container and what looks like a band of white feathers. James walks back over to the bed, but my eyes are on his gloriously hard and thick cock.

I lick my lips. I shouldn't look forward to sex with a client, but with James, I do.

"Honey dust," he says, and I nod.

I've heard of the sweet powder before, but I've never used it.

James uncaps the container and dabs the bunch of white feathers into it then leans over my body and softly, gently, tantalizingly, he dusts the powder over my shoulders and down my arms. He twists the applicator back and forth over my breasts, coating each one with what smells like raspberries to me.

"I'm going to lick every inch of your body clean," he says. Goose bumps break out over my sensitive skin, and I shiver in anticipation. "Then I'm going to fuck you until you're filthy with only my cum."

Yes, I want that so fucking bad.

Sitting back on his heels, he says, "Spread your legs."

My knees widen.

"Show me your pussy."

I reach down and slide the material over my swollen lips. James dabs more powder onto the feathers and then teases my wet pussy with them. I sigh in delight, and my back arches as he applies more dust.

"James," I say, but it's more of a plea. Talk about foreplay.

"You're fucking dripping," he growls, his eyes swirling with heat and desire, like I'm sure mine are. "I can't wait to be balls deep inside your sweet pussy, fucking it up."

Have mercy.

James places the feathers and dust on the mattress, capping the container so it doesn't spill. He kneels between my legs, leans down, and licks me through the lace. My back bows and I let out a moan against my will. Between his tongue and the material pushing into my pussy, pleasure soars through my veins. He grabs my thighs and holds them open while he's nipping at my clit.

"James, stop," I say, but another moan escapes me.

His head pops up from between my legs, and he almost looks high from indulging in me. "So. Fucking. Good." Then he's back down to business.

I'm so confused with what's happening and hate my body for reacting. I'm not supposed to respond to his touch like this, like *I want him to fuck me senseless*, but I do. God, do I ever. I need to quell the desire climbing inside of me. He reaches up and grabs my breast, twisting my nipple so hard it shoots a zing to my clit. I yell out in pleasure and reach for him.

I sit up and grab his face, forcing him to rear back and get on his knees. I climb onto his lap. My breasts are pressed to his chest, and I kiss the fuck out of his mouth, not caring that I'm a savage about it.

"Little fuckin' vixen." His voice is guttural, fingers digging into my ass as he breaks our kiss. His tongue leaves a wet trail over my neck as he begins licking me clean. "That's not how this works, sweetheart. Nice try, though."

James shoves me back, and I fall to the bed. He's securing my wrists above my head, hovering over me. His eyes are glossy, and I have a feeling mine probably look that way too. I'm breathing heavily as he says, "You've always had control when you fuck, haven't you?"

I nod. His cock rubbing against my pussy causes friction with the lace. He drags his swollen head along my wetness, and my breasts rise in response. I briefly wonder if I suck his cock if I'll taste the powder on him. I swallow hard and let out a moan so he knows how much I really am loving this. If I can make him come first, then I can after. Because I need to come and come hard and long.

"Most of the time a man can't find a clit. So yes, I have to be in control."

He lifts a brow and smirks. "Stop fucking boys and get yourself a real man."

"I'll put it on my to-do list," I say, and he chuckles at my response. I'm happy he's not as angry as he was when he first walked in. "I want to get off too, so I usually do all the work. I don't care, as long as I come."

We're both breathing heavily, our eyes locked on each other's. I've already said more than I should have, but I couldn't stop myself. It feels natural to talk to him.

James's head descends, and his tongue draws circles over my nipples before moving lower. I want him to take my teddy off so I can feel his tongue on my flesh, but his mouth over the lace is even more seductive, and I can see why he left it on. His tongue covers every inch of my body, and by the time he reaches my pussy, I'm out of breath and drowning in desire for this man. He licks me over the lace and then moves the material to the side and goes to town on me like he can't get enough.

"I need you to fuck me already," I admit to him. I don't even recognize my voice.

His phone makes a sound, and James scowls. He climbs off me, and I get up on my elbows, watching his backside as he walks away, taking him in. His masculinity turns something on inside of me, and it worries me. I can't fuck up this job, but I can feel myself wanting his mouth back on my body. The desire he rouses is more than just a craving. It's a fucking need I want to drown in.

James retrieves his phone from his pants pocket and reads something on the screen while he strokes his cock, squeezing the tip. I watch him, finding the way he plays with himself erotic. I look down at my blushing chest, my nipples aching—

"Motherfucker!" he yells, then grabs for his pants. He's dressed and out the door faster than I can say what the fuck.

Chapter 28

I slam into my apartment and call out for Natalie, thankful when she doesn't reply. I'm still too worked up over what happened with James at Sanctuary Cove. He left with a hard cock and without a single explanation, and here I am, trying to figure out if I'd just imagined it all.

Definitely not.

I rip my Burberry coat from my body and throw it across my bedroom. I didn't bother changing before leaving Sanctuary. I just grabbed my shit and tore out of there as fast as I could wearing the one-piece James left me aching in. Nothing screams hooker more than riding home on the subway in a trench coat and stilettos, but I'm too aroused still to give a shit.

The lace of my teddy presses into my clit and glides over my wet lips like silk. I rub my thighs together and moan under my breath. My body is on the edge of bliss and in desperate need of an orgasm. I reach between my legs and find that I'm soaking wet. Drenched.

Of all the clients I've had so far, none of them have made me feel the way James has. He just has a way about him. The thought of him and his cock makes me seep with shameless desire. He's got me so wet, needy, and fucking bothered that all I can think about is him. How he felt. How he would feel inside of me. How his cum tasted on my tongue. I want him to request me again and finish what he started. I'm thoroughly fucked up in the head.

I spread out on my bed and roll over onto my stomach, pushing my hand between my legs to cup myself. I sigh, loving how wet I feel. I grind my clit into the heel of my hand and bite down on my lip, clenching my legs. I'm so close. My sensitive nipples ache against the material of the lace teddy and my comforter, and I feel the orgasm steadily climbing when a sound catches me off guard.

Pausing with my hand on my pussy, I listen to the silence, my fingers teasing my lips. Shit. It's my cell phone. I groan inwardly. I can't catch a fucking break.

I climb off the bed and walk to retrieve it from my dresser where I left it before work. No personal cells allowed when I'm on the job.

I quickly swipe it open to read the text message.

Daniel: Hey, pretty girl. Any plans for tonight?

I smile to myself. He couldn't have texted at a more perfect time.

Me: Netflix and chill?

The reply bubble pops up immediately, and my chest tightens with anticipation.

Daniel: It's like you read my mind. LOL!

I grin. Of course, I can read his mind. It's my fucking job to know what a man wants.

I tell him to text me his address, and then I place my phone back on the dresser and walk to the bathroom to clean myself up. I need a quick rinse in the shower since I can still feel James's mouth all over me and my pussy.

Quickly, I turn on the shower and remove the lacy garment, and then I tie my hair up into a bun so I don't get it wet.

Stepping under the hot spray, I revel in it for a moment before I eye the showerhead. I was so close to finishing and still aching for release.

I shouldn't, but I can't stop myself as I reach for it. Not when James is all I see and feel.

Placing it between my legs, I aim the stream at my clit and almost fall over from the pleasure that rips through my entire body.

Yes, this is what I needed.

"Ahh," I gush, holding myself up against the wall. I wish James was holding the showerhead for me. Between the pressure of the water and the vibration, the visual of James's mouth on my pussy, the way my tongue felt wrapped around his thick cock, it doesn't take me long to come.

I have a feeling climaxing with him would be earth-shattering.

Breathing heavily, I release a sigh and stand upright to finish rinsing off. I could easily go for another orgasm, but Daniel is waiting and I plan to get lucky at his place.

Hopefully, I'll be sated then.

***

"Hey, Au—"

Daniel opens the door, and I attack his mouth, cutting him off mid-greeting. The door closes behind me, and I push him against it, plunging my tongue past the seam of his lips as my hands roam his body.

"Whoa, hey," he says, trying to slow me down. But he doesn't get far.

I reach for the hem of his shirt and yank it off him, tossing it to the floor. My hands are back on his stomach, feeling his toned abs.

Daniel laughs against my mouth, trying to grab my wrists to hold me back. "I don't usually have sex on the first date."

"Luckily this isn't our first date."

"Good point," he responds.

Kissing me back, Daniel threads his fingers through the hair at the nape of my neck, clenching around my loose locks. He tugs, pulling my head back, and I feel a jolt of desire to my pussy. I sigh into his mouth. We rip each other's clothes off as we cross the short distance to his bed. For once, I'm happy lofts are small.

I push him down onto his bed and climb over him and meet his gaze. Daniel's eyes are brown, not blue like *his*. Thank God.

"I want to ride you," I say, breathing heavier.

"Whatever you want, sweetheart."

Don't call me that, I want to tell him, but I don't.

"Grab my hips and hold me hard. I want you to be rough with me."

I need the fight. I need to feel bad and work for this.

"I don't want to hurt you," he says sweetly, and it just annoys me.

"It's okay. You can." I lean over him.

He shakes his head.

"Condom," I say, and he reaches into his nightstand for one.

I tear the foil packet open with my teeth and roll the condom down his erection, and then I climb on top and sink down on him. My head falls back and my eyes roll shut. A moan vibrates in the back of my throat as I feel him swell inside me.

Yes ...

Expelling a deep breath, I lift my hips and look down at James.

Shit. I mean Daniel.

I look down at Daniel and take note of his soft eyes. I can tell he wants me, but he's missing the hunger in them that James has, the hunger that just takes me higher. He holds my hips, guiding me up and down his cock, but he's gentle when I asked him not to be. He doesn't squeeze them, and his fingers aren't digging into my flesh the way I want them to, like when James held my legs apart and went down on me.

I squeeze my eyes shut. *Why can't I get James out of my head?*

My body picks up speed and I bounce on him, my heavy breasts moving with me. I'm worked up, but I'm not ready to orgasm just yet. Daniel grunts, his body stiffening. He finally grabs my hips the way I want him to and a lazy smile tugs at my lips. I'm getting closer. I glance down, and Daniel is already coming. His head is arched back, exposing the chords in his neck. His chest is flushed with desire, and I think about how James is just like this when he's about to unload, the sounds that erupt from *his* throat and the strength is *his* body.

A shot of pleasure goes straight to my clit as I imagine I'm riding James, and I'm finally coming too.

Only, I'm angry and confused for letting my Valentina side override my Aubrey side, and while I came, it wasn't enough. I don't feel sexually satisfied. Not even close.

"Don't move," I say, my voice a little raspy.

I pull off Daniel and turn around, guiding his cock back into my pussy again within seconds. I don't want to picture James's face while I fuck someone else. I need to focus on my pleasure, as Aubrey.

"Fuck, babe. This feels too good like this," Daniel says. "Fuck," he says again, drawing the word out.

I ride him hard and fast, the bliss spiking through me. I like it this way. I can feel his cock at a different angle, and it helps me focus on my orgasm. Closing my eyes, I feel another orgasm quickly rising inside of me and reach up to pinch my nipple. I twist it hard and apply pressure, my pussy contracting around his cock from both the pain and the pleasure.

"Oh, yes," I say, panting. "Fuck me harder, Daniel."

He does, thank God. He thrusts his hips rough and hard, and I finally start feeling the type of pleasure I need to feel sated. My pussy squeezes his hardness as I come on his cock. Daniel lets out a deep moan, and he orgasms again as we both fall into a pit of euphoria together.

Breathing heavily, I stay in place for a few seconds, trying to get ahold of myself. When I feel like I can move again, I climb off Daniel and fall back onto the bed. I watch as he reaches down to remove the condom and drops it to the floor. His cock is glossy with his cum, and I want to reach for it to stroke it, to feel it, but I don't.

"That was the last thing I expected when you walked in," Daniel says, staring up at the ceiling in awe.

"What did you expect when I said Netflix and chill? For me to read you a book while you braid my hair?"

Daniel barks out a laugh and turns over onto his side. "I didn't expect you to attack me when you walked in, that's for sure. You were like an animal."

"Sorry." I blush, feeling a little bad I acted like a raging nymphomaniac, all because of James. What is it about him?

He reaches over and brushes a lock of hair behind my ear. "Don't be. I like a girl who takes charge."

I lean over and drop a light peck on his cheek. "I couldn't help myself. You just looked so cute," I lie. It's not like I could tell him why I was horny as fuck. I had an itch that needed to be scratched.

"I like you," he says.

"Thanks. I hear I'm the life of the party." I smile.

He gives me a soft kiss on my lips. "I *like* you," he repeats quietly. "I know we've only been around each other a handful of times, but you've made me happy each time. I want to be around you more."

A blush climbs over my cheeks, and I take in the sincerity of his tone. He's cute and not bad in bed. And I really did have a good time with him on our date. He could be good for me. A good balance for my Valentina side. A bit of normalcy. Real versus fantasy. *Can prostitutes be normal?*

"Do you think if I hadn't ordered that coffee that day, would you have talked to me?"

His thumb grazes my jaw. "Yes. I was drawn to you the moment I walked in. You had this look on your face, like you were deep in concentration and debating life. I knew I had to talk to you and was going to find a way to make it happen."

"Daniel," I say, a bit embarrassed to know I was being watched. "You know how to make a girl feel good."

His lips tug up gently, and he blinks like he's thinking about the first time we met. "I had a feeling you were going to say no when I asked for your number, but I held out hope you'd come back. Not many women want a triple shot."

I swallow at the kindness in his tone. His touch is soft, his words even softer, and it shifts something in my chest.

"I'm glad you didn't give up," I say and lean into him.

He wraps his arms around me and rolls me onto my back. His eyes gleam as I feel his length hardening. My heart races with the way he looks at me. Much to my surprise, I like it.

He lowers his mouth to mine and kisses me, this time leaving me breathless.

Chapter 29

Christine asked me twice this week to see James, and I shot it down both times citing I had a lot of homework. One more, and she'd call me in for a reevaluation. I can't lose this job, but I don't know if I can see him again either. And at the same time, I'm not ready to give him up.

Truth is, I love being in his presence. I love the sound of his voice. God, the way he expresses his words, they sound like they're deep in his throat. The way he carries himself in a suit or nothing at all. But most importantly, he doesn't look down on me for what I do with my body. He didn't judge my decision to be an escort. He didn't make me feel less because of it when I thought he would. For all his "we're equal" talk on our first encounter, he made me believe it.

"Aubrey?" Daniel says, and I focus on him.

He studies me. I can tell he wants to ask what I'm thinking about, so I quickly conjure a lie.

"I'm sorry. I was just thinking about my grammy."

Fucking James.

"You're close to her?" he asks, forking some pasta.

He insisted he take me to Carmine's Italian Restaurant since I said I'd never been. He was nearly flabbergasted by my confession, and now here we are, sharing a family-size dish of penne alla vodka. It's enormous and tastes fantastic, except for the fact he wanted anchovies in it.

"I am. She's my best friend. I haven't spoken to her since I took her out for Thanksgiving dinner last week, and it worries me.

She looked like she was under the weather but tried to cover it up."

I'd noticed Grammy's steps were slower than normal, which she blamed on the weather and arthritis. And the cough she'd had a few weeks ago was still present. But her eyes lit up with surprise when I took her to Elio's Ristorante for real, handmade, fresh-to-order Italian food. The owner, an immigrant from Italy, was known for singing Italian Opera on Friday nights and holidays. Their baked clams and veal dishes were a favorite among customers. I knew she'd love it. There were even rumors the Gottis visited often. That's how popular it is. She was worried about how I could afford it and offered to pay a portion. I told her I had picked up an extra nanny shift just for the occasion then slipped a fifty into the bottom of her purse when she wasn't looking. I hated lying to her, but I could hardly tell her the truth.

"Why don't you surprise her with a visit? I bet she'd love that," Daniel says, and I can hear the concern in his voice. "Maybe take her out for lunch. What does she like? Bring her something that will make her happy."

His suggestion warms my heart, and I soften a little. I take a small sip of the Chianti he ordered for us.

"I probably should. She's obsessed with her cats, so buying something for them will make her fall over with happiness."

"Bring her some mice for the cats to catch."

"Daniel," I say his name firmly, and it's enough for him to get the hint.

His smirk is filled with charm. The way he tilts his head as he looks at me is endearing. He licks his lip.

"You know, I told my mom about you. She wants to meet you."

I freeze. I'm not ready to meet the parents yet. It never even crossed my mind for Daniel to meet Grammy.

"You don't think it's too soon? We haven't been dating that long."

I start counting the weeks in my head, but I'm so overwhelmed by the idea that I can't think straight. I take a long sip from my wineglass until it's gone, and Daniel watches, chuckling.

"I didn't ask you to marry me. Calm down."

"In other cultures, that's pretty much the same thing." My lips twitch. "It's like taking the relationship to the next level. What if she asks what I'm bringing to Christmas dinner that I didn't even know I was invited to until that second, which makes it totally awkward for us since we didn't even talk about it, and then she starts asking about us having kids one day?"

My eyes are wide and my heart is racing with apprehension. Now I'm really worried that this all will actually happen. I'm not ready for it or the lies I'll have to tell about being a nanny to more people. What if I end up loving his family?

Daniel shrugs then says, "So we tell her you're already pregnant with twins and you're bringing cheesecake."

Flattening my lips, I stare at him in both shock and horror. "You're evil!" I joke and laugh. "You're so bad. Here I am, panicking, and you're loving the fact that I'm suffering inside."

Daniel reaches across the table and grabs my hand. He laces our fingers together as he pours me another glass of red.

"You're adorable, and I love your reaction. My mom is just nosy. To be perfectly honest, I don't know if I'm ready myself. Whenever it's time to meet your grammy and my meddling mother, we'll decide together."

My shoulders loosen and I relax a little. Thank heavens. I'm a little caught off guard by how easy and gentle he is.

"Really? You're okay with not being ready?"

"Of course," he responds, almost insulted. "I'm not going to push you or anyone into something they're not comfortable with, because I would want the same for myself. You get what you give in life."

I nod slowly, agreeing with him. We spend a few moments eating in silence. I appreciate that he isn't pushing me into this. It's too soon, and I'm just not ready.

"I'm surprised you're not married yet."

Daniel seems like a good catch who actually cares about who he's with and what they want.

"I was engaged once a couple of years ago." Something darkens in his eyes.

I sit up a little straighter. We haven't talked much about past relationships. Not that I care to since it's in the past, and who he's been with doesn't bear weight on the present, but this is something entirely different. This is almost marriage.

"Can I ask what happened?"

He looks directly into my eyes. "She was a lying, cheating whore."

I take a small sip of wine then place my glass down.

Would escorting make me a lying, cheating whore?

I have money bands from the jobs with numbers in the double digits hidden in my room that I'm sure could be considered cheating to most people. Regardless of being emotionally attached to someone or not, having sex with another person other than your significant other is cheating. So I guess my answer is yes.

I don't respond, because what the hell do I say to that? Instead, I reach for my glass again and take a large swig, hoping it drowns out my guilt.

"She fucked my best friend for months until I found out. I walked away from both, and I haven't been in a serious relationship since," he says, his tone dripping with resentment. "Until you."

Of course, he goes after a woman who secretly sells her body for money.

With the exception of James, sex with my clients means absolutely nothing. It's just sex. Just a blow job. Just some fucking, weird-ass, kink fetish. None of it bothers me in the least, but something in my gut tells me Daniel wouldn't see it that way.

I decide right then and there not to tell Daniel about my

double life. When the time is right, I'll sit him down and tell him I've been doing this job since before I met him.

Exhaling a sigh, I finally say, "I'm really sorry, Daniel. I can't imagine how hard that was for you."

He shakes his head like his thoughts are dark and he doesn't want to go back there.

"There's only two things I expect in a relationship. Honesty and faithfulness. It's really not that difficult to be a decent human. There's nothing worse than breaking both when you're in love with someone." He pauses and looks away for a moment. "They got married, and then a year later, she cheated on him."

Daniel huffs under his breath, a revengeful sneer scarcely tipping his lips, and I get the vibe he's happy about karma being dealt.

Once the check is paid and we're walking hand in hand outside, I lean into him and he wraps his arm around my shoulder, holding me.

"I like this," I say softly. "Thank you for dinner."

The comfort between us is creating a warmth in my chest I wasn't expecting. Being with Daniel is easy, and I briefly wonder if this is how relationships are supposed to feel. My eyes fall on the people walking briskly around us, rushing from block to block. New York is such a rat race, and it feels good to not have to be in a hurry for once.

Daniel looks down at me, and I give him a sated, lazy smile. He returns it too.

"I like this, and I like you, Aubrey. All I ask is that you don't fuck me over, and I won't either."

"I don't usually do relationships, Daniel, but I'm trying for you." I swallow down the guilt eating away at me.

"You're trying, and that's what matters. Don't spread your legs for another man, and I won't dip my dick in another woman. We'll be golden. I'd like to be exclusive with you. I don't do well with sharing."

He's not asking for a lot. It's what's naturally expected of any normal relationship, but my stomach is roiling with unease because come tomorrow, I will be spreading my legs for a man whose name I don't even know.

My chest tightens, and I chew the inside of my lip. Maybe dating is a bad idea, but he keeps me feeling wholesome and happy and doesn't demand a lot. He's like that laid-back friend who just happens to be a boyfriend at the same time.

He's my sense of normalcy.

Just as we're about to make our way down the subway stairs and part ways, I see a young, skittish girl leaning against a dirty wall with a Styrofoam cup next to her.

I feel bad for her. She can't be more than seventeen.

Stopping a few feet from her, I reach into my purse and take out a couple of bills. I hope she uses the money to get a hot meal or maybe find a place to sleep, but judging by her looks, her first stop might be to score some drugs.

As I close my bag, Daniel places a hand over mine. He turns toward me, and I look up at him and meet hard eyes.

"Don't give her money," he says firmly.

My brows furrow, and I'm instantly annoyed at being told what not to do. Exhaling through my nose, I try not to overreact. I understand why he's against giving cash to the homeless. It's drilled into our heads at a young age to never give money to the needy on the streets, but I can't help it. I've always done it when I could, and now I try to do even more.

"I always give money back."

"That's not giving money back, Aubrey. That's feeding an addiction. She's just going to run and get high. If you want to give it back, donate to a church."

My eyes lower. "I don't donate to churches. They're corrupt."

"Then give to a homeless shelter, not the riffraff on the streets.

At least the money is being used honestly in shelters."

"What if I can be the one to change her mind?"

He shakes his head, his voice hard. "You won't be, and you know I'm right."

He could be right, but I still have to try.

Daniel exhales a strenuous breath and concedes. "I won't tell you what to do with your money, but I wish you wouldn't do this. She's young enough to get a job. She's just lazy."

Stepping around him, I bunch the money up in my hand and walk up to the girl with wild hair dressed in all black. No one knows what she's doing or thinking, but maybe she isn't going to get high. Maybe she won't run back to a pimp and give it to him. Maybe she's collecting it to get a bus ride out of New York, the city that will eat you alive if you don't know how to fight back.

Our eyes meet, and she looks at me with anxious, brown orbs. I instantly feel worried for her because she doesn't seem like the typical homeless who sleep on the street and are hooked on drugs and because she's so young and impressionable. She has a chance. I've never lived on the streets, but Grammy came awfully close to being evicted a few times. I guess I have a soft heart and don't wish a hard life on anyone, especially young kids.

I get close enough and reach out, her hand already open. I roll up the bills so Daniel can't see what I'm giving her and place them in her dirty palm. She won't know that I gave her a few hundred dollars until I leave because she sure as shit isn't going to count her money in public.

"You're better than this," I say softly. She nods, and I sense she knows I'm right. At least I hope she does.

Stepping back, I take Daniel's hand, and we walk down the stairs to catch the trains going our separate ways. It smells like urine underground, and there's even more homeless in here who are just trying to stay warm and make it to the next day. I'm not naïve. I know most are hooked on drugs and will run to get their next fix if given a few hundred dollars. While I understand why he's against it, it rubs me the wrong way that he would try to stop me from giving money to a young girl. It's my money, and it wasn't like I was trying to give cash to an obvious meth head. I try to find the ones who look like they still have a fighting chance or the ones who truly have no other option than to be on the streets. Besides, it's nobody's business but my own what I do with my money.

Chapter 30

"Shit. Shit. Shit," I say, barging into my apartment. I drop everything on the counter and run to my room in a panic.

"What's wrong?" Natalie says, walking into my room.

I turn around and look her up and down. "You're here?"

She grimaces. "I woke up feeling like shit, so I skipped classes today. I really wasn't in the mood to trek through the snow either. Why aren't you in class right now? This is so unlike you."

I start shuffling through my pint-size closet, shoving clothes back and forth.

"Christine texted me in the middle of class. She's offering thirty-three thousand for a new client."

Natalie frowns. "That seems like an awful lot for just one guy."

"I thought so too, but I didn't ask. I never do. I figured he's got some weird-ass kink. I've never gotten paid this much for one job before. How could I say no? Nat, I could take Grammy on a Caribbean cruise and get her out of the cold for a couple of weeks. Maybe that will help clear up her cough. I'll tell her I won a trip or something."

She chuckles, and my phone starts buzzing in my pocket. I grab it and read a text from Daniel.

"Shit."

"What's wrong now?"

"It's Daniel. He's confirming our date, but I need to cancel. What do I—"

"Grammy emergency," Nat offers.

I text it out and drop my phone, not waiting for a response. I look at Natalie, and she's already standing beside me, peering into my closet.

"So tell me, what do you need help with?"

I pull out a black two-piece—a lacy push-up bra with matching bikini panties. I decide I'll wear thigh-high lace stockings and garters. I look at her and place my ensemble on my bed.

"If you're feeling sick, you can lie down."

"Shut up and tell me."

"Do my hair while I do my makeup?"

Just under two hours later, I'm in Midtown, walking into Baccarat Hotel and taking the elevator up to the penthouse suite. I've yet to do a job this long, not counting James, and get paid over thirty grand for it. I'm a little edgy not knowing what to expect. I just know I don't want to fuck up.

Coconut oil. Throat spray. Percocet. Vodka.

I'm good to go.

What every working girl's arsenal requires.

Exhaling a slow breath, I try to remain calm as the elevator comes to a stop and the doors open. I pull off my gloves and fold them into my purse then walk to the end of the hall. Christine told me the door would be unlocked and to walk right in.

I step into the massive suite that's cloaked in darkness. The blinds are at half-mast, and the lights from the surrounding skyscrapers create an elegant glamour that lures me in. The aroma of vanilla coats the room, and there are orchids on every counter. Large white tiles, white bed sheets with a dramatic canopy, and a stunning crystal chandelier hang in the center of the room. I can hear the shower running and decide to pour a drink and wait for my new client.

Stepping up three stairs, I walk into the lounge room and come to a halt.

My heart drops, and I gasp quietly. There's someone already

sitting in the corner with a drink in his hand. He twirls it, and the ice clinks against the glass. I can't see his face, but his legs are crossed and his black shoes gleam in the dark. There's a subtle scent of cologne that's so alluring, I feel the attraction in my chest.

"You're a hard woman to track down, Valentina," the voice says, sending an all-consuming shiver down my spine.

James.

I swallow hard and walk over to him, trying to steady my racing heart. I'm both impatient for his touch but uneasy about how it will make me feel.

As I step closer, light from the window casts a soft glow over his handsome face, and our eyes meet. He's wearing a slate gray crisp dress shirt that oddly accentuates his mature age.

My lips part with a sigh, and I sober up as much as I can, even though my body immediately stirs with hunger each step I take closer to him.

"James. A pleasure to see you again."

"Yes, it sure is a fucking pleasure," he says, raking a heated gaze up the length of my body. "Tell me, why have you refused to see me?"

I blink, clearing away my Aubrey thoughts and slipping into Valentina. I step over to the glass table that houses a few bottles of alcohol. Lifting the decanter, I say, "James, you have to know I have other clients. I can only spread myself so thin." I pour myself two fingers of tequila.

"What do I have to pay to be your only client?"

I bite the inside of my lip and walk back over to him in my four-inch heels. I place my glass down on the table between his chair and mine. Unbuckling my belt, I remove my coat and place it over the arm of the chair. His eyes flare lower then. He unwinds and leans back, all the while staring at me like I'm a five-star meal and he's a starving man. I melt a little inside, loving how he stares at me.

"Getting right to the point?" I smirk and sit down.

He seems so relaxed and calm, but I can feel his tension, his desire, and yet he's as smooth as the jazz softly playing in the background.

"Since you hid from me, yes. Give me a number, and it's yours. I want you, Valentina. For my own. I'm willing to pay any amount. Want to do it privately and not through Sanctuary Cove? Even better. Name your terms, and I'll sign a contract. I'll draw up the papers myself. You want a monthly stipend? A condo in SoHo? The rest of your tuition paid for? Name it. There's nothing I can't make happen when I want something, and God, do I want you."

My heart skips a beat. Maybe I used my sexuality a little too much. I take a deep sip and look at him over the rim, allowing the pungent alcohol smell and taste to coat my throat. His words get to me, but I remember this is an illusion we give each other and nothing more. Still, I love that he wants me so bad. I love that he's willing to do whatever it takes to keep me. I love that we've yet to have sex and I've seduced him to his knees.

"Who else is here?" I ask casually. At least I tried to.

"A partner from my firm, a good friend of mine. He's the one who introduced me to Sanctuary Cove. When Christine kept telling me you were unavailable, I had him call and try to schedule you. Imagine my shock when he books you on the same date I was told you had filled."

"You're slick," I say, and he puts his hands out, as if to say he'll resort to any means necessary to get what he wants.

He's proud, and I can't fault him for that. I stare at him for a moment, trying to decide which angle to go with his statement. He's aggravated that his friend got through and he didn't.

"So we're having a three-way," I state. Wouldn't be my first time, but it would be as Valentina.

"No, sweetheart, we're not," he says, and I frown and angle my head. "I'm going to watch you."

My lips part with a small gasp, and his words heat the blood in my veins. My cheeks flame with want. I've never done that before, but the thought alone excites me.

"You're going to watch me fuck your friend?"

His eyes darken. James likes the idea. I just hope his friend is as attractive as James, or otherwise it might be difficult for me to stay in the moment.

"Do you have a problem with that?" he asks, challenging me.

I shake my head. "You know I don't. So you're not going to touch me at all?"

"I didn't say that." He downs the rest of his drink and places it on the table. His gleaming wedding band catches my eye, and I wonder why he wears it on appointments like this. "Come here."

I stand and take a few steps until I'm in front of him. Without waiting for him to tell me what he wants, I take the lead and climb onto his lap, pressing my body to his, kissing him hard. I knew James wouldn't be able to refuse me, and he doesn't. He fists my hair and grips my hips hard. I taste the expensive liquor on his tongue and suck his lips a little harder. His hips thrust, forcing me to grind into him.

This is exactly what I was trying to stay away from, this intensity between us, the way he holds me with fierce passion, how I moan into his mouth, how his touch paints my body with craving. How I can't seem to concentrate when I'm with him. I don't have to guess if James feels the same way. It's clear that he does.

He breaks our kiss, breathing hard into me. I'll have to tell Christine after this night that James can't be my client ever again. I'll have to give up everything he's offering.

"Why do you want me so bad?" I ask, short of breath.

"A few reasons. I think you're the type who needs a man to take the wheel and fuck you the right way. I can tell you think too much. Sex has always been an effort for you, and it's the one place it shouldn't be. Outside, on the streets, you're a woman with no filter who can hold herself up to anyone, which I fucking love, but in bed, I think you need someone to make you forget your name. I can do that. I want to be that man for you. Between the sheets, you should be saying, 'Yes, please, more, harder'—my fucking name and nothing else."

"Should I say, 'Yes, Daddy', too?" I ask innocently with doe eyes.

He barks out a laugh, throwing his head back, and I smile.

"See? This is why I want you. Little shit like that gets to me. You get to me, Val. You make me feel good."

I avert my gaze and look down. I'm feeling a little shy with the way he looks at me. All I did was act like myself, and he doesn't mind. Not even Daniel sees this side of me.

I hear the shower turn off, and the nervousness is back. Leaning down, I place a gentle kiss just under his ear. His hand holds the back of my head as he sinks a little deeper into his chair. A door opens, and his friend steps out of the bathroom.

"Thanks for getting me warmed up," I whisper. "Sometimes the vodka and Percs aren't enough. But you, James, will always be enough," I say, then turn around to sit on his lap, feeling his obvious erection against my ass.

Chapter 31

I'm purposely swiveling my hips seductively slow on James's lap. He grabs me, digging his fingers into my flesh and pushing me down hard on his cock. I sigh inwardly, my body already so hot with need. I know he said we aren't having sex—and I'm glad we're not—but I still want to make him feel good.

I take that back. It's not just about making him feel good. I want him to crave me. I want to seduce him until he's the one begging for me. I want to tease the fuck out of him. The thought of doing so fills me with adrenaline.

"So, this is the girl you've been raving about?" James's friend says eagerly as he walks over to us with just a towel around his hips.

He's not unattractive, but he's definitely not the man behind me. I don't ask his name, it's irrelevant really. I stand up to greet him.

"I hope all good things," I say cheekily.

James's hands find my hips. Fingers pressing into me again, he leans in and gives me the softest kiss above my ass.

"Only the kind of things a man wants to hear."

I'm not sure what that means, but since I've only given James a blowie, I assume that's what he's referring to. Reaching forward, I move his hand and unravel the towel, allowing it to drop in a heap to the floor. I look down at his length already covered with a condom and make a face of wow with my lips. Men ... They're so easy to understand.

He's not huge, thankfully, but a really good size. At least I'll be able to walk tomorrow.

"You ready for tonight? James is going to instruct me on what to do, and you're going to listen."

I feign a purr in the back of my throat. "Ready as I'll ever be. You guys do this often? Tag team?"

He doesn't answer. He threads his fingers through my hair and pulls me in for a kiss. The kiss is a bit sloppy, but I think it's because I can taste some type of liquor on his tongue.

I reach for him, stroking his already hardened length. He thickens in my palm, and I rub him a little harder, his hips surging forward. He palms my breasts that are barely covered by my demi bra and steps closer. I tease him with my tongue, my kiss, the fake moan I unleash on him. Behind me, I feel James stand. I hear his belt come undone and then the button of his pants.

Much to my surprise, his hand slips around my hip to my sex and his cock nudges my ass cheeks. His body is radiating heat through his clothes, and I want so badly to lean back into him, to feel him, but I don't. He drags my hair to the side, and his mouth is on the curve of my neck, kissing me softly, lapping his tongue in a sensual circle.

I've had threesomes before, but doing them while being Valentina is proving to be difficult. I know I need to make sure the clients come first, but I'm already hot and bothered from having these two men—having James—touching me.

I forget I'm kissing his friend as James's hand slides into the front of my panties and finds my clit. The cuff link on his shirt is cool and shocks my skin as he rubs my pussy. I shift in my stance, giving him access. His fingers slide through my bare seam and into my wetness. I moan enough for them both to hear me. Teeth score my flesh, and I stroke his friend harder, faster, trying not to focus on James's attentive fingers.

"She's fuckin' soaked, Reece," James says.

Now I have a name to put with the cock.

James slides two fingers into my wet pussy, and I flex around them, my back arching and my ass rearing into his hot waiting cock. There's barely any place to move with how close we're standing. James's thumb circles my clit, and I quickly feel an orgasm rising. I panic because I can't come yet, and I don't know how to stop him when a thought pops into my head.

Reaching behind me, I grip his thick cock and give it a nice squeeze. James groans under his breath. He's as hard as steel and hot as a flame. His fingers stop and his forehead drops to the back of my neck as he breathes hot air across my skin. James slaps my hand away and breaks my kiss with Reece to kiss me.

I lean back, angling my face toward James, as Reece reaches behind my back and undoes my bra with skilled fingers.

My breasts spill over, and it feels so good, freeing. I purposely bought a smaller bra to appear bigger, not that I really needed to with my full Cs.

Reece leans down and tugs a nipple into his mouth. I release a real sigh, my back bowing. He sucks hard enough to leave a bruise, and I like it. Soft touches are too tame for me, and now my head is a hazy mess of lust because all I can focus on is Reece's tongue twirling circles around my sensitive bud. I don't know who's palming my other breast and who's playing with my clit and fingering me. All I know is that I'm sandwiched between two men and falling into a dark, cavernous pit of pleasure, lust, and sinful desires.

"Put her on the bed," James orders huskily. "Take her panties off, but leave the shoes and stockings on. I want you to fuck her while I watch, but not yet. Let's get her ready first."

Reece does as James says, and in no time, I'm lying in the center of a plush bed, nervously excited for what's to come.

I reach my arms above my head, stretching, my hard little nipples in the air, my back arching. The glass of tequila is finally hitting me, and the Percocet is making me feel a little less modest.

James moves a chair closer to the bed then walks back over to the table at a leisurely pace. He removes his watch and pulls out his wallet from his back pocket, placing both on the table. Even in the darkness, his moves are stealthy as a panther.

Reece grabs a drink while I watch James unbutton his shirt and take it off, carefully placing it over the counter. I take in the length of his body as he sips from his crystal glass. He watches me, eyes boring into mine like we're the only ones in the room. His pants are still on, but the top button isn't fastened, and the color of his tattoos are dazzling in the lights filtering in through the windows. James is without a doubt a fine fucking man. Fifty-two or not, if we were both free of Sanctuary Cove and that wedding band, I'd fuck him all day every day.

James takes a seat in the chair he moved closer to the bed and spreads his legs to grasp his shaft. He's angled so he has a full view of my pussy and so we can lock eyes.

"Spread her legs," James orders. Reece climbs onto the bed, and James groans as he views my wet lips. "Lick her clit while you're fingering her pussy."

I clench my eyes shut in defeat. I know there's no way I'm not going to be able to come. Fuck, I just know it. Still, I work to fight it, except Reece's lousy kissing skills work wonders on my throbbing clit and I'm trembling from head to toe. He makes me even more wet. I pull on his hair and moan, feeling my orgasm climb inch by inch. I can only hope the way his fingers move inside my pussy is the same way his cock will—slow, hard, and teasing. If I didn't have high heels on, my feet would be digging into the mattress and my legs would be scissoring the sides of his body, but I'm immobile. I start panting, trying to think of any random thing to hold off my orgasm, but it doesn't work.

"Grab her wrists and hold them to the bed, Reece." Then, "Valentina," James snaps, and my eyes open. My wrists are securely locked to the mattress now. "Have you ever had two men lick you at the same time?"

I shake my head, but the thought makes my mouth water.

I want that to happen.

James stands and drops his pants to the floor. My stomach flutters as he walks over and stops at the side of the bed. His intense stare makes me yearn for his touch, and I see the truth. He wants me just as bad as I want him.

"Take my cock out and suck it."

Reece lets go of my hands, and I reach for James. I grab his warm cock and take him into my mouth. My neck is at an odd angle, but James leans in closer so I don't have to strain. I tip my head back, and as I do, James's fingers glide slowly down my neck in a massaging manner.

"That's it, relax your throat," he says soothingly and slips his cock deeper into my suctioning mouth.

The swollen tip breaches the back of my throat, and I swallow, trying not to panic and gag. Fucking spray isn't working, damn it. James groans, rocking his hips into my mouth. He's growing, thickening, and my pussy is aching to be fucked. All I can think about is how I wish it was always like this.

"Lift her ass," James says, pulling out of my mouth.

I'm so helpless, unsure of what will happen next. I lift my hips to hold myself up as James descends. His eyes are glazed over as he takes my pussy lips and carefully spreads them wide. He holds them open for his friend to lick me. A gasp of intense pleasure rips through me, and my thighs tremble. I lift my head up and watch. I'm overrun with euphoria at the sight of both men pleasuring me and how erotic this moment is.

Reece pulls back and licks his lips coated with my pleasure. His eyes are dilated, and I wonder what kind of drugs he's on when he slurs his words. "James, come taste this pussy. So fucking sweet."

"Yesss," I hiss.

They switch places, and then James is on my pussy. Stars explode behind my eyes, and a throaty moan rolls off my lips. His hands hold down my wrists while Reece is on one nipple and tweaking the other to the point of pain. If death by pleasure is a thing, then please kill me, because this is too much. My entire body is tingling, and I'm panting from the overwhelming sensations racking through me.

Holy. Fucking. Sex.

There's no stopping my orgasm now, and I wiggle my arms trying to break free because I want to press their heads into me, but James is too strong. Something about being restrained makes my heart beat faster.

"Oh, fuck," I pant, breathing heavily. I draw the word out, my eyes rolling shut.

James is holding my lips open, and I want to cry out from the hunger taking over my body. The pleasure is rising, and my blood is rushing through my veins so fast I can barely catch my breath. My hips are moving of their own accord. Reece nips my nipple, and I yelp. I need more, I want more, and suddenly I'm about to beg them both to fuck me.

"I ... I can't take it ..."

"Come in my mouth, Val," James says, and fuck it all, I do.

I come so hard there's no denying the moan is real. I couldn't fake one like this if I tried. James's tongue is wicked and tortures my pussy in all the right ways, making sure he wrings every ounce of pleasure from me. I feel my release slide down to my ass. My body is damp and I'm bursting with the most intense orgasm I've ever had, and I never want to come down. His tongue is wild, penetrating my entrance, as Reece now rubs my clit so hard it feels like there's a vibrator on it.

James pulls away and leans higher to kiss my mouth. My legs wrap around his hips, and I dig my heels into his ass so his cock grinds into my pussy. He drops his weight on me. I moan again, tasting myself on him. It's salty and erotic, making me even more aroused.

James breaks our kiss to stand and walk away. I blink a few times and reach out for him. Our eyes lock and my lips part with want. He notices, and I swallow hard, retracting my hand. James takes a large gulp of his drink, eyeing me until my heart can't stop pounding. I don't want Reece to fuck me, I want James to, and he clearly knows that.

"Turn over and get on your knees." He pauses, then addresses Reece. "Don't be easy on her. I have a feeling she can handle anything we throw her way."

Chapter 32

I do as he says, my head light and my limbs weak. I feel like I'm high. I mean, I kind of am. James is stroking himself, and it's incredible the way he sinks lower into the chair and twists his wrist, tightening around his glistening head.

Grabbing my hips, Reece doesn't hesitate, slamming into me in one motion. He lets out a long moan, his width warm inside me. I take a deep breath, trying to hold back from allowing myself to really feel. If he was as big as James, I would've split in two, but thankfully he's not.

Just like I hoped for, his thrust is hard but fast. His fingers are gripping me, digging into my hips, and I like the strength he exudes. I'm sure I'll have bruises tomorrow.

Pulling out, he slaps my ass then surges back in and holds himself there. I gasp, feeling the pleasure from it, and fall onto my elbows. My back arches at a steep angle, and I reach out in front of me, taking him deeper.

"She's fucking squeezing my dick," Reece grits out. "Fuck, she's so tight," he says and then starts thrusting faster. His thighs are slapping into my backside, but his strong hold doesn't let me go anywhere.

"Eyes on me at all times, sweetheart," James says. "Get up on all fours. Now."

I do and eye his stroking hand again. I can't not. The way James pleasures himself, how he swipes the precum to coat his thick head makes me wish I could be the one to do it for him. I contract around Reece, feeling my orgasm climb. I throw my hair over my shoulder to make sure I don't miss a thing.

"You're going to watch me while he fucks you," James says, and I nod, driving my hips back into Reece.

I need it harder. I want it harder.

"When you come on Reece's cock, your eyes will be on mine."

My lips part, eyes fluttering. The blood rushing through my veins is chasing a feeling I so desperately need yet shouldn't crave.

It doesn't take long for my body to reach the point of no return. I decide since I already came once, there's no difference if I come again. The truth is, I don't want to hold back. I like watching James while his friend takes me from behind. It makes me hot.

"Reece ..." I moan his name purposely, knowing James wanted me to say it. "Oh God, yes, harder. Fuck me harder."

I don't have to force those words. I actually want him to.

Reece doesn't hold back and fucks me with speed and precision, hitting the right spot each time, making me cry out in pleasure. He's a savage, and I didn't expect that from him at first sight.

Ask and you shall receive.

My breasts are bouncing, and James eyes them, licking his lips. I wish his mouth was on them and his tongue was rubbing my nipples. He's stroking faster and rougher, and I see his chest fall and rise and the muscles in his arm contract as he fucks his hand. The only sounds in the room are the ones our bodies are making, and it's the sexiest ballad I've ever heard.

"She's getting close, James. Her pussy ... Fuck, you gotta get in here."

My eyes snap to his. For a split second, I wonder why he hasn't. The dark desire in James's eyes screams that he's intoxicated with our performance, and that empowers me. Reaching for Reece's hand, I pry his fingers off my hips and force him to play with my nipple, placing it on me how I like it.

"Squeeze it," I beg. "Twist it, pull it, anything," I say, and

James's jaw locks down. "Give it to me," I say to both of them.

"Fuck, James, I can't hold on any longer. I'm gonna blow hard."

Looking into my eyes, James says, "Are you ready to come on Reece's cock?"

"Yes, James," I say, his name a purr on my lips. I can't take it anymore and need to come. "Please ..."

After a few more thrusts and strokes, James is groaning with ecstasy. "Come for me, sweetheart. Come on his cock and keep your eyes on me, imagining that's my cock fucking you right now."

My eyes threaten to roll shut at the thought, but I make sure I keep them open and watch. Twisting one nipple, Reece slaps my ass and drives in until he's balls deep. I come just as James does and feel Reece pulsating inside of me. It's a rush. I feel drunk taking all of Reece as cum coats James's straining cock and hand. I want to wrap my lips around his dick and swallow his cum down. There's a vein in his neck that begs to be licked. We don't stop watching each other. The room is filled with our heavy breathing and our bodies are spent from the pleasure that's been wrung from us.

Reece pulls out, and I allow my body to take over. I turn around and grab his face, kissing him hard and pushing into him until his back meets the bed. His eyes widen in shock. One of his hands is fisted in my hair, while the other roams over my back. I don't know what's come over me. Maybe having James watch us made me do it. I don't know.

I have a feeling that Reece probably took Viagra to last as long as he did, because he's still hard. I position him at my entrance and sink down on his length without asking. I don't need to ask—men never refuse pussy. Especially pussy they're paying thousands and thousands of dollars for.

"Fuck me," he groans in deep pleasure.

I grab his hands and place them on my breasts as I ride him into my next orgasm without holding back. I grind down on him, taking what he has to give. The sounds escaping my throat are not Valentina's, but I don't worry about that in this moment. His hips are jackhammering into mine as we both come together.

I collapse to the bed. My body is completely depleted while Reece is pulling off his condom at the foot of the bed, staring at my body like he's captivated by me. I feel sexy the way he eyes me.

Grabbing the bed sheet, Reece wipes himself clean.

"I bet she's got another round in her, James." Reece drops the blanket. Walking over to me, he places a kiss to my lips and says, "That was incredible. I can see why James was raving about you."

Then Reece is dressing and walking out the door in less than three minutes, while I'm still in a euphoric state and not ready to get up.

James makes his way to the bar and pours two drinks. He's got a nice ass, and I watch it bounce as he takes steps away from me. He's naked and comfortable in his skin, and I like that. Confident. He walks over and hands me the drink. His cock is still hard, unless that's how he usually looks. Sitting up, I take the glass as he sits down next to me. We both sip, watching, observing. My body is hyperaware of his presence, and I want so badly to climb onto his lap.

His eyes narrow and he says, "Come here."

Yesssss ...

I straddle his hips and push my pussy against his cock. A purr escapes my lips, my eyes lowering as I take a sip of the tequila. His jaw flexes and I lean in to kiss him, but he stops me by placing a hand on the curve of my shoulder and neck.

"Is there a reason why you blocked me from seeing you?" he asks, dragging his hand down to my breast.

He gives it a gentle squeeze, and I lean into his palm. I reach with my other hand to grab his cock, but he stops me. James places both of our glasses down on the nightstand then takes my wrists and secures them behind my back.

Yes, I love when he gets like this.

"I didn't block you, James. I just have clients. Pleasing everyone is a twenty-four-seven job, and I do my best in between classes."

"Why are you lying to me?"

"I've been lying since the day we met."

"Valentina."

"James."

When he grips my breast in a painfully delicious way, my eyelids threaten to lower, but I fight to keep them open.

"You can have my cock—we both know you're dying to fuck me, sweetheart—but only if you tell me the truth."

I swallow hard. He's not playing fair, and as much as I want to tell him why so I can finally have all of him, I can't do that. Not only would I look like a fool, but it would go against the rules. Even though there are times when I don't like my job, I don't want to lose it.

"I told you," I say sweetly, batting my fake lashes. "I have clients, James. I'm doing the best I can."

"And I fucking told you to name your price, sweetheart."

He's angry, but even so his voice elicits a simmering of need under my skin.

"My tuition is paid for. I got a full academic ride."

"I had a feeling you weren't any old broad. That doesn't surprise me. Name what you want, and it's yours."

"Why are you married?" I ask curiously.

"It's complicated. We're working through things."

"Working through things is code for fucking whores on the side?"

His jaw grinds back and forth. I know he doesn't like when I use that word to refer to myself. I can sense he's getting mad at not getting what he wants. But the thing is, I'll never give him what he wants. I simply can't.

"Well, this was fun. You can get the fuck off me now."

"No," I say boldly, a little hurt.

"No?" he says.

"James, please," I say softly, a whisper, Aubrey shining through.

I chew my bottom lip, and he watches then pulls it free. I really wish he'd stop pushing me on this topic. He has to know I won't cave. Leaning forward, he kisses me gently, unlike his usual passionate self, and it's still just enough to get me hot for him.

He's staring at my mouth. "Unless you're willing to give me what I want, we're done here."

"James," I whisper, "please don't do this."

He shakes his head. "Up. We're done here."

"Do you pay all of the women so you can own them?"

His eyes flash with rage. "I don't own anyone, Val. Everyone is free to come and go as they please. What I'm offering to you, I've never offered to any of them."

I don't believe him. He's pushing too hard.

"Do you question all of your whores like this? Push until you get what you want?" My teeth dig into my bottom lip again, rolling over it. "Why do you want this so bad?"

"I'm not fucking repeating myself. I've already told you the reasons why I want you."

James taps the side of my thigh, ushering me to move. My heart sinks into my stomach. I don't want him to leave. I want to be around him. The last thing I want to do is upset him, but I can't give him what he wants. I can't tell him the truth. Just thinking about it makes me feel foolish and stupid. No whore gets a happy ending with a client.

Reluctantly, I move off him, breaking our connection. I don't want to be anywhere I'm not wanted anyway.

"Where are you going?" I ask, watching him walk toward the table with his clothes and belongings. I sit against the headboard and place a big, fluffy pillow in front of my body. My shoulders fall forward in defeat.

James doesn't answer. He just dresses, finishes off his drink, and then buckles his belt. Walking over to me, he locks his eyes with mine as he slips his wallet into his back pocket. He leans over, places his hands on the bed, and kisses the top of my forehead. I swallow the knot in my throat, closing my eyes. He starts to walk away, and I feel a part of me leaving with him. I wish I could tell James what I feel for him, but I can't.

"We're gonna get too attached," I yell at his back before he leaves the room. My voice cracks a little, but that doesn't stop him from walking away.

"Too fuckin' late for that, sweetheart."

Chapter 33

I don't waste any time.

Pulling myself together, I get dressed and take a taxi to Sanctuary Cove, where I ask to speak with Christine. It's late and I have class early in the morning, but I can't wait any longer to put a stop to this.

I take in her ornate office while I wait, looking around at how exquisitely designed it is. I'm a little edgy, the effects of the pill and tequila still working over me. I don't want to get fired, but I need to get it out and talk to her.

I can't allow James to ever see me again. As much as it's going to hurt, it's for the best. Nothing good could come from us being together. Except maybe sex, but even that comes with emotional strings I'm not trying to tie in a bow.

A door opens, and Madam Christine walks in. There's no expression on her serene face, and I'm not sure how to handle that. I dig my teeth into the side of my cheek. Should I stand? Do I shake her hand and greet her? I hope I didn't interrupt anything.

She takes a seat behind her desk and leans back casually. I've never seen black hair so straight and sleek looking.

"I take it this is about your job tonight?"

My stomach knots, heart pounding. Fuck.

"Did you get a call? Someone complained?"

Her lips curve, but her voice is soft, pleased. "Quite the contrary, actually." Christine pauses and studies me. The way she stares makes me think she's trying to do a psychic reading on me. "You were praised. Not only did you get a very generous tip from

Reece, but from James as well."

I falter, my jaw bobbing. "I didn't know I was given a tip."

Madam Christine reaches into her desk and pulls out an envelope. She slides it across to me. It's about two inches thick of what I'm sure is hundred-dollar bills.

"I was going to call you tomorrow to come pick it up. Imagine my surprise when I learned you were already here."

"Thank you."

"James wants you as his own." I catch the slightest smile on her face. A rare commodity. "Do you know the pay involved with that? The requirement?"

I blink a few times, processing what she said. Christine is beyond thrilled. I can understand why. Her clients are being serviced, and she's getting richer off me. Only, she doesn't know the whole story.

I'm surprised. James got to her before I could. Even though he knows how I feel and where we stand, he still hasn't given up. He's desperate to have me, but all I can think of is the consequences.

"No, I'm not aware."

"It's a hundred thousand monthly allowance, a fully furnished and paid-for apartment wherever you choose, an American Express Black Card, and a personal driver. One year of your time is required. When that time is up, both parties can either go into a new contract or go their separate ways."

Jesus Christ. I almost don't want to refuse an offer like that. It's surreal to think that I could make over a million dollars in one year, but I know in those three hundred and sixty-five days that I would lose a part of myself I'd never get back. That's not something I think I could give to any client.

I avert my gaze and look down, shocked that I'm going to turn it down.

"What if I say no?" I ask quietly.

She lifts her hands as if to shrug. "Then you say no. I'd never push one of my girls into something they don't want. I'm not a pimp, Valentina. You come to me willingly, and you're free to leave at your own will. Of course, the money is fantastic, but being a full-time live-in girlfriend is demanding. You have to surrender part of yourself and be all in. It's technically a full-time job. I was told that if you say no, to offer three hundred grand a month."

My eyes widen and my jaw is hanging open. She can't be serious.

"My men don't usually offer that kind of pay," she says quietly.

I sit in silence, contemplating how to decline the offer but also tell her that I can't see James again. I'm sure anyone would say I'm stupid. How does one pass up over three million dollars just to be a live-in girlfriend? It's only a year, and I'd become an instant millionaire. I'd be set for life. So would Grammy. I glance down at my fingers I'm twisting together. When something feels too good to be true, it usually is. My emotional well-being is at stake and not something I can put a price on. The risk is too high. I'm already feeling attached to James. I can't imagine what a year would do to me.

It's the right decision to decline.

I release a soft, regretful sigh. Not even money will win me over this time.

"Christine, I'm going to decline the offer, and while I do, I don't want to take James as a client anymore."

"If you give up a client, you give up everything he offers in the future. There's no turning back."

"I understand."

Her brows angle and she tilts her head to the side. "Did he do something wrong? Hurt you? Make you do something you didn't agree to?"

Yeah, he made me fall for him.

My teeth dig into my bottom lip. It would be so easy to lie, but something tells me she'd see right through it, and I really don't want to do that anyway.

"No, I just think he should find another girl. It's best for both of us. We're already too close, and I don't want us to fall further." I exhale a heavy breath and let it all out. "James is a walking heartbreak waiting to happen. It would be too easy to fall in love with him, and I don't want that. I'm not looking for love, and I don't think he is either. We connected on a deeper level I think both of us didn't want to acknowledge, which is why I refused his last two jobs. I feel like I sound so stupid, but I'm not naïve. James pretty much admitted to me that he's in too deep. It has to stop before it goes further."

"Did you have sex with him?"

"No."

Her brows lift. "Interesting."

She doesn't say anything else, and it causes my stomach to harden.

"I'm sorry."

"Do not ever be sorry for using your head and playing it smart. It doesn't happen often, but there are clients and girls who do fall for each other. It never ends well. Never. Money can buy a lot of things, but it can't buy common sense. I'm glad you told me."

"He made me orgasm for him ... a few times. I tried so hard to fight it off—"

She shakes her head and puts her hand up.

Now I know why she has that rule that I thought was so stupid in the beginning. It makes sense now. That feel-good feeling is undoubtedly tied to emotion and something everyone chases. We all want to feel happy and carefree, and whatever causes that short-term feeling is one we will continue to seek, regardless if it's good for us or not. I've always loved sex, and if someone is able to give it to me how I like it, you can bet your ass I'd be going back for more. But tie in feelings, and it ruins everything and makes it all a complicated mess.

"Stop. It's impossible not to when you're both into each other."

I frown. "You're not angry? I'm not going to get fired?"

"Did you come for Reece?"

My cheeks heat thinking about how hard I orgasmed because of him, how incredible it felt, how I would do it again if I could. But I didn't really come for him then.

"I came, but only while I was watching James. If James wasn't there, I wouldn't have." I pause. "Well, maybe after Reece I might have."

"Then no. But I bet you understand why I have the rules I do now."

I nod. "I do. They make perfect sense."

"I'll make sure James is never one of your clients again. Do you want Reece on that list too?"

"No, he's not an issue. He's harmless." I chuckle, thinking about how I took control of him earlier and the look of elation on his face. "I do think he's secretly into submission, though, and would die if a girl took control." I give her a knowing look, and the corners of her mouth curve up. "He seems too macho to ask, you know?"

She nods, and her eyes agree. "They usually are. Thanks for the tip."

As I step out of Sanctuary Cove and back into the real world, my shoulders feel lighter, but my heart is undeniably heavier. I'll never see James again. The thought crushes my heart and makes me want to run back inside to change my mind. I won't, I know I can't, but at least I'll have the memories of the few times we were together to reflect on. Those will last longer than anything. I feel sick over it because deep down, I know a small part of me will always miss him.

As I eat up the pavement with each step I take, I keep telling myself it's better this way and that I don't regret my decision one bit.

I lie to myself.

I want to cry. I don't want to never see him again.

I regret my decision. Of course I regret it, but I know it was the right one.

Exhaling a tired sigh, I walk a couple of blocks to the subway and catch sight of the woman I usually see when I leave Christine's. I don't know what it is that draws me to her, but it's something in my gut that I can't fight.

She's probably just trying to stay warm and avoid the snowfall that's supposed to take place starting after midnight. I walk over to her, and recognition forms in her eyes.

My pockets are lined with cash, and I hand her a wad of bills. Her jaw trembles, and I feel for this woman as tears brim her eyes.

"Why do you always give me money?" she asks.

"I just felt like you need help, and I can do that for you. I know what it's like to struggle and go hungry."

She can't stop saying thank you and calling me an angel.

Yeah. I'm an angel with black wings, born with no morals or modesty, and legs for days that spread like holy water.

But at least I put them to good use.

Chapter 34

Ever since I was ten, Grammy and I have volunteered at a soup kitchen on Christmas Eve. She never had money to donate, but she taught me that time was more valuable. She'd say, "The holidays are hardest on the needy, and we have to give back, especially when they need our help the most."

I continued our tradition, even when I went off to college. Today I'm volunteering at a kitchen in the city, and then I'll go to her home in Queens and sleep there so we can spend Christmas Day together.

I offer a plate of food with a gentle smile to a woman holding a toddler. Something in my gut draws me to her. There's a story behind her eyes, and I can't help but wonder how she and her kid got to this point. I feel bad for them. No one should live on the streets, especially a child. I think about how that could have easily been me with my Grammy.

As I pass the next plate to a girl who doesn't look much older than eighteen, I'm reminded that there's a story behind every person's eyes. We don't know what these people have been through. I'm not naïve. I'm sure there are some who take advantage, but I like to believe most aren't like that.

Seeing so many women struggle makes me think about all the cash I have hidden at home and the money I make now, and suddenly, the idea running through me like a freight train, I know what I want to do with my degree after graduation.

I'm going to open a nonprofit shelter for women and children.

I finish my shift at the soup kitchen with renewed energy

and head home to clean up and grab my bags. Grammy is already asleep by the time I arrive. It's late and I don't want to wake her, so I quietly place my gifts under her tree and plan to cook her breakfast when I get up.

***

"You outdid yourself this year," Grammy says the next morning after we exchange gifts.

I swear she looks thinner since the last time I saw her, but it's hard to tell with all the layers she's wearing. It's a white Christmas this year, and even with the heat turned on high, she's standing in the kitchen sporting the fleece-lined boots I got her.

"Did you get more prescriptions recently?" I ask as she measures out her morning medication into a small ramekin.

There's a slight tremble to her hands as she carries it back to the kitchen table. I look at the colorful pills with a feeling of dread. There seems to be a few more than usual, and that worries me. She normally tells me when she gets new prescriptions.

She holds one pill up to show me. "My cholesterol skyrocketed." She places it down then picks up another. "The doctor gave me a new one for osteoporosis, and this one is for anemia. Apparently, my levels were low. And this one is for high blood pressure."

Satisfied that it's nothing serious, I take a bite of one of the cinnamon rolls I'd made from scratch then address her original comment.

"I told you I make good money now as a shot girl, and I wanted to spoil you." I had to tell her last month that I'd switched jobs when she questioned where the extra thousand in her account had come from. "When people are drunk, money flies, so I make sure to keep the shots coming all night."

"Aubrey," she groans. "I know what else happens when men are drunk, sweetie. I don't want anything to happen to you."

I smile at her concern. "All I do is flash my pearly whites, and the money rolls in. Nothing to worry about."

"As long as you're not flashing anything else."

Dread forms in the pit of my stomach from lying to her, but I push it aside and ignore it. What she doesn't know won't hurt her. She's my world, and the very last thing I want to do is hurt her.

"Grams, I want to spoil you and your cats."

Grammy's eyes soften with love. Taking the pills all at once, she gulps hard. "You played me, young lady," she jests, and I smirk. "Giving me gifts for my cats."

I chuckle and a smile spreads across my face. The way to her heart is through her cats. I may have gone a little overboard, but she deserves it. On top of all the cat gifts, I had a monthly food delivery set up for them.

"I did what I had to do. I figured it would be better on your arthritis not to have to lug those heavy boxes and bags inside."

"You have no idea. I didn't even know I could order a subscription thingy. I wish I had known sooner."

Swallowing the last bite of my sweet bread, I set my fork down. "I only just found out myself after I did some internet searching for 'lady in the shoe' gifts."

Her eyes twinkle with laughter. "Have I turned into *that* lady?"

"Uh, yeah, you have. But if they make you happy, then who cares?"

She looks over at her tabbies playing in the obstacle tower. "Life is too short to be anything but happy, Aubrey. You, my cats, you all set my soul on fire with love and so much joy. Those little fur babies love unconditionally, and it's something this world needs more of." She looks back at me with clarity in her eyes. "No matter how outrageous, how weird, how strange your view might seem to someone else, you should never settle for anything less."

I swallow hard and avert my gaze to her cats. I've yet to tell her about Daniel, but with good reason. I don't have to guess for a second that she wouldn't approve. She'd tell me to dump his butt—not ass, because she won't curse—and move on to another fish. While Daniel doesn't set my soul on fire, he makes me feel normal at this point in my life, and I need that. I'm not settling for good. I'm settling for just this moment, even if it is a little selfish of me. Daniel will never be my endgame. It's not possible after working at Sanctuary Cove, but that doesn't mean we can't have a little fun in the meantime.

"This is by far the best Christmas I've ever had," she says, her voice cracking a little.

Her words take me away from my thoughts, and I observe her while she looks at her cats with longing. Grammy is happy, and I know the tears in her eyes she's trying to conceal are from joy.

"It's one I'm going to cherish forever and ever."

Chapter 35

It's too early to be up. I'd tossed and turned all night again with all the shit on my mind. Lately, the lack of sleep has been worse, and I can't figure out why. It's like a glass of water sitting on the counter that starts trembling because of a grumble in the distance. The closer the tremor gets, the more it vibrates. Then it stops. Then it starts up again. It's unsettling, and I don't like it.

Expelling a heavy breath, I go straight to the kitchen and pour a glass of orange juice. It's mid-January, and I'm ready to get back to my schedule—and my life.

"I miss school. I can't wait for classes to start back up."

"Only you would say that. Winter break is too short for me," Natalie says.

She's sitting on the couch bundled up. The winter has been cruel this year, and as much as I love the cold, I'm ready for it to be over.

I drink a full glass, pour another, and drink that too.

"I need the distraction from the weird-ass clients I've had lately."

She looks over at me. A sly smile spreads across her lips. "Spill. We can exchange war stories."

I close my eyes and shake my head, trying not to think about last night. "I can't. I don't want to relive it."

"Bitch, you better tell me," she says then gets up and comes into the kitchen.

She pops a bottle of champagne and makes us mimosas. Then we take our drinks to the couch and get cozy under a shared blanket.

"I'm beginning to think Christine should make the men take a breathalyzer test before every job."

She frowns. "Why?"

"Last night, my client ..." I sigh dramatically. "He wobbled when he walked and was so fucking drunk that he was flicking his cigarette ashes into his sparkling pink wine and then drinking from it. It was disgusting, Nat. I'm sure he saw the look on my face because there was no way to hide my repulsion. I tried to get him to ash into something else, but he wasn't even making any sense and seemed content, so I let it go. He smoked—and then drank—a lot of cigarettes."

"That's Owen," she says, then casually takes a sip.

My eyes widen. "You've had him?"

"We've *all* had him."

My face pinches up in repugnance. "So this is a regular thing for him?"

Natalie nods but doesn't seem bothered.

"From what I hear, he lost his entire family during a home invasion many years ago. It was gruesome, and he's never been the same since. He's totally harmless, though. Honestly. I bet you didn't have to do any sex shit, did you?"

I shake my head. "No. I was surprised."

"He doesn't ever sleep with any of the girls or want anything sexual in return. He just wants someone to ramble to."

My heart softens a bit for him at that. "That's kind of sad."

"Yeah, he's a soft teddy bear and just never got over what happened to his family. I don't blame him."

I purse my lips. "Now I feel bad. I shouldn't have judged him. He was showing me picture after picture, but I couldn't understand what he was saying. Now I know they were of his family."

"Don't. We all were like that at first. Next time you'll know what to do. Just act really interested in his family, and he will be so happy." She tips the glass back, drinking the rest of the contents. "How's it going with Daniel? Lover boy giving you any good bonings?"

I look down at the bubbles in my glass. I thought being with Daniel would help me get over James. I was wrong. Three months after I confessed to Madame Christine, I still think about that silver fox. There is just something magnetic about him that I can't quite explain. Like one of those kismet moments that I'll remember for the rest of time. And I didn't even get to fuck him.

It's going okay, but I think it's time to break up with him."

"Not that I ever thought dating was a good idea in the first place, but what made you change your mind? I thought you were satisfied."

I shrug one shoulder, unsure. As I allow more time to pass, guilt festers inside of me. I've been lying to my boyfriend since the day we met. "I don't want Daniel to get too comfortable because I know he wouldn't be okay with a girl who turns tricks for a living." I also feel like I'm using him, but I don't tell her that. "His ex cheated on him and he's still sore about it. Imagine he finds out about Valentina and the sixty-one clients? I also wouldn't call the bonings good. They're not bad, they're just mediocre.

She nods her head, agreeing. "It's probably for the best. Sounds like the relationship has run its course for you."

"Yeah," I say. "Daniel was only supposed to be a fling."

All I feel is hesitation when I sit and think about it. I don't know what's preventing me from actually doing it. I guess I don't want to hurt him. But if I wait, and he finds out the truth, I know that will ultimately destroy him.

Natalie's phone rings. "Hey, Mom," she answers.

I pick up my phone and scroll through social media while Natalie talks on the phone. I'm grateful not to have to talk about Daniel anymore. He's a good guy and I'm a terrible girlfriend, and acknowledging that makes me want to climb down into a gutter where I belong. Maybe she'll want to go shopping in a little while and then go with me to Pilates later to take my mind off things.

"I love that idea," she says then frowns. "Ah ..." She nudges me, and I look up to find her eyes narrowed at me. "Yeah, well, I had plans that night with my friend, Aubrey. Maybe she can come too? You'll finally get to meet her."

I frown, lowering my phone. We don't have any plans coming up, not any that I can remember at least.

"Valentine's Day at La Grenouille it is. So romantic," she says, her voice syrupy. She hangs up, and I stare at her in question.

"What did you just agree to?" I ask.

She huffs and makes a face, then stands up. She takes both of our glasses, refills them, and then sits back down next to me.

"My parents are hosting a dinner. It's for some charity shit my dad's company does twice a year that they make me attend. They need a picture-perfect family for the night. Since you've gone supermom on me and want to save the world now, and I need a wingman, it's the perfect plan. Besides, who needs more saving than your own bestie?" She bats her eyelashes at me.

I give her a long stare. Ever since I told her of my plan to open a nonprofit, she's been calling me Supermom. I guess it's a step up from her calling me straight Mom in my nanny days.

"Really, Nat? I'm going to be standing there all awkward-looking, like the adopted daughter next to you and your parents."

"My mom and dad are a mess. One second they're good, and the next they're all weird and arguing. My dad cares more about his job than his family, so I doubt he'll be near my mom. He'll be busy trying to schmooze everyone who comes to the event. He's a dick and she's a sweetheart, but whatever. If I have to suffer, at least I can do it with my bestie beside me."

I sigh dramatically. I guess it wouldn't be a terrible idea since my heart is set on opening a shelter one day. It could be a good learning experience for me and a way to network.

"How many people will be there? How long is this shindig?"

She rolls her eyes and shakes her head. "I'm sure my dad will invite the whole city. The only plus is this restaurant has amazing flower arrangements and my mom is obsessed with them, so that's why my dad is hosting it there." Natalie shrugs. "She's happy, I'm happy."

"Why do you have so much resentment toward your dad?"

I've never asked many questions about her family because I felt like it was never really my business. All I know is the basics— only child who grew up in an affluent part of the city, Dad is a hard-ass workaholic, and Mom comes from a WASPy background.

Natalie averts her gaze and stares at the wall for a long moment, her mouth pinching tightly together. She licks her lips, and I can taste her loneliness when it comes to her dad before she even speaks.

"There was never a point in time or an event that divided us—we just never got along. I am my own person. I'm not a daddy's girl. I never have been, and I think he wanted that. My dad is a workhorse, and the people in his field see him as someone of power. He and I are similar in many ways, so we butt heads easily. I want to make my own decisions, whereas he thinks his are best. He wants to provide me with the life he thinks I want, and he thinks I should listen and be grateful." She looks at me. "It wasn't until it came time for college that my resentment turned to animosity. We said some hurtful things to each other that I'll never forget."

My brows angle together, sadness creeping its way into me. Natalie has a strong personality, so I can see how she would butt heads with someone who's like her. She's unyielding in her decisions, and once she makes her mind up, that's it. There's no going back, and I love that about her.

"I hope in time, things smooth out for you guys. It's kind of sweet he's hosting the party at your mom's favorite restaurant. It's an all-night thing?"

Guilt is written all over her face, and it's impossible to be mad. "Don't hate me!" she begs, pleading with the champagne glass between her hands. "I'll treat you to a spa day. No vag waxing this time, promise."

A slow smile spreads across my face. "Perfect timing. I wanted some time with my bestie today anyway."

Chapter 36

"First things first, we get a drink since I'm not going to know anyone here," I say as we step out of the town car.

Natalie gave me the rundown on the way to La Grenouille. We'll be mingling with the upper crust on the most romantic night of the year. I feel like I'm crashing a party, but Natalie assured me it wasn't like that. Plus, she said her mom really wanted to meet me. Surely it won't be as bad as I'm dreading inside.

Daniel wasn't too thrilled when I told him I had plans with Natalie on Valentine's Day. It's taken a few rounds of wild sex—for him, not me—to make it up to him, and then some.

Since becoming Valentina, I've begun to view sex as more of a chore. The intense, constant focus of the job has stripped me of feeling any real pleasure when it's on my personal time. Sex is not nearly as enjoyable, and orgasms are rare. Daniel doesn't even know the difference between a fake moan and a real one ... unlike James.

Ugh. I used to love any act of sex, and now I can take it or leave it. Maybe if I didn't have to work so hard to make sure others feel gratification, it would be a different story.

"It won't be as bad as you think," Natalie says, regaining my attention.

"I'm not worried with you by my side," I tell her. I just hate feeling like a third wheel—or fourth in this case—but then I remind myself if the roles were reversed, she'd be here with me, no questions asked. I stifle my thoughts and plaster a smile on my face.

We walk inside, and it's a sea of expensive suits and designer dresses that flock from corner to corner. Diamonds and dripping jewels flicker under the rose lighting, and the flowers are a soft contrast to the Botox-filled air I'm suddenly breathing in. A blend of vocal jazz and swing music plays softly in the background, and I feel like I'm transported to a Frank Sinatra music video as we make our way to the bar. Natalie had said the place would be dressed up like a wedding, we'd be doing cocktail hour, and then we'd be guided to another room for a sit-down dinner.

After the first sip of tequila and Sprite, I sigh dramatically—loving that first taste—and smile at Natalie.

Natalie downs her entire drink in one gulp then lifts one finger to the bartender for another. I angle my head to the side and smirk at her.

"Are you feeling better?" I joke.

"Much," she says, her eyes wide.

I can feel Natalie's tense energy. Her shoulders are bunched up, so I make conversation to calm her nerves. I never had to go through something like this with my parents, so it's new territory for me, but I'm going to try to make the best of it for her.

"My body is so sore but tight from Pilates. Like my legs are firm but they feel good. I think I'm going to try hot yoga next. You should come with me."

Natalie takes a sip from her glass then licks her lips. "My body is like coconut oil. Thick and solid on the surface, silky and wet on the inside."

I almost choke on my drink and start laughing. "Where do you come up with this stuff?"

She taps the side of her head, and I laugh again. "You know I resort to sarcasm when I'm uncomfortable. I don't even think that made sense."

"Who cares? I thought it was funny," I say, smiling. I feel my phone vibrating in my purse, and I know who it is before I reach for it.

"Danny boy?" Natalie asks.

I look down at my screen and nod. I read the text then hold up the phone for Natalie to see the flowers and chocolates he has waiting for me with a candle lit in the background.

"Still stringing him along?"

My stomach drops slightly with guilt. I really should break it off soon. But even knowing I'll never be the faithful woman he wants, I can't bring myself to let him go just yet.

"I'll stop by his place later and give him a happy ending." I slip my phone back into my purse.

"You don't have to whore yourself out for him, you know. He is your boyfriend, after all."

I purse my lips. Natalie gives me a knowing look but dives back into small talk about school and this being our final semester.

Just when I think she's back to her normal self, her shoulders pull back and her gaze fixates on something behind me.

My back tingles with awareness, and I can't tell if it's in warning or because I'm wearing my favorite bare-back dress that I only got to wear one other time before. My heart clenches at the thought of that day spent drinking and laughing and touching the one man I've ever truly wanted but could never have.

Holding the glass to her lips, she says quietly, "Incoming. Parentals. Act normal."

I chuckle, feeling the tequila swimming happily in my bloodstream. "You act normal, you nut."

Natalie places her glass down on the bar countertop, and I do the same as her parents stroll up. She exhales, and I want to tell her to wipe that expression off her face because she looks constipated.

"Mom, Dad, I'd like to introduce you to my roommate and best friend, Aubrey Abrams."

Swallowing, I inhale and turn to face them as they close around us in a small circle. My nerves are a little wired now, and I feel like I'm on a blind date.

My eyes lock with her mother's first, but I freeze when I catch the scent—a too-familiar scent—of lemon and bergamot.

No fucking way.

I can feel the weight and shock of his gaze on me. A chest-crushing wave of anxiety slams into me. I can hear my heart pounding in my ears and extend my hand out to greet her mom. A chill dances down my spine. I blink and focus on her, hoping I don't look as pale as I feel, struggling to form composure. I work to keep my expression neutral and force a smile, praying I give nothing away. Her mom's gaze is tenderhearted. She looks so identical to Natalie that it's startling.

"I've heard so many wonderful things about you, Aubrey," she says, her voice refined. "I'm Katherine, and this is my husband ..."

But I already know her husband's name before she says it.

I know what he tastes like, what he looks like when he's naked, the length of his cock and how he strokes it, every colorful tattoo on his chest and the meaning behind each. I know how his strong hands feel on my body when he's about to come, how his tongue feels when he licks my pussy.

I know him in ways that no friend should ever know her best friend's dad.

My eyes shift up to his, and my heart slows to a stuttering rhythm. He gives absolutely nothing away, and that somewhat eases the tightness in my chest.

I thought I was good at playing the game, but he's better than me. There isn't a look on his face that would hint at us knowing each other before now.

"James Riviera," he says, making the first move by putting his hand out. I hesitate for the briefest moment, then tentatively put my hand out to meet his. My palm slides against his large one, and I feel a spark pass between us, the same spark that's been there since the first day we met.

"It's nice to finally put a face to the name," he adds, eyes boring into mine.

Fuck. My. Life.

He asked for my real name once, and I refused to give it to him. Now he has it. I stare at him for a moment before a loud, boisterous laugh across the room startles me. I really don't even know how to act at this moment, so I go with the basics.

"It's a pleasure to meet you," I say automatically, returning his shake. "Natalie's told me so much about you guys."

James chuckles, and it ignites all the nerve endings in my body. A flush works itself through me.

"I'm sure nothing good," he jokes, but I know he's being serious.

"Oh, I'm sure it was all pleasant," Katherine says sweetly, patting her husband's chest. "Aubrey, that's a beautiful dress."

I glance down and then want to fall into a dark hole and never be found. It's the same dress I wore when I met James, the one he loved so much. The one I was wearing when he bought a five-hundred-dollar bottle of cognac and sucked my nipples as I rocked against his lap, feeling his dick.

God, if you're real, please strike me dead now.

"Thank you," is all I say, tight-lipped. I shoot a fleeting glance at James, but he's already watching me. My cheeks fill with heat because I know he remembers it too.

"So, you attend Fordham with my daughter?" he asks, eyes telling me he's purposely probing. He's smug that he can ask, but he's disguising it well. James sips his amber liquid, and I can't help but stare at his lips. "What are you majoring in?"

Another piece of information I'd once refused to give him. I take a deep sip and decide to order tequila neat next time.

"I do," I say, answering his first question. "We've been roommates since freshman year and have gotten along famously since." I look at Natalie, scrunching my nose, and she smiles. "I'm majoring in developmental sociology."

"Oh, that's an interesting major," Katherine says. "What will you do with it?"

"I'm undecided."

James isn't willing to let that slide. "You have to have an idea."

"She's undecided, Dad," Natalie repeats, the frustration in her voice clear.

I eye her, letting her know it's okay. "I've considered law school, but I'm thinking of starting a nonprofit organization for women and children." I pause. "Lawyers, as you know, are money-thieving liars. I'm not sure I have that in me."

Katherine pales and places her hand along her neck, but both Natalie and James laugh.

Looking at her mom, I say, "I apologize. Sometimes my humor isn't appropriate. Natalie told me her father is an attorney."

"That's very admirable of you," James says. Something tells me he's not just saying it, but that he actually means it. I let the comment roll off my shoulders and remind myself that this is all just a game to him.

"Thank you." I look at Katherine. It's too difficult to make eye contact with James. It makes me feel like everyone would know what's between us just by looking at how we look at each other. "It's astounding, the resemblance between you and Natalie," I say to her mother, trying to change the subject.

Katherine smiles proudly at her daughter. "Since the day she was born."

"Everyone thinks we're sisters when we're together," Natalie says cheerfully.

"You guys could definitely pass as them, that's for sure."

"What kind of nonprofit were you considering?" James asks, unrelenting in his effort to reveal all my secrets, and I want to murder him.

Before I can think of a reply, Katherine intervenes. "Will you excuse me? I need to use the ladies' room before we're seated for dinner. Aubrey, it's so great to finally meet you and I hope to see more of you soon."

I respond with a faux smile, my stomach twisting into knots of guilt. I never want to see her again. I hope I never have to. All I can think about is the fact that I've sucked her husband's dick twice and orgasmed on his tongue and how he watched and directed me to fuck his friend.

Shame fills every ounce of my body, and I suddenly feel nauseated. This is bad. This is really bad. My lungs are constricting. I feel like I can't breathe. I need to get out of here and get fresh air, but I can't excuse myself just yet.

"I'll go with you, Mom."

Eyes wide, I panic inside and snap my attention to Natalie, who gives me a pleading look. I can't refuse it either, seeing as I'm now harboring a scandalous secret that's going to haunt me until the end of time.

"My dad loves this boring talk, so you guys are perfect for each other. I'll be back soon."

Natalie pats my shoulder then scampers off with her mom. James watches until they turn the corner, and then he looks at me.

I look away, unable to make eye contact with him. I lean against the bar and signal for another drink, a double this time. Screw the single. James is facing the crowd, whereas my back is to it. He's close enough that I can smell his cologne and feel him without us even touching, and it awakens something inside of me I haven't felt since the last time I was with him.

Chapter 37

"And here I thought I'd never see you again," James says under his breath, only loud enough for me to hear.

Chills dance down my arms, and I hate that my body reacts to the sound of his voice.

I thank the bartender and take a huge sip.

"That was the plan," I say. "Man, is fate cruel. It always has a way of fucking me and never leaving me satisfied."

"Fate is definitely on my side tonight."

"You would think that."

He's quiet for a moment. "Why'd you do it?" he asks, his voice guttural, pained.

Fuck, my heart. I know what he's referring to. His voice screams pissed, but his question stirs my blood.

I angle my body toward him and look up, defiant. "Are you really going to ask me that?"

"I tried to find you."

"That doesn't surprise me after the conversation I had with Madame Christine and your outlandish offer. I'm glad you couldn't find me."

He stares down at me. "Why?"

My throat is tight, choking with emotion. The way he's looking at me—pleading with me—kills me, but I stand firm. Now I have no choice but to stand my ground. I did what I had to do.

"You know exactly why, James." When he doesn't respond, I say, "Promise me, right now, that Natalie will never find out what happened between us. She's my best friend and one of the few people I have left in my life. I *will not* lose her."

He still doesn't respond.

"James, please. Promise me."

His nostrils flare. "Does she work *there* too?"

My stomach drops, and I realize I can never, ever let the truth about that get out. I'd rather Natalie know about James and me before James ever found out that his daughter is a prostitute, high-end or not.

"No," I say forcefully. "She doesn't even know what I do, and she never will."

James bobs his head. He finishes his drink and orders us both a cognac. I can't blame him for drinking back-to-back. I feel like I need to be put out of my misery too.

"My offer still stands, you know."

I scoff, a heated breath rolling off my lips. "Wow. You're such a fucking dirtbag to say that at a time like this, with your family, your *wife*, in the same room."

He looks at me like I offended him. "Why? Was I a dirtbag to you before you knew the truth? You knew I was married. Nothing has changed."

My eyes widen in surprise.

"You have to know that offer is forever off the table now. I would never do that to Natalie. Speaking of, why do guys have different last names? Is she not your biological daughter?"

With different last names and no family photos in our apartment, there wasn't a single thing that would've tied his identity to her. Looking back on it now, that was a blessing in disguise.

His gaze roams over the sea of people. Lowering his voice, he says, "She's my daughter, much to her dismay. She got pissed at me before she left for college and changed her name to her mom's maiden name. It killed me when she did that."

"Doesn't surprise me. Natalie is so rebellious sometimes."

A small grin tugs at the corners of his mouth, his eyes beaming like a proud parent. "Would you reconsider my offer? She'll never know about us. No one has to know, not even Christine. It's between us."

My breathing slowly deepens, and I roll my lips between my teeth. The decision would be so easy. If it weren't for my damn job. If it weren't for my best friend. If we were any other two people, I'd take him in a heartbeat. But any temptation I might have had before this night would now have to be buried for good.

"I can't, James. That will never happen." My response is soft, and it hurts my heart. "I can't believe you're Natalie's father. If things were different, you wouldn't even have to make an offer and I'd be yours, but I can't do that to her. I just can't. This is already bad enough."

His wild eyes shift back and forth between mine. "I should've fucked you when I had the chance. You never would've walked away."

"James," I say in a desperate whisper, feeling those words hit deep in my bones. We both know it would've been too good, too addicting. A part of me is glad it didn't happen now.

Natalie makes her way back to us at that moment, and I send up a silent prayer thanking God for being on my side for once.

"Natalie, I was just telling your friend that I would donate to her nonprofit when she's ready to start it up," James says, still looking at me with pure desire in his eyes.

My spine tingles. Oh, he's good. He's really good.

Natalie's blue eyes widen, and a small smile spreads across her face. "That's very generous of you." She looks toward me. "How awesome is that, Aub? Dad picks two charities a year and goes ham on them. Now maybe you don't have to go to boring law school after all."

I sip my cognac stiffly. "Very generous indeed. I was just as surprised as you when he told me."

My phone vibrates in my purse. I set my drink down to take it out.

"Is it him again?" Nat asks, and I can feel James looming over me trying to read the text message.

"Him who?" James asks a tad too harshly.

"Daniel. Her lame doctor boyfriend." Natalie rolls her eyes, and I can see she's a little more laid-back with her father now that the liquor is streaming through her body.

I nod. "Yeah, he wants to see me."

"You should go."

I snap my gaze to her, surprised she would even suggest that when she'd begged me to come tonight in the first place. I promised her I would be here, and I'd planned to stay, even with my dark secret standing three feet away from me. But if she's offering me a way out of my personal hell without realizing what she's doing for me, I'm taking it.

"You sure?"

She nods, and a thankful smile spreads across my face.

"I'll walk you out," James says. "Natalie, you can find your mother, and I'll make sure Aubrey gets a car."

She reaches over and gives me a hug. Whispering in my ear, she says, "Thank you for being here. Now go give Danny boy the ride of his life."

I chuckle through my discomfort and hug her back. "You're so bad. Love you, chica."

Natalie walks away, and I turn to James, glaring at him. "I don't need my hand held to get a cab. Real slick, though."

"I'm very well aware that you're capable of holding your own."

My cheeks bloom with heat under his wandering gaze.

I sip the rest of my drink, my eyes trained on him, and then place the crystal down, anxious to get out of here. I don't like the way he's looking at me because it's making me feel all tingly and pretty and sexy, and I haven't felt that way since the last time we were together.

Swallowing hard, I say, "I can't say it's been a pleasure, James."

"I can."

"That's because I'm fucking amazing," I say sarcastically.

I huff under my breath and turn around, leaving him behind. He's getting to me so easily when he shouldn't have any impact on my emotions whatsoever. I retrieve my coat from the coat check and step outside, inhaling the dirty air. Anything is better than the stuffy floral scent inside, not to mention being within touching distance of James.

God, he looked divine tonight in the pale-pink dress shirt he'd left partially unbuttoned to reveal the lively artwork across his wide chest. What gave him the seal of approval from me were the navy-blue slacks that looked downright sinful on him. He has an ass that rivals David Beckham's, which is saying something, since I think James is at least ten years older and David's ass is perfection.

Before I can raise my hand to call for a cab, an arm wraps around me and pulls me into a small, dark alcove between the buildings. My back slams against the exposed brick, and then James's lips are on mine, our tongues tangling around each other's in a heated kiss. Tension crackles between us, and I know he feels it by the way he leans into me. My sighs are a soft melody as his hands paint my body with a worshiping touch.

"James," I whisper, breaking the kiss. "We can't do this. Please." My heart's racing, and I'm terrified. "I don't want to get caught."

"Agree to see me again, and I'll leave you alone for now," he breathes into me, his forehead pressed to mine.

I clench my eyes shut and shake my head. "No. You know I won't."

He slides his hands inside my coat and pulls my body flush to his. His hands are on the small of my back, cupping my ass and giving me a gentle but firm squeeze. A purr rolls off my lips, and I press my fingers into his shoulders. His erection digs into me, and I gasp, wanting to feel more. His lips meet my neck, and the fine hair of his beard tickles my skin. There's something to be said about a man who knows how to navigate a woman's body.

"Say yes." His voice is guttural, skating over my skin. "I won't take no for an answer now that I have you again. We don't need to go through Sanctuary Cove. It can be just us."

I frown, wondering again how he can even ask such a thing while his wife and daughter are inside waiting for him. He has to know I can't do that to Natalie, and I would think he wouldn't want to hurt her either, because that's exactly what it would do.

I push James away with every ounce of strength I have. "I need to go," I say and rush off before he can catch me.

There's a cab waiting at the curb now with a couple standing next to the open door, so I quickly step around them and jump in.

"I'm sorry! Family emergency!" I say, slamming the door shut.

Within thirty minutes, I'm back in my apartment, my former favorite dress a crumpled mess on the floor, and I have a large glass of wine in my shaking hands. My plan was to drink until I couldn't see straight and then stumble to bed, so all I'm wearing is a white tank top and black boy short panties. Guilt, shame, mortification—they all hit me with a force so strong it makes me sick.

I glance at the colorful hues of the dress that James loves. I never want to look at it again.

Walking over to the small window, I can feel the icy air seeping through the cracks. I stare down at the busy city in a daze, wondering how this happened. There are escort businesses all over New York City, but few as exclusive as Sanctuary Cove, so I'm not too surprised both James and Natalie ended up there. That means Madame Christine had known who he was when she paired him with me. How awkward it had to be for her to have to make sure she never accidentally scheduled Natalie with her father.

Had I known who James was, I would never have taken him on as a client. I'd have put a stop to all of this before we had a chance to make things complicated and messy, before we had the chance to dance together.

Tears burn my eyes, the emptiness in my chest suffocating my emotions. I need to forget everything. Every word, every touch, every look, every smile—pretend like it never happened. But it's hard to let go when he's all I've thought about since the moment I met him.

Pouring another glass of wine, I place the bottle down and cork it as a rapid knock sounds at the door.

"Natalie, did you forget your key again?" I call out as I pick up my glass. "I told you to check before we left." I unbolt the door and pull it open, and the blood drains from my face.

"Hello, Aubrey."

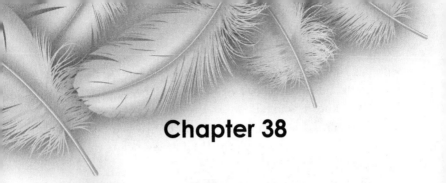

Chapter 38

He doesn't wait. He just pushes the door open and steps inside, shutting it behind him and locking it with the chain.

"You can't be here," I say. I stare at him with honest-to-God fear. "How did you find me?" I ask then regret my words. Of course, he'd know where his daughter lives, even if they have an estranged relationship. I place my glass down on the kitchen counter.

"I'm not done with you," he says, taking in the length of my body.

"How are you even here right now? Shouldn't you be at your event? How did you leave?"

He steps toward me, but I step back.

"I got an emergency call from a client. Happens all the time," he says, sounding a tad too proud of his lie. "My wife understands."

My jaw drops in shock. "You bailed on your charity shindig to chase after me? James, you need to leave. Natalie could walk in at any minute."

I'm panicking inside. If she walks in, there'll be no way to explain this. None.

James advances on me, and I retreat until my back hits a wall. The city lights filter through the window and illuminate his features. I take in his eyes that are full of determination, his skillful lips that are inching closer to mine, and I can't help but wonder how is it that this man, with his matching salt-and-pepper hair and beard, has me in knots and aching with desire for him.

Inhaling, I hold my breath as he closes the distance.

"She won't. I know she won't leave her mother until the night is over." He glances briefly at his Rolex. "Which means we have a few hours. I want to know why you did it, Aubrey. Tell me why you blocked me."

I swallow hard. I love the sound of my real name on his lips.

Shaking my head, I say, "You're far from stupid, James. You know why."

He raises a hand to my cheek, allowing his fingers to graze down the side to my jaw, my neck, and to the strap of my tank top. My nipples harden, and I know he sees it as he slips the strap down my shoulder. He palms my breast roughly, making sure he pinches my nipple, and I draw in an audible breath, my back arching as the searing heat travels through my body.

"I can't get close to a client for obvious reasons, and you're a complication I didn't want." I pause. "I still don't want it."

"Liar," he says, no doubt feeling how I'm trembling against him, my body betraying my words. "I'm a complication you need, sweetheart," he continues, his hands slowly moving down my waist to grab my hips.

His touch is seductive, and he leaves a trail of hunger in his wake for me to chase after.

"This is a complication we both need."

I place my hands on his chest to stop him, but it's a useless effort, as I'm defenseless against him. James lifts me with ease.

My legs automatically wind around his waist, and I fall into him. One of his hands skims up my back to cup my neck. I sigh at his strength, and he sees it. His other hand is under my ass, holding me up as if I weigh nothing. He presses my back to the wall to secure me and pushes his chest into mine. His fingers dig deeper into my neck, and my thighs tighten even more as a rush of desire slips from me. There's something about how he takes control with just enough power that makes me fucking weak for him.

I draw in a heavy breath. "I can't do this, James. I refuse to do this to Natalie. I love her, and I don't want to lose her. Her friendship means more to me than whatever this is."

My heart is racing, and I wonder if he can feel it. Bringing my hand to his face, I cup his jaw, stroking his beard and bringing him to me. My thumb traces over his bottom lip, and he opens to bite down. His mouth is too close, and I fight the urge to lean in and press my lips to his.

"Why are you pushing this?" I whisper.

"I wish I had a real explanation, but I don't. There's something about you that has captivated me ever since the first day we met. I haven't been able to stop thinking about you. Why do you think I kept requesting you? When you blocked me, I went fucking out of my mind."

I shake my head vehemently. I refuse to believe he feels the same way as I do. "It's because we didn't have sex. That's all it is. I'm a challenge, and the chase excites you. But you'll get over it and forget me in time."

His face turns hard. "No. Not even close, Aubrey. Yeah, don't get me wrong. I'm fucking dying to be inside you, but it's *you* who fascinates me. The way you speak your mind, the jokes you make, the way you carry yourself in a public setting. The way you challenge me—I fucking love that you do. You have a beautiful heart and a dirty mind. I like what you bring to the table." James applies pressure to the back of my neck, and my body melts into him like butter. A soft, breathy sigh expels from me. "You want a man who's real with you, Aubrey? You want honesty? My wife hates when I touch her like this, but you respond to it. I can feel your body light up under my fingertips, and it makes me curious to see what other reactions I can get from you. So excuse me for wanting someone who indulges in the things I do inside and outside the bedroom."

That's the thing. We indulge, and then we connect, and that leaves us with a side of feelings that will fuck us over in the end.

His words resonate deep inside me no matter how hard I try to pretend they don't. He's the flame on the tip of the arrow that's aimed right at my heart. I want to burn alive with him.

A few short moments pass between us, and he presses his lips under my ear, peppering me with warm kisses. My hand caresses his neck, and I can feel his throat move when he swallows, something that's sinfully hot to me. Moving higher, my fingers thread through his hair, and I hold him to me.

"You should go." My voice is husky. "I won't betray Natalie this way."

"I'm not asking you to betray anything. I'm only asking you to be mine for a little while," he says and closes the distance, pressing his lips to mine.

If there ever were a set of words that could break a woman's heart, that would be it.

He kisses me deeper, so fiercely that I almost yield from the way his tongue coaxes my own to respond.

"Are you really going to refuse to feel what we have? Let me tell you something—I'm not a fucking pansy. I don't do soft and I'm not that romantic, but this feeling in my chest is not normal. This craving I have for you is not fucking normal. You're all I can think about—you're what I want, what I need, like I need air to breathe. I've never had this before, and my gut is telling me to chase it. I'm not giving up on this ... *You*."

I blink, trying to sort out what's going on between us, knowing I need to push him away for good.

"What I have with you, I have with every client, James. I just know how to play the game. That's all it is and nothing more. I'm paid to give you an illusion, to create the ultimate fantasy for you."

"I don't believe you," he says against my mouth, unaffected by my harshness. "You're lying."

"You saw me with Reece. It's a deception of the mind and what we want our clients to see. I'm just really good at giving the illusion."

"I saw you had to tell him what your body needs. You don't do that with me. Will you really say that you can have a conversation with him the way you do with me? How about speak your mind and be real with him the way you are with me and laugh about it?" He shakes his head, and his lips brush mine. "When you kissed him, did you feel anything? When he touched you, did it consume your body as my touch does? Do you think about him as much as you think about me? When you fucked him, did you come because of him, or was it because of me?" He gives me a soul-searing kiss then. "Did you reach for him the way you reached for me? Yeah, I saw you reach for me, sweetheart. You don't have to tell me. I see it in your eyes. And I saw it that night."

I swallow hard, ignoring the truth and hating that he can read me like a book. He's completely right, and he knows it.

"Say yes," he demands.

"No," I whisper.

"Aubrey."

"James."

"How much money do you want?" he asks. "I told you once, I'll tell you again. Name the price for your time."

I run my tongue over my bottom lip, thinking of a number that would no doubt be outside his price range, knowing he won't take the bait. I need him to drop this and leave before everything gets even more complicated and painful.

"Ten million for one year."

"Deal."

"What?" I shriek. "No ... No. You're not supposed to say yes."

"Stick your hand in my left pocket," he says, looking me directly in the eye.

"No. You're not supposed to say yes, James. Just leave. Please!"

"Stick your hand in my left pocket," he repeats. Wary, I do as he says, and pull out a thin strip of paper.

LUCIA FRANCO

A blank check.

For the first time in months, the thought of being paid for sex makes me feel sick to my stomach. If it were anyone else, I'd say yes—not just yes, but *hell yes*—but coming from James, it doesn't feel the same.

Turns out, I really am no better than a working girl who takes twenty dollars for a blow job.

Tears sting my eyes, my emotions ready to burst through the dam. This is the exact reason why I put a stop to us a few months ago. I want him, and I want that money, but I never wanted to have him *because* of the money.

Feeling wrung out and thoroughly broken, I place a hand on his chest and force him back until I'm standing on my feet again. The agony of everything that's happened has reached its boiling point.

Looking into his raw, questioning eyes, I say through my teeth, "That was a test and you failed it. You're just like every other man with a big dick hanging between his legs. All you want is sex, and when someone refuses you, like I've refused you, it becomes a challenge. I'm just another conquest you'll get your fill of and then move on. The issue is, I have more to lose than you, and I'm not willing to risk it."

"You're really going to refuse that kind of money?" James asks, his voice rising. He looks about as lost and confused as I feel. "Don't be stupid and not take the money. You can live extremely comfortably and use it to open your nonprofit."

I stare at him, chewing my lip to keep my mouth shut.

"Do you want more? Is that it?" He puts his arms out and challenges me. "I'm a billionaire, sweetheart. There isn't a fucking thing you can ask for that I would say no to."

Shaking my head, I lunge away from him, but James catches up to me in two strides and pulls me around to face him.

Glaring down, he says, "Ten million now, and another ten

261

million when your time is up."

My jaw drops. I'm rooted in place, struggling to breathe. The money is just as tempting as the man in front of me. Why the fuck couldn't we have met in that coffee shop? Why couldn't he have been single and unrelated to my best friend?

Despite the pain, despite it all, I hesitate to refuse him, because Jesus Christ that's a lot of money for even a nun to turn down. He sees my indecision, walks around me toward the kitchen, and returns with a pen he grabbed from the counter. My jaw is slack as he starts filling out the check, but I don't stop him. When he's done, he drops the pen and turns to face me again, unphased by the numbers he'd just written down like he was writing nothing more than a grocery list.

I feel sick, because in that moment, I know what I'm going to do, even though I know it's wrong.

"It's right there, Aubrey. Take the fucking money. You know you want to. I can see it in your eyes. It's better this way anyway. Less complications."

We both know that's bullshit. James is angry now, but so am I, because he's right and it sickens me. My eyes shift to the check, lingering, then back to him.

"James ..." My voice cracks, and that's all the confirmation he needs.

He walks up to me, and I can feel the tension radiating from his body onto mine. "Which room is yours? The last thing I want is to fuck you on my daughter's bed."

Chapter 39

"Strip," James says, standing against my closed and locked bedroom door. His arms are crossed in front of his chest, the material of his shirt stretched tight around his biceps.

My chest is rising and falling rapidly with a million feelings. We both know I'm not shy about being naked, but I know in my heart that nothing good is going to come from this.

And yet, here I am diving headfirst into the fire. It's the fact that I just made a willing deal with the Devil that bothers me. I'm fucking over my best friend for cash.

Correction. I'm fucking her dad for cash.

Reaching for the hem of my shirt, I pull it over my head and drop it to the floor, and then I push my panties down and step out of them. His eyes blaze with need as he takes in my large breasts, and my nipples pucker in response.

"Take your hair down," he says, and I pull the rubber band free and drop it to the floor too. "Now, undress me," James orders, his voice low.

My heart pounds as I take two steps, and he drops his arms to his sides, standing up straight. My cheeks are flushed, my mind is racing with too many thoughts, and I wish it would stop. His knuckles graze softly down the slope of my waist. My stomach dips, and James hums his approval under his breath. I unbutton his shirt, pulling the material out of his dress pants and finishing off the buttons before I move on to his belt. There's an obvious bulge I can't ignore but want to touch. I think back to the first time I saw his cock and how big it was.

Tonight is going to hurt in more ways than one.

Unbuttoning his pants, I pull the zipper down as James's fingers reach up to pinch my nipple crudely. I gasp, feeling pleasure spike through me. My face twists in shame as pleasure seeps out of me. God, I really am a whore. I lean into him, pressing my forehead against his shoulder, and take a couple of deep breaths.

"You like it," he says, and I nod. I love it.

He does it to both nipples, and wetness seeps from my pussy. My trembling fingers finish with the zipper, and I reach around to push his boxers and pants down, pressing soft kisses to his chest and neck.

"You want me, don't you?" he asks, his voice gruff, but it's more of a statement. "You want me to fuck you."

He steps out of his shoes and pants, and I push his shirt off his shoulders.

"Look at me," he says, and I swallow hard. I'm apprehensive about looking at him, but I do. Our eyes meet, and for a split second, I'm lost in his gaze. "Shut your mind off and just focus on my touch."

"I don't know how," I whisper nervously.

Fuck. I don't know how I'm going to do this. I know I think too much, and right now my thoughts are in overdrive because of what I've agreed to, of what I want, and of what I know will be the thing that ruins my friendship with Natalie.

James slips his hand between my thighs and inserts a finger. It slides right in with no issue because I'm already wet for him. A purr vibrates in the back of my throat. He strokes me a few good times, and my lips part.

Barely moving his mouth, he says, "One thing you should know about me is that I love to eat pussy, another thing my wife hates. Get on the bed and pull your knees up." My jaw bobs, and I'm stunned into place. "Now, Aubrey. Where are your belts?"

I blink, a little confused. I step over to my dresser and reach inside to pull out a few belts, but something else strikes his fancy. He reaches into my drawer and pulls out a silk sash that goes to a robe I never use. He fingers the soft material then gestures to the bed. Once I'm on my back, James climbs between my thighs and reaches above my head, tying my wrists together before securing them to the wrought iron headboard. Sitting on his knees, he yanks my hips down so that I'm stretched out with no room to move, and then without wasting any more time, he lunges for my mouth and kisses me savagely. The silk digs into my wrists, silencing my mind. I moan into him, twirling my tongue around his, loving how he just takes my kiss without asking. Hiking my leg up, I wrap it around his back and tug him to me, needing to feel more. He grabs my hip and squeezes me tightly, and then he breaks the kiss and moves down my body until his mouth is fastened on my pussy.

"Oh, God," I moan. "James ..."

His palms are on my nipples, and he pinches them with no remorse while his tongue penetrates my pussy and his teeth move over my clit. The heels of my feet dig into the mattress, and my back arches from the pleasure racking my body. My fingers tighten around the silk belt. I'm hot everywhere, the blood in my veins sparking. I clench my eyes shut, focusing on the check now sitting in my nightstand, effectively killing my rising orgasm. I have to look at this as a job and nothing more.

Only, it's not that easy when I actually like the guy and because he wasn't kidding when he said he loves to eat pussy. James knows exactly how a woman likes her pussy licked, because he's doing everything, and I mean *everything* the right way. Wetness seeps down to my ass, and my thighs clench around his head. Biting into my lip, I start counting sheep in my head to push down the still-climbing orgasm.

"Come in my mouth," he says, his voice muffled. "I want to taste this sweet pussy again."

"No," I say, and my refusal only encourages him to ravage me.

Fighting it is getting harder and harder, and little sounds escape my lips. I want to let go, but I can't. James pulls back, and I exhale a loud gush of air, my chest rising and falling fast. Our eyes lock, and I know he can tell what I'm doing. His mouth is covered in my pleasure, and it's even on his beard. My gaze drops to his erect cock, and I swallow.

"Roll over onto your stomach," he says, his voice rough.

There's enough give in the sash that I'm able to do as he says. There's a dip in the mattress. He's sitting on the back of my legs, and I'm trapped to the bed, unable to move. His hands rub circles on my butt cheeks, warming them.

"You have such a nice ass. I'm about to color the shit out of it."

Then, without warning, a whoosh slices through the air and he strikes my ass with a belt. I gasp loudly, and before I can ask what he's doing, he spanks me three more times back-to-back-to-back. I've been spanked with a hand a few times, but the belt catapults me to a new level of desire I wasn't prepared for. I clench my eyes shut and focus on what he's doing and how much I love the sting. My back bows and my hips rear back. His hand plunges between my tight legs, and he inserts two fingers into my pussy. I let out a loud moan at how good they feel against my tingling skin. My hips move on his fingers as pleasure spreads through my body. My mind starts to go blank.

"James ... fuck," I whisper. "Someone is going to hear us." Like most New York City apartments, my walls are paper-thin.

"Let them. I want to hear you anyway."

I panic for a second. "What time does your event end?"

"Don't worry. I've already checked the time. I'll be gone way before Natalie gets back."

I release a breath, and he spanks me again with his free hand, his fingers on the other still inside my pussy, and it only intensifies the experience. I whimper, biting into my bicep from the intense amount of ecstasy roaring through me. Something in my mind cloaks me like a blanket, and my thoughts shut off after the belt blows across my skin in rapid succession.

A sensual moan vibrates the back of my throat, and my body melts into the bed. I'm lax and feeling better than I have in a long time. My nipples are sensitive as they scrape along the material of the blanket beneath me. My entire body is glimmering from head to toe with something I've never experienced. I'm on the edge of something deeper and want more. Exhaling a long moan, I feel like I'm high on ecstasy.

"That's what I want to see," he says, sounding satisfied, and I like that he is. "Listen to the sound of my voice and focus on my hands."

James removes his fingers, and he spreads his hand, sliding it up my back. With his lips pressed to the small of my back, he kisses his way up my spine, his warm cock dragging along the crease of my ass. My pussy aches for him. He moves my hair to the side and exposes my neck, and then he slips his hands under my chest to cup my breasts and massage them. His teeth sink into my shoulder blade, and my body erupts with a need unlike no other.

I moan. "Mmm ... That feels good," I say, trying to turn into him. "James, please ..."

"Tell me what you need," he says, his breath hot near my ear. "Tell me." He twists my nipples, and I pull on the silk belt. The material digs into my wrists, and my flesh is alight with a demand to be taken.

"I need you inside me," I beg. I feel like I'm high.

"Say it again," he demands, twisting my nipples. My hips rear back in reckless desire.

"I want you to fuck me like a ruthless savage with no morals and little integrity, James. Is that better?"

In the blink of an eye, my hips are raised in the air. He gives me a few good smacks to my ass before he's surging inside until he's all the way in, and I yell out and clench my eyes shut.

"Fuck," James says, his voice tight, and I feel the same way. His fingers are pressing so hard into my skin, I know they'll leave marks.

"Ahhh ..." I groan. He's bigger than my other clients, and it hurts to be stretched like this. My inner thighs are trembling, shaking from the shock. James doesn't give me a chance to adjust to him, but instead takes me rough and hard.

"You'll get used to it," he responds.

My orgasm is already here, and I rock back into him. I'm not myself, but whoever I am, I want to feel like this again, because I feel desired and sexy and like I'm being cherished instead of the other way around for once.

"I knew you'd feel good. Should've fucked you the first chance I got."

He's plunging into me with harsh strokes that cause my orgasm to rise higher and faster. Reaching around, he finds my clit, and my body shakes from head to toe. All I want is to fly. He doesn't rub the sensitive ball of nerves. He pinches it so hard that a bright shock ricochets through me. My hips arch and my knees widen so I can take him deeper.

"More. Harder. James, fuck me harder," I plead, and he does.

"I'm not pulling out," he says. I hear the strain in his voice, like he spoke through his teeth. "I'm gonna cum inside you."

"You fucking better not," I respond, and he chuckles. We both know I'm on birth control thanks to Sanctuary Cove.

James starts biting parts of my back, and combined with the pressure between my legs, I can't hold back any longer as gratification explodes inside every one of my veins. I come harder than I think I ever have in my life. My body tingles from head to toe. I pull on the silk restraining my hands, trying to break free, but James has me locked in place, and it only heightens the eroticism.

"Come on my cock. That's it, sweetheart, give me your pussy," he says, and the sound of his voice sends me into overdrive. "Fuck. I can feel you coming," he groans, rubbing my clit now, and the sensation is too much.

"Oh, oh, oh," I purr. "I've never felt like this." I'm breathless and floating on cloud nine.

Just as I start to come down, James pulls out and flips me over, and then he's back inside and looming over me. He kisses me, my body pliant for him. Lifting my leg, I drive a heel into his ass.

"That's it, take all of me," he says, surging into me, and then he bites my breast.

Back arching, I gasp. "James, fuck." I grit my teeth.

But he doesn't stop, and I'm okay with that. His hands are everywhere, all over me, and where he's not touching me, he's kissing me like it's his last day on Earth. I can't concentrate, but I think that was his point. James just wanted me to let go and feel the moment, and when I'm pretty much flying, it's impossible to think of anything else.

"James, let go of my hands. I need to feel you."

But he doesn't untie me. He reaches up and laces his fingers with mine and kisses me deeply, passionately, while he fucks me like a savage. I can feel the pressure rising again, and my whole body is damp with intense ecstasy. I'm on the verge of something decadent. I don't know what's happening, but I'm in seventh heaven from the nirvana ripping through me.

"Let go," he says against my lips, and I know what he means.

A couple of slow, deep surges, and we're both coming together. His cock twitches inside my tender pussy, and he rolls his hips into my clit, making me squeeze my thighs around him. I can feel the warmth of his release seep out of me, coating my thighs.

His hips slow to a steady rhythm, and he kisses me softly. "Fuck me, I haven't come that hard in years."

I swallow and chuckle. "Wow. You really know how to whisper sweet nothings in a woman's ear after giving her the best dick ride in town."

Chapter 40

"You're grinning at me. Wipe that smug look off your face." It only makes his grin grow, and now I'm smiling. "I'm serious, wipe it off and untie me. I can't feel my fingers."

Leaning up, James is still hard inside me as he pulls the sash loose. "Don't move your arms. They're going to be stiff."

Carefully, he lifts one arm and massages my shoulder. I watch him, and he seems very focused on what he's doing and making sure I'm recuperating. I wasn't joking when I told him it was the best dick ride. It was. I had a feeling sex with him would feel good, I just didn't think it would be *that* good, especially for a man in his fifties. My body is lax. I feel like I took a Xanax and I'm ready to fall into a deep sleep. He moves his attention to my other arm.

"Do you take Viagra?"

He stops and looks offended. "What the fuck made you ask that?"

"How are you still hard?"

"I'm not that hard right now," he says.

My brows shoot up. "Yes, you are. I know a hard dick when I feel one."

"That's just how I am when I'm around you."

I laugh so hard I have to hold my stomach, and I clench around his cock.

"So you see me, and your cock just shoots up like a pole? Like, bing, and it's a rod? James, that's so ridiculous. Don't ever say that again. That's like saying my nipples get hard when I see you."

He watches me for a second then looks at my chest. I follow

his gaze. There are teeth marks everywhere. His thumb grazes over them softly, his brows angled deep.

"What's wrong?"

"You fell apart in my arms," he says quietly, studying me.

Heat fills my cheeks. I did fall apart in his arms, and it was the most intense thing I can say I ever felt in my life. The kind of sex we just had isn't normal. And it's the kind of sex I've been craving and just didn't know it. It's dangerous and freeing and easily addicting. We were burning in the flames together, responding to the other's body as we came alive. All outside noise was forgotten in that moment. We felt every touch, every kiss, every stroke, every thrust. It sealed our relationship, whether we wanted to acknowledge it or not.

"I did. I've never had that happen before. It's like you cherish a woman's body. It was ... overwhelming to say the least."

He looks at me. "I do. I love all women and everything about them. If I had it my way, I would end my day just like this every day."

I would too.

"You made me feel wanted ... desired."

James frowns. "You typically don't?"

I shrug, my chest feeling a little empty now that I'm admitting how I feel. "I'm a prostitute. Where's the desire in that? Yeah, I know I have a pretty face and I keep my body in shape, but the way you touched me, you made me feel like you actually do desire more than just a place to stick your dick. Sex is meaningless for me. It always has been. But tonight it was different, and it made me feel different." I pause, feeling embarrassed. "I probably don't make any sense. Feel free to tell me to shut up."

His frown deepens. "Sex should never be meaningless."

"It always has been for me."

He muses over my response. "Sex is how you connect with another person. It's where you see their vulnerabilities and insecurities, where you want to make them forget everything but remind them you're there for them. When you're both into each other and understand each other's minds, it's a deeper connection. It's how the intimacy grows."

James pulls out but leans down so he's lying on top of me. I smile up at him, my cheeks aching from my grin. He's a big man, but his weight is like a security blanket on me, smothering my anxiety.

I wrap my arms around his shoulders and wish I knew what it is about this man that settles that edgy feeling inside my body and quiets the thoughts and fears in my head. He's the best anti-anxiety medication there is.

"It's like you just knew what I needed," I say.

"Are you trying to say you had a meaningful *dick ride*?"

We both grin, trying not to laugh. "It made a difference to me. Is that stupid?"

"No, it's not. How you feel should never be stupid, Aubrey. What I did with you tonight"—he looks away and pauses for a moment—"it's something my wife doesn't let me do. She doesn't let me spank her or tie her up. I definitely can't bite her and fuck her as rough as I did you. That only touches on the things I want, and need, but I never get. I have needs too. I have to be able to release the weight of my day, and when I can't, all it does is build up inside me. The pressure makes me tense, like a ticking time bomb. So I seek out women who will allow me to control them for a little bit, ones who won't call me a freak the way Katherine does."

My brows shoot up. "She called you a freak?"

He nods, and my heart breaks a little. Now it's my turn to frown.

It's never crossed my mind to call someone a name for their personal preferences, and it bothers me that the one person who should always have his side is the one who ostracizes him. What people do behind closed doors is none of my business, and I would never make them feel like shit for it. What I find gratification in, someone else might not, and I'm okay with that. It's what makes us all so interesting.

"The way you were tonight, I honestly can't imagine you any other way. You're definitely not the type to just lie there and take it, but I don't think you're a freak for that either."

"I can do that though, if that's what you need," he responds quickly.

Why did those words penetrate my soul? I know why. My gaze drops to his lips, and my heart softens for him. I gave him what he needed, so he'd do anything I want in return for that.

"It's called compromise, but a lot of people don't have that word in their vocabulary. It's all I do with her—compromise—and it fucks me in the ass."

"You watched me fuck your friend. I definitely don't think you're a freak, James." I chuckle softly. "I thought it was kind of hot actually."

His eyes darken, desire swirling in the depths. His jaw flexes. "Do you have any idea how much control that night required? Practicing control only heightens the pleasure, but that night almost broke me."

He licks his lips, and I have the urge to kiss him now. I want to, but I don't know if I should. I don't really know what this arrangement between us means actually. Do I wait for him to tell me what to do? Or do I just take the initiative?

"What are you thinking about?"

I swallow and tell him the truth. "I want to kiss you, but I don't really know if I should or not. I don't know what our deal means, what it entails, what I should or shouldn't do. I feel a little lost right now."

"Aubrey?"

"Hmm?"

"I know this makes me a heartless piece of shit, but my wife and I have an agreement. It's one of the only times we've really agreed on anything. To make the marriage work, she told me to fulfill my needs somewhere else. Keep it discreet and never bring it home. It killed me when she said that, because to me it shows she really doesn't care that I've done everything I can to make her happy and she won't do the same for me. So, I fuck random women. But with you, and our deal, I don't want you to ever hold back. So fucking kiss me like you really want to and do it whenever you want."

I blink, taken aback by this news. "Wait. She's okay with you being with other women?"

He scoffs. "No, she fucking hates it."

"Is she with other men?"

"I don't ask, but I don't think so."

"Then why are you married?" He doesn't answer, so I continue. "I love sex, and I get the feeling you do too, but how does that work when you don't mesh with your spouse? I would definitely go all Lorena Bobbitt on you if I were her, but then again, I don't think I could marry someone who has no interest in the things I like. It's hard to connect when two people don't like the same things, you know?"

He huffs. "Yeah, I do know, and I hate it. So when you want something, you tell me. When you want to touch me or kiss me, or fuck me, do it. Those are the rules."

My palm roams his naked backside. "You do have a nice ass for a man your age."

He raises his brows and grins. My cell phone chimes and James moves off me so I can reach for it. He sits up, and I stare at him while he picks up his pants. I grab my cell phone and see Natalie's name flash across the screen. I sit up against my headboard and cover my chest with the sheet.

My heart drops, and James takes in my face. I feel sick to my stomach as I text her back.

Quietly I say, "Natalie texted me. She's on her way back."

James slips his shirt on, his movements carefree like he isn't worried. Meanwhile, I'm a little terrified we're going to get caught. I study the lines around his eyes and see he's deep in thought. He fastens a few buttons then leans over and drops a kiss to my forehead. His tattooed chest is exposed, and he's looking damn good just like this.

"Don't worry. She won't see me leave, and she'll never find out."

I never say never.

Before he can pull back, I grab his collar and kiss him like I wanted to before. I rise to my knees and clutch his shirt tightly in my fists and press my lips to his. His arms automatically wind around my back, and one of his hands grips my ass. The way he grabs me makes my heart pound. I don't know what I'm doing or why, and I know I should run and tear up the check, but there's something about James that I'm not ready to let go of yet. He creates this fluttering in my chest every single fucking time we're together.

Breaking the kiss, I ask, "Why me? Why push for me when you can have any girl at Sanctuary?"

He brushes my hair off my shoulder and tips my chin up. As he looks into my eyes, I have to wonder if he's certifiably insane to attempt this thing between us.

"You have a backbone. You're sassy. You're smart. You're fucking gorgeous. You're resilient, and you'll do any kind of work to make a life for yourself. You're not ashamed, and you don't seem to give two fucks what someone thinks of you. Plus, I like the way your mind works." The way his voice washes over me like silk makes me hang on to every word he says. "I gravitated toward you in spite of all that. Katherine is the opposite. She's gentle, soft, and easy to walk over. You give me something to work with. I don't fuck with my coworkers, and the other girls I've been with 'yes' me to death. Fucking boring."

Licking my lips, I drop my gaze to his mouth, but he doesn't let me look away.

"Nope. Look at me."

I do. James kisses me one last time, and it settles my mind and eases the apprehension ruffling through me.

"I have a dinner coming up that I want you to come with me to. It's a cocktail thing for two merging companies."

"A work event?"

He nods. "If I have to suffer through it, I want you there with me."

My brows furrow. "People will know I'm not your wife, though. Aren't you worried?"

"Not in the least. Half of them aren't faithful, and my wife doesn't attend the events anyway."

I feel only a little relieved. I'm not sure why, when in the past I had no issue taking jobs like this from Christine. This shouldn't be any different, but it feels that way.

"When I call you, I expect you to be there. No excuses."

I swallow. The nervousness clenching around my shoulders creates unwanted tension.

"Get rid of the boyfriend who probably only does thirty seconds of damage to your pussy. He's not negotiable. Is that clear? You should also tell Christine you're taking a break. I want you to be exclusively mine."

Irritation simmers in my veins. My eyes lower. I'm not quitting my job for an entire year. He gets Valentina. Not Aubrey.

"James, one thing you need to understand outside of the bedroom is that I don't like being controlled or told what to do. I make my own choices. The only time you get to tell me what to do is when I'm Valentina or your cock is inside me. Deal?"

His eyes darken, and I can feel the rumble in his chest vibrate against mine. "We'll see about that."

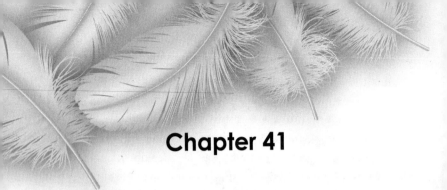

Chapter 41

"Is it summer yet?" Natalie asks dramatically. "This snow is starting to make me feel suicidal."

Every year, I swear the winter gets longer and colder. Still, I'd take it over the heat any day.

I glance out our small apartment window at the gray skies. It's been snowing for three hours straight, and I find it so peaceful to just sit and stare at it, which is what I've been doing. It clears my mind.

"I love it."

She throws a pillow at me. "Let's plan a trip to the Bahamas."

"When? We have school right now."

"We can go for the weekend. We'll leave after classes Friday and come back late Sunday. Just us. We can drink fruity drinks from a coconut and sit on the beach and do nothing. The conch there is fresh and the best. I love it, especially when it's fried."

"We know you love *conch*," I joke.

As much as I love the idea, it's not something I can do right now. Not after the deal I made with James last weekend. I haven't seen him or spoken to him since that night, and I'm not sure how to feel about that. While I'm kind of glad I haven't, he's been on my mind, and I can't help but wonder what he's doing right now or where he is.

I glance toward Natalie as she scrolls through her phone. Her legs are hanging over the arm rest of the couch, her UGG boots dangling while she lies on her back. Being in the same room with her these days has been difficult. I find it hard to look at her, hard to talk to her, hard to just sit next to her without feeling insanely guilty. The pressure in my chest steadily grows, like a giant divide that's trying to put distance between us. I can feel myself trying to pull away. I've contemplated countless times this week telling James this isn't going to work, but I know deep down that I won't. I have him—really have him this time—and I'm not ready to let go.

I sigh inwardly, exhausted with my thoughts. The snow is getting heavier and falling faster, holding me in a daze. Going to my classes has been the only time that's allowed me a moment of reprieve from my shame. I've immersed myself in homework. School has been more like a lifeline lately, until we got the notice that classes were canceled due to the impending snowstorm. Now I feel trapped and paranoid again, the guilt is eating away at me.

Natalie came home about an hour after James had left. She'd tried to talk to me, but I pretended I was sleeping. I couldn't look at her after what I'd done, not when I still felt her father's cum seeping out of me. For days now I've acted like I'm insanely busy with work and school when I'm not. I'm getting paranoid thinking I've made it obvious I'm avoiding her.

I'm not sure the mind fuck is worth the money.

Oh, who am I kidding? My dignity, and my sanity, is obviously worth twenty million dollars.

"What do you say? Wanna hop on a plane and hit the surf? We can fly first class and get drunk on mimosas then plant our asses in the pink sand and soak up the sun."

"I don't know ... I have a bunch of jobs coming up I already agreed to. Maybe we can plan something for the summer when we have more time."

She groans. "I'm going to join Bumble just to find me a new bestie because you're fucking lame."

I smile, knowing she's just being dramatic. Her cell phone rings, and I hear her greet her mom when she answers it. My face falls, my stomach tightening when I hear her voice on the other end.

Standing up, I walk into my room. I have a lunch date with Daniel that I need to get ready for, but first I'm stopping by Grammy's house to make sure she's stocked with necessities for the blizzard. I told her I would stay with her until the storm rides through, but she told me to stop babying her and that she has her cats.

Changing out of my clothes, I can hear Natalie talking to her mom. I don't want to eavesdrop, so I close the door, but her voice carries. I can hear the urgency in her tone.

"No, Mom, I'm sure there's a reasonable explanation for why Dad's acting like a dick. He must be on his period, because a few days ago you were going on and on about how wonderful he's been." She pauses, probably to listen to her mom vent. "I don't know why you're surprised. This sort of thing happens often with you guys, but just like those other times, it'll smooth out like it always does in a day or so." She sighs. "Yeah, I know, but you guys haven't come this far for nothing. What happened with counseling? Are you guys still going?" She pauses again. "Oh, good. Maybe you guys just need a vacation ..."

I don't want to listen to anymore, so I put on a playlist and get changed. Once I'm done and bundled up, ready to brave the snow, I step into the living room.

"Where are you going?" she asks.

"We're supposed to get eighteen inches of snow tonight. I have to make sure Grammy is taken care of, and then I'm going to Daniel's. He's been bugging me to come by all week."

Now more than ever I need to break up with him.

"I'll take eighteen inches and some snow right now." Her eyes twinkle, but there's no light in them.

"Everything okay?" I ask.

Natalie chews her lip as she looks back at her blank phone screen and stares at it. "Yeah, you know, all parents argue.

They're always up and down, but that's also because they're polar opposites."

"They say opposites attract," I offer, and she nods, though a sad smile fills her face. I'm not sure why I even said that. I guess to ease Natalie's worry, but maybe more so to feel a little better about myself.

***

"Grammy, I don't like the way you're looking. You're really pale," I say, studying her face. "You're basically translucent."

"Sweetie, I don't leave the house when it gets cold out," she responds, trying to make me believe her, but something is up, I can feel it in my gut. Unless it's the guilt still eating away at me, which it could definitely be. "Of course I'm going to look like a ghost."

"All right, well, eat that lunch while I unpack the car."

After taking the train and bus to her house, I borrowed Grammy's car to go stock up on the snowstorm essentials I knew she wouldn't have. She always assumes the storms won't be bad, but I don't like for her to risk it, especially at her age. Luckily I went when I did. It was slim pickings, but I got precut wood for her fireplace in case the electricity goes out, water, a loaf of bread, and a few cabinet staples. I even set up a company to come shovel the driveway and around her car.

"How is school going?" she asks once I put everything away.

"It's going. Only a couple of months left until I'm free like a bird and can fly around the world."

She's petting her cat lovingly, her voice soft as she speaks. "I'm counting down the days until I get to see you get that diploma you worked so hard for." Her chin quivers, and my smile slips.

Whenever there's a milestone in my life, she gets emotional, wishing my parents were here. I lift my hand, my fingers grazing over my mother's necklace I remove only when I go on a job.

"Have you figured out what you want to do with it yet?"

"Does anyone know what they want to do with their life?" I say, and Grammy just smiles. "I'm thinking I might move back in with you."

It's more of a joke. I don't need to move back in with her with the money I have now, but I would if she needed me.

"You know you can always come back here until you find the right job. I don't want you to do something that doesn't make you happy just to do it. Life is short, but it's a long one too. You should do what you love. This will always be your home, and I would never turn you away."

Exhaling a heavy sigh, I tell her what's on my mind. "I don't know what to do, Grams. I feel like I suddenly have to make this big choice, and I don't know which door I should open. Do I do what my heart is telling me to, or do I use my head and make the choice that's smarter? Take the path that will set me up with a good job and one I can supposedly be proud of that will make me money? I feel like I have one chance, and I don't want to mess up."

I tell Grammy about my idea for the nonprofit I want to open for women and children. She seems to love it and makes small talk about the times we volunteered over the years. Grammy starts coughing and reaches over the table and plucks a tissue to cover her mouth. The cough strengthens, like it's deep in her lungs. The sounds she's making worry me, and I rush to the kitchen to get her a glass of water.

"Are you okay?" I ask once her coughing subsides. She sips the water slowly, and I look at her with concern.

She points to her throat. "My babies shed so bad. I think a piece of cat hair tickled my throat. Every once in a while that happens, and it sounds like I'm hacking up a lung. Thank you for the water."

I grimace, my mouth twisted up.

"Cat hair doesn't cause a wet cough, though, or for you to

cough as long as you did."

She glares at me. "Are you suddenly a doctor?"

I flatten my lips. "No."

"A vet?"

I don't answer her.

"Then leave it be. I had a tickle in my throat. That's all."

I bite the side of my lip. "I can't help that I worry about you."

"It's not your job to worry about me. Now listen," she says, petting the cat in her lap a little too aggressively now. "Do titles mean anything to you?"

My head angles to the side. "What do you mean?"

"For instance, is it important for you to be able to say that you're a CEO, or a doctor, or a director of some company?"

"No, not really."

"Would it make you happy?"

"I don't think so?"

"What if it could guarantee to make you wealthy?"

"Well, money does make the world go round, so I say yes."

"But is money worth sacrificing your happiness and your future for a job that has the potential to make you miserable, one you despise having to wake up and go to every day?"

I counter her. "What if I learn to love my money-making, amazing job title?"

"What if you don't learn to love it? What if you spend years wishing you had opened your nonprofit instead?"

I consider her questions and realize I'm in a bigger jam than I thought. I don't want to be unhappy—no one does—but I want security.

I shift on the couch, a little uncomfortable under her unyielding gaze. I wonder when I became obsessed with making money. I feel a little blindsided by it. Financial security has always been my ultimate goal, and now that I have it, I don't see myself stopping. Natalie was right. The escorting world is addicting once the cash starts to flow in. I want as much money as I can get.

"Honestly, it's a tough one. I don't care about the title, but money comes with a good job title anyway. And isn't that why everyone goes to school, to get the best job they can? To live a comfortable life without worry? To travel the world and buy a house in the boring suburbs and have two-point-five kids one day?"

"Aubrey," she says, a little disappointed. "If you aren't happy in the end with your decision, how will any of that bring you happiness? Because it's what you're supposed to do? Says who? I'll never tell you not to do something, and I won't make the choice for you, but I hope you sit down and really think about what you want and make the right decision for yourself and no one else. Lord knows we didn't have a lot over the years, but I had a job I loved, and even though you had so little, you didn't know any better and were always smiling. People think they need money to make them happy, but what people forget is that we create our own happiness. Whether you have ten dollars or a hundred, that happiness is still created inside you."

I exhale a stressed breath, feeling so overwhelmed. " I want to open a nonprofit. I feel like in my heart, it's the right thing to do."

"You're your own boss right now. Do what you feel is right. Patience and trust in yourself are what'll give you happiness and a place where you want to be, and that's something you can be proud of in the end. If you focus on good things, good things will come to you. I know it might not seem like that right now, or maybe when you were younger, but life has a way of working out the way it's supposed to. You'll see."

Leaning over, I give Grammy a long hug. She feels cold even with the layers of clothes. I reach for the blanket behind me to drape over her shoulders, and then cuddle up to her. She pats the side of my head lovingly. Her fingers are icy, but I nestle closer to her anyway. The tightness in my chest feels a little lighter sitting next to Grammy.

"Since when did you become so wise?" I ask, watching her pet the little fur ball on her lap.

"It comes with age, my dear. One day you'll understand."

Chapter 42

"Are you going to stay over? I'd love for you to stay for once," Daniel says, his finger dragging lazily down my arm.

For once. I grimace inwardly, thankful he can't see my face. He wraps an arm around my waist, holding me to him. Daniel nestles closer to my back. I never stay over, no matter how many times he's asked me. I feel bad, but I like my privacy. While I should stay over sometime soon, it won't be during a damn blizzard, where I'll be trapped.

"Maybe next time I will when I'm a little more prepared," I lie, kind of.

"What's this from?"

I lift my head and look down at my arm.

Fuck. A bruise from James.

I'd purposely stayed away from Daniel this week, telling him I had my nanny job. James had left teeth imprints on my breasts and back, which resulted in little bruises. I smiled every time I saw them. Most of the marks and discoloration are gone, but I guess this one needed a little more healing time than the others.

My body warms, thinking about what his teeth had done to me, how he'd made the pleasure intensify when he bit down and surged inside me simultaneously. I squeeze my thighs together, pushing back the desire that's finally climbing. God, what's wrong with me? I couldn't even get off when I had sex with my boyfriend, yet here I am wet and ready at just the thought of James.

"Huh. I must've walked into a door or something."

"Or one of the kids you babysit bit you."

"What do you mean?" I frown and look harder. Oh my God. There's an obvious mouth imprint.

I decide to shrug it off and act blasé. "Oh, I wouldn't be surprised if that's what happened. I've told you the kids are little fucking monsters."

"Maybe the parents should have the kids tested to see if there's a learning disability there."

I turn over to face Daniel. "They're just kids. I wouldn't think anything of it."

"Some kids can't express themselves and bite to get the frustration out, which can lead to more behavioral issues."

"There are no behavioral issues." I feel defensive over the fake kids for some asinine reason. "And honestly, how many kids can express themselves at two years old? They're normal little monsters. If I were their parent, I wouldn't worry. Maybe if they were seven I would, but two? Come on. It's not like they walk around just chomping on people."

His eyes harden like I offended him. "I'm a doctor, Aubrey. I see things like this all the time. They need to be evaluated. You should take the issue to the parents."

I'm a doctor. Ugh. Gag me.

I swear Daniel wasn't like this when I first met him, but I feel like lately he's been showing this closeted, loftier side the more comfortable he gets. I can't fucking stand when people walk around announcing what they do for a living, as if they should be held to a higher standard than normal folks like myself. He's acting like a know-it-all.

Plastering on a cheesy smile, I roll him onto his back and drop a kiss to his lips. "I'll bring it up to the parents for you, but I don't want to talk about it anymore."

Internally, I'm cursing James for that bite mark. This is so ridiculous, but since I live a lie when I'm with Daniel, I guess it's par for the course. Sadly.

Daniel holds the back of my head and guides my lips to him. My hair falls around us as he says, "Thank you," and kisses me. "Sometimes the physician in me comes out, and I don't mean for it to."

The candor in his voice relaxes the tension in my neck, washing away the sour taste in my mouth. I can tell he means it, and now I'm wondering if I'm just projecting because my guilty conscience is making me edgy. I'm finding fault in things that probably don't need to be looked at.

Sitting up, I straddle his hips and the sheet slides down my back. I grab his hands and place them on my breasts, wanting to feel him. He gives me a tender squeeze, and I lean into his palms.

His eyes lower, teeth digging into his bottom lip, and his hands move to grip my hips. "If I didn't know any better, I'd say you love sex. Are maybe even addicted to it."

I rock my hips insanely slow, dragging my pussy over his hardening length a few times so he feels that I'm wet and ready.

"Is that your diagnosis, doctor?" I say, slipping into my Valentina voice.

"I love when you ride me," he groans, and I purposely pull my hips back to capture the tip of his cock and push my swollen sex over his length. His jaw flexes, nostrils flare. I can tell he really does love it. "I want you to turn around and sit on my cock like that."

A sigh escapes my throat at the thought.

"Stay the night."

I tilt my head to the side. "Daniel ..." I say softly.

He sits up and presses his chest to mine. Wrapping his arms around my shoulders, he says, "Stay with me, and I'll do anything you want. I want to wake up with you in my arms, Aubrey. Stay the night, please."

"What if we get snowed in for three days and you want me to leave but I can't?"

"Won't happen," he says. "I've been asking you to stay for a while now."

"I like to sleep naked."

"No complaints here. Next."

"I snore."

"I know you're lying. Next."

"I kick when I sleep."

"I'll kick you back."

My head falls back, and I start laughing. Daniel presses his mouth to my neck and places sweet kisses down the column to my shoulder. My laughter changes into a hum.

"Is that a yes?" he asks, his voice deep.

I hesitate for a long moment. "You're going to regret it."

"Somehow I doubt that," he says then reaches between us and enters me in one swift motion.

This time, I climax.

***

"Aub? Where the hell have you been?" Natalie says the moment I walk into our apartment two days later.

Throwing my keys onto the table, I give her an apologetic look as I place my purse down and tug my coat off.

"I'm sorry. My cell died, and Daniel has a lame Samsung. I didn't have a charger, and I wasn't going out to buy one in the crazy weather."

Her jaw drops, eyes widening. "I almost put out an Amber Alert on your dumb ass. Why didn't you call me from his phone?"

I give her a droll stare. "I did. You didn't answer."

"No, you didn't."

"I did," I say. "I called the night I decided to stay."

Natalie picks up her cell phone and scans it. Shaking her head, she says, "You're crazy. I don't have a missed call from you."

I frown, thinking back to that night and how drunk we'd

gotten. My face twists up into a smirk of embarrassment.

"I wonder who I called, then, because someone got a drunk message from me, and apparently it wasn't you."

She shakes her head and grins. "You got a special delivery. Some package."

"I did?"

"I put it in your bedroom."

We both walk into my room, and there's a big white box with a satin bow wrapped around it. I'm dumbfounded, wondering where it came from.

Pulling off the lid of the box, I place it on the bed and find a card lying on top of the black tissue paper.

"Oh, so seductive," Natalie says, her voice animated.

I take the card out and read it with Natalie leaning over my shoulder.

A limo will pick you up at 8 p.m. on Saturday. Looking forward to seeing you again. Expect to stay the night with me. Until Saturday, sweetheart.

A knot forms in my throat. My stomach plunges to the ground. I instantly feel sick.

James.

Thank God he didn't sign it.

"Who's it from?"

"Ah, Daniel. No wonder he pushed to have me sleep at his place. He must've wanted to surprise me," I lie through my teeth. "He mentioned some dinner event for his work." Not necessarily a lie.

I place the card on the bed, move the tissue around, and pull out another box. Inside there's a pair of sky-high rose gold pumps that shimmer against the window light. They're classy and scream sex rolled into one.

"Red bottoms. Nice, so he's got taste. What else is in there?"

There's another box, this one a little heavier, and I already know what it is. Flipping the top back, there's a matching strapless cocktail dress covered in rhinestones.

"Wow."

I pick it up and hold it to my body. I glance down. It's heavier than it looks, but small, and I don't know if my boobs will fit inside. It's just as gorgeous as the shoes. I can't wait to try it on.

"Okay. What kind of money does Danny boy make? Because that's a Badgley Mischka dress, and not off the rack either."

"You can tell that at first glance?"

"Oh, yeah." Her eyes drop to the black tissue. "Oh hey, there's another box."

"Take it out and open it," I tell her, holding on to the dress still.

Natalie does, and we both gasp at the glittering jewels inside. Dainty diamond teardrop earrings that will complement the dress perfectly, along with a slender ring. Leaning over, Natalie looks inside the box and riffles through some more then turns around and walks out without saying anything.

Fuck. My. Life.

The next time I see James, I'm going to have to set some boundaries, like not sending gifts to the apartment I share with his daughter, regardless if they're anonymous or not. I feel nauseated. Even though I know this gift is for the event he mentioned, I can't live on eggshells, worrying if he'll try something like this again.

"Here. You're going to need this," Natalie says, storming back into my room with her hand out. She's holding her favorite beige Chanel clutch. A vintage she paid an exorbitant amount of money for.

"Oh, Nat, I can't."

She shoves it at me. "Nope. Take it. You need a purse, and this one will complete your outfit. Trust me."

Hesitantly, I take it and thank her. A tightness spreads throughout my chest from the guilt consuming me. I try to take small, inconspicuous breaths so she doesn't notice the panic attack rising inside me. There's a throbbing on the side of my head near my temple, and I'm terrified I'm going to break.

Natalie clucks her tongue in approval.

"I don't know what you're doing to keep Danny happy, but whatever it is, keep doing it. That dress is going to look stellar on you. Oh! Let's do natural makeup. Does he like your hair up or down?" When I don't respond, she leans around to look at me and says, "What's wrong?"

I shake it off, eyeing the bounty. "Nothing. I'm just surprised is all. Down. He likes my hair down," I say quietly.

"Perfect. We'll do loose, wavy curls. When he sees you, he's not going to be able to take his hands off you."

Natalie squeals. She's so eager. If I was in a better mood, I would've made fun of her for it, but I'm not.

"I'm so excited for you! I bet he fucks you senseless in the limo before you even get there." She rolls her eyes and fans herself. "So hot."

Natalie elbows me, and I offer her a timid smile. I'm too ashamed to look at her.

If she only knew she was actually talking about her dad.

Chapter 43

My fingers are jittery, fucking butterflies wreaking havoc in my stomach, and no matter how many times I told Natalie I didn't need her help, she insisted on being there.

I have to give it to her ... She made me look absolutely stunning. Ethereal, almost.

I'm a filthy fucking piece of shit best friend.

I should've taken a shot before I left, but I knew James would want to have a few drinks, so I held off. But, dear God, my nerves are fraying at the ends right now. I've done this sort of thing many times before with other married men, so technically it's nothing new for me. I shouldn't be this worked up, but I am. Worse than ever.

I have a plan, though. First, I'm going to give him a piece of my mind. Second, I know he's going to want sex, and while I'm cool with that, I won't allow myself to orgasm. I'm not going to tell him either, I'll just have to fake it. If I wasn't attracted to him the way I am, then it wouldn't be an issue for me to come. But I am, and that only complicates things. Sex creates this sense of euphoria in me. This addicting desire I want to chase. I'm terrified of getting attached to that feeling and him. Add emotion to the equation, and it's a recipe for disaster and not something I'm interested in cleaning up.

Exhaling a deep breath, I step inside the swanky bar and glance around. There are mostly couples here, but I can see a few single patrons. The conversation is low, intimate, and I feel the pull to James before I look for him.

Our eyes meet and my lips part. All the air leaves my lungs. My heart thumps at the sight of him leaning against the bar on his elbow looking fine as hell.

Jesus hates me. I swear he must've been like "let's test her principles tonight", because the way James is looking makes me forget my plan. The floozy in me is coming out, and for a second, I let her spread her legs.

I've seen him in a suit before, but this one is all black, including the shirt and tie. My gaze openly rakes the length of his muscular body, instant thirst consuming me. The way this man is looking makes me want to get lost in him for hours. I want to climb him like a tree and dig my claws into him. His salt-and-pepper hair is brushed back, giving him a polished look, but it's his gaze that reduces me to a stationary object. All I can focus on are his searing blue eyes and the way he's stroking his beard while he stares at me, like he wants to devour me in front of everyone.

James Riviera is the definition of sex.

He subtly crooks two fingers at me to come hither, and I all but drop to my knees and crawl to him.

Someone's obnoxious laugh knocks some sense into me. I start walking toward him on steady legs, telling myself I'm Valentina right now, and that's what he's going to call me.

"Sweetheart," he whispers in my ear, his arm going around my back. His breath is hot, and it tickles my neck. "You're fucking killing me in that dress right now. Exactly what I'd imagined you'd look like." Tipping my chin up with two fingers, he drops a soft kiss to my lips, and my eyes flutter shut. "Your legs and those shoes are going to look sensational wrapped around my hips. Tonight, I'm fucking you against the window—from behind—and maybe against the wall, or in front of a mirror, with those shoes."

"I love when you talk dirty to me," I say, my voice husky.

A smirk starts to form on his face, but it stops when he sees that I'm shooting daggers at him.

"But, James, let's get one thing straight—never, ever, have anything delivered to my place again. You know, where I live with your daughter? You're a fucking dickhead for that one."

I reach for his glass—probably another favorite obnoxiously priced cognac—and drink the entire thing. He just raises his hand and waves two fingers at the bartender, then looks back at me. He's too suave for his own good.

"Do you know that she stood right next to me as I opened the gift? Yeah, she did. And she insisted she wanted to help me get ready, which she did, thank you very much. All I could think about is what a shit friend I am that she's helping me get ready to see her fucking father. What else could I tell her? That it's from a client? Then I would have to explain what that—"

James slams his mouth to mine in a hard kiss, grabbing the back of my head and clutching my hip. He doesn't ask, just takes, and slips his tongue into my mouth, stroking me the right way, enough to make me forget just for a second that I'm aggravated with him.

I can taste the alcohol on his tongue, and I kiss him back with the same drive.

"Does she know?" he asks, pulling back.

I blink rapidly and stare up through my voluminous lash extensions. "No, obviously. She'd murder me if she found out."

James slides a drink my way, then picks his up and sips, watching me. "Then that's all that matters. Let it go." My nostrils flare, and he sees it. "I won't do it again," he adds.

I frown. "Really?"

"Yeah. I'm too old for games, and I don't do miscommunication. You want to talk it out? Let's do it. The makeup sex will be that much sweeter."

I grimace and shake my head, trying not to grin. I wish he didn't make my heart race for him. "I should've expected that."

"I wasn't thinking. I should've been, but I just had this vision of you, and it's all I could see." He eyes my body, and God, I love the way he looks at me. "You really do look incredible."

"You look pretty dashing yourself. My first thought was I wanted to climb you like a tree," I say casually, like I'm talking about the weather. I sip my drink.

James laughs. I can tell he likes when I say things like that to him. "I clean up well," he jokes. Licking his lips, he says, "I figured we'd meet here before the event and go over a few things."

"Good idea. I have a request too."

He puts his hand out, encouraging me to go first.

"Only call me Valentina. Please, don't call me Aubrey."

He frowns. "In general or just tonight?"

"Well, I would prefer in general, but definitely if we're out somewhere."

His brows lower. James seems offended, but I try not to make anything of it. There's no need to make it personal.

"What else?" he asks tightly.

I purse my lips together. "I can't think of anything right now. It was just the package at my apartment and the name thing."

"Did you break up with the boyfriend?" he asks.

"What boyfriend?" I respond.

He nods and reaches for my hand. My heart kicks up a notch when he laces our fingers together and gently tugs me closer. I really need to dump Daniel. I don't know what's holding me back.

"No one is going to question you. It's just like the first time we met."

I nod quietly. I know he's right.

"You'd be surprised how many people don't bring their spouses to events, including women. They're just as bad."

I reel back, a little bothered. It's sad how easy people cheat.

"Is anyone faithful these days? God."

"Being in a committed relationship is more than rainbows and butterflies. It takes more work than people expect. Communication and compromise is where it's at, but no one realizes that until it's too late."

Damn. He has a point.

"How depressing. Thank God I never plan to marry."

His brows bunch together. "Really?"

"Ah, yeah. Just based on my line of work and what I've seen, I'd rather be single forever."

"Until you find that one person who just gets you in every aspect of your relationship. That's when it'll be worth it."

"What else?" I ask, needing to move on. I highly doubt I'll be able to find a two-in-one man after all the men I've been with and one who is okay with what I do. It sounds like a pipe dream and not something I want to focus on because it'll just make me depressed. Not that I ever planned to get married, as I'd said, but I would never lie to my spouse about my past either. With my luck, one of my clients would end up being a brother—or father—to my imaginary husband.

The bartender asks if we'd like another drink, and James declines. We leave the bar and make our way to the elevator.

"I would never censor you, but please try to refrain from talking about the size of my cock this time, if you can."

I blush and briefly roll my lips between my teeth. "He had it coming."

"Val," he warns.

"He did!"

James just stares. I can see the laughter in his eyes, but he holds steady, and I concede.

"I make no promises, but I'll try not to say anything." As we step into the elevator and the doors close, I can't help myself. "I wasn't wrong, though. You are hung like a stallion and fuck like a beast." I laugh, and so does he.

***

Three hours of making small talk with his coworkers, and James has hardly left my side. We've been upstairs in a small, intimate private room that overlooks the city. Floor-to-ceiling windows, this one-of-a-kind skyscraper view is something I've always wanted to experience. I find myself gazing out the window while James talks. Every so often he gives me a little tug, and I smile at him. There's an open bar, and the display of towering hors d'oeuvres is picture perfect. James keeps offering to get me food, but I'm rarely hungry on jobs, something I keep reminding myself I'm on. I think it's the nerves that just get to me, and even though I'm a little more relaxed now, my stomach is a mess.

James gives me a little squeeze. His arm has been wrapped around my back with his hand resting on my hip the entire time, like he doesn't want anyone to steal me away. His possessiveness is appealing, and I blush when he drops kisses to my temple. He's even included me in conversations, something my other clients rarely do. I'm to be seen, not heard, a few have told me. The conversations are a drag. Talk about politics and who's positioning for partner, who closed which case and how much money a firm made, who was arrested for embezzlement and fraud. So much schmoozing and ass kissing that I have to wonder if they recognize it for what it is ... Ladder climbing. It's boring as hell, but I remind myself that for ten million dollars, I'll make it look like I'm eating out of the palm of their hands.

After all, money talks.

No one has talked down to me like when Philip did, which is a plus. It's something I worry about when I go out on jobs because I'll want to defend myself when I can't. I guess that's what the booze and pills are for, to relax me so I don't say something I'll regret. Funny enough, though, it's not usually the men who say anything. They just look at my client with envy. It's the women who are the worst.

Like this one woman who hasn't been able to take her eyes

off James. I'm not jealous. I'm secure and confident in my skin, but she's grating on my nerves because she's clearly eye fucking him. He's looked at her a few times.

"Thank you for coming with me tonight," he says, looking down at me. He turns me to face him so we're chest to chest, and his hands dance down my waist and swoop over my lower back. "You've made it bearable. I hate these things, but it's a must for work, you know? Keeping face is why I am where I am. No one is going to take what I have or try to one-up me."

I smile pleasantly at him, my hands flat on his chest. "It wasn't as bad, but James? If you look at that woman in the hideous yellow frock one more time, I'm going to bite your dick when it's in my mouth tonight," I say, my voice sugary sweet. I pat his chest and flutter my lashes through the knives I'm throwing at him. "Understand?"

Amusement dances in his eyes, and I can see the grin behind the beard. He's smiling, but I'm not playing. I don't know where this is coming from, because it's not usually me, but with the way he looks tonight, I want to plaster myself all over him and tell everyone he's mine.

But that's the thing. He's not mine, so I don't know why I even said anything. I'm annoyed with myself and wish I hadn't spoken up, but I just hate the way she's looking at him.

Cupping my jaw, he pulls my mouth to his. I gasp right before his lips slant over mine, and I lean into him. He kisses me slow, deep, showing me that I'm all he wants, and he does it in a public setting.

"Valentina?" he says against my lips.

"Hmm?"

"Shut the hell up."

I nod and chuckle. "I'm just saying, if you want her instead tonight, I saw a hot waiter I wouldn't mind screwing in the kitchen."

James leans down and grabs my bottom lip between his teeth, tugging it hard before he kisses me again. I draw in a breath as his tongue erotically circles mine. I get lost in his strokes. A throb resonates between my legs, and my heart rate kicks up a notch. I love and hate the way he kisses me. He knows exactly how to silence my moronic thoughts and get to me.

"You want that little fuck?" he asks, shrugging nonchalantly.

James is possessive. He's as confident as I am, and fuck, it's a turn-on.

"Bring him to our room, and I'll show him how a man handles a woman like you. I guarantee you won't be saying his name by the end of the night. You both will be calling me Daddy."

Chapter 44

I laugh so hard my stomach hurts. His grin sends a current of happiness though my veins. I love this back-and-forth banter we have. It's hot and exciting and fun. It's too easy for us—natural—and kind of addicting.

"I'll get us another drink. Let's circle the room, and then we'll head out," he says. "I'm dying to get you out of that dress."

"Whatever you want, *Daddy*," I say in my Valentina voice.

His eyes widen. "I see that look in your eyes. Don't even think about calling me Daddy in front of anyone."

I grin so big my cheeks hurt. "You take the fun out of everything. First no big dick talk, now this? What shall I ever do?"

"Sorry to interrupt, James," a man says next to us. "Mind if I have a word? There's a matter I'd like to discuss with you."

James looks at me, and I tell him I'll get us our drinks and see him in a few.

While I wait on the bartender, I take a seat on an open stool and pull out my cell phone and quickly check my messages. They're all from Daniel. He wanted to see me tonight, but I told him I was doing an overnight nanny job and wouldn't be back for two days. I won't be gone for two days, but I know I'll need a day to recover. He wasn't thrilled, going as far as making a nasty comment about the parents, but I ignored it. I feel bad, but this is technically a job, so in a way I don't.

"What did you have to do to get a man like that?" the woman in the yellow frock askes, staring openly at James from across the room. She wants him so bad I can taste it.

I place my cell phone back in my purse, not retuning any message to Daniel, and give this woman a honeyed smile.

"He's a hunk of meat on two legs, isn't he?" I say, playing her. "What's hanging between those hips, though?" I blow out an exaggerated breath and make a face like I've never seen anything so big in my life. "Too bad he bats for the other team."

Her face falls, and I revel in it.

"You're lying."

I shake my head. "He's got a mouth like a Hoover and a trunk like an elephant. I've seen it in action and experienced it a time or two myself when he's let me. It's something to marvel at. I bet he gives better head than you."

Her face twists up like she sucked on something sour. She scoffs and gets up, stalking away just as James walks over to me.

He looks at her as she passes him and frowns. James unbuttons his jacket before sitting in her empty seat. He places a hand on my knee and swivels my chair to face him so that my crossed legs are between his.

"What did you tell her? She looks like her dog just died."

I nod, giving him a grave look. "She's heartbroken. I told her you bat for the other team and that you like it when I wear a strap-on."

James barks out a laugh, and I smile in return. I know he's not mad. One plus about this particular agreement with James is that I can be myself. I get the notion that not many other men would be okay with my crude thoughts the way he is. It's just another reason why I adore him.

Lifting his glass to salute me, he says, his eyes gleaming, "Your ass is mine tonight."

***

Our clothes are on the floor in a trail of passion the second we step into his grand suite.

Within two minutes, James is surging inside me. His strokes are hitting all the right spots most men can't reach inside me. It's a struggle not to allow myself to sink into the decadence of this man. It feels too good, and I'm fighting off the orgasm, as usual. Every time I feel the pleasure drawing closer to the surface, I close my eyes and breathe steadily through my nose.

"I swear you have more testosterone than a teenage boy," I say, breathless.

"Is that a complaint?" he asks, wrapping my hair around his fist and yanking my head back.

His mouth is on my neck, and if he sucks any harder, he's going to leave a hickey. Right now, he has me pressed against the window as he takes me from behind. My hands are flat to the cold glass, and every time I exhale, a frosted little circle forms in front of my mouth. The cool air causes my nipples to harden, and a soft moan escapes my throat as he drives in and holds stills. Fuck my life. I love this pressure between my legs so much. It's a painful kind of pleasure—need—that I fall into.

"I'm just shocked you haven't come yet," I say.

James groans near my ear like he's in ecstasy. "I only come once you do, sweetheart. Never before."

Valentina, you're up.

"Why didn't you say so before? I've been waiting for you," I say and start putting the act on like I'm getting closer. I don't make it obviously fake the way porn stars do, just enough to sound genuine, which isn't hard with James. I'm so close, but I hold off. Moans and purrs leave my parted lips, and I call his name, telling him I'm coming all over his cock that I can't get enough of. I tell him to take me harder, and he does, and that nearly sets me over the edge for real. The hold on my hair tightens and his thrusts deepen, but I don't feel him come. He just slows to a stop, let's go of my hair, then pulls out.

"You didn't come," he says.

I freeze from his stiff voice but quickly recover. There's no way I was a bad fake. Impossible.

"I did."

He turns me around to face him. I can't help but take in his beautifully toned naked body before my eyes meet his. He's not angry, but he's not happy either. Strength and sexuality ripple from him, and it makes me want to reach out and touch every inch of him.

"You want to try that again?"

I frown. "I don't understand," I say, my heavy breathing matching his.

"I know what your pussy feels like when you come, and it didn't do shit."

My lips part. The sound of his voice sends chills over my body. I'm instantly annoyed that he can tell, but more so at myself for not giving a better performance.

"James, that's ridiculous."

He counters me, and it makes my heart pound. "Are we going to start lying to each other already? Because a year contract is a long time to harbor resentment. It turns the sex sour, and as you know, intimacy is a huge factor in my life and why I'm willing to pay whatever it is you want to have that intimacy with you."

I swallow, a little insulted, a little hurt. Flattening my lips, I tell him again. "James, I did come."

His eyes harden. "I can't get off if you don't, sweetheart, and you definitely didn't. Your satisfaction is what makes me hard as a fucking rock. What do you need from me? Tell me so I can do it."

My chest constricts at his words. He wants to make me feel good, and here I am trying to not allow it. His gaze pierces my heart, and I prop my hands on my hips, looking away. I can't tell him I don't want to finish, because that sounds just plain fucking strange, but I know that if I do come, it'll only pull me closer to him and I don't want that. I can't afford for that to happen because then I'll fall even further for him. It's clear that my needs are his needs, and that's just not something I'm used to. It's new territory for me. My heart is telling me to put a wall up to prevent the inevitable hurt.

From what I've come to understand, there are two things that are an absolute must in a relationship for everyone: intimacy and trust. Intimacy is the bottom lock on a door. It can be toyed with and sometimes popped open for others to enter if there isn't a strong trail of communication. Trust is what seals the relationship and keeps it solid, the bolt that keeps both people locked in and makes that intimacy build. I can't afford to be trapped when he has the key. A year from now when he unlocks that door and says goodbye, I'm walking out with the clothes on my back and an eight-figure check. I'm not asking him to throw away the key, but I'm not trying to start anything more either. I feel like that's what will happen if I let go and really give myself to him. I don't see why I can't just give him the sex he wants and nothing more.

Swallowing, I soften my voice. "I don't need anything else from you, James. Everything you do is perfect."

"Did you forget that I work with liars every day? I can smell them a mile away. What I don't understand is why you would lie about this. What am I doing wrong?"

Instead of answering, I reach out to grab his still erect cock and step closer to stroke him. I offer up a sweet smile then drop to my knees and take him into my mouth before he has a second to say anything else.

Blow jobs. Catnip for men.

James groans deep in his throat. His hand fists the hair at the back of my neck, and he rocks into me slowly. I suction my lips around his cock and place my hands on his ass to hold him to me. I can taste myself on him, and it's oddly erotic.

"You know I love your mouth, but you're doing this on purpose to avoid the conversation," he says then leans forward to place his other arm on the window to hold himself up.

Wrapping my tongue around his warmth, I pull back with a pop of my lips and focus on the tip for a second before taking even more of him.

"Fuck, Aubrey." His voice is guttural, and I love that I can make him sound like that.

Suddenly, he pulls out. I wipe my mouth with the back of my hand and sit back on my knees, wondering what happened. "Get up."

James turns and walks to grab a chair. He picks it up and plants it right in front of a floor-length mirror. He takes a seat and spreads his legs, his sack heavy and full. He leans back and looks over at me. My teeth roll over my bottom lip, scraping the skin.

Standing, I walk to him. He holds his hand out, and I take it, feeling that glow fill my chest again. There's something in his gaze that steals my breath as he guides me to stand between his legs and turns me around to face the mirror. His palms spread over my hips, caressing me, and he leans forward to kiss my back. His beard tickles my already heated flesh, and it only heightens the touch.

"I love your body," he says between kisses, his voice low and raw. I watch him in the mirror. "I think about you all the time, you know. I love how your eyes flutter shut when you're about to orgasm, the little purr that comes out when you're coming, how your body turns lax and you just get lost in the moment. Let me show you why I get off when you do," he says, his teeth nipping my waist. "Spread your legs."

Chapter 45

Guiding my hips, James grips his cock and enters me slowly.

I hold my breath as he pulls my back to his chest as he slides all the way in. We both groan in unison at the warmth and friction. He picks up both of my knees and places them on the outside of his, making me fully exposed and vulnerable to him in this position. My inner thighs start to tremble, a violent shock reverberating throughout my body. I let out a soft sigh. I grab his legs to ease some of the sensation, but he takes my hands and pulls them behind his back, then spreads our legs wide enough that my toes can't reach the ground anymore. That dreamy haze takes over my body, and I'm tingling from head to toe, falling into an abyss.

"Leave them there," he orders, his voice reminding me of a lazy Sunday morning.

Fuck, it's too much, especially seeing us in the mirror like this. I squeeze my eyes shut and let my head fall back onto his shoulder. James skims his hands up my body, and he settles deeper into the chair—and in me. He wraps one hand around my waist, the other coming up to cup my throat. He applies pressure, fingers pressing into the column of my neck, and a warmth fills me, a sense of security and comfort I can't seem to explain. I relax into his body and allow myself to feel all of him. I allow myself to succumb to him for a few selfish moments.

"James." His name is a plea on my lips.

"There's something to be said about two people coming together," he says, his voice raw as it caresses down my neck. "The day could be shit, the absolute fuckin' worst kind of hell, but when you're with that person who just gets you, who makes you feel good just by smiling at them, who knows what you like and likes it too, none of that shit matters anymore, because when you're lost inside them, everything fixes itself. Sex is like breathing air for me, and I think it may be that way for you too."

I open my eyes and meet his gaze in the mirror. He's watching me, waiting for a response. I nod in silent agreement.

Unhurried, James starts slowly thrusting inside me, my skin pricking in response. At this angle, it's different, better, deeper, and so fucking good. Tightening his hold on my neck, his fingers at my waist move and find my clit, and he ever so slowly circles it. My eyes roll shut, and I let myself focus on the rapture slowly consuming me.

"Let me show you what you do for me that my wife can't. What no woman can but you. Let me show you why you fucking drive me insane. Let me show you why I need to be inside you. Why I want you. Why I need you all the time. Open your eyes and watch us."

Lifting my heavy lids, I watch as our bodies move together in the mirror in flawless harmony. My jaw slackens as James surges inside of me. The width of his cock from this view is frightening. From this angle, he looks painfully large. Yet, he's just perfect for me.

"You just want to be inside me because I'm new and fresh. That's all it is, James," I say, trying to downplay his words, but I can barely get the words out myself as I watch us with unabashed lust. "I think you want me even more now only because of who I am."

He drives into me hard and rough then pauses. I try to move my hips away, but he pushes me down. My entire body lights up, and I let out a loud, gasping breath.

"I wanted you way before that and you know it, so don't put words in my mouth and create dumb shit that's not there between us, sweetheart," he says, unwavering. "I won't allow it."

It's too much, too hot, too erotic. My thighs start shaking again and my heart is beating so fast from the desire rushing through me that I start rotating my hips on his, grinding down. I'm suspended in his arms and at his mercy, and I kind of love it. God, I want him to bend me over and take me hard. I want him to slap my ass and pull my hair and fuck me until I can't walk. Between the way he's touching me and the way he feels inside of me, my orgasm is back and climbing fast.

"James, please," I say, begging. He doesn't know I'm begging him to stop, though.

"Tell me why you lied."

I suck in air between my teeth and grind my jaw. "Please."

"Tell me."

I cave and tell him the truth because it's inescapable at this point.

"Christine doesn't want her girls to indulge in pleasure at Sanctuary Cove. I'm not allowed to orgasm at least until the client does since I'm being paid an exorbitant amount of money to meet their needs. This helps to keep me from under performing and getting attached. Plus, what I want doesn't really matter. This isn't for me or about me. I like the rule—it's usually not hard not to come anyway—and it helps keep my mental space in check. But with you, it's the struggle of my fucking life every time."

"Guess what?" he says, and my eyes meet his hard ones in the mirror. "We're not at Sanctuary Cove, and our deal is just between us. There's no reason for you not to give me everything."

My heart can't take it. I shake my head, and he just keeps gliding in and out of my pussy like he owns it.

"But I need to keep it that way. Emotionally it's important for me, and I think you understand why. I'm trying not to get attached to you, and viewing you as a client helps me keep everything separate." I pause, holding my breath. "I don't want to come."

James leans in and peppers kisses over my neck. The way he's with me makes it so easy to think what we're doing is more than what this is, that he actually likes me romantically. It's stupid, I know it is. It really is just sex, but there's something hidden under his touch that fires up my soul when he's with me that's hard to ignore.

"Sweetheart, I think it's safe to say we're past both those points. You're coming, and you got attached to me the moment you started refusing me as a client months ago. You just don't want to admit it."

I clench my eyes shut. I hate that he's right. "I don't want to lose myself."

James turns my head to face him. Our lips are so close, the rawness shifting between us undeniable. "Then get lost inside me, and I'll take care of us. I need you to, because I'm already lost to you. I'm fucked, Aubrey. When our time is up, I'm not going to be able to watch you walk away. I don't know what our future holds, but I do know I want you in it."

James captures my lips with his, and then we're lost to each other. What he says is exactly what I fear because I feel the same. My heart is about to burst. He's swelling inside of me, and even though he told me to leave my hands where they are, I reach up to cup the back of his head so I can kiss him with the same passion he gives me. James fills me completely, hitting all the places he shouldn't.

"Just let go," he whispers against my lips.

James keeps his thrusts at a steady rhythm, building an incredible rise roaring through me. The pleasure makes me want to scream at the top of my lungs, it's so good.

"Let go," he orders again, his voice low and in control. "Fly with me."

I shake my head, breathing heavily, relentless in my effort to fight it.

His fingers stop circling my sensitive clit, only to pinch it so hard I see stars ... And then I'm coming. I let go then, allowing my body to revel in this man. I moan out his name, pulsating around his cock. The pleasure is divine. James thrusts a little harder, but not faster, and starts to come with me.

The way our bodies move together, it's beautiful and all-encompassing. There's no way to contain the whimpers in my throat as I climax around him. Skin sinfully flush against skin, our lips are painted in passion and the sex is forming a tether between us that I've been fighting since the start.

And yet, right now, I don't care. Right now, I live in the moment with him.

"James," I whisper against his mouth. I don't know what I'm asking for or saying. I wonder if he can feel the somersaults my heart is doing. "What was that?"

"Look at us," he says, and I do.

My chest is flushed, my breasts full and nipples rosy pink. James is still swollen and deep inside me. Thick white cum seeps out my pussy and onto the chair. There's so much, and it's so overwhelmingly sensual that I can't stop looking at us. I clench my pussy around his cock, and he groans. James loosens his hold on my neck, and I melt into him. I'm sated, knowing this incredible feeling is something I can't put into words.

His nimble fingers gently, tenderly, sweep over my clit. My stomach dips, and I exhale a breathless sigh when he uses his fluid to caress me. I feel like I'm floating on a cloud, like I'm high, and I don't want to move.

"This is how I want you," he says, his voice laid-back. "I love how you're open to me and letting me just touch you."

I want to say something slick, like *Ten million you can do whatever you want,* but I don't. Truth is, even without the money, I would let him touch me like this.

"I could stay like this all night," I say quietly.

"Don't hold back with me, Aubrey." My gaze lifts to his. Fuck. I don't know why those words tug at my heartstrings, but they do. "I like seeing you explode. It makes me feel good to see you happy."

"I feel like I should get up and do something for you. Like I'm supposed to be taking care of you."

"Stay where you are. This is exactly what I want," James says. "Do you want to come again?"

My teeth dig into my bottom lip, and I nod. "I'm not far, but I can wait for you so we can finish together."

"No, I just want to watch you in the mirror like this. Don't use your hands and try not to move your hips. I'm not going to drive into you. Just focus on how you still have my cock hard and how my fingers move slow while I tease the fuck out of your clit. It's about control, a slow fucking burn, and if you hold still and let me take care of you like this, I promise it will be better than anything."

Licking my lips, I think about his words and how anxious I am. How I've never had a man just play with me before, but it's something I could get used to.

"James?"

"Yeah, sweetheart?"

I guide his free hand to my nipple and show him how I like it played with. I capture his lips with mine and I don't hold back as I kiss him. He senses a shift in my actions and surprises me by meeting my desire. I kiss him deeply, madly, and freely, giving all of me, knowing there's no chance fighting it anymore.

"I want to fuck you so bad right now," I say, my voice raspy. "God, you make me feel so good."

"Slow and steady. I'm going to make you come on my cock like this." He pinches my nipple, giving it a little tug, and my back bows from the pain. "I can't wait to feel your pussy tighten around my cock and watch your body unravel in the mirror again. It's so fucking hot. I can stay like this all night and into the morning, if

312

you want."

"I want what you want," I say automatically, and I do. "Honestly. If you want to sit just like this and play with me, who am I to say no to that?"

I give him a lazy smile, and he returns it. He switches up his motions and moves his fingers in a circle, then a soft pinch, and back to a circle. He does this a few more times until I'm gasping and trying to kiss him again, but he won't let me. His mouth is just as bad as his fingers, and while he doesn't kiss me, he does. Just our tongues twirl erotically around each other's, and I can feel myself growing even wetter.

"God, James, how do you do it? I'm so close," I whisper. James slowly, and just right, pushes in a little deeper, and I'm coming again. "Ah, oh …"

"Don't move," he says then lifts his eyes to watch in the mirror. My nose grazes his neck, and I close my eyes, letting myself fall into the intensity of the orgasm.

James was right. Letting go of my control and transferring it to him is empowering. I'm shocked by how the release crashes through me and takes over my body.

Little gasps and pants exhale from my throat as I ride the wave, ride James. My breasts lift into the air with each breath that fills my lungs. I swoop my arms under his and latch on to his biceps, and my legs wrap around his calves as the pleasure racks through my body violently. What James can make me feel, I could almost cry from it.

Chapter 46

James took control of my body all night long in front of the mirror, continually insisting that he gets off by making me feel good. I decided before I fell asleep that I would treat him in the morning. I never thought anything could be so erotic, but last night was intoxicating and something I wish I could have all the time. Although, I guess for the next year I can, but afterward ...

Blinking, I brush the thought away, not wanting to think about that just yet.

Like most men, he's asleep with raging morning wood. I already know what I'm going to do, but before I climb on him, I allow myself to take in his naked body while he sleeps.

I don't know what time we went to bed—it was late—but it didn't take long for us to fall into a deep slumber. Limbs entwined, I don't think either one of us moved for hours.

As I watch the sunlight cascade over his masculine form, I wonder what goes on behind closed doors with his wife, because the way he took me last night was like a man starving to fill a need to care for someone. It's not normal, but I understand now why he pays for sex. No marriage should lack something like intimacy. His longing, his desire for something deeper, echoes through my veins. I want to give him what he wants. Almost like a craving in me to make him happy. Is it in his touch, the way he looks at me, and accepts all of me without disgust? Or how it just feels so damn natural between us that I want to give him everything he wants?

Or is it just the fact that he's paying me?

I sigh, wishing I knew.

"Are you gonna get up and fuck me, or are you gonna be lost in your thoughts all day?" James asks, his voice still groggy.

I start giggling, not expecting that. "You knew I was awake?"

He peeks at me with one sleepy eye and smirks. My heart feels full looking at him.

"Yeah, sweetheart."

The smile falls from my face a little at the nickname. I like when he calls me that, but now I wonder if he calls the other girls that too.

"What's wrong?"

I shake it off, casting my gaze down. "Nothing," I say as I get up on my knees and straddle him.

James helps me, and I can feel the weight of his eyes on me. He places his hands on my hips as I reach for his cock and slide down on it. We both groan at the warmth of us connecting, like it's where we're supposed to be, and take a moment to allow that powerful feeling to spread through our veins.

"Look at me."

My eyes shift to his.

"Tell me."

I swallow, licking my lips. "I just wondered if you call all the girls sweetheart, and then I realized it's dumb to even wonder that because it's none of my business."

He thrusts into me, pulling my hips down to meet him. "Only you."

"Liar," I gasp.

"I don't even call Katherine sweetheart. I don't call her anything, actually. You're the first woman I've wanted to give an endearment to in many long years. Just felt natural, I guess."

My cheeks bloom with heat, and I feel stupidly giddy. I smile at that. James sits up so we're chest to chest, and then he takes control. I love how he knows exactly what both of us need—and like. It doesn't take long until we're both climaxing on breathless moans and sighs.

I fall back onto the bed and smile dreamily up at the ceiling. "What a way to wake up," I say. After a few minutes of blissful harmony in his arms, something dawns on me. My voice lowers to a quiet tone, slowing the pulse of my heart. Unsure. "What are you going to tell your wife when she asks why you didn't come home?"

He's quiet for a moment. "Nothing. She won't ask," he says, and it intrigues me.

I roll onto my side to look at him. I lace my fingers with his and fold our hands so they're pressed to my chest. "Really? I'd want to know where the hell my husband was all night."

"She doesn't question me. I don't question her. This is nothing new, trust me."

"But why? I don't understand why anyone would want a marriage like that," I say.

James sighs deeply and looks at the ceiling, lost in thought. His fingers tighten around mine. "Where we come from, divorce isn't an option. You have to remember, I'm in my fifties. It was a different time then. Once you get married, you stay married. It's just how things were done."

"So, what? If you divorced you'd get twenty lashes? I don't understand."

James goes into detail about both their backgrounds, how her family is just a step below the Kennedys, but no one knew who he, or who his family was, the way people did hers.

"The problem is that the heat of the moment resulted in a pregnancy. Twenty years ago, when you came from a well-heeled background like her, the only way to cover up a pregnancy was to claim love and marry. Natalie is the only reason we're married, and so we stay together for her. I came from a low-class background, which humiliated Katherine's family. They paid my family quite well to stay quiet. Marriage was not something either of us wanted. Yeah, we were both attracted to each other, but it was nothing more than a few hot drunk hookups and that was it. Believe me, we tried to make it work for years through counseling, but it just wasn't in the cards for us. Turns out, we don't do it for each other when we're sober."

"So that's why you have a membership at Sanctuary Cove," I state in understanding.

He nods. "She thinks something's wrong with me. Like there's some deep-rooted issue that stems from childhood bullshit because I'm too dominant for her. She wants a soft lover—"

A burst of laughter flies from the back of my throat, and I cover my mouth.

"What's so funny?"

"You're anything but a soft lover. I could tell that the second I met you."

His eyes twinkle when he leans over to look at me. "Don't tell me that bothers you and you're only with me for my money."

"No. I mean, at this point, the money is just a plus to me." James stares at me, blinking a few times like he's lost in my eyes. Lowering my voice, I palm his jaw and tell him the truth. "No, it doesn't bother me, James. I actually like the way you handle me. Not because I like it rough, but there's something about the way you touch me that makes me forget everything on my mind. Your hands understand my body in ways no one ever has. I have this notion that sex is stress-relieving for both of us, like there's an understanding, a connection, and it just works. I've never experienced anything like that before you, so now it's going to be something I always seek. I don't think I'd like a soft lover. That being said, I think you could probably do rough but soft sex and it would be really incredible."

James leans in and gives me an emotional kiss, one filled with need and acceptance. His hands roam every inch of my body he can reach, and I draw closer, only for him to break the kiss and lie back.

"The one and only time I got hands-on the way I like it, she said she felt like she was being assaulted, that it came off as rape, and hitting a woman to have sex is repulsive. I never touched her like that again. I would never hit a woman. I have certain tastes my wife doesn't approve of, and I hate when she tries to make me feel guilty for them. I need a rougher kind of sex, but she doesn't fulfill my needs, so I look for it elsewhere."

I think it's hot when James is dominant, but I don't tell him that right now. It's not the time.

"But you fulfill hers."

"Yeah," he says. His voice is low and so empty that it hurts my chest. "Do you have any idea how hard it is to have sex with your wife and hate it? I want to be able to connect with my wife, but I never will."

I feel bad. I know what it's like to have bad sex. I can hear in his voice how unhappy he is, and I want to try to fix it.

Gently, the next few words I utter are spoken with hesitation. I don't want him to get the wrong idea, like I'm being pushy or intruding, but maybe he needs to be reminded.

"It's the twenty-first century, James. I don't think anyone would care if you guys divorced. It happens every day."

He shakes his head. "The divorce rate is high these days because millennials have an argument and can't talk it out. Ten seconds later, they're googling where to find a quick divorce lawyer and crying about it. I've never had a reason to file because I've never found that one person who just does it for me mind, body, and soul. Part of the agreement was that we stayed married for a period of time. After that time was up, we just sort of stayed. Divorce is messy and costs a lot of money."

It's cheaper to keep her, I want to add, but I don't. "That's because you haven't really had the chance to find that person."

"The one thing we both actually agreed on was to give Natalie a good family, so we've made it a marriage of convenience and stay together for her. Katherine's tried too, but we're just oil and water now. She does what she wants, I do what I want, and everyone stays happy."

I frown. "But you're not happy."

"Far from happy, which she knows." He pauses. "I'm happy with you."

"You're not getting any younger, James. Wouldn't you want to spend the time you have left searching for that person? I would think being alone is better than that. I'm sorry. I know this is none of my business. I probably shouldn't say anything."

"Believe me, I've considered divorce a time or two. The only thing I want is for someone to want me the way I want them. To want all of me, not just a few parts of me. I want to connect emotionally and mentally and just have fun with someone. Life's too fucking short. If I search for that specific person, I won't find them."

He has a point, but I'd rather be alone than stuck with someone who isn't my match in every way. That's not the kind of life I want to live, and I feel bad for the people who do.

"Can I ask what happened with you and Natalie? If you don't want to talk about it, you don't have to. I'm just curious."

James remains quiet for a long time. I kind of feel like I'm intruding on my friend's privacy, but given the nature of my relationship with James, I feel like I need a little more background.

"I said some pretty shitty things to her a few years ago that I can never take back. We were arguing about college and her future. The conversation got heated, and Katherine wasn't helping the situation. I told her she was ungrateful and ..." James hesitates for a moment like it hurts him to speak. "I said I wish her mother would've had the abortion." He closes his eyes, remorse etching his face. My jaw drops at the thought of such cruel words being spoken. "I didn't mean it and regretted it the moment I uttered the words. Of course, Katherine confirmed that I wanted one. I'll never forget her face that day. It was like Katherine was proud to tell Natalie." He sighs. "It's been pretty tense ever since."

"You asked for an abortion?"

He nods. "I told Katherine she should have an abortion so we didn't have to marry, but she refused. I'm glad she didn't listen to me. Everything changed for me when the moment came and I got to hold my daughter for the first time. She's been my world ever since, and everything I've done has been for her. It wasn't that I didn't want Natalie. I just wasn't ready for a child with a woman I barely knew and then be forced into a marriage I didn't want. I was barely thirty, and my life took a fucking nosedive. Now Natalie looks at me with disdain and thinks I never wanted her." He's quiet for a long moment. "I only want the best for her and to give her the life I felt she should have. I went about it the wrong way that day. I'd already had a massive fight with Katherine that I was steaming from. I said things in the heat of the moment I can't take back."

The creases between my eyes deepen from the sound of sorrow coming from his voice. There are so many things I want to say to James.

"You'd feel pretty shitty if it were you, wouldn't you?" he asks, sounding so far away.

My teeth dig into my bottom lip as I put myself in Natalie's shoes.

"Yeah, I would. Natalie and I, though? We're polar opposites. I can see how she would stay mad. My parents died in a car accident when I was young, so my grammy raised me. If those words were spoken to me, I wouldn't ever be able to forget them, but I do know what it's like to miss a loved one I'll never get to see again, so I tend to get over things a little differently. Everyone says things in the heat of the moment that we regret. If we can learn from that, then we can forgive and be a better person. I try not to stay mad too long. All it does is harden the heart."

"Natalie holds a serious grudge toward me, which is another reason why I haven't divorced her mother. Katherine doesn't want the problem to get worse and thinks it will if we separate. I kind of do too. The tension between my daughter and me eats away at me every damn day, so I suffer through this depressing fucking marriage, hoping one day she'll come around. If I divorce her mother, I don't think Natalie will ever have a change of heart with how she already feels." He takes a deep breath. "I think that would be the straw that breaks the camel's back."

"You do realize Natalie isn't a child anymore. She's an adult, and I'm sure if you talked to her, told her the truth, it wouldn't be as bad as you think."

He turns over onto his side to face me. Pulling me so I'm nestled against his body, he lies halfway on me and continues. "It's a risk I'm not willing to take. I love my daughter too much for that. I don't want to lose her completely."

I glare because I know he's not that stupid. "A divorce is something you can work on with her. But I'm telling you right now that if she ever finds out about us, I don't think there's anything you could do to fix it. Not to mention, she's going to think you cheat on—" I stop short. "Well, you do cheat, even though you have an open relationship, but your wife doesn't mess around."

He twirls a lock of my hair between his fingers. He watches his movements, his gaze so far away that it bothers me. It's a side I've yet to see of him.

"Natalie will never know," he says quietly.

My stomach knots at the thought, and all my guilt comes thundering back tenfold. I pray she never does, because even though I know better than to get in bed with her dad and the consequences it brings, I still did.

I take a deep breath and exhale. "I hope she never does either."

Chapter 47

Pulling my cell phone out, I glance down to see *Blocked Caller* on the screen. I don't typically care to answer numbers I don't know, but I've been getting calls from this one all week, so I decide to put an end to whoever's on the other end.

"New York City Sperm Bank. You squeeze, we freeze. This is Valentina. How may I help you pump one out today?"

"Val." The voice sends chills down my spine to the tips of my toes. "It's James."

I smile. "Oh, I know it's you," I say, feeling relieved. I'm walking up the stairs and opening the door to the school building.

"How'd you guess?"

"No one calls my cell and says Val, for one thing. Plus, I love the sound of your voice. You could be across the room and I'd hear you and know it's you. How'd you get this number?"

"When you were sleeping last weekend at the hotel, I got it."

I smile. "Sneaky. I'm glad, though. I was wondering how you would get ahold of me. I'm about to walk into class right now. Can you call me in an hour and a half? I have a small break in between classes and can talk then."

"How about I meet you for coffee? I just need to see you."

I hesitate for a minute. Natalie will be around this part of town too and I don't want to risk it, but I do want to see him.

"That sounds good. Just not over here. How about—"

"I'll text you the place. Don't worry, no one will see us."

My shoulders loosen. Pulling open the heavy door to the lecture hall, I say, "Sounds good. See you soon."

"Later, sweetheart."

I smile to myself, eager to see James. That light and airy feeling inside my chest stays for a good portion of class, until I get a text from Daniel asking to meet me at our coffee shop.

Guilt racks me once again. I'm going to give myself an ulcer at this rate.

I lose focus on what my professor is talking about and stare at the text messages. I shouldn't feel as anxious as I am to see James. I *should* feel like this for Daniel. I mean, I do, but it's just not the same. Not even close.

I stare down at my cell phone, blinking, trying to figure out what I'm going to do. I decide to tell Daniel that I have plans with Natalie, but I'd love to see him for dinner later. I haven't seen him in days, and I can tell he's getting antsy. We agree on a late dinner so I can do some homework beforehand.

I shove my phone away and decide not to check it again until class is over. I'm bothered that I'm happy. My heart is conflicted, and I hate that I'm learning to lie to the people I care about so I can please everyone. I'm seeing two men today. Both I like, both are vastly different, and both make me happy to see them. One sets my heart on fire. The other balances me. I can't explain what's going on or how this happened, but all I know is that if I don't get my emotions straight, I'm going to slip and fall.

And I have this feeling I'm going to hit the ground hard and alone.

***

"Is this the Aubrey side I've wondered so much about?" James asks as he rakes a gaze down the length of my body. I step up to him, and he kisses my forehead.

"This is schoolgirl Aubrey." I smile up at him.

Ripped jeans, Toms, and a loose, off-the-shoulder sweater with a stack of books in my arms. It's finally warming up, so I didn't bother with a coat today. I look around at the coffee shop that's about ten minutes uptown. "I only have thirty minutes, and then I have to head back to class."

"Not enough time, but I'll take what I can get. You look so fucking adorable. I want to take a bite out of you."

I flush and bite my lip. After we get our coffee, James guides us to a little booth in a corner. I place my books on the other side of the table, and we sit next to each other. I sling a leg over his thigh so my foot is dangling between his legs and nestle close to him. He drops an arm across the back of the booth.

Reaching up, I palm his cheek and turn his face to mine. I press my lips to his and give him a kiss that feels natural. His hand finds my inner thigh, and he gives me a tender squeeze, which sends my heart running.

"What was that for?" he asks, breaking the kiss.

I shake my head and shrug. "Nothing. No reason. Just saying hi."

A shadow crosses his eyes. "Hey," he says in a low voice, and it makes me want to kiss him again. So I do. "How are classes going this week?"

"Exhausting." I take a sip of my coffee. "I'm looking forward to finally being done with college, to be honest. And here I wanted to get my master's or go to law school. I think my brain needs a rest before I jump into anything else."

"What happened to the foundation you wanted to start?"

I glance at James. "You remembered that?"

He pulls back, almost like he's offended. "Yes, of course. I thought it was a great idea."

"Really?" I say, perking up. "I feel like you're the first person to tell me that."

His brows furrow. "Who else did you tell?"

Averting my gaze, I look down at our drinks. I haven't told Daniel yet. After his response to me handing out money to the homeless, I don't want him to discourage me, and I think he would do just that. I feel like he'd say it's a waste of time or something along those lines.

"I told my grammy, but she's biased." I smile to myself. "She supports me regardless, but when there isn't anyone rallying next to you, it kind of sucks the joy out of it."

He nods in understanding. "You should know that I was serious that night when I said I would make a donation. Sure, I was trying to find a way to get to you too, but I meant what I said. Whenever you're ready, just let me know."

"James, I can't take a donation from you."

"Why not?"

"Because that's mixing business with pleasure, and that never works out well."

His eyes glimmer. "Sometimes that can make for the best recipe."

I laugh nervously. "Yeah, said no one ever."

He squeezes my thigh again. "Give it some thought. My firm picks two charities a year, and I'd like to make yours one of them."

I swallow back the knot in my throat. "Why did you want to see me today?" I ask, changing the subject. I'm not ready to have a conversation like that just yet. Mainly because I can't tell if he's actually supportive or if it's just a way to keep us together after our time is up.

He sighs deeply and looks ahead. "Work. It's been a stressful week. I love being a lawyer, there's something new and exciting all the time, but some days it just gets to me, you know? Especially when people need direction over every little fucking task. We have some attorneys fresh out of law school who feel entitled to everything, some seasoned but utterly fucking clueless. I'm not going to baby them, but fuck, I wish they'd use their heads and think before asking a question. I'm trying to prepare for a case coming up that can take my firm to the next level. I don't want to be bothered every second of the day."

I pat his chest then rub it soothingly. "Try not to take it too personally. You have to remember you were once a novice too and probably were the same way, even though I'm sure it would kill you to admit that."

He looks down at me and smirks.

"Anything I can do to help?" I say.

"Have dinner with me tonight?"

Leaning in, I give him a peck. "I can't. I'm sorry. I have plans with Natalie," I lie. "But what about this weekend?"

His face falls a little and I feel bad, but I can't cancel on Daniel again.

"I have a place out east I use when I need to get away. Come stay the weekend with me. Friday night to Sunday night. Just me and you, and we can do and go anywhere you want."

My brows lift in surprise. "You mean you don't want me naked and willing all weekend at your mercy? My, James, I'm slightly offended."

He chuckles. "Well, I'm sure I'll have you on your back at some point ... But I just need to be around you." He lowers his voice. "You're a ray of light for me, Aubrey. I see things differently, clearer. Things I want, things I need to change. I don't feel stressed when I'm with you. I feel a sense of relief. I feel like I can fucking breathe again."

I smile, though something inside my chest tightens and I can't figure out what it is.

"Better yet, let's go to Aspen for the weekend," he suggests.

"What?" I laugh, a little nervous. "Where did that come from?"

He shrugs. "I have a place there too. We can go skiing and then sit in front of the fire at night."

A huge smile spreads across my face. "Why did I instantly think of an old Harlequin romance book cover?"

We both laugh, and he gives me a little nudge.

"What do you say? Come away with me." He doesn't beg, but I can hear the plea in his tone. I want to give in to him. It's so easy with him, and I forget I have to be careful.

The temptation to be alone with James all weekend is strong. I want to go, but I hate lying to everyone I care about. But the way my body is craving to be with just him, I realize it's worth it for me.

"I've never been skiing before," I say quietly. "We might have to use the bunny slope."

"Whatever you want, as long as I can have you to myself all weekend."

Glancing at James, I nod. Our eyes lock, and I feel myself weakening further. I know he sees it, because I can see the same feeling mirrored in his eyes.

My heart is in danger. His heart is in danger. I realized this months ago when we met, which is why I tried to put distance between us, but something as simple as spending a half hour in a little coffee shop solidifies it.

I'm fucked.

***

"What do you mean you have plans this weekend? The entire weekend? When am I going to see you again?" Daniel asks, the annoyance in his voice clear. I don't blame him, though, so I don't argue. After all, I'm lying to him, and I feel like shit over it. Maybe he'll break up with me instead of the other way around.

"I have to work," I say apologetically. "The family wants to go to Nantucket, and they need me to babysit. How about Monday after class, I come right over and stay the night? I'll go to school from your place the next day."

Daniel places his red wine on the table, but he doesn't let go of the stem. He stares at it, his eyes hard. We just finished eating Thai at this little hole-in-the-wall restaurant, and our night was going smoothly until now. Disappointment is written clear across his face. The last thing I want is to dampen the night, so I need to figure out how to make this right.

"I have to work late on Monday, so I won't be home."

I shrug, trying to find another solution. "So meet me at our coffee place that morning and give me your key. I'll make dinner and have it ready by the time you get home."

He lifts his eyes to mine, and a hopeful smile tugs at his lips. "You can cook?"

I flatten my lips, trying not to laugh. "I can barely boil water. I was just going to order out and take the credit for it." I joke, and a huge smile spreads across his face, easing the tightness in my chest. "However, I was going to set the mood for you ... Maybe slip into something nice and give you a massage after a long, hard day at work?"

Daniel reaches for my hand across the small table. Lifting it to his lips, his eyes lower as he gives me a little kiss to the top of my knuckles. "A for effort. I'll be counting down the hours until I get to see you again."

Chapter 48

"Natalie, I'm screwed!" I yell Friday morning.

I woke up early to pack so I'd be ready when I got out of class, but now I'm a frazzled mess and I can't think straight. I'm so stressed about this weekend. My gut is still screaming that it's not a good idea to go away with James, but my heart is saying to put one foot in front of the other and shut the fuck up because this is what he's paying twenty million for. I'm eager to be with him, but I have so much shame filling every inch of my body that it's hard to function.

"That makes one of us. What's wrong?" she asks, holding her coffee as she walks into my room. Her eyes widen, taking in the scattered clothes all over the place.

"I have a job out of town all weekend, so I told Daniel I'm nannying in Nantucket. He's not thrilled, so I'm dealing with that, and now I don't know what to pack."

She glares at me. "So? What's the issue? You have to be getting at least fifty grand to do a weekend event like that. Maybe more. Just make it up to him with sex."

"That's the plan. I just feel bad."

The real issue is I need to get my lies in order for her too and that makes me more edgy than anything. In case she sees Daniel by some odd chance, not that I think she will, I need to make sure my double life is lined up on both sides so I don't get caught.

"Why?" she asks. "I'd take the money and lie too. You've been working a lot lately."

It's true. Every night this week, Christine has offered me a job, except the night I had dinner with Daniel. I've taken them all, but the last time I spoke to her, I told her I wouldn't be available this weekend. Thankfully they've all been uneventful quickies, but I've been busy nonetheless.

"I need the distraction, honestly." My cell phone rings. "Hand that to me, please," I say as I lean over one bag to squish it down so I can pull the zipper closed.

Natalie picks up my cell phone and reads the screen. Handing it to me, she says, "Blocked caller? Who's that?"

Blood drains from my face, and my fingers start trembling. My heart is racing so hard, I feel like I'm going to be sick.

"Are you going to answer it or just stare at it like your grammy found out you bang men with cannibal fetishes for hush money?"

Blinking a few times, my jaw bobs until something pops into my head. I offer a courtesy laugh and quickly switch my phone to silent.

"Ah, it's no one. Just some telemarketer that keeps calling. They leave messages in Spanish, so I know they have the wrong number."

I pocket the phone and prop my hands on my hips and exhale a sigh, avoiding her gaze.

"Why don't you skip class today so you can pack and then go to a spa to relax before you leave? I can feel you from here, and you're stressing me out."

I drop my arms. "Can't. I have to go to class. One of the professors is going over what'll be on the final exam, and I need to take notes. I'm just nervous to be going away with a client for the weekend."

"You have any Percs left? Want mine? Maybe you should take one now."

My eyes light up. "I do! That's a good idea. I think I have two left. I'll have to get more from Christine soon."

Going to my desk drawer, I take the bottle out and break one in half. I wash it down with a sip of my coffee and pack the rest.

"Okay. I think I have it all set until I get home. I can't help but feel like I'm forgetting something. I need to get to class." I look at her. "Will you be here when I get back?"

"No, I have three jobs tonight back-to-back-to-back, and I'm booked all weekend."

My brows shoot up. "How are you going to manage all that?"

She gives me a sly smile, and I shake my head. Natalie walks over to me, and I give her a big hug.

"I'll see you when I get back."

Her eyes twinkle with trouble. Turning away, she walks out of my room, but not before saying, "Don't do anything I wouldn't do."

***

"You rented a private plane for us?" I ask as we take our seats. I look over at James in surprise.

"I want you to myself the entire weekend. That means no one breathing over us in first class."

My cheeks flush. "You already have me. You didn't have to do this."

"I know you've never been on a plane before. I wanted the first time to be a memorable one."

I study him, my heart melting at his thoughtfulness. It had to cost an arm and a leg to charter a private plane, and yet he doesn't even bat an eye. Sometimes I forget that he's a billionaire.

"I've never left New York," I say. "Do you rent private planes often?"

"Only when the time calls for it, and before you ask—no, I don't do it for the others at Sanctuary."

My brows drop, eyes lowering to slits. I definitely was thinking that.

"I know you're the possessive and jealous type—"

I gasp. Reaching over, I cover his mouth with my hand. His beard tickles my palm. James grabs my wrist, grinning, and pulls me closer to him.

Eyes wide and playful, I say, "You bite your tongue, Mr. Riviera. I am not either of those."

"You're such a liar," he teases, pulling my hand down. "So you're saying that if I took another girl from Sanctuary Cove to, say, Hawaii next week on a private plane, you won't have an issue?"

Okay. Maybe I am a little possessive over him. The thought of James with another escort chaps my hide and does makes me jealous. I can feel my heartbeat speeding up, and it makes me want to slash tires. I need to act cool and reserved to play it off. I don't want to be that girl, even though I kind of am. Sitting back, I brush the nonexistent lint off my jeans and then look ahead at the ivory bucket seats, purposely avoiding him. I have no right to be up in arms if James actually does go to Hawaii with another escort when I'm still dating Daniel and working at Sanctuary Cove behind his back. It's a bit hypocritical of me.

My voice is quiet, scornful, with a hint of mockery, even though I attempt to mask it.

"What you do in your spare time is none of my business. If you found another girl who can take care of you better than I can, more power to you. Get it, baby."

He's quiet for a moment. "Get over here."

"No." I purse my lips and fold my fingers together.

"Aubrey—"

"No."

"Get. Over. Here. Now."

I don't respond, and James gets out of his seat to kneel down in front of me. He spreads my knees apart and scoots until he's as close as he can get. Leaning back casually in my seat, I wonder what he's doing. I'm annoyed, and I know it's because of my feelings for him, because of the lies I'm telling everyone. The lines have blurred, and there's no sharpening them. I shouldn't care that he could be with other girls, but holy shit does it do something to my heart that I wish it wouldn't.

James grabs my wrists and pulls me to him so I'm only a few inches from his face. We're about the same height at this angle.

"I'm just playing with you. I think at this point it's clear where you stand for me, but it's nice to see where I stand with you. Makes me feel good."

I swallow hard and lick my lips. It hits me that I've never really said how I feel about him, but that's because I've been working to keep my feelings separate and not get too invested for obvious reasons. But everyone needs to be reminded that they mean something, and now I think I should tell him.

Or maybe not? I'm so conflicted.

"If you need someone—"

"All I need is you, and I mean that," he murmurs, cupping the back of my head. He kisses me, bleeding his words into me so I feel them. And damn, do I ever. "I don't need, or want, anyone else but you."

My heart is pounding so fucking hard that I cave.

"I like you, James, more than I thought I did. More than I should, and it's killing me inside. If you want to hire other women, obviously I can't say anything since this is just a deal we have going on, but that doesn't mean I wouldn't want to carve her eyes out with a plastic spoon and offer them to you on a platter to show you that I'm better than her."

His chuckle is raspy. "I think we both know this is far more than just a deal, sweetheart. Tell me, if there was no money, no friend or daughter, and I met you at a bar without going through Sanctuary Cove on a random Tuesday night, would you still be here with me?"

I nod without hesitation, my gaze vulnerable. "You know damn well I would be."

His eyes soften, and he looks at me with a tenderness that shouldn't be there. The truth is, I would be here with him, and I would still want more with him. I have deep feelings for James I tried so hard not to acknowledge because I know nothing good can come from them. They're rooted to the walls of my ribs, the feelings growing stronger every day, wrapping around each bone, connecting him to me for good.

"I wanted more before I knew the truth of who you are, and now it's only amplified into something more. I hate that we're stuck and that nothing more can come out of this, because I like you too much, James. It's God's honest truth. I fucking like you so much, and I can't bear to lie to you and say that I don't." I pause then say, "I'm not going to hold back how I feel anymore. Not while we're together. And I promise not to get all *Fatal Attraction* on you either."

James captures my lips with his and kisses me deep, full of untamed passion. I know I'm falling in love with this man.

My arms wrap around his shoulders, fingers threading through his hair. I put all of myself into him and our emotional kiss, letting him feel just how much he means to me.

Breaking the kiss, James gets up and scoops me into his arms. He takes a couple of steps and lays me down on the bed in the back of the plane. He gets comfortable between my legs and stares into my eyes. His gaze is piercing my heart because I know he feels the same way for me as I do for him.

"No one has ever done it for me the way you do," he says. "The universe is cruel for putting us together, but I don't feel bad because what I feel when I'm with you is what I've been looking for my whole life. I just never knew it until I met you."

I blink a few times, breathing a little harder. I need this man something fierce. "James?"

"Hmm?"

My jaw trembles. "Make love to me?"

"Sweetheart, I've been making love to you all along."

Chapter 49

I nestle closer to James, smiling against his neck. I'm sitting on his lap naked and wrapped in a flannel blanket. We've been watching the snow fall for hours now, with the most incredible snowcapped-mountain view I've ever seen.

We both woke early and reached for each other without uttering a word. In the mornings, I find I like to give him a slow ride, and at night I like when he sets the pace. It works for us, especially since he loves sex just as much as I do. I feel like I'm back to enjoying it the way I did before I became an escort, only it's better than ever before, and I have James to thank for that.

"I can feel you smiling," he says, his voice like gravel.

I pull back and look at him, grinning from ear to ear.

"I'm really happy," I say. "I know this sounds stupid, but I could sit here all day with you and just watch the snow fall. We can drink coffee, or hot chocolate, and maybe some cognac later in front of the fire when the snow is really coming down. It's so peaceful. Being in your arms makes it that much better."

He kisses me. "I like this no holding back. Tell me more."

I laugh. "No, your head is just going to get big. What are we doing today?"

James eyes my bare shoulder and fixes the blanket so it's covering me. We're sitting in the coziest kitchen nook I've ever seen, with plaid pillows all around us. The floor is heated, and the seat cushions are so large it's like being on the couch.

"Well, we can stay here if you want or use the bunny slope I rented for us."

My brows raise. "Just for us?" He nods, and excitement rolls through me. "I can't ski to save my life, so this is going to be fun! When do we leave?"

He grins, and it melts my heart. "Anytime you want."

"Really? Can we spend all day on it?"

"Yes," he says.

I'm so ecstatic that I lean in to give James a big smacking kiss. I moan into his mouth, loving that he always kisses me back with the same passion. Swiveling around, I move to straddle his hips, but he stops me.

"You don't have to give me sex every time I do something for you," he says, frowning. "Seeing you happy makes me happy. I don't expect anything in return." The way he speaks, sounding pained, means my actions hurt him, and I don't like that.

Still, I take his thick cock and align it with my pussy, teasing the tip. His nostrils flare as he guides my hips down. Eyes locked, our mouths fall open and we both sigh in bliss. I rock my hips slow, feeling his cock swell inside me. His fingers thread the hair at my nape. He tugs, fisting a clump, and my eyes grow heavy. We can't look anywhere else but at each other.

My hands glide over his shoulder and chest. "I like having sex, James, and I want to have sex with you. I think about it all the time, how you make me feel when we're together, how you make me see stars," I say, moaning and feeling the desire rise. "Sometimes I can't even concentrate on anything else but you and the way our bodies move together." I lean in and say against his lips, "Damp sheets, flesh against flesh, your cum dripping out of me ..." He growls, and I fucking love the sound of it. "I know this makes you happy, and it's what I want to give you because that makes me happy. It's called working together." I lean in to tug his bottom lip between my teeth. "And honestly, I just really love the way you fuck me. I was kind of hoping you'd use your belt again later."

"Where have you been my entire life?" he says before slamming his lips to mine and leaving me breathless.

***

"How can you balance in five-inch heels but barely stand in skis on a baby slope?"

I laugh so hard I have to grab his arm to steady myself. "Skills. I got skills, baby," I say, standing up. "I feel like I'm going to slide everywhere."

"Did you ever play sports? Ballet?"

"Nope. My grammy couldn't afford it. I can't throw a ball, and I can't catch one. The only balls I can handle are the big ones hanging between your legs. The only rhythm I have comes from drinking tequila, and then I'm suddenly a backup dancer for Beyoncé. I can twerk with the best of them. That's about it."

"What the fuck is twerk?"

I can't help the laugh that erupts in my throat.

"What?" he asks, confusion etched on his face.

I'm grinning so hard my cheeks hurt. "Your age is showing, James."

James just shakes his head and grins. "Okay. Hold my hand, and we'll go slow."

He helps me on the slope, giving me instructions and thankfully not getting impatient with me. By midafternoon, I have it down for the most part, only my stomach is so sore from using muscles that never see action beyond the bedroom. My cheeks are a little chapped, but the cool, icy air is breathtaking. I want to stay outside and just take in the beauty of it all. I hope one day I'll be able to do something like this again. I love the snow, but there's something about the mountains and trees that captivate me. I find them inspiring.

Much to my surprise, James can navigate the slope better than I expected. I sit at the top of the hill and watch him glide over the powdery snow like a pro. Well, a pro to me. He's smooth, and I can't take my eyes off him. After a couple of rounds, he comes to sit next to me.

"What are you thinking about?" he asks, a little breathless. He removes his goggles, and there's a red outline around his eyes.

"How incredible the world is and that I hope to get to see it all one day."

"What's stopping you?" he asks, scooting closer to me.

I shrug, looking at him. "I don't know. School? Life? Work? Responsibilities? What holds anyone back from doing what they want?"

"Don't take this the wrong way, but between the money you've made at Sanctuary Cove and our deal, you can go anywhere in the world you want."

I'm not offended, so I give him a small smile to show that. "I'm going to use that money to start my foundation and buy my grammy a house. I just have to figure out a way to do it without her questioning me."

James watches me. "This foundation is something you really want to do?"

I nod. "Yes. I can't ignore the feeling in my stomach that's saying to do it. Like it's a calling. There's so many homeless in New York, and considering I was almost homeless once, I know what it's like to hold that fear and panic close to my chest. When we're going to eat next, if we'll have heat in the winter. If I can help at least five people, it will be worth it."

"What if you traveled before you started it? That way you get the best of both worlds."

I glance down at the snow. I'd love to travel first, but I don't know if I will. I look back at James.

"Do you think it's stupid? Tell me the truth. Or do you think I should continue my education?"

He runs his hands through his hair and shakes his head. "I'll always be one for continuing education, but starting a foundation is not a stupid idea. Not one bit. If it's what you desire, who the fuck am I to tell you no? I think it's a fantastic idea. You're going to have to jump through some hoops to start one, but the money I gave you can be written in the form of a gift, so it shows you have some sort of income. My family, though not nearly as important as Katherine's, was always donating and supporting charities. Might not have been much, but it was something. I wasn't born with a silver spoon in my mouth, but my family always gave back to the less fortunate, which is why I do so now twice a year. I don't have to continue it since they're long gone, but I like to. Good deeds bring more good deeds."

"It's going to be a lot of work," I say quietly, realizing that I've settled my mind on it. My gaze moves across the tops of the mountains.

"You're not unfamiliar with working hard for what you want. The struggle is nothing new to you."

I laugh and huff at the same time. "It's not, that's for sure."

***

After skiing, we sat in a hot tub that overlooked the slopes, and then James took me out. We sat side by side in a dark booth, trying to come up with names for my foundation while we ate an exquisite dinner. Once we arrived back at his cabin, James used one of his ties to blindfold me. I gave him the best blowie of his life, and then he spanked me with his belt. There's something about giving an amazing blowjob that brings a man to his knees. I had James in the palm of my hands when I gave him permission to manhandle the fuck out of me and fell into that deliriously blissful high of pain and ecstasy he's so good at giving.

"Would you like another glass?" James asks, standing up.

He walks around the couch, and I look down at my empty tumbler. "You know, you don't have to get me drunk to take advantage of me."

He leans over the sofa and gives me a big kiss. My hand finds the back of his head, and I hold him to me. His lips move down the column of my neck, and my nipples harden in response. I breathe in through my nose, drawing him in.

"You're insatiable," I say, giggling.

He pulls back and smirks. "Me? What about you?"

"Sex is addicting when it's done right." I smile up lazily. "I'm not denying it."

As James pours us both another glass of his tawny drink, I get up and lay the blankets and pillows in front of the fire. We're still naked, but neither of us are shy about it. I lie in front of the flickering fire and place my hands under my head, watching the flames lick each other. The heat is heaven, and I feel myself warming. James walks over, and I take in his body. His tattoos come alive against the firelight—captivating, moving—and I can't tear my eyes from him. The colors are moody, like they're speaking. His art is something to appreciate.

James places our crystal tumblers on the floor next to me and drops to his knees, spreading my legs. They fall willingly, and in seconds his mouth is on my pussy. My back bows and I moan, my hands threading through his hair.

"Baby, I need you in me," I tell him through clenched teeth. "I'm already so close, and I want you to come with me."

James climbs up my body and thrusts inside me, filling me. I feel like I should be adjusted to his size by now, but I'm not. I'm a little tender and it's tight, but I take all of him without reserve. Our sighs create a sinful melody while his moans leave an imprint on my heart. It doesn't take us long before we fall over the edge, him coming inside me.

Kissing me, he pulls out and rolls to the side, taking me with him. Warmth seeps from me, sticking to my thighs, but I can't be bothered to clean up when James is playing with my hair. I'm drawing lazy circles on his chest, noting that something seems off with him. I can feel how tense his body is against mine when it shouldn't be. I look up and rest my chin on his chest, only to see him staring at the ceiling and frowning.

"What are you thinking about, baby?" I ask, my voice soft.

Lifting his head, he looks into my eyes. "That I finally have a reason to leave my wife."

Chapter 50

I finally have a reason to leave my wife.

I can't get those words out of my head. It wasn't supposed to be this way.

Squeezing my eyes shut, I fold my arms and drop my head to the desk of the cubby I'm sitting at in the library. Exhaustion hits me hard. I'm so tired from the stress that comes with a lie this heavy. I can barely eat, and nighttime is the worst because my mind is running. My chest feels tight, like I'm having mini panic attacks. I rub the pain away and take deep, slow breaths.

The best plan I could come up with to quell the babble and anxiety was to lose myself in clients from Sanctuary Cove, booking myself every night to avoid seeing Natalie. It's the last thing I want to do, but in some strange way, it helps remind me of what I am—a prostitute and nothing more. By the time I get home, Nat's either sleeping or working. I'm out of the apartment before the sun rises, going to a coffee shop to study, and when she sends me a text, I don't respond immediately.

I can't get James out of my head. It's like he's tattooed himself under my skin, and I'm trying to hide it from Natalie, feeling as if she might read the truth on my face if she saw me.

This life sucks. I want him. I need him. I miss him.

I can't have him.

I can never have him completely.

Glancing at the time on my phone, I stand to gather my books. I so desperately want to skip class today just to sleep, but I know I'd only regret it. I step outside and make my way toward the grouping of school buildings, when my phone rings.

My heart flutters at the sight of *Blocked Caller*, and I'm quick to answer.

"I was just thinking about you," I say, smiling into the phone.

"I miss you," James says. I love the early morning roughness in his voice.

I chuckle lightly. "You just saw me a few days ago."

"That wasn't enough. I need to see you every day."

I shake my head as if he's standing right in front of me. "You're terrible."

"When can I see you again?"

I bite the side of my lip. "You make the rules, not me."

A long stretch of silence, then, "Aubrey."

The way he says my name is enough to cause me to stop walking. It was a bullshit comment to make, and we both know it.

"I'm trying, James," I say, my voice a little shaky. "I'm just having a week where the guilt is eating away at me more than usual. I can't sleep. I can't focus. I'm avoiding everyone like the plague and trying to stay busy. I'm tempted to come clean with Natalie, but I know deep down it won't go the way I hope it will in my head. And, well, I just miss you."

Tears sting my eyes. I'm talking a mile a minute, and I'm on the verge of a breakdown. What's wrong with me?

"Sweetheart, it kills me to hear you like this. Do you have plans later?"

Swallowing, I shake my head and keep walking. "I don't know ... I was going to try to sleep after class, to be honest. The stress is exhausting."

"I'm going to text you an address and time within the hour for you to get a deep-tissue massage. Go to the appointment. It'll help loosen you up a little."

I hold the phone tight to my ear. I've never had a massage before. "You don't have to do that."

"I know I don't have to do anything. I want to."

"That's really sweet of you," I say softly.

I hear someone knock on his door through the phone. "Come in," he says, holding the phone away from his mouth. "Yeah, I got the case file right here," he says to whoever it is. "I gotta go. I'll talk to you later?"

"Yeah," I whisper. "Later."

Only later, I don't make it to the massage. I don't make it to the rest of my afternoon classes. I drop everything when a seven-one-eight number calls to inform me that my grammy is in the hospital. I silenced the number since I was in class, then stepped out to listen to the voicemail. I left immediately.

"Grammy, you're sitting here with machines making noise and an oxygen mask over your face. You look terrible, and your only concern is your cats?"

There's a grayish sheen to her skin and puffy circles under her eyes. The only concern she should have is getting healthy. If I didn't love her so much, I would yell at her. When the hospital called to tell me she was brought in after the neighbor below her in the basement rental heard a loud thump and went to check on her, I thought I was going to have a heart attack. The neighbor told the hospital she fainted. Grammy denies it. Regardless, having bronchitis is no joke, but at her age, it worries me even more.

"Aubrey! I'm all they have! If I don't come home, they'll go into a frenzy."

"They're cats. They only worry about when their next meal is coming," I say, deadpan.

She looks truly upset and hurt, so I offer a solution I really hate but know I'll suffer through, because she's Grammy.

"What if I pick up all your little fur balls and take them to my place? I'll probably need to borrow your car, if you're okay with that. I'll park it in the city somewhere, but at least they'll have me."

Her eyes soften. "You'd do that for me?"

"I'd do anything for you. Of course."

"Natalie won't mind?"

"Nah, I doubt it. Do you know when you're getting out?"

"I told them I'm fine and don't need to be here, but you know how hospitals are. They want to test everything just to run up the insurance."

I'm not amused. "Grammy, you collapsed. You definitely need to be here and have tests run."

"Honey, I have a bruise on my foot and they want to X-ray it." She uses her hand to wave where the light bruise is, annoyed. "All that happened was that I tripped because one of my cats was in my path and I didn't want to step on her. That's where the bruise came from. It's not like I can't walk. They're making a big deal out of nothing."

"You fainted."

"I was coughing and tripped. I didn't faint."

I concede. I'm not going to argue with her, not when she's trying to hide the slight shake in her hand or the way her shoulders lift to catch her breath. Standing up, I shuffle through her purse for her keys. She gives me a rundown of how much her cats eat and how often and what toys they like. I just nod and listen, then lean down to give her a kiss on her head. I want her to rest, and if something as simple as taking care of her cats makes her happy, I'm going to do it the way she likes.

"I'll be back tomorrow to check on you after class." We both know she won't be out tomorrow either, not until the infection clears up at least. I just worry with her being here and already sick that she could catch something else.

"I don't need a babysitter. I'll be fine." She coughs.

"Love you, Grams."

"Love you too. And Aubrey?"

I turn around to look at her. Our eyes meet. There's something in her gaze that makes my stomach stiffen.

"Thank you."

I linger at the door, my heart not wanting to say goodbye. Smiling, I blow her a kiss and leave. As I'm leaving the hospital, I take out my cell phone to see a slew of missed calls from James. I know he's wondering why I didn't go to the appointment. I'm sure he's worried, especially since I keep missing his calls, but right now I have too much on my plate, so I put my phone away.

Who knew cats needed so much shit? I'm sneezing like crazy and my eyes are watering. It took a stupid number of hours to make sure I had everything then forever to trick the cats into their crates. The last thing I need is for one of them to attack me while I'm driving, which, given my luck lately, would totally happen.

As I sit in bumper-to-bumper traffic, I'm reminded why I don't have a car while living in the city. It's beyond aggravating, and I'm antsy wishing these morons knew how to drive. I reach for my phone and dial up Natalie.

She picks up on the first ring, and I sigh in relief.

"The caller you've reached is unavailable. Please try again later." She hangs up.

I call again.

"Please leave a message at the tone. Beeeep." And she hangs up again.

If she wants to play like that, I'll just text her instead.

Me: Felicia

Nat: Felicia isn't here at the moment, but if you leave a message at the beep, she'll text you back. BEEEEP!

I'm seriously going to slap her now. Still, I play along since I know why she's acting like this.

Me: Felicia answer your text. I know you're there. Feliciaaaa! Wow, this is how it's gonna be? Ok FINE just send me a text when you get "back" .

Nat: If you would like to leave a callback number, please do so at the end of this message.

Me: 212-fuck-you

Nat: I'm sorry. That is not a valid number. Please try again later. Thank you.

Me: 212-fuc-kyou

Nat: Your message has been recorded. Thank you.

She's upset with me, so I don't get angry with her. I've been dodging her all week. I deserve it, but that doesn't mean I have to like it. A few minutes later, she calls me.

"Hey," I say.

"I'm going to put out an ad for a new bestie, because this week, you've totally sucked."

I look at the row of taxis in front of me and stare. "I know. I'm sorry. Things were just busy with school and work."

"Yeah, yeah, yeah. What's up?"

I give her a quick rundown about what happened with Grammy.

"Ram Jam!" Her tone is so apologetic that it kills me. "You should've said that in your text! Now I feel like shit."

"No, don't," I say, moving a few feet but missing the next light. "I know I've been MIA, and I'm sorry."

"I was just giving you a hard time on purpose. Whatever you need, I'm your girl."

I chuckle lightly. "I'm going to need to double park to unload the car. Can you wait by the curb with this stuff while I find a garage to park in, and then we'll bring it up?"

"I'm already walking downstairs. But just so you know, I highly doubt someone is going to swipe four cats and a scratch tower taller than your fucking Jolly Green Giant ass as they walk by."

I smile sadly. "Thank you."

"I'm gonna have to hit the weed pen and get wine drunk if I'm going to live with more pussy."

"You and me both," I say, laughing.

Chapter 51

"Hey," I say, my voice groggy.

"Where've you been? What's going on? Why are you ignoring me?"

I can tell James is both angry and worried, with good reason. I know I should've answered one of his many calls last night, but instead, I put my phone on silent and set up the cats, and then I had a large glass of wine with Natalie.

"I'm sorry. I had a family emergency with Grammy." I yawn, not wanting to get out of bed just yet. Thank God tomorrow is the weekend. I'm so mentally and physically exhausted that I just want to sleep, but I don't know how I'll get any rest with Grammy on my mind and seeing Daniel later.

"Is she okay?"

I hesitate. I want to tell James what happened, but I feel like if I do, that opens another door for us, and I'm not sure that's a good idea. Yet, the urge to lean on him for support is strong. I want to tell him, and I want him to tell me everything is going to be okay.

"Everything is fine. She'll be okay. I just got tied up yesterday."

"I was worried about you," he says. I can't help but wish he was here holding me.

My voice is quiet. "Sorry for worrying you."

"Do you want me to reschedule your appointment?"

"Yeah, but I'll let you know when. I can't do it right now. I have too much on my plate."

"What can I do to help you? Name it."

Closing my eyes, I pet the kitty curled up on my stomach,

absorbing his warmth. "Nothing, but thank you."

"Can you at least tell me what happened?"

I swallow. "I don't want to talk about it just yet."

James is quiet for a moment. He doesn't like my response. "Are you in bed? You sound like you just woke up."

A sleepy smile pulls at my lips, and I turn onto my side. "Yeah, I have to get up, though. I have class soon. I never stay in bed this late, but I was just too tired to get up."

He hums in the back of his throat. "Waking up next to you is the best way to start my day. Can I see you later?"

The smile slips from my lips. "I have plans later." Those plans are sitting with my grammy then getting obliterated on wine when I get home.

"What about this weekend? I need to see you again, Aubrey."

"Aubrey! This little cute fucker is scratching the couch!" Natalie yells from the other room. "Come get it before I pull his claws out with my teeth!"

I chuckle into the phone. "I gotta go. Natalie is yelling for me."

"Give me an answer, sweetheart. I want to see you. Just have dinner with me. I think you want to see me too. Wherever, whenever. You set it, and I'll be there. An hour is all I'm asking for."

I stare at the wall in front of me and wish that what he said wasn't the truth. I do want to see him, and technically, I can't say no because of our arrangement. I clench my eyes shut feeling the pressure even though there is no demand in his voice. Duty calls.

"Of course" I say softly.

"He just pissed in my thousand-dollar shoes and stared at me while he did it. You have until the count of three, and then I'm skinning him!"

Chuckling, I jump out of bed.

"I'll call you back about when and where?" I ask James but

hang up before he has a chance to respond.

***

"Nat, where are you?" I say. I'm walking out of the hospital and feeling too emotional right now. The day dragged on, which allowed me to get deep in my head, and I need to shut my thoughts out now.

"Where do you want me to be, baby," she says, her voice seductive. "I'm willing and ready for that pipe."

I bark out a laugh. I needed that.

"There's something mentally wrong with you. Do you say that to your clients?"

"When the mood calls for it, I do. You know how men are. I only say it when he has a turtle head between his legs, though. I let him feel himself for a minute." She laughs. "Only the big boys get called Daddy."

I shake my head as I walk to the bus stop. Never a dull moment with her. "I need to get drunk. Like hammered—the kind where I forget what I'm talking about mid-conversation."

"Bad visit with Grammy?" she asks, sympathetic. Her tone softens.

I swallow back the emotion climbing the back of my throat. I sat with her for hours after class, even though she didn't want me to see her like she is right now. I told her too bad and that I was staying, and then I showed her the pictures I took of her cats at my place and she seemed to relax a little. I left out the comments Natalie made, though. Before I left, the doctor on call pulled me aside to tell me they're running additional tests because some results of prior tests raised concern, something about raised inflammatory levels, so they just wanted to double-check before they give any diagnoses.

"It wasn't the best. She looks even paler, if that's possible. I'm kind of worried. They're concerned about her lungs and that she could possibly catch pneumonia."

"Oh, yeah. Pneumonia loves old people, especially in hospitals. I'm sorry, Ram Jam. Your gram is a tough cookie, though. She'll pull through. Just get your bony ass home, and I'll have everything ready."

I stand at the bus stop with a group of people thinking about Natalie's last words. I don't want to what-if anything, but I can't help it.

My jaw trembles. What if Grammy doesn't get better? What if she gets sicker and doesn't pull through? A gust of wind blows by, and my hair coasts around my face. Glancing up, I see the lights blinking at the top of the bus as it slows down for my stop. People rise to stand and step close to the curb.

Sniffling back my emotions, I refuse to let myself go there anymore. I need to think positive. Positive thoughts bring positive energy. She's all I have, and if anything happened to her, I don't know what I'd do with myself.

After the bus ride to the station, I catch the train back into the city then take the subway to the street closest to my place. I had enough time to stew on my thoughts and decide that once my feet hit the streets of the concrete jungle, I'm not going to allow myself to worry about it anymore because everything will be just fine.

It has to be.

A girls' night is exactly what I need, and I'm getting a little excited to just chill on a Friday night like Natalie and I used to do before everything got complicated—Christine and James complicated. I need to balance my shit out and for someone to bring me back to my center. A night with my best friend is the perfect medicine, and then I'll top it off by hanging out with my real boyfriend tomorrow. If he's available. Taking out my phone, I look for Daniel's number.

"Hey, baby," he says. I don't think it even rang.

I smile. "Hey, handsome. I feel like I haven't spoken to you in forever."

He laughs. "I figured you were busy with work and school. I didn't want to bug you, but I will say I had a plan that if I didn't hear from you soon. I was coming for you."

Now I feel a little bad that he noticed. It's been almost a whole week—if not more—since I spoke to him last. My priorities have been messed up, and it's time to take responsibility for them. I also need to get my heart straight, and that starts with figuring out what to do about Daniel.

"I'm sorry. It's all my fault," I say with disappointment. "Yeah, this week was a pretty rough one. It's like you sensed it. Grammy was admitted to the hospital the other day, and school is just weighing me down." Among other things, but I don't say it, obviously. "I can't wait to graduate."

"Aw, babe. I'm sorry to hear that. What hospital is she at? Maybe I can help somehow?"

I soften and give him a quick rundown of her illness as I navigate the street. "She's at Jamaica Hospital. I'm going to visit her again tomorrow."

"Want me to go with you?"

I smile to myself. He's a good guy, and I can tell he just wants to help. "No, but thank you. However, I was going to see if you wanted to come over tomorrow and hang with me?"

"Netflix and chill?" he says, his voice piqued with interest.

"You're such a typical guy." I laugh. "Whatever you want. How about I text you once I leave the hospital? Around midafternoon?"

"Sounds good. I'm glad you finally called. I was missing you."

"Daniel," I draw out his name. "I'll make it up to you."

We hang up right as I'm walking into my apartment. I feel a little better about talking to him, almost normal.

"Nat?" I yell out, but she's already walking toward me holding two double shot glasses. Shaking my head, I drop my purse onto the table and take the glass. My eyes light up.

"What is—Ohhhh, you got pizza!"

She lifts the glass to toast me, and we throw back the shot at the same time.

"I'll take let's get wasted for two, Alex," Natalie says, her face pinched up.

"Give me another," I say.

"One step ahead of you, sis," Natalie says then steps aside and there's two glasses waiting for us.

I shake my head and start laughing as we take the other shot. "You're a terrible influence."

"And yet you love me anyway."

I nod. The tequila burns the back of my throat. "I feel like I can blow fire from the burn."

"That sounds like a personal problem you need to address, Ram Jam."

"Come with me. I gotta change real quick."

Natalie follows me into my room and sits on my bed, lighting up a blunt. I frown. She usually just uses her weed pen.

"Did you roll that?"

"Nope. Got it from my homie," she says, watching the flame burn up the tip. She's focused, and I can't help but giggle at her concentration.

I change into comfy yoga pants and a baggy sweater then take a seat next to her. Natalie takes a few puffs to get it started then hands it to me. I take a deep inhale, too deep, and feel my throat starting to tickle.

"Fuck," I mutter, blowing the smoke out, knowing the coughing is about to start. I hand it back to Natalie, and she takes a rip. "I forgot what it's like to hit a blunt." The pens are so smooth.

And ... I start coughing, which only makes the high hit quicker. After what feels like the longest coughing fit of my life, I look at Natalie. She bursts out laughing.

"What?" I ask, my eyes feeling heavy.

"Your eyes are bloodshot. Let's eat, and then I'm going to get you drunk and you're going to confess your love for me."

After a couple of hours, the pizza is almost gone and we're both on another level of stupid, giggling nonstop about nothing. It reminds me of when we met and the friendship first started. I miss this with her. Not necessarily the high and drunkenness, but just hanging out with my bestie without anything hanging between us. I'm feeling extremely vulnerable right now, and I'm tempted to feel her out about the dirty secret I'm hiding, but I'm not sure I can.

"You wanna talk about Grammy?"

I shake my head, a little sad. "Not really. I think I'll just get emotional about it, and I don't wanna cry."

"Daniel?"

"He's coming over tomorrow. Netflix and chill."

"I thought you were going to break up with him," she says.

"It's complicated."

"Good to know. I'll be gone. I have a job, so it's perfect timing. Just make sure you put a sheet down on the couch and don't get cum on it."

"I'll never understand how someone as pretty and sincere as you can have the most vulgar mouth."

"It's always the ones you never suspect who have the filthiest minds."

I giggle. "It's true. You're ratchet."

Her face lights up like I just gave her the biggest compliment of her life, and we both fall over cackling.

"There is something seriously wrong with you," I say.

She lights up the blunt again. Lifting her eyes to me, she takes a hard pull, the embers a crimson red.

"You're just realizing that now? I sell my body for a living, and I don't give two fucks about it. You'd think I have daddy issues, but I don't," she says through the smoke.

James.

And there goes my reserve. I feel a splintering down the center of my chest thinking about him. Drinking on a torn heart is a recipe for a hot mess. Alcohol forces me to acknowledge James for what he is and what he'll never be. It's such a fucking lonely feeling.

"Question. Have you ever had a client you felt yourself growing attached to? Like you liked what you guys did together and how he made you feel?"

She nods, and a shadow casts across her eyes.

"Yeah, once."

My brows shoot up. "Really?" I wish she had told me this before. "When?"

"When I first started out. He became a regular client of mine, which was the worst thing we could've done. He was younger than most men at Sanctuary and in great shape. His body was to die for."

"What happened?"

"Eventually I told Christine he couldn't be my client anymore."

"No way."

She nods. "I had to. He was married, but we fell for each other. We started meeting more often, and not through Christine either. It was hard to fight what he made me feel, the way he touched me, like I was a real lover to him. We let that feeling consume us." She pauses. "I wish we never had," she says softly.

Slack-jawed, I sit here stunned as I listen to her speak.

"Do you ever think about him?"

"All the fucking time. Some days my chest hurts and I have to tell myself to stop being a little bitch. I can't even walk down specific streets in the city without looking for him."

"Really? How did I not know this?"

"I don't talk about it because what good is that going to do? I can't have him. End of story. I have to keep telling myself that any relationship formed inside the walls of Sanctuary Cove is doomed from the start."

I swallow. She's right, and I don't like it.

"But if there was a chance you could have him, would you?"

Taking a deep breath, she says, "That man is who I compare all other men to. If there was some wicked way it could work, I'd ride his ass all the way to the courthouse and sell my soul just so he could love me for the rest of my life."

My brows raise. "This is a side of you I've never seen before."

"There's a client like that for you, isn't there?" she asks.

My stomach tightens with anxiety. "Kind of." I look out the window, nervous to talk about this knowing I probably shouldn't. "I get this feeling in my chest when he's around that I can't explain. The way he talks to me ... touches me ..." My face falls a little, and I lower my voice. "He makes me forget it's only a job."

Natalie sits up and looks directly into my eyes. "Aubrey, break it off now. I'm serious. This is for your own good. I know how easy it is to get lost in the illusion that this John wants something more with you. He doesn't. Sanctuary Cove is a façade built from money on lies. Trust me, speaking from experience, I fell hard. You don't want to fall down that hole and get your heart broken the way I did."

I study her. She wants me to listen, pleading with me to take her advice. I recall Madame Christine saying something similar the night I told her that I couldn't work with James anymore.

The problem is, it's too late. I'm already in deep, and so is James.

Natalie takes a sip of her mixed drink and then a drag of what's left of the blunt. Blowing it out, she looks at me again and says, "Well, that escalated quickly."

Chapter 52

"Your phone's ringing," Daniel says from my living room.

I walk over with a bowl of popcorn. "What does it say?" I ask as I sit down.

"Blocked caller."

I look back and forth between his eyes and the phone in a panic. I swear I'm going to have heart failure by the time I'm twenty-five.

"Probably a telemarketer," he says. "I wouldn't answer it. I've been getting a lot of those lately."

Exhaling a stiff breath, I agree with him and reject the call, and then I place the phone facedown and on silent. I've ignored all calls from James since last night even though I said I would see him and call him back. Instead, I got drunk with Natalie. I needed a break and to escape my mind. I feel bad considering we have a twenty-million-dollar arrangement, but after James told me he finally had a reason to leave his wife, I haven't been the same. That wasn't part of the agreement.

Natalie was right in a way. It is a sick fantasy. I just hope when I do talk to James that he won't be upset with me for dodging his calls. I'll have to tell him about Grammy and explain myself in hopes he'll be understanding.

"Wanna watch *The Notebook*?"

I look at Daniel with skepticism and sit back. "Are you for real right now? Why the hell do you want to watch that? Do you have a secret crush on Ryan Gosling? Because news flash, he's taken, and with a baby, and that baby mama is *hot*," I say, and he grins.

Daniel chuckles and wraps an arm around my shoulders. "I don't, but I just thought you might. It's a chick flick. Doesn't every girl want to watch that?"

My head tilts to the side. "That's sweet of you, but I need something funny after being with my grammy."

He cups my jaw and gives me a little kiss. His eyes soften. "Still feeling down after seeing her?"

I nod, my lips a thin, flat line. Grammy's coloring was much better, and while that makes me feel a little better, I can't help but think the worst since she's still in the hospital. She's antsy to get out, and I feel the same way for her. I want her back in her home with her cats where I know she's safe.

"They're still running tests. How many can they possibly be running?"

"A hospital isn't going to release a patient without covering every inch of the floor. If they don't, that's a malpractice suit waiting to happen."

Makes sense. "They found something in her lungs," I say quietly. "They're going to do some pulmonary tests."

Daniel tips my chin up and looks into my eyes. "Hey now. That test can be used for something as simple as allergies. Don't get all worked up, and do not look shit up on the internet."

A small smile tugs at my lips. "Too late. I saw that sometimes it's needed for bronchitis, which is what she has, so that's what I'm going with and trying not to think the worst."

"See? They're just checking off all the boxes. Given her age, they have to, Aubrey."

"Yeah, okay. You're probably right," I say and lean in to hug him.

Daniel strokes my back, his fingers dragging lazily up and down. It feels so good.

"Thanks for trying to soothe me," I say softly. "I'm just worried. Grammy is my everything."

He leans in to kiss the top of my head. After a few minutes of silence, he says, "There's something I want to talk to you about."

His voice is low, serious, and that immediately raises flags inside me. That tone, and statement, means something more. Like taking the relationship to the next level. Heart racing, I pick my head up to look at him just as a knock sounds at the door.

"Hold that thought," I say, holding a finger up as I get up to answer it.

My jaw drops, and my heart plummets into my stomach.

Everything inside me lights up at the sight of James.

My eyes lock with his, and for a minute, it's just us and no one else. His gaze softens, and a grin spreads across his face. My body gravitates toward him, igniting my blood, knowing what he's capable of. I've missed him, but I didn't realize just how much until now.

"Everything okay, Aubrey?" Daniel asks from behind me.

James's smile slips. His gaze lifts above my head, and his eyes harden.

I didn't hear Daniel get up off the couch or walk over to me, but now he's standing behind me with a hand on my hip.

I stare up at James, unable to form words. He studies me, and I plead with him to not open his mouth through my nervous gaze. Not that I think he would, but the thought does cross my mind.

"Can I help you?" Daniel asks, because I'm still stupidly speechless.

"Ah, this is James, Natalie's dad," I say, recovering.

"Nice to meet you, sir," Daniel says and extends his hand.

James shakes his hand, but his eyes are trained on me. I swallow thickly, praying he doesn't spill our secret. My heart is pounding against my ribs.

"Would you like to come in? Natalie isn't here right now. I don't know when she'll be back. Aub?" Daniel asks, looking at me.

I open the door wider in an inviting move, only he doesn't

come in.

"Nice to see you," James says stiffly.

"Same. Yeah, so she's not here and won't be back until late tonight, actually. Did you try to call her?"

Thank God my voice remains steady.

James dips his chin once. "She didn't answer," he says, his interrogative gaze boring into mine. I have a feeling he's referring to me. "I have something important I want to discuss with her and need to do it in person."

My heart climbs into my throat, and it feels like there's a knot around my neck. "I can tell her tonight when she gets home if you like?"

"Just tell her I stopped by. I'll try calling her again." James looks at Daniel, and I hold my breath. "Nice to meet you."

James turns around to leave, and I shut the door.

"Ready to watch a movie?" Daniel asks, and I exhale, feeling relieved that Daniel didn't pick up on the awkwardness.

We're sitting back on the couch getting cozy and situated. I raise the remote control to play the movie when Daniel speaks. My stomach is a giant fucking mess now, my thoughts running in ten different directions. I can't focus. In all the years I've lived with Natalie, her dad has never once come by. I'm panicking inside because now I know James was really coming to see me. But he saw Daniel, the boyfriend he told me to break up with.

"I was thinking, and you don't have to give me an answer now—in fact, I want you to think on it first."

I sit up and look at him, cautious.

"After you graduate, I was wondering if you wanted to move in with me. I really like you, Aubrey, and I'd like to take this relationship to the next level."

My brows shoot up to my hairline, and my eyes widen in shock. Jaw bobbing, I'm speechless. I don't need this right now. Daniel just stares, chuckling like my reaction is cute.

"Move in with you?"

His smile turns timid, uncertain, and I feel bad. I don't want to make him uncomfortable. But I also do not want to live with him. I was supposed to break up with him!

"Yes. Live with me. As in share a home, a bed. As in I get to see you all the time."

My chuckle is flighty. "I'm sorry. I know that. It's just so unexpected. Really? You want to live with me? I'm kind of a disaster, and I work weird hours."

"I do. If it's what you want."

I bite the side of my lip, and his gaze falls to my mouth. I need to lie.

"Can I think about it? I've lived with Natalie for so long ... I'd have to make sure she has a roommate first, how I'm going to support my part of the rent, what I'm going to do with my life—"

"Babe. That's why I said think about it. I don't want you making a decision you'll only regret."

Nodding, I smile shyly at him and nestle into his side. He drapes his arm over me. I like living with Natalie and don't see myself moving out any time soon.

"Aubrey ... Aubrey ..." Daniel says, gently shaking me.

I open my eyes, heavy with sleep, and blink.

"Did I fall asleep?" My voice is groggy.

He smiles sweetly at me and brushes my hair back. "You did. It was pretty cute. I don't think you made it past the first ten minutes of the movie."

Sitting up, I rub my face. I didn't realize how tired I was.

"I'm sorry. I don't know what happened. I just got so comfortable on you that I guess I fell asleep." Leaning into him, I wrap my arms around his stomach and get closer. "You're so warm. Lie back down," I say, pushing into him.

"I wish I could, baby, but I got called into work. I have to go."

Unhappy, I grumble under my breath, and he chuckles.

"Boo. Stay here. We were supposed to chill all day."

"I know, and I hate that I have to leave, but duty calls. I have to go." Daniel stands and kisses the top of my head. "How about I call you when I get out later? I don't know what time it'll be, but I'll call anyway."

"Fine." I huff and move to stand, but he stops me.

"Go back to sleep. I'll lock the bottom lock when I leave."

I nod then lie back down. Daniel grabs his cell and wallet, then gives me one more kiss. He covers me with the blanket before he walks away and out the door.

I can feel my body falling into a deep sleep, the weight pulling me under. Just as I'm about to doze off, there's a knock at the door. Groaning, I stand and go to answer it.

Chapter 53

"James? Hey," I say, looking up at him. "What're you doing here again? Natalie isn't back yet."

My heart is racing. I have a feeling he came back for me and not his daughter.

"I know," he says gruffly then pushes himself inside and shuts the door.

Fuck. I close my eyes. My stomach flips backwards and the hair on the back of my neck rises. I'm slightly annoyed he just barged in, but I let it go because I have a feeling I know where this is going. Taking a deep breath, I open my eyes but James is already staring at me. His gaze is hard, his blue eyes accusatory. I take in his disheveled dress shirt and windblown hair. The colorful tattoos outlined in black I love so much are peeking out and capture my attention. I stare at them for a moment.

"Who's Daniel?"

My eyes snap to his. The moment of truth is here, one I wanted to avoid. If only I had broken up with Daniel, or called James back, then this wouldn't be happening right now.

Quietly, I say, "My boyfriend."

James turns to stone in front of me, unmoving. Rage burns through his gaze, and it hits me smack in the chest. "What do you mean your boyfriend? What are you talking about?" he says, eyes narrowing.

I shift on my feet and prop my hands on my hips. "Wait a minute ... Did you wait outside until he left?" James stares at me, ignoring my question. His body leans to the side in his stance.

"You did, didn't you?" I say, surprised.

"When did you get a boyfriend, Aubrey? How long have you been with him?" he asks through gritted teeth.

I look from one eye to the other. I'm going to be sick. "Did you really come here looking for Natalie, or were you looking for me?"

"Answer the question."

I'm quiet for a moment. "It's really none of your business to know anything about him."

His blue eyes flare. Wrong choice of words. I shouldn't have said that, because James is downright seething now.

"I have every right to know about him."

I shake my head. "No, you don't. You don't have access to my personal life."

"I told you when we went into this agreement to get rid of the boyfriend and to stop working at Sanctuary," James says, his voice raised and loud.

I'm steaming mad. He's acting like I just took away his favorite pacifier. I want to tell him to grow up. "I've been with Daniel since before we agreed to anything, and I wasn't going to stop working just because you said so. I have a deal with *you*, when I'm with *you*. Not a deal that controls my entire life. You're paying for Valentina, not Valentina and Aubrey. Did you really think I was going to let you own every second of my day for the next year? Was I supposed to drop out of school too because you said so? What I do with my personal time is none of your business. You told me you don't own the girls you're with. And anyway, you're married, remember?" My gaze drops to his left hand, and I lift it to show him his wedding band. He yanks his hand away and steps toward me. I rear back and square my shoulders. "I'm not a fucking dog, James. I don't heel because you blinked your goddamn eyes."

"For twenty million dollars, you'll do exactly what I say and what I want, whenever I want. If I want you to get on your knees and suck my dick in the middle of Times Square, you fucking will. If I want to watch you fuck two men at the same time, you will. I said no work and no boyfriend. Those were the only things I asked, and you couldn't do that or be honest with me. I don't ask for a lot. Instead, you keep spreading your legs for money you don't need and have a baby boy on the side."

Rage pours out of me. "You have a fucking wife! What does it matter if I have a boyfriend or a job? None of that stops me from doing what you want."

"Actually it did stop you. You've been blowing me off and ignoring my requests to see me." He pauses. "Are you still at Sanctuary Cove?"

Eyes wide, I drop my jaw. I don't answer, and he mimics my gaze.

"Yes, I am," I admit.

James lets out a mocking laugh that sends a shiver down my spine. "You really are a whore, aren't you?"

"Fuck you!"

That one hurt. I draw in a thick gasp of utter disbelief. Of all the things James could say, he goes for the one thing that would hurt me the most. He knew, more than anyone, how I felt about selling my body.

My emotions are quickly climbing, and I can feel the burn of tears in my eyes. He sees it and doesn't even apologize. Being called a whore in the manner he used it denotes a dirty, disgusting woman living on the streets giving blowies for a two-dollar hit of crack. It makes me feel cheap, like a real piece of garbage.

I'd worked so hard to keep a stable and somewhat normal, balanced life while working for Christine, trying to prove to myself that what I do is just like any regular job. Prostitution is the oldest working profession in history, after all. But James just swiped all of it away with a few words.

"Get the hell out," I say, my voice a whisper but full of venom.

"That's exactly what you are, though," he pushes. "I give you any amount of money you want, and you still whore yourself around after I asked you not to. You're a fucking prostitute, Aubrey. *Valentina.* Whatever the fuck you want to be called today. You're just another pretty face with the ability to suck a dick better than most sluts. That's all," he spits. "I should've known better." James lifts his shoulders and shrugs like he just parted the sea and it was no big deal.

My eyes lower to slits, and I'm trying really hard not to cry. "That's all I am? Really? I give you things your wife can't give you, that *no one* has ever been able to. That's why you paid me, because you know I'm fucking good for it. And now you're mad that I give them to my real boyfriend too." I pause, a devious smile tugging my lips up.

I step toward James until we're a few inches apart. The tears that threatened to fall shrink back, and my voice turns to syrup as Valentina emerges. He stares down hard, nostrils flaring, and I can't help but love the hate pouring out of him.

"Oh, I see what happened here," I say. "You're sexually frustrated, aren't you? Was your wife a shitty lay last night? Did she just spread eagle while you gave her soft, weak thrusts so you didn't hurt her saggy little honey pot? Is that why you're here wagging your pecker around like you own me, because you couldn't come the way I fucking make you come?"

Reaching out, I cup James's cock and give him a good squeeze. I grin. "Well, well, well, will you look at that? A hard dick, and all I did was talk back to you."

I tighten my grip, but he smacks my hand away. In one swift motion, James lifts me up and slams me against the front door, his mouth on mine, tongue delving into my mouth. His chest is pressed to mine as it heaves.

"You don't deserve me," I grit out, breaking the kiss. "I'm just a trashy whore anyway, right? I thought you were different, but you're not. You're just another fucking sleazeball looking for a tight pussy."

I'm no match for his strength as he maneuvers himself so that he's got both of my hands captured in one of his while his teeth bite into my nipple. I gasp loudly as pleasure sears through my body. My ankles lock around his waist, thighs tightening. My shorts are damp, and I'm ashamed because what he said about me is true. I am just a whore, no matter how much I dress it up.

"Next time think before you speak," he says with my nipple between his teeth. He uses his tongue to wet my shirt, and my hips move in his hold. My nipple hardens and my eyes threaten to roll shut. It hurts so much that it feels fucking divine.

"James," I warn.

Flattening his tongue, he licks a hot trail up the column of my neck, and I almost sigh from it. Goose bumps trickle down my spine. I wiggle free and unlock my ankles, pushing him back so I can stand, and then I shock us both by slapping him across the face.

I shouldn't have done that. I blink, unsure what to do now. James takes both my hands and raises them above my head, securing them to the door. I try to wiggle out. His grip is so tight, I'm going to lose feeling in my fingers. He presses his body into mine. Bending his knees, he rolls his hips so his erection thrusts against my clit. My jaw falls open, a soft sigh spilling from my lips. He takes advantage and locks his mouth over mine, kissing me like he has every right to. He's brutal, hard, making sure I feel every bit of him from the inside out. James is a beast and he doesn't let me come up for air. His cock is straining through his slacks and rubbing my pussy until I'm finally giving in. I moan into his mouth, kissing him back just as rough. I bite down on his lip as my hips surge toward his. We both groan into each other. "You're soaked," James says then unbuckles his belt and pulls his zipper down. His pants fall around his ankles in a heap.

I don't want to be controlled by money over every aspect of my life. That was never the plan. He's paying for Valentina. Aubrey isn't for sale.

I break the kiss. "I'm not changing my life for anyone."

"Yes, you are. You're mine, Aubrey, no one else's," he says, yanking down my little shorts. "Just like I'm yours."

When he notices I'm not wearing underwear, I grin like the cat who ate the canary.

"Fucked Daniel earlier—you know, my boyfriend? Planned to fuck him senseless all day."

It's a lie. I didn't have sex with him earlier. I'm just mad and want to hurt James the way he hurt me.

His eyes darken, and it excites me. "I'll show you how to fuck someone senseless."

He thumbs my clit in circles, and my knees go weak while he roughly penetrates me with two fingers. It doesn't hurt me, though, because his touch does nothing but bring me pleasure. Taking his cock, James strokes my sex, willing my legs to spread. I fight my moan, and he lifts my leg, hiking it up over his hip, and then he surges into me in one long, hard stroke. I yell out as I stretch to fit his width, the sharp, wonderful pain taking over my body.

His mouth is on my neck, beard drifting over my skin, and I whimper. Pulling out, he thrusts back in.

"How can you say those things to me and still fuck me?"

"You mean after I spoke the truth?" he says, his words hot. "That's what you are, though. You're a fucking whore who I just happened to fall in love with."

I clench around him. A little gasp escapes me. Tears fill my eyes, and before I can stop them, one slips down my cheek. "Don't say that," I whisper, my chest burning. "Take it back."

He looks at me, eyeing the tear. "Take what back? It's called honesty, sweetheart. You should try it sometime."

My jaw is trembling. "James ..."

"Yes, sweetheart?" he responds, pushing in a little deeper.

My pussy is pulsating around him, wanting more and wanting him to leave.

"Take it back. Now."

"You'll let me call you a whore, but saying I love you is too much for you to handle?"

I don't want to hear that he fell in love with me. It's a lie. It has to be. He can't possibly feel the same way about me as I do him, because then it will ruin everything.

"Take it back," I repeat.

"Which part? Say it."

James thrusts all the way in again and lets go of my hands. My arms fall to my sides as he grips my hips to pick me up and shove me down on his length so I can't move. He's thick and warm, and I feel like he's splitting me in two, emotionally as much as physically. I place my hands on his chest and run them up to tangle them in his hair. He leans into me, his mouth hovering over mine.

"How's this for honesty? I was going to leave my wife for you. I thought I'd finally found someone who gets me, but she's still fucking men behind my back. Even after the millions of dollars I've given her. Goes to show that money can't buy everything."

"Stop it," I say as another tear falls.

"Say the words and I'll leave her," he begs and then kisses me.

James doesn't hold back and starts driving his hips against mine. I meet him thrust for thrust. He's rough and we're desperate. Together it makes for a hunger like no other. He grips my thigh so tight my hips instinctively roll into his, making sure I get all of his length. I sigh and moan, hating that I caved and loving what he gives me despite the hurt he's caused.

"It'll never work that way. There's no use in talking about it."

James knows I'm referring to Natalie. It's soul-crushing, but it's the truth.

"I'll make it work. Just say the word, sweetheart. I'll leave her tonight and make things right if I know I can have you forever."

I shake my head vehemently. How could he want me after he discovered Daniel? After what he said to me? James is crushing my heart. I want to say yes and I know there's no way I can. I can't say the words because I know they'll never come true.

"James, please ..."

"Say it."

"I can't. You know I can't!"

"I know you love me just like I love you."

A tear slips from my eye. He kisses me again like he's determined to win me over. Ecstasy rips through my body, igniting his pleasure at the same time. We're both coming hard, nails digging into skin, moans and grunts fill the air as his cum blows inside me and I milk his cock for everything he has. We're floating into oblivion together, left with another mind-blowing orgasm better than the last time.

He doesn't waste any time. He pulls out of me, leaving a clear line of his cum dripping behind. James pulls his pants up and fastens them. I'm slumped against the door, my fatigued body in a stupor. I tug my shorts on, my thighs quivering.

I watch as he walks over to the counter and pulls something out of his shirt pocket then reaches across the counter. I frown, trying to see what he's doing, but he's done faster than I can blink my eyes. He turns toward me and walks my way, closing the distance in three large steps. My gaze drops to the counter, and my heart splits down the center.

A check.

Glaring down at me with resentment so thick it chokes me, he says, "That's the balance I owe you. It's safe to say this little arrangement we had is now over. If you won't give yourself to me completely, then we're finished."

My lips part, my eyes wide. I step out of the way, and James leaves, walking out of my life. All I can do is fall against the door in a slump and cry my eyes out.

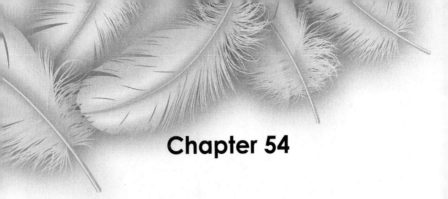

Chapter 54

I skipped class all week, citing the stomach flu. The days were long, the nights longer. It was the first time in all four years of school that I didn't show up to class and couldn't have picked a worse time. Finals are coming up, and graduation is around the corner. I need to be there. Instead, I laid in bed, lethargic, crying on and off.

When the tears weren't flowing, I was in an unblinking daze staring out my bedroom window, which is what I'm doing now. Daniel tried to come over to check on me multiple times, but I wouldn't let him. I just wanted to be alone.

My feelings for James run much deeper than I thought. Even though I'm still reeling with anger over the things he said to me, it doesn't change the fact that I'm madly, head over heels for him. I keep thinking about the way he left me, the hurt and real love in his eyes as he walked out. He took my heart with him.

I exhale a fatigued sigh. I can't imagine if we'd gone the whole year what state I'd be in at the end. More time together would've made things complicated, but I guess they already were.

I clench my eyes shut, hearing his words replay in my head for the hundredth time this week, how he wanted to leave his wife for me. How I'm a whore he fell in love with. I know I should look at the dissolution of our clandestine agreement as a blessing in disguise, but it's also undeniably heartbreaking. We were hopeless from the start.

Sitting up, I reach for my vibrating phone on my desk. I look down at the screen and see Madam Christine texting me again.

Shit.

I've refused all jobs this week, telling her I've been sick. I send her a quick message saying I'm on the mend and that I need to talk to her. I've been thinking a lot about escorting and decided I never want to go through feeling like this again.

I can't work at Sanctuary Cove anymore.

Between the guilt of lying to both Natalie and Daniel, it's for the best. I know it is. I made a shit ton of money before the deal with James, which meant I didn't really need to keep doing it anyway.

I get up to use the bathroom, and then I make my way to the kitchen to get a glass of water just as a furious Natalie storms in. The door flies open and hits the wall. She reaches for it and slams it shut.

"Aubrey!" she screams. Fuck, my ears.

"I'm right here," I say quietly behind her.

She jumps, holding her chest, and I'd have laughed if I wasn't feeling so miserable.

She looks at me, and her face scrunches up as she takes in my appearance. "You look like death."

"Love you too. What's up?"

Natalie stomps to the cabinet. She takes out a tall shot glass and pours tequila. A few drops spill onto the counter.

"My dad is a fucking psycho," she says then throws the shot back. "I hate him."

I swallow hard. She offers me a shot as she's pouring another one, but I decline.

"What happened?" I ask, nervous.

"Remember how I thought it was strange that he stopped by? Now I know why he came by last week."

I frown, holding the glass of water to my chest. I had to tell her James stopped by in case Daniel let it slip.

"He wanted to tell me himself that he filed for divorce."

My brows shoot up and my jaw drops. Divorce? I didn't think he'd still go through with it.

"Exactly," she says at my expression. "And with some bullshit excuse too, which makes no sense because my mom said they were working on their marriage and everything was going really well. She's devastated because she's been so happy. I know every marriage has issues—theirs certainly did—but he blindsided her with the papers. She says it's unexpected, and I kind of agree."

My eyes widen in utter shock. He already had her served? So maybe he had been coming to see me but also Natalie too. I'm not sure what to think, and I try not to allow myself to feel anything, but my heart is fluttering crazy fast. Talk about mixed emotions. I didn't know they were still working on their marriage. James never mentioned that, and while I feel even worse now, there's a part of me that's thrilled with the idea he'll be free. I knew James was serious about us, but I don't understand how he thought it would've ever worked. Paranoia seeps through me. Maybe if I'd answered one of his many calls this week, I would know, but I hadn't, and now I'm even more perplexed.

I swallow back my tangled feelings and paste on sympathy. "I'm really sorry, Nat."

She shakes her head and takes another shot. She's staring at something behind me like she's lost in her thoughts.

"I don't understand ... he was so calm when he told me. My mom was crying nonstop. He's already moved out to someplace on the east side, said things haven't been working between them for a long time now. He decided they needed to move on separately." She looks my way, downright baffled. "It doesn't make sense." Her nails tap the counter frantically. "Something is missing. I just don't know what yet."

"What was his reason?" I feel like if I don't ask something it looks bad, but being the lying best friend that I am, I feel wrong for asking too.

"He says their marriage hasn't been good for years and it's to the point that they hardly speak. He says they've had some type of agreement but it's between them and refused to tell me. I asked my mom about it, but she won't tell me either. She's distraught, which makes me so angry at him to see her that upset. My mom is as gentle as a ladybug." She shakes her head. "I can't get over the fact that he filed for divorce and moved out so quickly."

I can't either.

I'm hesitant. "Does it bother you that they're divorcing?"

"Yes and no. Of course, it bothers me a little bit, but that's because I just feel terrible for my mom. She has a slight drinking problem, so I hope this doesn't set her over the edge. When I went to see her, she was drunk as fuck, but I didn't say anything because her husband of twenty-plus years left her, so I felt like she deserved a pass, you know?"

I nod. I can't not agree. I'd be the same way regardless of if the marriage had already been lost for years.

"I guess the actual divorce doesn't bother me? I don't know. I'm not a child. I can see things differently. I wouldn't want to be locked in a marriage I don't want to be in." She pauses. "I don't ever want to get married."

I frown, agreeing with her, and give her a hug. I wonder if James would've still filed for divorce if I hadn't come into his life. Their marriage wasn't ideal from what he'd told me. They didn't see eye to eye or have the same interests in much, but I still don't like the thought of being responsible for them separating.

But I am the reason. I know I am, and it kills me. Now that James and I are through, I hope our secret stays buried forever.

Natalie eyes me, and I hold my breath. I decide to change the subject. "Daniel asked me to move in with him."

Her jaw drops. "Are you going to?"

I shake my head. That's the last thing I want. My phone rings, and dread fills my stomach. I hope it isn't James at a time like this.

"Let me grab that real quick."

I run into my bedroom before the ringing stops and pick up my phone, frowning at the unknown number.

"Hello?"

"Ms. Abrams?"

"Yes?"

I sit on the edge of my bed with the phone clutched in my hand, my stomach cramping with the worst fear of my life. I'm staring blankly ahead, in shock, listening to the doctor at Jamaica Hospital tell me I need to come in. My heart is pounding in my chest, beating so hard I can barely hear what the doctor is saying. One of Grammy's cats rubs up against the back of my arm. I reach for it, bringing it close to my heart.

"Aub?" Natalie says, walking into my room.

My eyes shift to hers, and she looks at me with concern. Quietly, I say, "The hospital called. They want me to come in to go over her test results."

Her frown deepens. "They can call you and ask you to do that?"

I nod. "Grammy has me listed on her medical papers in case anything happens. She's fine right now, but the doctor wants to go over her results with me." I swallow back the tears rising to the surface. Something isn't right. I can feel it in my bones.

The cat purrs against my neck, rubbing its head on me as if it knows I need support. It's the nicest cat, except when it wants to sleep on my chest in the middle of the night. I glance down at it, deciding I'm going to sneak the furry little beast into the hospital.

It took about two hours to buy an animal duffel bag to conceal the pet and get to the hospital, but I'm finally sitting next to my grammy at her bedside. She knows why I'm here. I'm trying to be optimistic before we speak to anyone, but it's difficult when I take in the yellow coloring of her eyes and how pale she looks.

"Grammy, I have a surprise for you," I say, reaching down by my feet. I unzip the bag. "I smuggled your cat in."

She starts laughing, and her face lights up. Right there, that moment, that look, is worth the risk of getting caught. To see her smile and her eyes dance with happiness is everything to me.

"Does the hospital know?" she asks quietly.

"Heck no."

She giggles. I lift the cat and stand to hand it to her. The white fur ball with blue eyes curls up against her and nestles into her arm. I smile seeing the love the two have for each other as I sit down.

"Oh, Aubrey. This is the best surprise you could've given me," she says, her voice shaky. "I wish she could stay with me. It's lonely at night."

My heart aches for her. "I told you I would stay the night."

"No." She shoots me down. "You have school and work. I'll be fine here. I'm not really alone anyway, with the nurses pricking me every few hours for blood." She pets the cat lovingly. "Isn't graduation coming up?"

I nod. I know she's changing the subject. I let it slide.

"It's a little over a month away. You better be out of this hospital and there with me. I'm looking forward to taking a few shots with you afterward."

She chuckles. Her smile is so wide that it makes me feel good. "Honey, I wouldn't miss seeing you graduate for anything. I'm so proud of all the hard work you've done to get where you are."

After a couple of hours spent talking with Grammy, she drifts into a peaceful sleep. Carefully, I place her cat back in my carrier, drape a jacket over it, and then seek out the doctor. He pulls me into his office and has me take a seat across from him. I place the pet carrier down and pray the cat doesn't make a sound.

The doctor leans over his desk and threads his fingers together. I watch his movement with an impending sense of dread.

"Are you aware of how ill your grandmother is?"

I frown. "I know she has bronchitis."

He studies me for a moment. "She told me she doesn't visit her physician often. Is that true?"

"She only goes if she feels really sick. Otherwise, she just fights any infection off herself." I pause. "She's stubborn like that."

"Did she ever seem sick? Tired? Out of breath? Weight loss? Complain about pain?"

I shake my head. "I live in the city, so I'm not around as much as I used to be. She does have a cough I noticed, but nothing else." I shrug. "She wouldn't have told me if she wasn't feeling well, though."

He blows out a long, heavy breath, and it makes me tense. There's a tightness in the way he speaks, cautious and careful. He tells me in detail about the scans and lab work, the reasons he requested them in the first place, and then reads the results. It's a lot to process, and I almost wish I had James here with me to go over it.

Leaning forward, the doctor hands me copies of the reports to reread when I get home.

"What does this all mean?" I ask, looking down at the papers as I flip through them. I look up when he doesn't respond, and his face softens with regret.

"I'm sorry to be the one to tell you this, Aubrey, but your grandmother has lung cancer."

Chapter 55

Every day since the doctor diagnosed Grammy with stage four lung cancer, I've been by her side each chance I've had.

She opted out of chemotherapy and decided to let nature run its course. I cried and begged her to consider changing her mind. She said she's too old to go through such drastic treatment and wants to spend whatever time she has left with me and her cats instead of in crippling pain just to live an extra year, if she's lucky.

Her decision broke my heart.

I decided I wouldn't read anything online, even though I almost caved a few times. It'll just mess with my head. The cancer has metastasized. Knowing that pretty much answers every question I had. I can't blame her for not wanting to go through treatment. If I was pushing eighty, I wouldn't want to do it either. Doesn't mean I have to like it.

The truth is, I fucking hate it. I want to push her and force her to do the chemo, but I can't. I won't. It's her decision, but it's breaking my damn heart.

I haven't stopped crying. It's only been seven days, but those seven days have been the worst of my life. I've kept it all bottled in and cried when no one was looking. I didn't tell Natalie. I was already dealing with the guilt of her parents' divorce, and I couldn't bring myself to lean on her for support. How shitty of me that would've been. The pressure inside my chest is growing by the day, my anxiety higher than ever at night. I hardly sleep. If I'm not at the hospital visiting Grammy, then I'm at school or in the library doing homework.

I also decided against leaving Sanctuary Cove, thinking the forced distraction would ease the pain, if only for a short time. Every day I take a job from Christine. Once visiting hours are over, I become Valentina.

"Are you okay?" Natalie asks as I step out of my room.

She's sitting on a high-top chair at the kitchen counter doing homework. I eye her coffee mug and can't even bring myself to laugh. I LIKE BIG BALLS AND I CANNOT LIE. I slip my crossover purse over my head.

"Yeah, I'm fine."

"You don't look fine." She taps her pencil on the counter. "How was last night?"

I realize I need to cover up my emo mood before she digs and I unleash everything I'm holding in. That's the last thing I need to happen.

Reaching inside the refrigerator, I pull out a bottle of sangria and pop the top. I offer Natalie one, and she takes it. Gotta love six packs of pre-made, sugarfied sangria.

I turn around and lean against the fridge. "I've had the strangest clients all week. I don't even know what to think. It must be a full moon or something. This one guy wanted me to slap his balls until they were red. I didn't want to at first because I didn't want to hurt him. You know how guys are so sensitive there? You look at the dick the wrong way and they're practically singing soprano. This guy, though, he took it like a champ and came four times. I've never seen anything like it."

She takes a sip and nods. "Been there, slapped that." We chuckle. "That's actually fairly common. I had one guy who filled his dick with saline before I banged his balls around."

I grimace in sympathetic pain, wondering why any man would want to do that. "This other guy wanted me to tell him how I lost my virginity while he was dripping sweat all over me. He sounded like a horse as he was fucking me."

"Did you?"

I smirk. "I got the feeling he was a bit of a creepo, so I made up a story and told him my teacher in ninth grade taught me how to have sex. He was super into it."

She shakes her head in disbelief. "Men are so weird. They like the strangest shit. I have a client this week I have to call every two hours to make sure he's still wearing the pink diamond butt plug I put in him. He only takes it out to sleep and shit."

My face scrunches up in disgust as we trade war stories. "I have no words."

"I told him to buy a vibrator and sit on it with the plug still inside him. He said he can't because he came in his pants too many times the first day and isn't bringing a change of clothes to work."

I almost choke on my sangria.

"I'm telling you, we could write a book about our adventures as sex workers."

"We can call it, The Chronicles of Valentina and Natalia," I joke and finish my drink. I place the bottle on the counter and reach for my vibrating phone.

Blocked Caller.

A deep sadness runs through me. James calls me every day, and every day I decline it. Crazy enough, the one person I wanted to lean on when I discovered the news about Grammy was James. I wanted to run to him and cry on his shoulder and feel his arms wrapped around me and have him tell me that everything was going to be okay.

"You all right?"

Swallowing, I nod hastily and stuff my phone away. "I'll be back later. I'm going to help Grammy home from the hospital and get her settled in. I'll come back and get the cats afterward. I figure discharge will take a while, and I don't want to leave them in the car, even if it's cool out. She'll have my head for that."

Since Grammy waved her rights for treatment, the doctor

suggested a nurse come in a few times a week to check vitals and make sure she's taking the prescription medication. I want to be there to meet the woman.

"I'm gonna miss this little shit," Natalie says as she picks up a cat and pets it.

"Yeah, you're gonna miss a cat the way you miss a yeast infection," I say then blow her two kisses and leave.

***

Who knew how much time and stress the day was going to bring.

I'm not complaining, since I'm spending it with Grammy, but between the time it took to discharge her, the prescriptions I fought over with the pharmacist who insisted they weren't covered by insurance, city traffic, dropping her off at home with the nurse, picking up all the cats and their stuff back in the city, and then driving back to Queens ...

I'm fit to be tied and could use a stiff drink.

Only, stiff drinks make me think of James and his expensive cognac. I think back to when we first met and how we hung out all day like we'd known each other for years in that underground private room, sipping his favorite drink and picking at food. I'd thought he was crazy to want to finish off a bottle. We did, though, and it was one of the best days I'd ever had being a whore, as James had so sweetly called me.

I close my eyes as I sit in the parked car in front of Grammy's house. There was such venom in his words the last time we were together. I keep thinking about why it hurt me so much to hear him call me a whore, and I think it's because he accepted me, the real me, from the beginning, just like I did with him, knowing he was married. It didn't bother him that I get paid for sex. James got all of me. It's why this separation hurts so much, why I can't eat or sleep. Why I've been falling into a deeper pit of depression each day. He took a part of me without asking, and I didn't even know it until it was too late. I've never given myself freely the way I did with him, not even with Daniel, and I don't know how to deal with that missing part of me I'll never get back.

I sigh inwardly and take out my phone when I see a message from Natalie asking to borrow a specific calculator. I send her a response telling her it's in my desk somewhere and to shuffle shit around until she finds it.

Daniel asked me earlier if he could see me tonight. I told him once I'm done with Grammy, I'd let him know when's a good time. I sent a quick message saying that he should bring over a bottle of tequila in about two hours. He responds pretty quickly and tells me he'll bring wine. I'm finally going to break up with Daniel. There's too much going on, and ultimately, I don't love him.

Getting out of the car, I walk up to Grammy's house carrying all the cat carriers and let myself in.

I almost burst into tears at the sight before me. Our gazes meet, and I force a smile. I can tell she's trying to remain strong for me, but I need to look just as strong for her. I squat down to hide my sadness and fumble with opening the pet cages. The cats run free, and one sprints onto her lap. I smile at the image of them.

Crossing the distance, I place a kiss to the top of her head. "I hope you're not giving the nice lady a hard time."

There's medical equipment everywhere, bags of clear liquid, a wheelchair, and vials of medicine. Grammy is seated in a tattered recliner while a nurse checks her blood pressure. The woman smiles up at me then focuses on her task at hand. There are black and blue marks at the creases of Grammy's elbows where blood was drawn repeatedly from her fragile body, and a new IV is sticking out the top of her hand.

She scoffs. "I don't need any of this. I'm fine. I feel great. Honestly."

I smile. "You're such a bull. Let the lady do her job. Did you eat while I was gone like I said to?"

She eyes me with guilt, and I laugh. "I didn't have an appetite," she says.

"You're eating before I leave. I'm going to bring in the rest of your cats' stuff, and then I'll make some soup for you."

"You're an angel," she says.

Once I unpack her belongings and set up, I'm standing in the kitchen warming something up when the nurse comes in to introduce herself.

"I'm Ms. Shelly, and I'll be one of your grandmother's hospice nurses on rotation."

I almost drop the pan I'm holding.

"Hospice?"

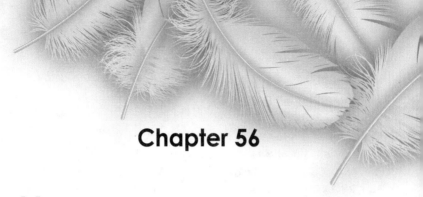

Chapter 56

Ms. Shelly looks at me in confusion. "Were you not aware?"

I blink a few times. "I knew there would be a nurse. I just didn't know it would be from hospice."

Her smile is gentle. "Your grandmother made the call herself from the hospital. I'll be here four times a week to monitor her condition and check how well her medications are working to relieve symptoms. I'll also be communicating with her doctor should anything arise."

The fact that Grammy called hospice makes me sick to my stomach. No one makes that call unless it's serious and they absolutely have to. My jaw trembles and I sniffle, sucking back my emotions. I try not to think about how her cancer is terminal. The only plus I see about hospice is that I'm relieved someone will be here for her when I can't be.

"What about at night? Does someone stay?" I ask, my voice a little shaky.

"We can. We can do shifts if it makes you feel better."

I nod. "It would. If you're here that many days a week, the cancer must be worse than I thought. She just doesn't want to tell me. I'd like someone to always be here for her."

"We'll have to modify the paperwork—"

"Don't bother her with that. Whatever it is, I'll take care of it. The papers and cost, anything she needs, I can take care of."

Ms. Shelly smiles appreciatively. "She's lucky to have a granddaughter like you. Now when you're done, I'd like to show you a few things if you have time?"

"Of course. Would you like a bowl of soup?"

Ms. Shelly politely declines. I prepare a bowl, then carry it out to Grammy.

"You didn't tell me you called hospice."

She sits up, scooting close to the table. "I didn't want you to worry. I may be hardheaded, but I'm not dumb. Hospice is here to help ease my pain." She takes a sip of her Tuscan soup. "This is delicious. Thank you, Aubrey."

I smile sadly. I didn't make the soup. It came from a can.

"Do you want me to stay the night? I was thinking I would."

"No, absolutely not," she says firmly. "You're not going to baby me because of a few words the doctor said. I can handle myself—plus, I have Shelly here." She takes another bite then says, "In fact, it's late and you've been helping me all day. Why don't you get going?"

My brows lift. "Are you kicking me out?"

"Yes," Grammy says, but not with any meanness. "I love you, but go home."

I chuckle lightly. After Ms. Shelly goes over everything she brought and explains what her role is, I kiss Grammy on the head and leave. As I'm walking down the block to the bus stop, I text Daniel, telling him to meet me at my place in an hour or so, and then I dial up Natalie.

"Hey," she answers.

I frown at her tone. I know it's only a three-letter word, but it sounds clipped.

"Hey! I'm on my way home and need a drink so bad. Are you busy?"

"No."

I hesitate for a second. "Oh, okay. Well, Daniel's coming over with wine. I thought we could all hang out and order Chinese?"

"Sure."

My frown deepens as the bus draws closer. "Is everything

okay?" I ask again. "You seem off."

"Yeah. Everything is just dandy."

Something is definitely wrong. There isn't a hint of playfulness in her tone like there usually is.

"Okay ... Do you want me to pick anything up before I get home?"

"No. I'll just see you when you get here," Natalie says then hangs up the phone.

Pulling the phone away, I glance down at the blank screen, wondering why her tone seems so grim. It's totally unlike her.

An unsettling feeling coils in my stomach as I climb onto the bus and take a seat. Maybe she had a job gone bad and wants to be alone, and here I am telling her Daniel is coming over with wine.

After a few transfers and a couple of blocks, I'm finally unlocking my door. I push it open to a somewhat dark apartment. It's oddly quiet, and I reach for the light on the side of the wall. Placing my purse on the counter, I shrug my jacket off and turn to hang it on the back of the door when I spot Natalie behind me, sitting at the table. I jump, grasping my chest.

"Jesus fucking Christ, Natalie!" A harsh sigh bursts out of me. "You scared the shit out of me. What are you doing?"

She's staring, her severe gaze probing mine. Heat prickles down my arms, and my veins fill with dread, a laden weight rooting me in place.

"Is everything okay?" I ask. "Did something happen?"

She sits back, still glaring. She unfolds her arms, and I see a little white piece of paper between her fingers. I can hear the material rubbing together as she straightens it out and flips it over.

I hardly breathe when I view the front of it. The world fades around me, sound drowning out as my eyes focus in on the pale blue rectangular piece of paper with angry scribbles on it. My lips part and my throat is dry as cotton.

It's the last ten-million-dollar check James wrote me. I never deposited it. I placed it in my desk drawer under a few things and shut it. I was going to give it back, but I was too distraught to think since that day and forgot. Then I got the news of Grammy's cancer and my head hasn't been right since. She must've found it when she was looking for the calculator.

"What is this?" she inquires.

Her gaze ... it says everything. I try to swallow, but my throat is tight.

"Natalie," I say softly.

"What is this?" she repeats, enunciating the words to a point.

She slowly stands and walks over to me. She holds the check up to my face. My eyes run over it. At the bottom where the memo is, James wrote "services."

Fuck.

My gaze shifts up to hers. I need to think before I speak, but I can see in her gaze that her mind is already made up.

"It's not what you think." Dumbest words ever spoken. "It is ... but it isn't." My voice staggers with guilt.

"Don't try and play me for a fucking fool. A ten-million-dollar check? Services? How long have you been fucking him?"

I flinch.

"How long?" she yells then smacks the check to the counter. "Did you go after my dad after you met him? Saw the money and lavish world and decided you wanted it for yourself?" Her eyes light up, like everything has just clicked into place. Her lips part with a gasp. "You're the reason," she says under her breath. "You're the reason my dad moved out. The reason for the divorce."

I shake my head vehemently and draw in a heavy breath. "No, it's not like that. I swear."

"It is, though. That's exactly what it is. When did this happen?"

I'm silent, unable to speak.

"Answer my fucking question because I'm about two seconds

from losing it completely."

This can go one of two ways. Honesty is the only way to set the truth free, but honesty is going to be what ruins everything. Harboring a dark secret and telling the truth is a double-edged sword for a friendship.

"It started about eight months ago," I say.

Her eyes widen in shock and confusion. "How? You only just met him a couple of months ago."

I lower my voice to show her that I don't want to fight with her. "I didn't know he was your dad until the charity dinner. I met him before that."

She blinks a few times. "When did you start fucking him? Before you knew he was my dad or after?"

My jaw trembles, tears filling my eyes. I try to blink them back. I feel like I'm splitting in two. I know if I tell her the truth that our friendship will be over.

An eerie calmness settles over Natalie. It spreads like wildfire, and it frightens me because I can feel the blazing heat seeping from her. I'm trying to think of what I can say that might help this, but nothing comes to mind.

Her head bobs subtly in awareness, her gaze accusatory. "It was after, wasn't it? You slept with him after."

I nod, and before I can see what's happening, her hand is flying toward my face. My head whips to the side as a gasp is torn from my lips. I reach up to hold my face and stare at her. She's absolutely seething, but what kills me is the devastation in her icy glare.

"My dad offers you money for sex and you take it? Knowing he's my dad? Knowing he's married? What kind of person are you? You're supposed to be my best friend, Aubrey. I've always been there for you, and this is the kind of thanks I get? What did I ever do to you to deserve this? My parents have been married for twenty-two years. Then suddenly you come along and he has an affair? I know you're the reason he filed." She shakes her head in loathing. Her voice keeps getting louder and louder with every question she asks. "How do you do that to someone you care about? To me? How do you fuck him and then look me in the eye for months like nothing ever happened?"

I roll my lips between my teeth. The tears have broken free, streaming down my cheeks. "I'm so sorry."

"You're not sorry. If you were sorry, you wouldn't have kept spreading your legs. You're just sorry you got caught."

I look at her. "I *am* sorry. It's been killing me inside since the first—"

I stop myself.

Her eyes widen with fury. "Since the first what? Say it?"

I purse my lips together. "He wrote me two checks. That's the second one."

A shadow casts across her eyes. Disgust. Hatred. Outrage. "Twenty million? He gave you twenty?"

I nod.

"How many times did you sleep with him?" she asks through gritted teeth.

I swallow thickly. "I didn't keep track."

"I know you know. You always keep track."

I shake my head. That, I would never tell.

"I pray my mom doesn't know what you did, because if she does, there will be hell to pay. I hope that despicable man I can't even call my father spared her of that. I want you out of my life and out of my apartment. You're not a friend. You never were a friend. I would never, ever do that to you, no matter how much money I'm offered. A friend doesn't sleep with her friend's dad behind her back and then console her when she tells her about the separation. You're a fucking piece of shit, a home-wrecking slut. I fucking hate you."

Something about her tone and words set me off. I know she's

upset—she has every right to be—but she doesn't get to slap me and break me down with names.

"He didn't even know me as Aubrey until I met him at the dinner. Believe me, I wanted to tell you. I just didn't know how."

She scoffs, appalled. "You wanted to tell me, but instead you thought sleeping with him was a better idea? Do you see how messed up that is? Who are you?"

I don't want to throw James under the bus, but I need Natalie to see it's not all my fault and that I didn't chase him down.

"I met him through your club, Natalie. He's a member of Sanctuary Cove."

Her eyes lower to slits. "You're lying." She shakes her head, a mocking laugh under her breath. "Anything to save your ass. Where's the other half of that check?"

"In my bank," I say, my voice full of shame. "I forgot about that one"—I motion toward the check—"but I wasn't going to deposit it anyway."

"There's nothing you can say that will help this situation."

"Ask him. Go to your father and ask him. Did you even talk to him before you started making assumptions, or did you just decide to jump down my throat first? I know I fucked up big time, but I didn't chase James after I realized who he was like you think. Christine paired us up. That's how it started. Your dad was already cheating before I came along."

"There are eight million people in this scummy city, and you go after him?"

I don't say anything.

She's right, I could've said no. I tried to say no, but in the end, I couldn't deny him.

Still, I need to show that it wasn't planned.

"It's really not what you think. I'm not lying, Natalie. I met him through Sanctuary Cove."

Clarity fills her eyes. Covering her mouth, Natalie draws in an audible gasp. She takes a step back.

"Oh my God. He's the one, isn't he? The one you were obsessing over."

My heart is hammering so hard that my ribs ache. The look in her eyes says it all when it clicks together. All I can do is look away.

Chapter 57

Natalie throws her hands into the air. "Un-fucking-believable," she says, turning in a circle. She looks back at me, eyes wide and in utter disbelief. "So when you asked if I'd ever fallen for a client, you were talking about my dad?"

Her voice is starting to crack, and that only makes me more upset because the last thing I ever wanted to do was hurt her. I was hoping by ending it with James that it would pass with time and our secret would stay hidden. I should've known better. Secrets, lies, affairs, they never stay buried. They always come out and ultimately destroy the ones we love.

"Yes," I admit. "I was. I felt that way about him even when I didn't know who he was to you."

Natalie can't stop shaking her head or looking at me with such disdain. It's heartbreaking. I step toward her, only for her to take a step back like I'm carrying a disease she doesn't want to catch.

"I don't see how we'll ever get past this. I know now you're the reason for my parents splitting, because they were fine, and then suddenly, they're not. I'll never trust you again. A cheating loser and slut for a friend. You two are perfect for each other."

There's rapid knocking, and we both look at the door. Natalie looks at me. Scoffing under her breath, she asks, "Does he know about my father? About your work yet?"

Eyes wide, I shake my head as she reaches for the doorknob. A sly smirk tugs at her lips and her brow raises to a peak.

My body runs cold and sheer dread consumes me. "Please,

don't say anything. Let me tell him myself."

She ignores my plea and welcomes Daniel in. "Hey, Danny boy, what a pleasure it is to see you tonight." She lays it on thick and a tad sarcastic, but luckily he doesn't recognize it. She shuts the door.

Daniel walks toward me, but my gaze is on Natalie. I silently plead with her as he hugs me, but the look she's giving me makes me nauseated.

Daniel pulls back. I can barely meet his gaze. "Hey, babe ... Is everything okay? You look a little pale."

My jaw bobs. I'm struggling to find the right words as his brows grow deeper while he stares at me. I swallow hard. The air is so thick with tension that I'm convinced he can feel it. He looks back and forth between Natalie and me, confusion clear on his face, and places the wine on the table behind me. Thank God he doesn't see the check.

"Ah, hey," I say, my throat dry.

"Is this a bad time? Should we reschedule for another night?" he says, giving my forehead a kiss.

"Perfect timing, actually," Natalie says. She crosses her arms in front of her chest.

My heart drops. "Natalie, don't. Please."

She walks over to us so we're in a circle. Daniel keeps looking between us. The hatred spewing from her runs wild, and I'm choking on it so bad I feel like my heart is going to stop.

"What's going on?" Daniel draws out.

"Please, Natalie," I beg through clenched teeth.

She glares at me. "Are you going to tell him, or am I?"

"Natalie, *stop*."

Daniel takes a slow step back. His brows lower. I can feel his hesitation, and it's making me even more nervous.

"Tell me what?" he says, his voice raised.

There's a long beat of silence. I look at my best friend and see the torment in her eyes. She doesn't want to tell Daniel—that's not her style and we both know it—but she's so hurt right now, she's blinded by revenge.

"Aubrey was having her cake and eating it too." She pauses, nodding more to herself. "She was eating a lot of it."

Her voice is like syrup, and a slight smile curves the corners of her lips. Natalie walks over to the bottle of wine he brought and uses her electric wine opener.

"What's she talking about, Aub?"

I'm stunned speechless. She pours three glasses and hands them out, eyeing me with contempt. Clearly unsettled, Daniel takes a nervous sip, and Natalie follows. I don't. I can't.

"Your amazing, wonderful girlfriend right here has a side job. Has she ever told you about it?"

His brows deepen. "The nanny job, right?"

Natalie snickers. The sound grates down my arms. "Oh, you silly thing. Aubrey isn't a nanny. At least not anymore." Her nostrils flare. "You want to tell him the truth yet, or should I continue?"

"Natalie, just stop it. I know you're upset, but don't do this."

Casually, she takes another sip of wine and then eyes Daniel.

"College student by day, high-priced hooker by night." She pauses. "I just found out that Aubrey here has been fucking my dad for millions of dollars on the side."

A gasp gets lodged in my throat. I'm speechless. I'm hurt. I'm angry. I know what I did was horrible, but I didn't take my best friend as a tit-for-tat person.

The silence is deafening until Daniel barks out an incredulous laugh. Lifting the wine glass to my lips, I down the whole thing as I watch Natalie march into my room. Within seconds, she's walking back out carrying one of the boxes I use to hide the money I'm paid from my clients. She drops the box onto the table and flips it open. Bands of bills are stacked inside. Some wrapped in cash, others ripped open.

I swallow and look at him with panicked eyes. "I think you should go. How about I just call you later?" I place the glass down and try to get him to move, but he stands firm.

"She has an odd sense of humor, that one," Daniel says, grinning as he sips his wine. He thinks she's playing around. How sad that his perception is quickly about to change.

Natalie pauses and snaps her eyes to Daniel. "You think it's a joke?" Natalie lifts up an empty wrapper. I lunge for it, but she moves it out of my reach.

"Natalie, stop!"

Daniel is staring at me. He places his wineglass down. "Aubrey?" he asks warily.

"Natalie, don't do this! Stop!"

Natalie flips it over, her eyes sparkle with retaliation. "This is a ten-thousand-dollar money band with the number seventeen written on it. I remember when you got your first ten grand." She flicks it to the counter, and the paper drifts lifelessly like a feather. She picks up another. I grab the band and crumple it in my hand, crushing it. "This is a thousand ... probably just a blowie."

"A blowie?" Daniel says. The humor is gone from his voice. "Aubrey?"

Tears are dripping down my cheeks. Natalie reads two more, then grabs a handful of the bands that still have money in them and throws them to the table. My heart is shattering into a million little pieces. I hate that I'm so mad at her when I have no right to be, but I am. I'm fucking furious. I didn't think she'd stoop to this level.

"If that isn't enough ..." She reaches for James's check and smiles as if she just bought Girl Scout cookies. "Here. Read it if you don't believe me."

Daniel takes it. His brows lower and he frowns. "James Riviera? As in the attorney? Services?" He pauses. "Ten million dollars?"

LUCIA FRANCO

"Yeah, that's my pop," Natalie says, almost proudly. She pours another glass of wine and takes a large sip. "She was fucking him for months, and now my parents are divorcing. He actually gave her twenty mil, by the way."

Daniel is staring at the check. He's pale, quiet, like he doesn't want to believe it.

"I can explain."

He looks at me in utter shock and drops the check like it's on fire. My stomach is in knots, and I feel like I'm going to vomit.

"Is it true? You sleep with men for money? You're a prostitute?"

"Oh, it's true," Natalie says. "I'm the one who got her the job. Her name is Valentina when she's not Aubrey, and she gives the most fabulous blow jobs."

I give her a scathing look. She just shrugs casually.

"You're not a nanny?" he asks me, brows furrowed so deeply together. "You lied to me? This whole time?"

The hurt look in his eyes makes me feel like the real piece of shit that I am. I'm rendered speechless and have a gut feeling there's nothing I can say that will fix this. He'll never understand.

Natalie answers for me. "She used to be a nanny. Not anymore. She hasn't been a nanny in, like, almost a year. Right, Ram Jam?"

My jaw is trembling, heart is sick with grief.

"When? How?" He shakes his head. "Wait. All the times you had to babysit those kids or go away for the weekend, the stories you told me about them, were they fake?" My lips are pursed together. His eyes widen to large orbs, and his jaw drops. "You lied about all of it?"

Exhaling a heavy breath, I shake my head. "I can explain everything if you let me. It's not what you think. I had this job before I met you."

Daniel steps back, his eyes widening in repulsion. "You're really a prostitute?"

I nod my head. "Yes," I whisper, admitting the truth.

He draws in a harsh breath. "You have sex for money? The entire time you've been with me, you've been cheating on me with other men, *for money*?"

"For *good money*, Danny boy," Natalie adds. I wish she'd just shut the fuck up. "I wouldn't be surprised if she has around five hundred thousand saved by now. Well, add twenty mil to that."

His eyes bulge. He draws out his next set of words. "Five hundred thousand dollars? What are you doing for that kind of money?"

Natalie lets out a mock laugh. "You don't want to know. Some raunchy shit."

"That's enough!" I yell at Natalie.

I look back at Daniel to explain, but he puts his hand up to stop me. My heart sinks. I knew he wouldn't accept this type of work, but I didn't expect the look of repugnance on his face either. The way he's staring at me makes my skin crawl with filth.

"You're a fucking prostitute, both of you—"

"I don't have a boyfriend, though." Natalie chimes in, looking pleased. "Or bang my best friend's dad. Or split up a marriage."

I'm not a violent person, but I'm very close to slapping her if she doesn't shut up.

Daniel points his finger at me. "There's not a single thing you can say that will make me see this situation any differently. Nothing at all. We're through. You're fucking disgusting. I tell you my ex-fiancée had an affair with my best friend, and here you're doing fuck knows what with God knows who behind my back? To think I wanted you to move in with me so we could take it to the next level." He rakes a repulsed gaze down my body. "Would you have brought men to my house?" He pales. "Holy shit. Have you been tested? I bet you're a walking STD."

"Daniel, please. It's nothing like what you're imagining, trust me. It's just sex that doesn't mean anything."

"What about her father? Huh? If you can throw your best

friend under the bus, I can only imagine what you'd do to me."

I avert my gaze to the floor.

"I want nothing to do with you. I regret meeting you. I wish I hadn't pursued you. I thought you were different. There was a light about you, but now I wonder if you were playing me the whole time. Have a nice fucking life, you despicable, pathological, lying, fucking piece of trash."

Daniel storms out the door, slamming it behind him. I stare for a moment in a state of disbelief. Natalie makes a clicking sound under her breath. I look at her and wonder where we go from here.

The blow is devastating. I knew the risks when I took them, but I didn't expect an impact of this magnitude. I thought I would be done with James before Natalie could find out. I thought I could break up with Daniel before it was too late.

I'm sickened over my actions, too blinded by the hush money and all I've never had. I blink a few times trying to wrap my head around what just happened. I just lost my boyfriend, and my best friend, in less than a half hour.

"I hope you're happy," I say.

"Oh, I'm only just getting started."

Chapter 58

"I'm sorry to see you leave," Madam Christine says, sitting behind her desk. "Are you sure it's what you want? We could put you on a freeze until you're ready to come back."

I hesitate, even though I know what I need to do. Working for Sanctuary Cove has done nothing but cause problems. Problems caused by my greed.

"Is it wrong to say yes and no?"

She offers a small smile. "It's hard to walk away from easy cash like this. You'll never make it anywhere else. Why do you think I'm still here?"

"Yeah," I say under my breath. "Isn't that the truth."

"You're welcome back should you change your mind."

I swallow. "I don't think I'll be back, but thank you." I reach into my purse and grab my work phone. I slide it across the table.

"Thank you," I say again and then stand and walk toward the door. I pause with my hand on the knob and turn around. "Did you know that James is Natalie's father?"

Her lips curve just slightly. "Of course I did. You were everything he wanted, and I was happy to make the money. I knew the moment we met you were his type. I was eager to set you both up, but I had to test you first. I thought I was going to lose him as a client because no one was satisfying him until you came around. He nearly lost his marbles when I told you were unavailable."

I just nod. I can't even be mad. Not after I stooped so low to make money, too. I'm not any better.

Walking out of the club for good, I step onto the street, my gaze immediately looking in that dingy corner for the woman who's always resting there. She's not there, and while I'm relieved, I also can't help but wonder if she's okay.

I walk down the street to the nearest train station and take the next one to Queens. It's only been two weeks since I lost Natalie and Daniel, the longest fourteen days of my miserable life. I haven't bothered calling Daniel to attempt to fix things. I knew he wouldn't answer my calls, and I knew that nothing I had to say would matter. I was going to break up with him anyway. I guess I got what I wanted.

Natalie, on the other hand, is a different story.

I've tried talking to her multiple times. She won't give me the time of day. I don't blame her, but I had hoped she'd give me a chance. "You're still here?" is all she ever says and walks away.

She's made it very clear she wants me to move out. Now that school is over and graduation is around the corner, I'll start looking for a place to rent. I couldn't focus on that and packing, final exams, and attempting to reconcile things with Natalie at the same time. It was too much on top of stressing over Grammy. I've barely been able to handle anything else.

Taking a seat on the bus, my phone vibrates in my pocket. My stomach tightens, hoping it's Natalie since Grammy knows I'm on the way to her house. I pull it out and read the screen.

"James," I say under my breath. I've missed him so much.

I stare at the *Blocked Caller* flashing across my screen. I haven't answered one of his calls since that awful day. I want desperately to slide my thumb across the screen, but I don't ... and I won't.

I decline the call and pocket my phone as the bus comes to a stop. I get off and make my way toward Grammy's house and let myself in. Something feels off, but I can't place what until I step in further. Cats. I smell soiled cat litter, which is not something Grammy would've ever allowed.

Ms. Shelly turns the corner and walks toward me in her navy-blue scrubs. She's a little grim-looking, and that doesn't help the feeling in my stomach.

"Hey," I say, a little concerned by the smell. "How's Grammy?"

Her face pulls down. "She's resting. She's had better days ... today isn't one of them." Ms. Shelly pauses. I can tell she wants to say something. "Spend time with her."

I frown. "Where is she?"

"In her room."

"Thanks," I say and walk to the back of the house. Slowly, I open the door. The room is dark, dreary. The blinds are still pulled shut, and I don't like the way the air tastes stale. My chest tightens as my mind goes *there*, but I quickly brush it away.

"Grammy?"

She's lying in bed with three cats surrounding her. Her head turns toward the sound of my voice, and she smiles, though it's weak. It's hard to return the smile when I see the battle in her eyes. She's worn out. Anxiety clogs my throat from the fear of losing her.

"Aubrey," she says softly.

I take a seat on the side of her bed. My emotions are climbing pretty fast at the sight of her. She looks like she's worsened overnight. I don't want to cry, but it's hard seeing her like this.

Grammy reaches out for my hand. She's cold ... and feels fragile. "How you doin', honey?"

"Oh, you know, same old." One corner of my mouth tugs up. Tears blur my eyes. "I came to tell you I got everything situated for graduation so you can be there. I have a wheelchair in place and made sure I got Ms. Shelly a ticket too so she can be there with you."

Fuck. I can't even say the words without my voice cracking. I hate this state of unease cultivating in my chest. We've talked about this day for years, and now that it's finally here, I'm dreading it. It feels like an ending to a story I'm not ready to say goodbye to yet.

"I don't need a wheelchair," she says, and that causes me to laugh. "I can walk just fine."

"I know you can. I just want to make it easy on you." I take a deep breath. "I have a car service set up for you too, so there's nothing you have to worry about. The ceremony is in a few weeks."

She rubs my hand with her fingers. "I'm so proud of the woman you grew up to be," she says.

I'm nothing to be proud of.

"I really am. I love you, Aubrey Abrams."

If she knew the truth, she'd be so disappointed in me.

"I was thinking afterward I can take you out to lunch to celebrate. Any place you want, you name it," she says, and some for reason that causes me to break down.

I lean forward to hug her, and I just start crying. I can't help it, and I can't stop the tears. I burrow my face into the curve of her neck and just hold her. I breathe in her familiar scent.

"Aubrey, honey. Don't cry. There's nothing to be upset about. This is a joyous occasion, and I plan to have a drink with you right after."

Damn it. My tears are coming in harder and harder, my heart thumping rapidly.

"I love you," I tell her, my voice muffled. "Thank you for everything you've done for me, Grammy." I need to let her know I'm so grateful. "Just ... I love you."

I lie down next to her and hold her hand. My jaw is quivering as more tears threaten to spill over my eyelids.

"Raising you, though bittersweet, has been the highlight of my life. I wouldn't change a thing, other than to have your parents here. I wish I could have given you more."

I draw in a shaky breath and try not to cry again, but I can't help it.

"You did give me everything. You gave me what mattered

most. Guidance and love. You taught me to respect people and give back to those who are less fortunate than us. You instilled good qualities in me, ones I'm grateful for."

"I just wish I could have done more," she says. I can hear the regret in her voice, and I hate that for her.

"I plan to open that shelter we talked about for homeless women and children one day," I tell her. I know it would make her happy. "What do you think I should call it?"

"You're really going to do that?" Her voice quivers.

I pause for a moment and look at her. "I am. Do you think I shouldn't?"

"I think it's a wonderful idea, and if it's something your heart desires, then you need to do it. I just want you happy and to love your life, and if helping others makes you happy, then you do it. I honestly love the idea."

I give her a kiss on her cheek. "Thanks, Grammy. Your support means the world to me."

"Honey, if you want to start a business shoveling cat poop, I would support you. I wouldn't love the idea of that kind of work for you, but I'd still be by your side rooting you on."

Silent tears run down my temples. "Pick a name for me," I say.

"Oh, you just gotta put me on the spot, don't you." She laughs, and it causes her to cough. She leans to the side to cover her mouth with a tissue. There's a little blood, and it sounds like she has to breathe in deep to cough and catch her breath.

"I'm sorry," I say once it subsides.

"Bite your tongue. It feels good to laugh. Do me a favor and reach into the nightstand and get the box with the bow. I got something for you to wear to graduation."

My throat immediately clogs up again. "No," I tell her. "Give it to me after graduation."

"Don't make me get up and get it."

"Give it to me after I graduate, when we have our drink," I

repeat, my voice a pleading whisper. It's like a bad omen. I know if she gives it to me now, then she won't be there that day. I can't chance it. I just can't.

"Aubrey, please, I want to see you wear it when you walk across the stage."

I close my eyes, knowing I don't have it in me to fight her when her voice is so weak as she pleads with me. Sitting up, I pull the drawer open and reach inside. There's a little white box with a satin bow. I turn back toward Grammy, hiking my knee up onto the bed. I lift my eyes to hers. She seems so tired.

"Ms. Shelly helped me look on the internet. She used her phone ... Lord knows how she could even read on that thing, but when we came across this, I knew it was the one. Go ahead and open it."

My hand hesitates on the end of the bow. Grammy sees it and places her hand over mine. I look at her.

"Please, for me."

I nod, fighting the tears. Pulling the ribbon, I let the ends fall to the side and push the top of the box up to reveal a rose gold necklace. My lips part on a sigh. It's two rings, one large, one small, intertwined and attached to a thin chain.

"It reminded me of us. We've always been attached at the hip—well, until you went off to school. I'm the smaller circle, though. You've always had a larger-than-life personality."

Tears blur my vision. "It's beautiful ... I love it. Thank you so much."

"I got that color to match your mother's necklace. I thought you could wear both of them together."

My fingers run along the chain I'm wearing. "Grammy, you didn't have to get me this."

"I know I didn't have to. I wanted to."

I smile at her. Picking up the card it's attached to, I read the printed letters. "Oh, the places you'll go," I read aloud. There's a longer message at the bottom, and by the time I'm done reading it, there are tears in her eyes, which only make my already unstable emotions worse.

"Put it on," she says quietly, and I do.

The horseshoe necklace my dad gave my mom fits in the center of one of the circles. It's like we're all together again.

"Wherever you are, wherever you go, you'll have all of us with you."

She's right. It reminds me of us too, and it makes it that much more special to me.

"I'll cherish it forever."

Grammy smiles, but I can see the fatigue in her eyes. She lets out a heavy breath.

"It looks beautiful. Exactly how I imagined it. I can't wait to see you graduate with it."

Chapter 59

I decided to stay with Grammy all night. I cleaned up her litter boxes, something she fought me tooth and nail on, and then I made her dinner. She was only able to take four bites until she refused any more, saying she was full. She fell in and out of slumber, and when she'd wake, she'd look for me. Something in my gut warned me not to leave. Ms. Shelly set up the oxygen tank for her, and we fell asleep side by side, holding hands, with her cats surrounding her.

I'm so glad I listened to my gut.

Grammy died peacefully in her sleep.

I knew before I opened my eyes she wasn't here anymore. I laid in bed praying I wasn't right, but when I heard the soft sound of one of her cats crying, my worst fear had been confirmed.

Ms. Shelly allowed me as much time as I needed to say goodbye, and when hospice came to take Grammy's body away, she held me tight in her arms and let me cry on her shoulder until there were no tears left to give. It felt like a part of me left the world when she did.

Then, Ms. Shelly handed me an envelope.

An envelope I'm staring at while I sit by myself in my cap and gown with a diploma in my hand. I've brought the envelope with me everywhere since that day, but I just haven't been able to bring myself to open it. I know what will be written inside, and I'm not ready to read her handwriting or feel her words just yet. It's too fresh. Too real and too heartbreaking.

Ms. Shelly offered to come to my graduation, but I told her

she didn't have to. She surprised me right before I left with flowers and a heartfelt card with some encouraging words. She gave me her phone number and told me to call her whenever I needed her. I thought it was incredibly sweet.

Now I'm sitting in a room with other graduates and their smiling and laughing families. I'm not crying for once because I know Grammy wouldn't want that, but I need to get out of here before I lose it. I've yet to go a day without tears, and today has been by far the hardest for me.

Standing, I take off my cap and gown and fold them into a bag. I switch my high heels to a pair of flats so I can walk comfortably to the train station. Just as I'm about to place the envelope in my bag for safekeeping, I feel a vibration. Frowning, I retrieve my phone and look down at the screen.

Blocked Caller.

My heart clenches. I swipe the screen open and read the text message.

> **Blocked Caller: Congratulations, Aubrey. The offer still stands for your nonprofit when you're ready.**

Those damn tears fill my eyes, and I sniffle. I shove my phone back inside my bag and grab the rest of my stuff. My jaw trembles, my chest tight once again. James has been relentless with his calls. My life is in shambles, and I'm not trying to complicate it further by talking to him. When I decide I'm ready to open the foundation, I'll do it on my own. It's not like I don't have the money.

Swallowing back my emotions, I glance up, and for a moment I meet Natalie's gaze.

My lips part at suddenly seeing my best friend. She's not staring at me with harsh blue eyes like she's done over the past couple of weeks. She's looking at me with confusion. Her gaze shifts around me. I turn away. I've been completely alone and in the dark about Grammy's death, and seeing Natalie brings too many feelings back to the surface.

As fast as my legs can handle, I'm rushing from the congested room in desperate need of fresh air. I step outside and power walk a few blocks before I'm on a train and headed back to Queens. The moment I step inside Grammy's house, I do exactly what she'd planned to do and pour two shots of her favorite sambuca. I inhale deeply then lift one of the glasses to my lips, my hand shaking a little.

"Cheers, Grammy," I say to myself, then take her shot as well. I grimace over the gross black licorice taste then slam the shot glasses to the table. Goose bumps break out over my arms.

I glance around the quiet kitchen. The fucking tears start again, and my heart can't take anymore. I break down and cry hysterically. I'm sobbing harder than I have yet. Fat tears drip down my cheeks and into my mouth. I feel like I'm dying inside, and it'll never get any better. I don't understand how I'm supposed to go on with life like everything's okay. It's not okay. Nothing is okay. It wasn't supposed to be like this. She should've been here with me. I should've been celebrating with my best friend. But now they're both lost to me, and I'm alone.

I'm sliding to the ground, crying my eyes out with her cats all around me like they know I need them. Maybe Grammy was right. Maybe her cats needed her as much as she needed them, because I sure feel that way right now. I don't know what I'm going to do, but whatever it is will involve her fur balls. She'd want that, even if I do suffer from severe allergies.

I'm pretty drunk by late afternoon when my cell phone rings. I'm in no mood, and if I see *Blocked Caller,* I just might lose my shit altogether.

Reaching into my bag, I grab my phone and see it's a number I don't recognize. I'm a little relieved it's not him.

"Hello?" I say.

"Ms. Abrams?"

I frown. "Yes, who's calling?"

"This is Nicholas calling from the funeral home to let you know your urn is ready a little early."

I clench my eyes shut. Today is just not my day.

"Thank you," I say quietly.

"I understand there will be a small service held here a few days from now. You can come in whenever you like to spend time alone with her. Otherwise, please come in a few moments early to discuss the final payment. If there is anything you require, let us know so we can accommodate you during your time of need."

I nod, more to myself than anything, and tell him I'll be there an hour early and hang up. I wasn't going to hold a funeral, but Grammy had friends who would want to say goodbye, so I opted for a small celebration of life.

Exhaling a heavy breath, I place my cell phone on the table and spot the envelope hanging out of my bag. I blink, debating whether I want to open it. One of the cats rubs up against me, its tail wrapping around my leg. I glance down as it looks up at me. I swear it's telling me to rip the Band-Aid off and just open the damn letter already.

Taking a seat on the plastic-covered chair, I pour another glass of the licorice-tasting alcohol then run my finger under the seal. My stomach is a knotted mess of nerves as I pull out the letter and flip back the folds.

I reread the letter multiple times until the words are blurry and there are teardrops on the paper smearing the ink. I place it on the table and drop my head into my hands. I'm nauseated, and I can't seem to catch my breath, like I'm going to have a panic attack and vomit at the same time. Her will is enclosed, and so is the original diagnosis.

Grammy had cancer much longer than I was aware. She said

she knew I had a lot on my plate and didn't want to add more to it, so she kept it a secret. She felt it was the right thing to do. Apparently, when she found out about the cancer, it had already spread to multiple parts of her body, but she wasn't going to treat it because the survival rate was still too low. Grammy said she hopes I'm not upset with her and hopes one day I can forgive her for keeping the illness from me. She said she's going to miss me so much, that I was the greatest thing to happen to her, but that she's happy she can be with my parents again and how all three of them will be looking down watching over me.

Oh, and she wants me to watch over her babies. Like she even has to ask that.

I'm both upset and so angry that I stand and throw everything off the table in a rage. The cats scamper away in a panic. I scream, letting it all out. If I had known any of this, I would've done what I could to help her. I would've spent more time with her. I would've talked to her more, tried to be around to help more. Hunted down the best doctors. Anything. Now the guilt is eating away at me, and there's not a damn thing I can do about it. I thought she looked sick. I thought something was wrong with her, but I didn't push the issue because she'd insisted she was fine.

I'm crying and crying, hugging the cats and sneezing, when I hear a ding come from my cell phone. I get on my knees and scrummage for it, looking underneath everything I'd tossed to the floor to find it. I'm a little drunk but need more to drink. I don't want to feel anything more for the rest of the night.

Locating my phone, my heart sinks when I see Natalie's name on my screen.

I swallow hard and swipe a shaky finger to open her message.

Nat: Hey.

Hey. Three letters that have the power to make me want to

respond. Three little letters that have the power to make me feel all sorts of ways. Three stupid letters that make me miss my best friend so damn much.

But I don't respond. I know if I do, I'll just end up opening up to her and crying even more. She won't want to hear it, though, because she hates me. And since I know how mad she is, I'm sure she's wondering when I'm going to move my stuff out.

Instead, I just close my phone and attempt to clean up the mess I made. An hour or so later, after everything is locked up, I climb into Grammy's bed with her cats and cry myself to sleep.

Chapter 60

The celebration of life felt a lot longer than the two hours it was. The smiles and stories I heard about Grammy made me happy but also filled me with a deep sadness unlike anything I've ever felt. She didn't have a lot of friends by any means, but she had so much love surrounding her I wasn't aware of. For that, I can find a little reprieve.

I've been sitting alone for about an hour now in the front of the room staring at the best urn the funeral home had and a picture of Grammy. I take a tissue out of my purse and wipe my tears away, then crumble the tissue in my hand. My jaw quivers a little. I'm not ready to leave. When I step outside those wooden doors, it'll feel like I'm leaving her behind. I'm not ready for that. The thought makes me sick to my stomach, so I stay longer. Another round of fresh tears slip from my eyes. Just as I'm patting them away, I hear the door open behind me. I'm sure the director is here to tell me it's time to go.

Only, it's not the director. It's Natalie. And a whole slew of fresh tears fill my eyes when she takes a seat right next to me and holds my hand in hers. She doesn't say anything, and neither do I. She just sits with me and allows me to silently cry.

"I thought it was strange that I didn't see Grammy at the graduation," she finally says, her voice quiet. I can tell she's crying.

"She died a little over a week before graduation."

Natalie tightens her hand in mine. "You should've told me."

I flatten my lips. I don't say anything. It's hard to find words when I'm struggling inside with all the wrong turns I've made and the people I've let down. I couldn't call her and tell her, not after everything that's happened.

"I'm not okay," she continues, and my heart breaks a little further. "We're not okay. We're not friends, but I loved Grammy too. I wanted to be here for both of you."

I nod over and over. I won't argue with that.

"Thank you."

I take out another tissue and hand her one, and then I take one for myself. We wipe our tears and sit quietly for a little while until the director does come in and tell me it's time to close up. He informs me I can make arrangements to come back and pick up the flowers and photo tomorrow if I like. Since it's already so late, I agree to do that, thank him, and then take the urn and walk outside with Natalie.

As we step near the curb, I can barely make eye contact with her. My guilt is worse than ever, knowing she still came here for me.

"Thanks for coming," I say then exhale a heavy breath. I look at her. "I'll make plans to move my stuff out of your apartment soon. Just give me a little time, please. I know I have no right to ask for anything, but I am for this."

She bites her bottom lip and looks away. She hesitates. "Do you want to get coffee?"

"Really?"

She nods, her lips pressed between her teeth, and we start walking side by side.

I take her to a little café around the block, and we order two cappuccinos. We're sitting across from each other, stirring the light-brown foamy liquid. I know she wants to talk, but getting the first few words out are always the hardest.

"Natalie," I start the conversation. "You have to know I never meant to hurt you."

She inhales deeply then looks at me. "It's a strange feeling. I don't think you meant to hurt me, but you did. You hurt me more than anyone ever could. I want to come back from that, but I don't know how I can."

My jaw trembles, and I bite down on my lip. "I know. And for that, I'm so sorry. It's the last thing I wanted."

She takes a sip then places her cup down. She looks me directly in the eyes. I hold my breath.

"Why? Why did you do it?" The anguish in her voice crushes my heart. "Please, give it to me real, and don't bullshit me."

I shake my head. "I never bullshitted you, Nat. I didn't. I was telling you the truth when I said we were paired for a job through Sanctuary Cove. I didn't know James was your dad until I met him at the charity function."

"So the guy from the club you were falling for, the one you liked too much, it really was about my dad?"

I nod, and she scowls, so I quickly continue, hoping it defuses her temper. "But I didn't know it was him at first, I swear. He'd been a member of the club for a while."

"But you didn't actually sleep with him when you were on the job. You slept with him afterward, after you knew he was my dad."

I nod and try to speak, but she puts a hand up to stop me.

"What was the turning point? What made you go through with it and keep seeing him? Didn't you ever think about how much this would hurt me?" She's not angry. She's genuinely upset and wants to know the truth. Her jaw is trembling, and that causes more tears to fill my eyes. "You have to know I'd never do that to you."

I flinch. The worst part is, I do know she'd never do that. But then again, I didn't think I would either.

"Just fucking say it, Aub, Tell me the damn truth. I deserve to know."

So I tell her.

"You knew I connected with a client. You knew how he made

me feel. He tried to see me over and over until he outwitted me."

I tell her about the night with Reece, how James tricked me, how he said he was already falling for me. She's as pale as a ghost and looks like she's going to vomit.

"I went to Christine that same night. I told her I couldn't take him as a client anymore. Just because I ended it doesn't mean I ever stopped thinking about him. Did I ever think I'd see him again? Absolutely not. So imagine my shock when I meet him standing next to you. Why do you think I left?"

"You were going to see Daniel."

"I never made it there. I went home, but James followed me."

Her jaw drops in disbelief. Eyes wide, she says, "He was there with you while I was at the event with my mom?"

I nod.

"Un-fucking-real."

"I told him to leave, to go back, but he pushed ... and I missed him." A tear slips out, and I quickly wipe it away. "He thought it was some weird way of fate working out."

"But you had a boyfriend," she reminds me.

I take a sip of my coffee, feeling bad for how Daniel found out. He didn't deserve that.

"I didn't love Daniel, and it was wrong of me to lead him on. He was a means to pass time. You knew he was more of a thing to help keep my head on straight and accept the fact I was a prostitute."

She bobs her head to the side, agreeing with me.

"Anyway, James was relentless and told me to name my price. He'd been telling me for some time to name my price, even before we knew the truth. I always said no because I knew where it would lead. Then he said it again in our apartment that night. I was so worried you were going to come home that I finally caved. I liked being around him. I liked our conversations. I liked that he was persistent. I threw out that ridiculously high fucking number, assuming he'd say no."

She lowers her voice. "He said yes."

I nod. "He said yes, and then he upped it."

Her gaze drops to the table. She plays with her napkin, folding the corners and rolling it up.

"What was your price?"

I hesitate. I can see the indecision in her eyes. She wants to know but doesn't want to know. Softly, I tell her the truth. "I said ten million. He pushed it to twenty knowing I wouldn't say no."

Her eyes meet mine. "That's a lot of money but chump change to him." She huffs. "I guess I can't blame you for taking the money. Who says no to that?"

"I thought for sure he'd say no. He immediately said deal, then said he'd give me an additional ten. I thought I could do it for a year and then we move on our own ways. I didn't think it'd be so hard, not if I looked at him like a client from the club and nothing more. I should've known it wasn't like that." I look her directly in the eye. "I almost told you, you know. I tried to distance myself from the both of you. I felt so bad for lying all the time about where I was, what I was doing. I think there was a point when James and I both knew we were in too deep but just couldn't get out. It was strange, like we knew, but we didn't want to face the facts because we knew where it would take us."

"Do you love him?"

I immediately avert my gaze.

"Look at me and tell me, Aubrey."

I lift my tear-filled eyes, and her face falls. I nod.

Natalie's quiet for a long time. I don't regret telling her the truth, and in some strange way, I think she appreciates it, even though it hurts both of us.

We both finish off our cappuccinos. "I'm so sorry. More than you can ever know."

"Let me say something ... I'm not okay with this, and I don't know if I'll ever be, even though I have the facts. I spoke to my parents separately."

My eyes widen, heart pounding a little too hard in anticipation.

"I didn't tell my mom about you. I figured I would spare her any more heartache, but if you hadn't been set up with my dad, I do believe my parents could've worked things out. I definitely don't think he would've filed for divorce if you hadn't agreed to the private deal. So for that, I place blame on you because you could've said no and walked away. My mom told me they had an agreement and that it hadn't been as great as they made it look for a long time. She knew about his affairs, and he kept them discreet. While I never knew a thing—though I know the truth now—it still doesn't make what happened okay." She licks her lips. "My dad's story is pretty much identical to yours. I honestly hate him for what he did." She pauses, and there are tears in her eyes, which make mine well up too. "I hate you a little too. I mean, you were my best friend. Why did he have to go after you? Did he hate me that much?"

I shake my head to correct her. I try to speak, but she stops me again.

"I know he doesn't. It just fucking hurts, okay? I feel like I didn't know anything about them."

I drop my head, ashamed. Natalie moves to stand, and I look up when I hear the chair slide back. My brows furrow. She smooths out her black dress and levels a stare at me.

"The divorce is final. All I can say is that I hope you and my dad are happy now. I don't know if I can ever accept this, but I do miss you, and I hope one day we can try to be friends again. I'm not sure it'll ever be the same, though." She swallows then says, "I'm terribly sorry for your loss. Grammy was a good woman, and I can't imagine she'd be happy about what you did. Even though I do kind of hate you right now, I'm still here for you if you need me."

I nod and look down again. Her words are laced with so much emotion, I don't even recognize her. She meant every word, and I can't even be mad about it.

Chapter 61

"I'm glad you finally responded to a message," James says, handing me a tumbler. He takes a seat across from me.

"You can't seem to take a hint, can you?" I say, only sort of joking.

I take a deep sip, needing all the liquid courage I can get. It's been two weeks since I spoke to Natalie. I feel like it's time to put everything to rest, even though my heart is going to shatter into a million pieces again for it.

He shrugs an unforgiving shoulder and looks me directly in the eye. "What can I say? I'm a man who knows what he wants."

I glance around, taking in his apartment on the Upper East Side. It's bright and airy, with neutral blues and gentle grays that create a tranquil feel.

"Is this place new?"

"No. I've had it for years actually. It's where I live, alone." He pauses. "This is where I asked you to meet me before we went to Colorado."

I nod and look back at him, my heart racing even faster now. He's not wearing his wedding band, and his blue eyes appear at ease. He's too damn good-looking. He makes me ache for him just sitting there, and it kills me because I can't have him, in his dark, distressed jeans and a polo shirt that teases me with his tattoos. He's always been the silent, sexy type, and he wears it well. I rarely got to see him in short-sleeved shirts before, and now I just want to cover him up so no one gets to see him like this. I want him for myself.

"You look good," he says.

I give him a droll stare. "I look like shit, James. I'm on weird terms with Natalie, and my grammy died. I feel like death inside, and I know I look like it. So cut the act. I don't look good."

Guilt crosses his face. "Natalie told me what happened."

I squeeze my eyes shut and wave it away. I haven't cried in a few days, and I'm really trying not to right now. Tipping back the rest of my drink, I place the glass on the table and then reach inside my purse to pull out his check. I slide it across the table. His brows angle toward each other when he sees it.

"Take it back," I say.

"No. It's yours."

"I don't want it, especially not after what you said to me. We didn't finish out our deal anyway, so I didn't earn it."

His eyes lower to slits. "Don't care. It's yours. If you don't want it, then rip it up, but I'm not taking it. Is that why you finally came here? To give it back?"

He's angry, but I'd rather his anger than his love. "One of the reasons."

"What's the other?" he demands, finishing off his drink.

"Do you really want to play this game? Why do you think, James? You're not a stupid man."

Steel eyes stare back at me. "Say it. I want to hear it come from you. Let me hear the words."

My chest tightens just thinking about it, but I know what I need to say. Drawing in a deep breath, I pray I can get this out.

"We're through. There's no more deal, no more us, no more you calling me all hours of the day, no more text messages. It's over. It has to be this way. After today, please don't contact me again."

"No."

"I really want Natalie back in my life, and if this is how it has to be, then so be it. I'm cleaning up the stupid mistakes I've made."

His jaw flexes. "And I'm a mistake."

Oh, hell on earth, I can feel the tears climbing. My stomach is twisting with torment. I thought I could handle this, could stay strong.

My tongue glides over my bottom lip. "I want to call you a mistake, but I won't. You're not a mistake, but what we did was a mistake. I'm no longer an escort, and I don't have a boyfriend anymore. I'm just trying to get right with God and Natalie, and this is the first stop."

He huffs then smirks. "Boyfriend couldn't handle your job?"

"Thanks to Natalie, no, but that's beside the point. All I've done is lie and hurt people I care about, and I'm not doing it anymore. That's never been who I am."

He sees I'm not playing and sits up straighter. "Is it because of what I said? Because you know I didn't mean it, Aubrey. People say things out of anger. I did, and I'm sorry. I regretted it the moment I said it, and I can promise you it will never happen again. Please tell me you don't think I meant it."

I swallow thickly. I truly don't think he meant it, but it still doesn't change the course of action.

"It doesn't matter. It's the truth anyway. What's done is done. And we're done, James."

He brings his hand up to stroke his beard. I hold my breath. James looks away, and I take note of his salt-and-pepper hair and how it actually suits him so beautifully.

Shit. Don't go there.

I clench my eyes shut and tip my head down. As odd as it sounds, I love that he's a silver fox. He rocks that look.

"Is this what you want? Tell me. Do you want this?"

I meet his stare. No, it's not what I want. I feel like I'm dying inside knowing I won't ever see him again.

"It doesn't matter what I want." My voice breaks. "It's what it is. Let it go."

His eyes flare. James slams his glass to the table, and I jump. "Yes, it does. It matters."

Shaking my head, I push my chair back and stand. Jaw trembling, I don't know how I'm going to walk out of here.

"I've said all I needed to say." I reach for my purse.

James finishes his cognac and stands. Taking his tumbler, he rears back and whips it across the room, shattering it against a wall. My heart stops. Something inside me cracks as the crystal pieces fall to the floor. I break down crying. James rushes to me, and I can't help my arms going around his neck. He scoops me up and hugs me tight. I haven't been held since my life turned into the shitstorm that it is, and it feels good, so fucking good, especially coming from James. I cry in his arms, hating that this is goodbye, because it is. It's goodbye, whether we want it or not.

"Sweetheart, don't do this." His voice breaks me inside. He doesn't want it to end either, and it hurts so fucking much. "Don't do this. Things are different now. So different. It can work. *We* can work. We'll figure it out. I'm begging you not to do this."

My chest is on fire with emotion, with longing, with wishing things could be different. Maybe in another lifetime it would be, but not ours. We found each other at the wrong time.

Sniffling, I pull back to tell him I have to go, but he surprises me by pressing his lips to mine.

"Please, let me kiss you," he begs, like he needs me so badly.

I shake my head.

"Open your mouth."

I shake my head again as more tears fall. I'm afraid to kiss him. Afraid of what it could lead to. Afraid of what it would make me feel that I can't have. I want James Riviera, but I can't have him.

"Aubrey, please ..."

He's breaking just as much as I am. I don't know how I'll recover from this because this goodbye is so very unwanted. Our story isn't done, but the book is being forced closed.

"James," I breathe out. "I have to go. Let me go. Don't make this harder than it already is."

Finally, he releases me, but he doesn't release the hold on my heart. I'm crumbling inside, my chest shattering into a million pieces, and I don't know how I'm going to deal with it. How I'll live without ever seeing him again. I know what heartbreak feels like since Grammy passed away, but this is a different kind of heartbreak that I've never experienced. My chest rises and falls fast. James cups my face. Using the pads of his thumbs, he wipes away my tears and ultimately nods.

I make my way to his front door. My breathing deepens with each step I take. I place my hand on the knob and pause, knowing that when I walk out, I'll never see him again.

I look over my shoulder, but he's already walking toward me. Holding my breath, I look up. Our eyes meet, and I see the same look in his eyes that I feel in my heart. James places a small kiss to my forehead then opens the door for me.

I take a step and hesitate.

"If you don't leave now, I'm going to make you mine forever. It's what you want. It's what I fuckin' want, and we both know it. Last chance, sweetheart."

Tears well in my eyes as chills trail down my arms. I want him to yank me inside and make me his, but he's giving me the choice, and I have to make the right decision this time, even if it rips me apart.

Silently saying goodbye to the one thing my heart truly wants, I nod and step outside then hurry down the stairs to the street. I look back over my shoulder one last time, but James is already slamming the door shut.

And just like that, we're strangers again.

I take my time walking to the train station, allowing my eyes to freshen up and the tears to dry. I'm going to see Natalie at our apartment that I still haven't cleaned out. I don't want her to see me like this. That would allow her to ask questions, and while I didn't do anything wrong this time, I still don't want to give her a reason to think I did.

As I'm walking up the familiar steps, I take out my compact mirror to check how I look. I quickly apply some powder to hide the redness then stuff it away. I stand at our door and take a deep breath before knocking three times. I technically still live here, but I don't want to walk in either.

She opens immediately, and I hold my breath when I see her. Tears blur my vision. It feels like all I've done is cry lately, and now isn't any different. Something flashes in her eyes, and I almost regret coming over until she opens her mouth.

"You're fourteen fucking days late, bitch. God, you really know how to give someone a complex," she says then throws her arms around me to give me a giant hug. I gasp, and we both start crying happy tears as I step inside. "I almost had to hunt your dumb ass down," she adds.

"I'm sorry! I didn't know if, or when, you'd want to see me, but I couldn't hold off any longer. I miss you, and I'm sorry, and I want our friendship back," I say without taking a breath. "And I swear on my life I'll never talk to James or see him again. I just really need you in my life, Nat. I need my bestie."

Her navy eyes soften, and a few tears slip out. "I was never going anywhere. I just needed some time. You just gave me too much time." We both giggle. "We're more than just friends, Aub. We're like soul sisters, *wet* sisters, our own little gang, each other's tribe, my squad. Whatever you want to call it. How can we be epically fucking amazing when one half is missing? Answer. We can't. You're stuck with me for life, Ram Jam. I just needed a little time."

I always knew Natalie was a real, honest-to-God friend, but it is then that I realize what kind of person she is deep down inside. She's a better person than I am. I don't deserve her, but I'm lucky to have her in my life. A real friend accepts all the imperfections and lifts you up when no one notices that you fell. One who's always there with a shoulder to lean on, who can forgive even the biggest mistakes that hurt more than just one person.

I may have lost my grammy, but I've gained an angel for a best friend.

Epilogue

"Cheers to the hardest working broad in the city I know," Natalie says.

I smile from ear to ear. Our champagne glasses clink together, and we sip our mimosas. We're sitting at a little café overlooking the Hudson River having brunch.

"I can't believe it's finally open. I'm so excited for you."

I grin even bigger, feeling a bit bashful. "Right? I can't either."

This morning I cut the ribbon on Sanctuary, my nonprofit organization, with my best friend by my side.

"How do you feel about it?" she asks.

"Honestly? It's surreal. I really thought with each roadblock, it wouldn't happen. I started to lose hope at one point."

Natalie's lips turn down, and she nods. She knows. She was right there the whole time, watching how upset I was over the number of broken bridges I had to cross. A year and a half it took from start to finish, but now it's up and running, and in two days the doors will open to homeless women and children all over New York City.

"I couldn't have done it without your help," I say. "Thanks, Nat."

"I wouldn't have it any other way. I know how much it means to you, and I know Grammy would be proud."

"I hope so."

I smile and glance at the murky river. After the day I showed up at the apartment, we had another long talk through tears and cheap wine that made us sick the next day. There were too many memories to throw away and a bond that we knew couldn't be found with anyone else.

It was a little rocky at first. We both were testing the waters, being careful with each other, but eventually, we fell back into our natural, sarcastic ways. We argued here and there, but within six months it was put behind us and we've been good ever since.

I never went back to Sanctuary Cove, but Natalie is still there. She tells me all the time she's going to give it up, but that lasts only until she gets another really insane payment. Then she tells me next time. I laugh and tell her she's going to have a roast beef–looking vagina by the time she does leave.

Every few months, she asks me if I'll ever go back. My answer is always no, quick loads of money be damned. Like Natalie told me at the beginning of our senior year of college—more money, more problems. She wasn't kidding. The grass really isn't greener on the other side.

The only positive that came from working in the sex trade was that I used a good chunk of the cash to open the foundation, which wasn't easy to prove at first. It was that ten-million-dollar check I got from James that secured the deal in the end since he'd proved it was a gift. I didn't speak to him about it, though. Natalie did that for me. She claims he was happy to help.

I never ask about him. Ever. And Natalie never mentions him. It's one of those things that's always there but is never spoken about. I think about James often, and I still miss him something fierce, but my friendship with Natalie is more important to me. I won't go down that road again. I'm not sure I could handle the heartbreak a second time.

"Want to order Chinese tonight and get drunk at my place?"

I tip my glass toward her. "Sounds like a rad plan. Is my bed made up with clean sheets?"

She laughs. "I just ironed them for you."

I never moved back into the apartment, but Natalie insists

on keeping my room the way I left it. I joke that she's like a mom waiting for her child to come home from college. She's been amazing to me and beyond forgiving, so every couple of weeks I oblige and make her happy by sleeping over. That's only after I make sure Grammy's cats are taken care of.

Yeah, I still live there. The landlord had no intention of selling, but I offered him an over-market price and he accepted. On days when I'm lonely and down, I feel like she's there with me and I need that.

"Let's play a game," Natalie says, taking me away from my thoughts.

My eyes light up. I already know where she's going with this. She orders us another round before we start. It's Bottomless Mimosa Saturday, which means anything is possible.

"Are you going first, or am I?" I say.

"You."

I scan the sea of tables and point to a guy. Natalie studies him then gives me a side-eye smirk.

"He's a yuppie writing a book about Justin Bieber's music that's set in 1720 but found a way to time travel to his concerts. He swears it's going to win the Nobel Peace Prize."

I stare at her, perplexed. I'm at a loss for words and just start laughing. "Where do you come up with this stuff?"

She giggles. "I have no idea. It was my first thought."

"Okay. My turn."

Natalie looks around and points to an elderly woman with pale-blue hair wearing a SAVE THE WHALES shirt.

"Too easy."

I finish off my champagne and orange juice and pick up my fresh one.

"She used to be an astronaut but never made it to space, only worked on the shuttle. She dyes her hair the color of her favorite planet, Neptune. She's even named her kids after the planets, which her husband hates. She said, 'I pushed the kids out of my hoo-ha, I pick the name,' and the husband decided he wasn't going to argue with her."

"How ... nerdy. Kinda cool. Kinda agree with her."

We both laugh, and I pick a guy out this time.

Natalie says, "That's my future ex-husband times two."

I shoot her a confused look. "Times two?"

She smiles. "He won't be able to get enough of me and will marry me twice, only to see that I'm still the crazy fucking lunatic he married the first time and divorces me twice. Still calls for one-night stands."

I study the guy she picked out for me, how he's alone and taking pictures with an expensive-looking camera.

"He's a serial killer but just hasn't gotten caught yet. He pretends to take pictures of nasty pigeons, but he's really scoping out his next victim. You know how people say you walk past at least one murderer in your lifetime? That's him. I bet you're his next victim."

Natalie glares at me for a long period of time. "Bitch, please."

I laugh out loud, loving this game. "You'd kill him first."

"That escalated quickly," she says and laughs.

"How about her?" I say, pointing to a girl with large gold hoops and gorgeous, shiny black curls.

"She looks like she fucks her best friend's dad."

I give her a bland stare. "You're such a fucking asshole."

Natalie's head falls back as she cackles. "What! She does."

"You had to go there, didn't you?"

Her lips twitch like she's trying not to smile. She doesn't understand that her joke makes my heart ache, but I smile anyway.

"I couldn't resist," she says.

I look back at the poor girl. "If the dad was as hot as yours ... I don't blame her. I'd bang him until I couldn't walk and I'd have to sleep for a week."

"Ahhhhh my innocent ears!" she cries, covering her ears with her hands.

I feel a little better seeing that we can finally laugh about what happened. I thought it would be a sore subject between us for the rest of time, but I got lucky. Mainly because we haven't spoken about it much, but if she can be playful like this, then I know everything will be okay in the long run.

"Can I ask you something?" she says, and I nod. "Why don't you ask about my dad?"

My smile vanishes, my heart clenching. I reach for another drink. She doesn't normally bring him up, and now I'm getting nervous, wondering why she wants to know. I don't want to say the wrong thing, but I don't want to lie either.

I look at my flute, unable to make eye contact with her. "What good would it do? Chicks before dicks for life. I made that mistake once, and I learned my lesson."

"Do you ever think about him?"

I lift my guarded eyes to meet hers. I'm a little nervous and tap my foot incessantly on the floor.

"Why are you asking me this? I really don't want to fight, Nat."

"I'm honestly just curious. It's been almost two years since you guys were actually together. After everything I know and what we've talked about, I'm just surprised you never ask to see how he is."

I swallow hard, trying not to get emotional. I don't ask because it will just hurt.

"Yeah, I do. I think of him a lot, and I try not to," I admit, my voice low. "But it doesn't do me any good to talk about him, so I don't." I attempt to change the subject. "How's your mom?"

She rolls her eyes dramatically. "Better than ever. She's been hooking up with some pool guy she hired. It's crazy. I've never seen her so happy."

My brows raise. She can't live in the city if she has a pool, but I'm relieved to hear her mom is doing well. Makes me feel better, in an odd way.

"Where does she live now?"

"Out in Suffolk County. She bought a mansion that has a huge beach inspired, saltwater swimming pool with a magnificent grotto and waterfall. There are no steps to her pool. You just walk into the water as if you're at the beach. She even has a tennis court on her property and hired a full-time chef. I met the pool guy. He's a widow and doesn't look like he could hurt a fly. They play cards together on the weekends."

"Awe, that's good. I'm happy to hear that."

Her mouth tugs to one side, and she smiles. Natalie's phone dings, and she picks it up to read an incoming text message. "Yeah, I'm honestly really happy for her," she says, her fingers skating over her phone. When she's done, she takes a deep breath and squares a look at me, and I frown.

"You know I'm on good terms with my dad now, right?"

I nod. James and Natalie hashed things out shortly after we reconciled our friendship. I didn't ask questions, just took what she offered. Listening to her tell me how they talked made me so happy for her, even if I was dying inside missing him.

"I know. That's one positive thing that came out of what I did at least."

She checks her phone then says, "Listen, I'm not pushing for this because it's just fucking weird, but I'm so sick of seeing you and my dad mope around like lovesick losers. You're killing yourself with work. He's depressed and acts like his life is over. I know you're sad and haven't dated anyone since lame Danny Boy. I know you miss my dad, just like every time he asks me how you are, I know he feels the same way and misses you. Obviously you guys had something that was real, no matter how disgusting I think that is."

"He asks about me?" I say, too quickly and too hopeful.

She rolls her eyes. "All the time. That's kind of why I'm asking you about him."

I shake my head, trying to stop her. My heart is pounding in my chest, and I'm worried this kind of conversation is going to cause a fight. It's the last thing I want. It's too good to be true.

"Natalie, it's fine. Really. Why are we even talking about this? Just let it go. I'm never going to put us in that situation again. I promise. Your friendship means more to me, and I don't want to lose you."

She gives me an exasperated look. "Will you shut up for a second?"

I sit up a little straighter. "I haven't seen him. I haven't spoken to him. Nothing, Natalie. I swear."

"I'm gonna throw my mimosa at you."

I purse my lips together. "Go on."

"Like I said, I'm not pushing for this because it's just weird as fuck if I did, but I'm tired of seeing you guys look the way you do. I know you're hiding it from me how you feel about him. He asks about you constantly. If you want to talk to him ... you can. I won't be upset."

I just stare at her, unblinking, trying to figure out if this is a joke. My heart is hammering like a beat to a techno song against my ribs. All I can hear is the pounding in my ears and feel the pressure building.

"Say something."

"I'm not ruining our friendship again. It's fine. Thanks, but no thanks. I won't do it."

She leans in, her brows furrowed in disbelief. "I just told you I give you my blessing to bang my dad."

"It's not worth it," I say. I just can't risk losing her or going through the heartbreak again. It's too much suffering for one person to handle twice.

"I've given it a lot of thought. Everyone is in a good place right now, and I don't see why I should stop you guys from being together, if it's what you want."

I'm at a loss for words. I'm not sure what to say. I'm having a hard time processing what she just said.

"Talk about things escalating quickly. What if it leads to something more?"

"Well, I'm not gonna fucking call you Mom if that's what you're asking," she scoffs and then takes a sip. "And I sure as fuck don't ever want to hear about sex shit with you guys. I have to draw the line somewhere."

A surprised laugh escapes me, and she grins. Happiness surges through me, but I fight to keep it at bay. I'm not getting my hopes up, even though I can feel happy tears burning behind my eyes.

"Are you sure you're okay with this? Like really okay?" I ask, my voice hopeful. I'll ask a hundred times if I have to.

She places her glass down and levels a stare at me. "No. I was just kidding actually. I was seeing where your head's at."

My lips part in shock, heart plummeting to the floor. I had a feeling it was too good to be true. I'm a little hurt. I know we joke all the time, but not where it hurts the other person.

"That was cruel," I say honestly. "How would you feel if I dangled a stack of bills in front of you and then said you couldn't have them?"

Her lips twitch, and now I'm just getting angry. It was downright mean to do that.

"Would I do that to you? Seriously. I'm just playing with you, Aub. I know I have my moments, but I wouldn't purposely set out to hurt you. I was being real. I want you guys to be together, if it's what you want, and I think you want it." She pauses. "You want it, don't you?"

I nod, feeling a little torn. "I do. I miss him so much, but I'm worried it'll get weird between us."

She smiles appreciatively. "As long as we don't hide anything from each other, it won't. Promise. I was serious when I said you have my blessing."

We talk a little more, and by more, I mean I repeatedly ask her if she's sure she's okay if I speak to her dad. We have a few more mimosas, then pay the tab.

If someone would've told me that this is how I would spend my Saturday after opening my nonprofit organization—talking about my best friend's dad and how I can see him romantically—I would've laughed in their face. I want to see James as soon as possible, but it's been a long time and he was angry with me when I left him.

I sigh, hopeful. My heart is a wild mess.

Leaving the restaurant, we step outside to the curb and hail a taxi. Natalie has a day job with a client and needs to leave to get ready.

"Listen, I gotta cancel tonight," she says.

I frown. "Why? We just made plans like an hour ago." I was looking forward to hanging out. Sometimes the nights get lonely, even with all the cats.

She shrugs and digs into her purse. "I know, but I have a feeling you're going to have plans later."

I blink in confusion. "What?"

Natalie looks over my shoulder, and a smile tugs at her lips. Her eyes are filled with a tenderness and joy that causes me to freeze.

Just as I'm about to turn around and follow her gaze, I feel him. Lips parting on a gasp, I'm rendered speechless. My hand flies to my stomach, and I hold myself. My breathing deepens. Natalie's soft eyes meet mine for a brief second, and she gives me a gentle smile.

James walks up to us, and my world stops. I focus on only

him, unable to look away. Leaning in, he gives his daughter a kiss on the head and then a hug. They greet each other. I stare, wondering if this is real or not. Natalie finally gets a taxi. We say goodbye, but it's a blur because all I see is him.

I haven't seen James in so long, and I don't know how to react. I don't know what to do, what to say. The only thing I do know is that after nearly two years, he still makes my heart beat the way it did the first time we met.

James turns to look at me. He smiles. He looks like he did the day I left him, wearing dark jeans and a polo shirt that cups his biceps. His tattoos are on display, and he's still rocking the silver fox and beard look.

Fucking man is too good-looking for his own good.

We're standing on a street in one of the busiest cities in the world. People are rushing all around us, cursing that we're standing in their way. Horns are blaring, and the ground is vibrating from the underground train. Yet, all I see is him, the man I've loved since the moment I met him. James Riviera.

He studies me, his eyes roaming my face. He takes a step toward me. "Hey, sweetheart."

I choke back a swallow, eyes softening. My heart is about to pound out of my chest.

"Hey" is all I can think of saying.

"I've missed you so fucking much, Aubrey. I haven't been the same without you."

My jaw is trembling, and my lips part. I have to replay his words in my head because it's almost too good to be true.

"I've missed you too. I'm so sorry about everything. I never wanted it to end the way it did, but it had to. And I refuse to lose Natalie again or go through suffering a broken heart the way I did when we parted ways. So tell me now if you want something more or if this is just for fun, because I have to be honest and tell you I don't think my heart could handle another hammer shattering it again to a million pieces—"

James yanks me forward and brings his lips to mine. "Open up for me."

I don't hesitate.

He thrusts his tongue into my mouth and kisses me deep, stroking me with untamed passion. We both moan in unison and clutch each other. Strong arms wind around my back. James tugs me closer, kissing me hard, kissing me like we have a lot to make up for. He presses his body to mine, and I revel in it. I want to get lost inside this man like we never left each other. His fingers tangle in my hair, and then he fists a chunk of it in his hand. I melt into his chest, kissing him back with the same intensity.

"God, how I've fucking missed you," he says, breaking the kiss. He's breathing into me just as heavily as I am him.

I look back and forth into his steel-blue eyes. My fingers are shaking and my knees are weak, but it doesn't matter because I have the man I love more than anything in the world holding me up.

"I never stopped wanting you, James. I thought about you every day, hoping I'd see your private call on my phone. It never came." My jaw trembles. "It never came," I say again, this time my voice cracking.

His blue eyes soften with regret. He kisses my lips once more, and I breathe in his woodsy, bergamot scent I've missed so much.

"You have no idea how many times I dialed your number, only to hang up. Every damn day was a struggle to keep my distance. I've been holding out hope that in time we would find each other again."

Pressing my lips to his, I softly whisper, "We met by a cruel chance of fate. Becoming your lover was part of the job, but falling for you ... I had no control. I didn't stand a chance."

"Do you remember when I told you about moments and how they're priceless?" he asks, brushing his nose with mine. I nod. "I want to make the rest of them with you."

I draw in a breath before he kisses me deeply, passionately, setting my world ablaze for him.

"Let me take you to dinner. I know this little underground place where we can sip ridiculously expensive cognac and talk all night long."

I smile up at him. "I'd love that. And I even have the perfect dress to wear."

THE END

Acknowledgements

To my husband and two sons, thank you for putting up with the long hours I spend working at the computer, and never complaining about it. Most importantly, thank you for supporting the unconventional stories I love to write and rallying me on to keep going. I couldn't do this without you.

To my Jill and Keena, writing *Hush Hush* could not have happened without the help from both of you. You encouraged me to step out of my comfort zone and were there to brainstorm with me when I got stuck. I find myself smiling when I reminisce about the conversations we had over these girls and their lives. We laughed so hard. Those are *moments* I will cherish forever. Thank you forever.

Vashti Dawn, Nadine Winningham, and Amber Hodge, you each played a completely different yet integral part in writing *Hush Hush*. You cheered me on while I took a chance on a wild story that had been marinating in my head for years. Your feedback was priceless. I love this book so much and have you to thank for that.

Thank you to the readers who pick up my books and give them a shot. It means the world to me. Your support matters and makes a difference. Thank you for all the love and messages, tags, cool graphic edits, and videos. You guys are the real deal and make writing so fun.

About Lucia Franco

Lucia Franco has written over a dozen romance novels. Her emotional stories often include an age gap and forbidden love.

Her novel *Hush Hush* was a finalist in the RWA 2019 Stiletto Contest. Her novels have been translated into several languages.

Lucia resides in South Florida with her husband, two boys, and five pets. She was a competitive athlete for over ten years – a gymnast and cheerleader – which heavily inspired the Off Balance series. When she isn't writing, you can find her at the beach getting slammed by waves or wandering through her butterfly garden.